WAR BEGINS

THE ALPHA-OMEGA WARS

C.J. HANSEN

WAR BEGINS

Copyright © C.J. Hansen 2020

ISBN 9798683153410

The right of C.J. Hansen to be identified as the author of this work has been asserted in accordance with Section 77 of the Copyright, Designs and Patents Act 1988.

All rights reserved. No part of this publication may be copied, reproduced, stored in a retrieval system, or distributed, or transmitted, in any form or by any means without the prior permission of the author, nor be otherwise circulated in any form of binding or cover other than that in which it is published and without a similar condition being imposed on the subsequent purchaser.
Thank you for respecting the author of this work.

Edited by: Alex Florea

Cover Design by: Mecob Design Ltd

Cover images: © Shutterstock.com © iStockphoto.com

For

Hannah & Emily

With many thanks to Lucinda E, Alex H, Trevor H, Ash K, Jay B, Jamie O, Tanuja K, Michael J and Lee H

And with special thanks to Alex Florea, for all her invaluable advice and support – thank you!

Preface

Background to War Begins

(This preface provides all the background needed for readers who are new to the Alpha-Omega Wars. Further background detail is available in the appendix, for those who would like it.)

Secret journal entry by James Lawrence, Knight of the Order:
*"**London, 27th August, 1884.**
This evening I was party to a discovery made by Grand Master Edmund Warwick, which shocked me to my very core. The greatest threat we have ever faced to the future of the world has been revealed. The discovery came during my niece Anna's first instruction session, when she related the details of a dream she had as a young child. If correct, the findings may foreshadow our irreversible descent into the Omega World."*

* * *

Anna Lawrence was born with an unusual ability. She could see other people's auras. And by observing a person's aura, she could understand their true nature. Soon she learned that others could not see what she did. It scared them. They persecuted her, so she began to hide it. Then, aged fourteen, she discovered that an old family friend, named Edmund Warwick, shared her ability.

He explained that it was a rare power possessed throughout history by a small, hidden group called the

Knights of the Order of the True Path. This power usually revealed itself only upon reaching adulthood. He knew of no-one who had ever developed it so young.

Mr Warwick told of a secret struggle that had raged since the dawn of civilisation. On one side, the Order's mission was to move the world to an ideal state for all. The Alpha World. Opposing them were forces led by beings not born of this world, fighting to create a very different kind of existence. A world where nothing that lives here today would ultimately survive. The Omega World. Mr Warwick explained that these Alpha-Omega Wars lay behind many crucial events in human history. Understanding what was at stake, Anna vowed to fight for the Alpha cause. She began her instruction, which was led by Mr Warwick, a senior knight in the Order. He was assisted by Anna's uncle, James Lawrence, also revealed to be another prominent knight. This training would include mental combat – the art of combat using auras.

Anna learned that beings not born in our world sometimes appeared here. Amongst the deadliest were Satals. Hugely powerful creatures, their mission was always to shift the world towards the Omega state. On each occasion they caused untold death and destruction, and large numbers of knights were required to defeat them. Satals always took horrific forms, and they lay behind legends of beasts and monsters in most cultures. Since ancient times, their actions had brought about many of the most devastating events in human history.

Anna shared the details with her two mentors of a severe nightmare she experienced when she was six. Five figures had suddenly appeared on a hilltop. Anna's focus was drawn immediately to the eyes of the largest of the five. The 'whites' of its eyes were blood red. The irises were black as night. A deep red glow emanated from the pupils. Young though she was, she knew it had been real. She had seen, and had been seen by, the greatest evil imaginable. Eight years on the dream still haunted her.

Mr Warwick's interpretation of the nightmare stunned him, and shocked her uncle. What she had seen had indeed been real. Four of the figures were Satals. The largest was a being thought only to exist in the legends of the Order. A creature of unimaginable power, called a Gorgal. This ultimate enemy had sought Anna out upon its arrival. Never in history had five such mighty Omega creatures appeared at once. It threatened a final, fatal shift in the balance of the future, towards the Omega World.

Anna lived with her mother. Her father had died when she was very young, and her mother had grown highly protective. She knew of the Alpha-Omega Struggle and reluctantly agreed to Anna's instruction, but forbade her from leaving the house for any other purpose. Anna felt trapped. To meet her friends, she had to slip out unseen. Her best friend was called Rebecca Thompson. Anna was secretly in love with Rebecca's brother, Timmy.

From her friends, Anna heard rumours of a horrific monster, named the Beast of Highgate by the newspapers, which was believed to be behind a series of savage killings in London, around Highgate and Hampstead. Witnesses called it a demon from hell, possibly Satan himself, prowling the night streets. Mr Warwick later confirmed that this was, in fact, a Satal. Anna also heard from her friends about a mysterious man named Faulkner, rumoured to conjure up the Beast through evil rituals.

Faulkner had hired a gang of local criminals to do his work. Rough though they themselves were, they were known to live in fear of him.

In a blissful summer encounter with Timmy, Anna learned that he shared her feelings. However, once home again, she struggled to get a message to him. When at last she managed to, she was devastated to learn that he no longer wanted to see her. Finally, a meeting was arranged. She slipped out of her house to see him, but then Timmy failed to appear. As she returned home, a rough boy she knew, called Billy Gillespie, approached her for help.

Gillespie told her that Faulkner was hunting for his older brother, Kenny, a member of Faulkner's gang who had failed to follow orders. Faulkner had already killed Kenny's best friend for this, and threatened Billy with his life if he did not reveal his brother's location. Anna was stunned to hear that Faulkner *became* the Beast when he killed Kenny's friend. If true, this would mean Faulkner was a Satal, one of the five figures from her dream.

Unknown to Billy, Faulkner was following him. He was on the brink of catching them both, when Anna realised and concealed Gillespie. Once they thought Faulkner had gone, she urged Gillespie to escape London.

As Anna headed home, she looked back at the retreating figure of Gillespie, just as a huge creature with a horned head swooped out of the foggy night sky and snatched him away. It was the Beast of Highgate.

Anna fell to her knees in the empty road, devastated. One thought dominated her mind. Whatever it took, Faulkner must be stopped.

War was about to begin.

WAR BEGINS

'Interrogate yourself, to find out what inhabits your mind and what kind of soul you have now. A child's soul, an adolescent's, a woman's? A tyrant's soul? The soul of a predator – or its prey?'

'The soul becomes dyed with the colour of its thoughts.'

- Roman Emperor Marcus Aurelius
(AD 121–180), *Meditations*

Prologue

Deep underground, in a land many hundreds of miles from London, an enormous figure slowly became visible, lit dimly by the light of a single, flickering torch. It lay motionless on a giant slab of stone. The bearer of the flame lit four other torches, one by one. Together, their light provided shadowy illumination to the raw, rugged rock walls of the cave.

The torch bearer was joined by two more shadowy forms, one on either side. The figures bowed before the slab and began to chant. The sound was unlike any that a human has ever made. It possessed a quality that would have made the bravest hero tremble to their very core. It was a sound not born of this world, and its purpose was to strengthen the one whose sole aim was to bring about the world's complete and final destruction.

The day was near. The disciples' master would soon rise, to lead its servants on their apocalyptic mission. They chanted on into the dark, deadly night.

1
The Menace of Faulkner

Anna finally reached the foot of the steps leading to the large front door of her house. She had never felt more relieved to see the place. For the longest time, this house had seemed almost like a prison. Now it meant safety.

The day had been one of crushing disappointment. The night filled with extreme danger, and ultimately, with tragedy. The outside world had become a terrifying place, and Anna Lawrence, just turned fifteen, longed for nothing more than to be locked safely away from it again. No doubt there would be trouble waiting for her inside, too. But this would be trouble of a more familiar, domestic kind. Trouble that she could handle now.

She took two steps, then stopped dead in her tracks. From somewhere far away through the foggy night, an unearthly scream reached her ears. It was a sound she knew only too well. A sound that meant death. She bolted up the steps. The door was mercifully unlocked and she dived through it, slamming it shut behind her with her full weight. Breathing heavily, she leant against it for a moment, then staggered forward into the house, and to whatever reception lay in store.

Anna was braced for the scolding of all scoldings from her mother. Instead, to her enormous relief it was the tall, dashing, dark-haired figure of her Uncle James who stood there. He had been away from London travelling, and she did not know he had returned. He wore a heavy outdoor cloak and clutched a top hat. Both glistened with damp in the gas lamplight.

"Oh, thank goodness you're back!" she exclaimed, running to him.

"Anna!" he replied, his face lighting up in a way she had never seen before. "Where have you been? I've been out searching!"

"I went to see a friend," she started. She caught a sterner look entering his eyes. "Yes, yes, I know, I shouldn't have gone out alone, but it was… well, it was necessary. On the way back I got waylaid, and then I almost got trapped by Faulkner… and then I saw the Beast!" The words started to tumble out of her. Then, at the memory of what had followed, she burst into tears. Her uncle threw his hat and white gloves onto a nearby chair and began to comfort her.

"There, there, Anna, it's all right. You're safe now. Don't try to speak yet. Let's get you warm. I'll let your mother know you're safely home."

Anna was soon sitting beneath a blanket in the drawing room, in front of a roaring fire. Her uncle returned and closed the door, informing her of her mother's relief. She had agreed to let Uncle James speak with Anna first.

Anna explained what had happened, from the point Billy Gillespie had approached her for help. She recounted their conversation, including how Billy's brother, Kenny Gillespie, had crossed Faulkner, and that Faulkner had attacked Billy to find out where his brother was. She explained that Faulkner had tracked Billy down as far as the deserted garden, using some kind of connection he had established with Billy's aura. She described how she had shielded the boy's aura from Faulkner using her own, and how they thought he had given up his search and left them. Her uncle said next to nothing as she spoke, interrupting only to verify certain facts. It was clear from the look in his brown eyes, though, that his focus was absolute.

Finally, she relived with horror the moment she saw Gillespie in the distance, violently snatched away by the Beast, after she had left him. Her eyes welled up again.

"Is it possible he might still be alive? Is there something we can do to save him?"

Uncle James took a deep breath. "I'm afraid there's nothing that can be done for young Gillespie now. As you know, the beast that took him was a Satal. Satals are not like humans. They are creatures of the Omega World. They are utterly ruthless and devoid of compassion. They are single-minded, they know no mercy and they kill without hesitation, or remorse."

"But uncle, is there no chance…?"

"Alas, no, I do not believe so. Once the Satal got what it wanted from your companion, I'm afraid there was only one fate awaiting him. I'm sorry to be so blunt, but there's no kind way to say it. When a Satal takes on the form you saw tonight, its purpose is to kill. It is already too late."

Anna had already known this in her heart, but her uncle's words still hit her like a sledgehammer.

"But it's my fault, uncle! I should never have stopped shielding him. He would still be alive if I hadn't let him go. I've been such a fool, and now he's dead!"

"Anna, Anna, listen to me." Her uncle's tone was kind but firm. He gripped her by both shoulders and looked into her eyes.

"This is in no way your fault. You didn't know what you were getting into. You had no idea how to deal with a situation like that. We haven't even begun to prepare you for an encounter with such a mighty enemy.

"But-" Anna started to protest.

"It is truly impressive that you were able to understand what was happening, and how to shield Gillespie from Faulkner, at all. That was remarkable intuition on your part."

"But it wasn't enough!"

"It was all that could be done. You delayed the inevitable, and you gave the poor boy some kindness and support in his final hours. No-one could possibly have expected more of you. If Gillespie hadn't met you tonight, Faulkner would have caught him that much sooner."

"Do you really think so?" Anna looked at him through tear-filled eyes.

"I know it. It's right that you grieve for the loss of your companion, whatever kind of a fellow he may have been. That's as it should be. But please do not blame yourself anymore. Nothing more could be done against an enemy so formidable."

Her uncle fell silent for a moment, before continuing.

"Well, if it wasn't already very clear, I hope you now understand that going out on your own is simply no longer safe. This behaviour will not do."

"Yes, uncle." Anna looked down at the floor.

"In many ways, I feel you have let Mr Warwick and me down badly, despite all our warnings. I'm sure I don't need to tell you the state that your mother has worked herself into this evening?"

Anna was hit by a new broadside of guilt. She noted her mother had chosen not to see her yet.

"I trust you are under no illusion as to just how much danger you were in tonight?"

She swallowed hard and shook her head.

"I shall not labour that point then. But you will need to accept that your mother, Mr Warwick and I now have no choice but to guard you even more strictly than before."

Anna did not like the sound of this. But she nodded. Now was not the time to resist. She looked up at her uncle's face again. She was relieved to see it finally losing some of its sternness.

"As for what you've told me, we can only guess at Faulkner's motives for tracking Gillespie."

"Do you think he was trying to find me?"

He paused. "No. I don't believe he was using him as bait to capture you. Because if he had known that you were there, he would never have left that garden until he had hunted you down. You were singled out by the Gorgal when it entered this world. You would have represented an infinitely greater prize for Faulkner than the Gillespie brothers."

Anna shuddered, as she always did at the mention of the Gorgal, their ultimate enemy of the Omega World. The thought of that being from her childhood dream, with its terrible, penetrating red eyes, still terrified her.

"No, I am certain Faulkner had no idea he was so close to capturing you. I believe he began to track Billy Gillespie in order to follow him to his brother, Kenny. No-one can expect to cross Faulkner in the way Kenny

Gillespie apparently did and avoid the consequences. Faulkner will have found it easy to extract his location from young Billy if he knew it. Regardless, he will have had all Kenny Gillespie's regular haunts watched."

"So you don't think Kenny Gillespie will escape?"

"Not unless he possesses a great deal more cunning than I give him credit for. No, I'll wager it's only a short matter of time now before he's hunted down. I'm afraid the tragedy of the Gillespie family will soon be complete, if indeed it is not already so."

The reality of this struck Anna. Kenny Gillespie was a strong, rough and frightening young man. He himself had struck fear into many people. But even he had been completely powerless against the infinitely more evil enemy now at large in their city. She felt exhausted, but the night's events had started to forge a new resolve within her. She would play whatever part she could to stop Faulkner. To stop him from doing to anyone else what she had failed to prevent him doing to Billy Gillespie. And to do that, she must learn everything she could.

"What Billy told me tonight, about Faulkner actually being the Beast of Highgate, not just someone who conjures up its appearance... that was true, wasn't it? Faulkner didn't just summon that Satal tonight. Faulkner *is* the Satal, isn't he?"

Uncle James did not reply.

"But if he is a Satal," she pressed, "how does he appear as a man? And how does he turn into the Beast and back again? Uncle, please tell me. I need to know."

He hesitated. "Mr Warwick returns from his travels tomorrow. We are planning to recommence your instruction straight away. We'd better wait for that.

Personally, I would prefer to answer your question now. Indeed, I think we should probably have discussed these things long before, but Mr Warwick has strong opinions on this subject. Since we do not have long to wait, I suggest we do so."

Until now, Anna had always been content to move at her mentors' pace, to listen and not to challenge too much. She was naturally shy, and they were older and knew so much more than she did. But the experience of that night had changed everything for her.

"I'm sorry, but this can't wait, uncle. I was almost captured by Faulkner tonight. I wasn't ready, and I was almost done for. I know I will be hidden away, but we just can't be sure it won't happen again. I have a feeling that I may still have to face him, despite all our efforts to avoid it. I must be ready."

Her uncle gave her a long look that she could not read. He did not speak. Anna was struggling to explain the urgency she felt. Certainty coursed through her.

"Uncle, sometimes I – I sense things, very strongly. And these things, they often then seem to happen. And I sense that an encounter with Faulkner is coming, and it may be soon. I will do my best to avoid it, of course I will, but I need to be ready. And right now, the first thing I need to know is if Faulkner is a Satal."

She had never spoken this way to him before. She would never have dared. At first she thought he might be taken aback. But rather than resume the scolding or make one of his usual jibes about her impertinence, he continued to look at her, steadily. Then, he nodded.

"All right, Anna. In your studies, you will learn about the particular abilities of people whom we call Seers.

They are sometimes able to foresee certain aspects of the future. It is one of the Powers, like the ability to see auras, but much rarer. You are unique in so many ways, it would not surprise me if you are already developing some such abilities. If you feel the need for this knowledge so keenly now, I will not stand in the way."

Anna nodded. Her pulse raced.

"The answer to your question is yes. Faulkner is the Beast of Highgate. He's one of our deadliest enemies from the Omega side. He is a Satal."

Although Anna had already believed this to be so, the confirmation was still significant.

"I will also tell you this," he continued. "We are now but a few weeks away from the day when Faulkner and his gang will come face-to-face in battle with the might of the Order. Mark my words Anna, before the year is out, we will rid the world of this Satal for good. Then no-one else will ever have to suffer the fate that befell Billy Gillespie tonight. Please take heart from that."

With that, Uncle James drew the discussion to a close and bade her goodnight.

Anna was relieved that the Order was planning an attack on Faulkner soon. She was also delighted to hear that her instruction was about to resume. No matter what her uncle said, Gillespie had come to her for help, but she had failed to prevent the Satal from carrying him off to his doom. Previously it had been her mission to find out who this mysterious Mr Faulkner was. Now she knew. He was something far worse than she originally could ever have imagined. She had a much bigger purpose now: that evil monster's downfall, once and for all.

The idea was terrifying, but she owed it to the memory of Gillespie not to fail again. Not for revenge, but to stop anyone else falling to the same fate. Faulkner must not be allowed to ruin any more lives. The advance of the cursed Omega forces must be stopped. It was vital that she received the rest of her instruction. It could not come soon enough.

It would also give her something to take her mind off the crushing disappointment of Timmy's rejection, which had been confirmed by his failure to show up that day. She had no idea how her shattered heart would come to terms with that. Part of her felt like it hated him for it. But in truth, that was because the rest of her still loved him. The more distraction she had from thinking about that, the better.

Anna wearily made her way up to her room. She considered paying a visit to her mother, but she trusted her uncle had already reassured her sufficiently about her safety. Right then she did not have the energy to face another telling off.

Even troubled thoughts of Timmy, Gillespie and the Satal could not prevent her from falling into the deepest of sleeps. The last thoughts to crawl across her mind were those of the upcoming battle, and that Faulkner must be stopped.

* * *

The following day, Kenny Gillespie's body was found. It took the police a long time to identify him from his remains, so horrific were his injuries. "Beast

Strikes South of the River!" screamed the newspaper headlines. Faulkner had caught his prey.

2
Ambush

Anna's instruction was led by her uncle and the elderly Mr Warwick, a very senior knight and a lifelong friend of Anna's family. To everyone outside the Order, Mr Warwick was known only under his alias, Mr Barton, a kindly old bookshop owner. Anna's training sessions were always held in the back room of his shop.

Of all her training that November, 'The Nature of the Essence' was amongst the topics she most looked forward to. As a child she had discovered the word 'aura' to describe what she could see. She had recently learned that the correct term for aura, used by the Order, was 'essence'.

"As you already know," Mr Warwick began one such session, "the appearance of a person's essence represents their fundamental nature and character. As you would expect, there is a huge amount of theory associated with this. That includes what its state means, both for its owner and for the world, and about the right ways to think and act to improve the state of our own essence, and those of others.

"Of central importance is this: if everyone could achieve an entirely pure essence, the Alpha-Omega Wars would finally be over, and the world would attain the pure state of the Alpha World – the World as it Was Meant to Be. This is the ultimate goal of all of us in the Order of the Knights of the True Path. It is a subject to which we shall return many times."

Anna nodded. As he was speaking, she had instinctively shifted her focus to view the two men's auras. Auras were always located close to a person, usually at a height somewhere between the top of their heads and the bottom of their chests. Both the auras that she observed now were a considerable size, Mr Warwick's being the larger, and both were dazzling shades of blue. There was almost no other colour present in either, and particularly in Mr Warwick's – the surest indication of a good person. Anna had seen various colours in the auras of other people. Above all, the one she most feared was red. Red always signified evil. No-one, including Anna, could ever see their own aura.

"However," Mr Warwick continued, "we are planning a special training session on essences tomorrow evening. For once, it will not take place here in the shop."

He explained that although the purity of a person's intentions and actions were the principal way to achieve a pure aura, it was not the only way. It could also sometimes be achieved through the positive thoughts and emotions generated by outside stimuli, albeit always only temporarily. Feeling deeply moved or uplifted by a work of art or a piece of music, for example, was something that humans could experience uniquely, amongst all the creatures on earth. The old man explained that feeling exhilarated through the experience of music and the other arts was one way to come close to experiencing, just for a short time, what it would be like to exist in the pure Alpha World.

Anna was startled to learn that at such times, people's auras could change to a purer blue, and become less blemished, just for a time. However, such transformations were only temporary. Just as people found it difficult to sustain those exhilarated feelings for any length of time afterwards, the aura usually reverted to its former state again before long. The change could only be sustained if the experience led to a long-term change in the person's nature, thoughts and actions.

"It is one of the tragedies of our world as it is today that we may glimpse the ecstatic state of being that should be ours in the Alpha World, but that we can never sustain it. At least, not yet."

Anna said, "You mentioned a special training session?"

"Yes, that's right. Tomorrow evening, there will be a special piano performance at the Royal College of Music. As part of your instruction, you will get to see for yourself the temporary positive effects that music can have on the essences of the audience."

Anna nodded. "Where is the Royal College?" she asked.

"It's in South Kensington, not too far from your uncle's rooms. I hope you will enjoy the event. In our busy lives, it's important sometimes to experience the glimpses that we can of what the Alpha World would feel like. This is likely to be the last safe opportunity for you for some time. We know Faulkner and his right-hand man, Mortlock, are away from London for the time being, so I should like you to take it."

"Thank you, Mr Warwick." Suddenly Anna felt apprehensive though. Would this be one of those 'high society' occasions? They always filled her with dread.

Her uncle must have noticed. "Don't worry Anna, I'll be there with you. Besides, the star of the performance is a young lady not so many years older than you. One Miss Alexandra Greenwood. Another reason for wanting you to go is so that you can meet Alexandra. She is also a student of mine in the Powers."

"Oh, I see," said Anna. That sounded interesting. Another girl who could see auras.

"Miss Greenwood is one of our bright hopes for the future of the Struggle," her uncle continued. "I should very much like for you to get to know her. It would be good for you to get another young lady's perspective on the path to becoming a knight."

"Yes, I would like that," said Anna.

"Unsurprisingly," Mr Warwick added, "your uncle, being the very well-connected socialite that he is, has been invited to attend, accompanied by one guest. So, young Anna, you are being offered the seat that would otherwise no doubt be occupied by one of your uncle's many high society lady friends!"

The old man cast a jovial grin at Uncle James, who raised one eyebrow.

"I feel honoured, Uncle, that you sacrificed such a chance for me!" Anna joined in.

"Well, there will be plenty of other opportunities!" He returned their grins briefly, before immediately growing serious again.

"Before going any further, however, there is something very important we must discuss."

"What's that?" Anna frowned.

"You will need to dress appropriately. There will be some important people there. If you are to accompany me as my niece, your appearance must live up to the part!"

He winked, but Anna knew him well enough to know he was only half joking.

Despite her initial interest, as the time drew closer Anna felt less and less keen to spend the evening somewhere where people were going to judge her on her appearance. Her confidence in her powers might be growing, but that confidence did not extend in any way to her outward appearance. She was also not looking forward to having to make polite conversation either, with people she had never met before and probably never wanted to. She never knew what to say, and always felt awkward and foolish. But this event was clearly one that both Mr Warwick and her uncle felt would benefit her instruction, so she would go.

To her surprise, her mother provided her with a long, sapphire-blue dress of the most expensive-looking material. Anna was struck by its beauty. She liked it very much, though naturally she liked it far less when it was on her. Her brown hair was tied up fashionably, and that did make her look older than she was, but no amount of praise from those in the household could persuade her she didn't look foolish.

As she prepared to leave, Anna noticed her mother was waiting for her. She appeared to have tears in her eyes. She smiled briefly at her daughter, then she turned away and was gone in a moment. Anna could not for the life of her understand why she might be crying. Even Anna herself didn't think she looked quite that bad! The image remained with her. They barely spoke at all these days. One day soon they needed to have a proper conversation, to try to repair the relationship. It would not be an easy dialogue to initiate. She would need to pick the timing carefully.

Anna felt acutely self-conscious leaving the house. Her only comfort was that, where she was going, there was no chance any of her friends would see her. If they saw her looking like this, she would never hear the end of it. Her uncle, for his part, looked immaculate in his eveningwear, complete with top hat, white gloves and walking cane. She just managed to stifle a giggle as he bowed to her formally, then fired her a wink.

Jim, the junior butler of the house, was waiting outside the door to see them off. "Have a wonderful evening, mistress Anna," he said cheerfully.

"Thank you, Jim. I'll try!" she replied, although right then, not falling headlong in the ridiculous shoes she had been given to wear would be wonderful enough. Jim was always kind to her, and she liked him very much. She shifted her focus to look at his aura, as she often did when she saw him. It was as pure and blue as ever.

"Excuse me, sir," said Jim, turning to Anna's uncle. "A message arrived for you a short time ago, and I've not had a chance to give it to you." He handed him a sealed envelope.

They passed down the front steps of the house to their waiting carriage without any falls, much to Anna's relief. Once inside it, Uncle James immediately opened the envelope.

"It's from Miller. He's one of the Order's spies watching the enemy's house up in Eagle Street, in Highgate. We've rented some rooms on the upper floor of a building on the opposite side of the road, with a view overlooking it. We have someone there at all times now, watching their comings and goings."

Anna's mood changed instantly. That was the house where she had first seen Joseph Mortlock. Mortlock had once been Mr Warwick's best friend, decades ago, before he was turned to the Omega side. He was the first person she had ever seen use their aura to stab that of another person, to try to kill them. He had served at least two Satals before Faulkner that she was aware of.

She examined her uncle's face for clues as he read the note. A moment later he sat back in his seat, looked out of the window and muttered what sounded like a curse under his breath. He bit his lip, deep in thought.

"What is it?" Anna asked.

"The message says that Jake Grimes and Angus McCain, better known charmingly as Slasher McCain, are back in London. They were spotted entering the Eagle Street house this afternoon." He continued to look out of the window.

Anna waited for more, but the silence lengthened. "Uncle, who are those people? Jake Grimes and, what was the other name... Slasher...?"

Her uncle returned his gaze inside the carriage and looked at her for a moment before responding.

"Slasher McCain. Like it or not, you're involved with these matters now. I'll tell you who they are."

Anna nodded. She felt herself growing tense.

21

"Jake Grimes and Angus McCain are two of the most unpleasant characters you are ever likely to come across. They were part of a gang of villains who struck fear into large swathes of London during the last Satal war, guided by the unseen hand of Mortlock and his Satal master of that time. There were more than a dozen in that bloodthirsty group, and they were responsible for some of the most heinous crimes of the last fifty years. Their minds were twisted and their actions fuelled by the influence of the Satal of that time."

Anna's eyes widened. "That must have been an awful time."

"It was. Some of the gang met their end in that war. Others were captured and are now in jail. However, a number were never caught and escaped oversees. As of course did Mortlock himself."

Anna shrank back in her seat.

"There will be time aplenty to furnish you with details of that rotten bunch another time – Johnny 'Cut-Throat' Hyde, Albert Dobbs, better known as the Southall Strangler, Gianni Moretti, the so-called Butcher of Naples, who came all the way to London from Italy to join the Struggle here. I doubt London has known a more vicious gang of criminals than that which the last Satal assembled in this city to wreak havoc and mayhem, with Mortlock at their head. Their names live on in infamy to this day. And then of course there was the Black Widow…" Seeing Anna look up at this unusual name, he added quickly, "but hers is a story that must wait for another day."

The carriage swayed gently as it made its way over the cobbled streets towards Kensington.

"So were Grimes and McCain as bad as the others?" asked Anna.

"Yes. They were amongst the worst of them. They would harm you as soon as look at you, and cause pain without a second's thought. The young ruffians you have encountered so far, the likes of Kenny Gillespie, may have been nasty pieces of work themselves, but they pale in comparison. For Gillespie had no knowledge of the Powers. The members of that last Satal's gang, McCain and the others, they all did. This made them many times more dangerous than the roughest of normal men. They were *Turners* you see, like Mortlock, though not quite so high up in our enemies' ranks."

"Uncle, why would anyone become a Turner? I mean, why does any person with the Powers want to fight for the Omega side? Surely if the Omega side wins and the world does become the Omega World, the Turners will die too, along with everyone else? I've never understood this, ever since you first told me about Mortlock."

"Yes, that is a fundamental question. It's a very complex subject. It involves the frailties of human nature and the manipulative ways of the enemy. But one important reason is usually that they come to put their own, sometimes relatively short-term, gains ahead of everything else. They reach a point where they place no value in society, have no care for the well-being of others and have no interest in whether the world continues beyond their lifetimes or not. If they serve their Omega masters well, they can receive rich rewards and lead lavish lifestyles for the time being. They may imagine it's worth risking the world's eventual destruction for that. For a descent to the Omega would not happen overnight.

It might take years of painful destruction before it is complete."

Anna nodded, a little stunned as she took this in.

"You'll learn all about these things soon enough. But suffice to say that, although Turners try to justify their actions to themselves in various ways, the truth is their minds have been twisted one way or another to use their gifts in the direction of the Omega World. This makes them amongst the vilest and most dangerous of our foes. A person strong in the Powers, once turned, can become a most terrible and dangerous weapon for the Omega cause."

"And now two of them have returned to join the battle ahead…" Anna's voice had grown small.

"So it would appear. Jake Grimes was believed to be behind some particularly brutal crimes during that last Satal's reign of terror. And as for Angus McCain… well, suffice to say he wasn't known as 'Slasher' for nothing. It was due to his liking for bladed weapons, and the uses to which he liked to put them. Slasher McCain is evil to the core. A very nasty piece of work indeed."

Anna sat even deeper in her carriage seat.

"It is a sign of the times we are in that these treacherous villains have come back, like stinking rats returning to their lair." Her uncle's voice had grown stern. "I shudder at the idea they might attempt another reign of terror here, now. But this time we will act soon and put an end to them, once and for all, before they can put their evil plans into effect." He landed a powerful blow with his right fist into the palm of his left, making Anna jump. The jovial mood of a few minutes earlier had gone entirely.

"Are you sure Faulkner is nowhere near now?"

"Yes. Both Faulkner and Mortlock are out of London. We have spies tailing them. They are making various preparations for the upcoming war. That's why we judged it safe for you to attend the concert tonight. We felt certain that Faulkner's regular henchmen wouldn't act without the presence and direct guidance of their leaders. However, I now wonder if that's precisely what they wanted us to think. I must confess, tonight's news concerns me gravely. I'm no longer sure this evening's plan is such a wise idea."

He remained silent for the rest of the journey, staring fiercely through the carriage window. His jaw tensed repeatedly as though he was contemplating what to do next.

Presently, their carriage drew up outside the Royal College of Music. They alighted and Anna's uncle asked the driver to wait for them. Anna was both amused and slightly taken aback by the amount of eye contact that came her uncle's way from the many ladies in attendance. Anna had heard all about his legendary socialising when she was growing up, but to witness first-hand the attention he generated was something else altogether.

As they neared the grand entrance, she did her best not to reveal how out of her depth and clumsy she felt in her flowing dress and awkward shoes. She was surrounded by a growing throng of very finely-dressed people. The age range of the audience was considerable, but the average was younger than Anna had expected. There were a good number who looked to be in their late teenage years or early twenties, perhaps music students from the college. All around them, the air was filled with excited chatter.

Uncle James was evidently in his natural environment. Anna marvelled at how widely known he was, and how easily he dealt with all-comers, subtly adjusting his manner to put each at their ease. When she had heard about her uncle's social life, it had usually been in a disapproving tone from her mother. Seeing him in action now, she appreciated the considerable skill involved. No doubt about it, he was a fascinating study.

Anna wished some of his skill would rub off on her, as she was introduced to his acquaintances, one after another. She found herself tongue-tied and shy. Often, she was unable to pursue the conversations beyond the initial courtesy and a "how do you do". One thing she did notice was that several of the younger male audience members seemed to be making more eye contact with her than she knew what to make of, or to do with. They were boys around her own age or a little older, who her uncle explained were young music students.

She could not deny a slight tingle of excitement at this unexpected attention. This was always immediately accompanied by guilty thoughts of Timmy though, followed quickly by the certainty that she was misreading the situation anyway. But after a while her uncle remarked in a whisper, "You seem to be making quite an impression. That little shy act you put is having quite an effect!"

'If only it were an act,' thought Anna to herself, but she said nothing, merely smiling and then looking the other way by means of escape.

Her uncle took the trouble to introduce her to one person in particular. It was a blond-haired young man with a slightly pointed face, who looked about twenty, called Percival Gladstone. He was apparently a close friend of that evening's performer. Mr Gladstone appeared extremely enthusiastic to meet Anna, saying amongst other things that he was "deeply honoured to make her acquaintance", and giving her the lowest of bows. Anna thought it all a bit over the top, but she curtseyed and smiled politely in return, nonetheless.

Uncle James may have been socialising effortlessly, but he still seemed far from his usual self. His serious demeanour returned the moment each conversation was over, and at every opportunity he looked all around them, subtly, but fully alert. The message about Faulkner's gang members was clearly still at the forefront of his mind.

There was an announcement that the concert would start shortly, and everyone was asked to take their seats. In the distance, near the exit, Anna caught sight of Percival Gladstone again, talking to an older man with a big, drooping moustache. As she watched, Gladstone peered over his shoulder as if to check that no-one was watching him. Then he slipped out of the auditorium. Anna was wondering why he should be leaving just as his friend's performance was about to start, when her uncle touched her arm gently and whispered in her ear.

"Anna, I think we should leave. It will be a shame to miss the performance, but with tonight's news about our enemies I think it's simply not worth the risk. I asked our driver to wait outside for us. I suggest we return straight home." His face remained calm, but his voice betrayed a growing tension.

Anna's own pulse quickened. Moving against the tide of people coming to take their seats, they hurried back up the stairs, out of the hall and straight back to the main building entrance. Uncle James increased the pace further as they passed through it and down the stone steps leading to the road. All around them, a familiar, ominous, swirling fog was beginning to descend.

Uncle James was the first to realise that something was not right. He scoured the road ahead looking for their driver. He was nowhere to be seen.

"I don't like this. I specifically asked him to wait because I thought we might not stay. There's something wrong. Come on, we need to strike out on foot. Quickly!"

This was the last thing Anna wanted to hear. Her shoes did not seem designed even for walking in, let alone running. But there was no mistaking her uncle's urgency now. She did her best to keep up, gripping his arm with one hand and hitching her long dress away from her feet with the other. The fog was starting to swirl around them.

At the first opportunity, Uncle James led them across the road, then he took a side street. He continued to peer all around them, and at the next junction took another turning. Anna guessed he was trying to lose anyone trying to follow them from the concert venue. 'Just as long as he doesn't get us completely lost as well,' Anna thought to herself. But he knew this part of London like the back of his hand.

As they pushed on through the fast-thickening fog, Anna became aware of a strange, muffled sound. At first, she thought she had imagined it. Then she heard it again. It was the soft sound of music, played on what sounded like some kind of violin. But the tune was unlike any music she had heard before. It was an eerie sound, soft and swirling, but carrying a hint of menace. Just like the mist, Anna thought. The last time she had seen an evening as fogbound as this, she had come within a whisker of capture and almost certain death at the hands of Faulkner, in the garden with Gillespie. She quickened her pace.

The music was neither distant nor very near. Anna's first thought was that it could be a music college student, practising. But surely no college would teach music like this. It was a strange tune indeed. It was mournful and haunting, and Anna could not shake the thoughts it conjured in her mind. Thoughts of terror, and of death.

Uncle James also seemed affected by it. He took a firm grip of her arm, whispered to her to stop, then looked all around them, listening intently. The sound was starting to have a deeply disturbing effect on Anna. She peered about her, looking for the player.

Suddenly, her uncle set off again, now at a rapid pace, tugging at her arm to keep up. Her shoes were cutting into her feet, but she pressed on. She could still hear the music behind them. She peered desperately over her shoulder, fearing what spectral form she might see. Still nothing. Mr Warwick had taught her always to keep her aura disguised when she left her house, to make it appear smaller and less pure than its true form. The only thing no-one could do was to make an aura appear larger than its true size. Now, she made it smaller still.

They ran into a small square. They were halfway across one side of it when Uncle James stopped dead in his tracks. Three silhouettes were just visible ahead of them at the far side, lit faintly by the gas streetlamps. No-one moved. The sinister melody continued, suddenly growing faster, more manic and more discordant. Then, abruptly, it stopped.

As if in response, the three shadowy forms began to move slowly towards them through the fog. They were fanning out, the leftmost figure moving towards the far side of the square. Anna's uncle wheeled them both round, only to find three more figures now slowly emerging from the gloomy mist on that side of the square, too. They were moving with careful, crouching steps. Two of the three were already fanning out to the right. High iron railings lined the side of the road just to Anna's left, guarding an even higher terrace of buildings.

They were trapped.

3
The War Begins

Anna shifted her focus to what she could make out of the strangers' auras. Visibility in the fog was very poor now, but her worst fears were realised. The overriding impression was of red.

"Uncle," she whispered, "I don't know if you can see their essences yet, but they're not good."

"I don't need to see their essences to know that! Quick, get behind me." He turned to face the middle of the square.

Anna did as she was told, immediately moving between her uncle and the railings. He swept his cloak away from his arms and brandished his sturdy walking cane, ready. The six figures continued their stealthy movement, gradually completing the semi-circle around them. Their forms were more distinct now. All appeared to be men, and each carried some kind of weapon.

Then Anna spotted something that made her blood run cold. The unmistakable glint of shiny metal, coming from the hand of the figure furthest to their right. It came from a blade, over a foot long. 'Slasher McCain,' she recalled her uncle's words. Veteran of the last Satal war, and 'evil to the core'. Was it him? The man began to slowly slice the air in front of him with the weapon, as though eager to live up to the reputation that had earned him his name.

Anna shrank further behind the tall figure of her uncle, wishing desperately for some means of escape. Her uncle, however, did not take a step back. In contrast to how Anna was feeling, he seemed to be gaining in stature. She sensed him expanding his chest. He appeared to be challenging the men, daring them to take him on. Anna was reminded of a painting from India that hung in her house, of a mighty tiger preparing to strike.

The six figures stopped moving forward. They were looking back at him, all held in check for now. Slowly, Uncle James raised his walking cane and pointed it in the direction of the figure furthest to their left. He fixed him with a piercing stare. He made the same gesture to the next figure, then the next, as though giving each of them one final, deadly warning. When he reached the adversary furthest to their right, the man with the blade, he held the position for longer. He was singling this one out for particular attention. His breathing was even, and his aura dazzling blue. Anna's fear had been starting to get the better of her, but her uncle's presence and strength gave her courage. She slowly stepped out from behind him and stood by his side.

Still none of the figures moved. It was as though, despite their greater numbers, it was they who now felt intimidated. The man to the far right broke the silence, barking a single word: "Move!"

The gang edged forward towards them, all crouching as though ready to leap forward, or back, at any moment. Anna shot a glance at her uncle. He whispered to her to keep calm and to hold her ground until he told her to move. She looked back at the approaching figures.

Their auras were growing more distinct. And a collection of disfigured, misshapen specimens they were. None of them was more than very roughly spherical. Some contained great pockmarks, and all were black and brown with significant stains of red. Anna's stomach contracted. She fought to control her feelings. She remained standing resolutely by her uncle's side.

Repulsive and villainous though these auras undoubtedly were, in truth, five of them were of no great size. She peered more closely at the aura of the sixth, the man she presumed to be McCain. Sure enough, his was significantly larger than the others. It was also by far the most scarlet.

Uncle James appeared to be waiting until the approaching men reached a certain point. "Now!" he suddenly hissed to Anna, then he bolted forward, straight towards the one of the men in the middle ahead of them.

As he ran, the semicircle of figures immediately contracted faster towards them. The man directly ahead was the only one to stop, shifting his stance to prepare for the onslaught. They reached him in moments. Uncle James's walking cane moved fast, outmanoeuvred the man's weapon and struck him somewhere on his body. Anna's main focus was on his aura, though. With some wonder she saw it stretch out from him and instantly find a grip on the more sluggish aura of his adversary. He twisted it, contorted it powerfully, then threw it roughly aside. The physical and mental actions were simultaneous, but Anna was certain it was the mental contact that left the attacker helpless and sprawling on the ground. They rushed past his unmoving body and on into the foggy darkness of the square.

The brief scuffle had slowed their progress a little, and before they could escape the next attacker was on them. Anna gasped as from her left-hand side a particularly ugly specimen of an aura, resembling a rough, black and brown rock smeared with blood, came crashing into her uncle's pure blue one. He stumbled heavily, and for a moment it was only Anna's grip on his arm that kept him from falling. Regaining his balance and composure fast, he jabbed back at the attacking aura with his own, catching it squarely. The speed and ferocity of the hit sent it backwards, taking its owner's body with it. He tumbled to the ground, gasping for breath.

Anna took in all that was happening, her mind racing at lightning speed. She had noticed how her uncle's aura had contracted before he landed the blow. It had been like clenching a fist. Over her right shoulder she glimpsed the deformed aura of the next attacker bearing down in his direction. This time she reacted herself, visualising her own clenched aura moving in an uppercut towards the underside of the man's. She felt the hard contact. The effect was as dramatic as that of her uncle's blow seconds earlier, stunning the assailant and sending his physical body to its knees, doubled up in pain.

They pushed on. Anna finally shed her shoes and ran barefoot on the cold, wet cobblestones. They were approaching the far side of the square when she felt a crashing blow, as though a huge weight had been slammed into her chest. The unseen strike to her aura knocked all the breath from her lungs. She was thrown off balance completely, and fell face down onto the cold, damp cobbles. Gasping, she looked back up in time to see the craggy face of a rough-looking man, wearing a grim, murderous expression, bearing down on her with a metal bar. His aura was contorted into a shape resembling an axe head and it too was heading directly towards her. She reacted instantly, rolling her physical form away from the oncoming blow and visualising her aura moving in the same direction. This time there was no agonising sensation deep inside. The sound of metal on stone came from a foot away.

Anna was stunned by this sudden, shocking aggression. What could make people be so evil? Anger flared within her. Anger that she channelled into a surge of power. She looked up at her attacker, just in time to see his short, rusty metal bar now being used to parry a powerful blow from Uncle James's walking stick. Anna's uncle landed a mighty blow on the man's repulsive aura with his own, and Anna did the same from below. She dragged herself up to her knees and watched the craggy-faced man hit the ground like a stone, all consciousness gone.

Anna's cheek stung from where it had struck the cobblestones and her frozen feet hurt, but her uncle tugged her back up. They resumed their escape towards the dark entrance of a side street ahead. By now the final duo of the six had overtaken them, moving to block off this route. Anna glanced behind them again. Two of their assailants still lay prone, but the other two were slowly moving towards them again.

"Behind us, uncle!" she warned.

He slowed to a stop. It looked like this would be a fight to the end now. Immediately he made his move. At lightning speed, first he struck ahead at the man with the largest aura with both his cane and his own aura, knocking him backwards and leaving him stunned. He wheeled round with a sweep of his cape to his left, parrying the blow of a mace from behind him with his stick. He landed a devastating blow on that man's aura, knocking him out cold. Even as his opponent was collapsing into a crumpled heap, Uncle James had already spun round again and was moving rapidly in Anna's direction to protect her from the third assailant. He was just in time to see the man's scruffy form pushed over, senseless, to the ground by the far slighter figure of his niece, who had landed a huge, decisive blow of her own on his aura.

"What on earth…?" her uncle started.

The fourth man lunged at her. Before her uncle could intervene, Anna clenched her aura and aimed a huge hook at that of the oncoming man's. He was much too slow to avoid it. Anna dived out of the way as the man's momentum took him past her. He fell to the ground doubled up, and did not move.

Her uncle raised his left eyebrow and corner of his mouth in a very brief smile of approval. Then he wheeled back to face the first attacker he had stunned. It was the man with the largest aura, who carried the machete. He was the last of the six still standing. Anna could clearly make out his face now. He had recovered some of his poise and looked altogether more menacing than the other five put together. Anna was sure now that this must be Angus 'Slasher' McCain.

He looked to be a number of years older than her uncle. His features might once have been considered handsome, but now they wore the marks of a life spent living hard and pursuing evil. Most prominent was a scar that ran diagonally, almost from the brim of his flat cap at the top-right of his forehead, across the bridge of his nose and down across his lower left cheek to his jawline.

Anna's uncle moved between her and the man. McCain's eyes glinted in the gas lamplight, which grew brighter and dimmer by turns in the swirling mist. Slowly, he began to smile.

"Lawrence, I see you've lost none of your fancy moves." His rasping accent was unfamiliar to Anna. "But you don't scare me, you know that, don't you? I've faced you before and lived to tell the tale, and I'll do it again. But, tell me Lawrence, who is *she*?"

His voiced turned almost to a hiss as he raised his evil blade in a gesture towards Anna. Then he began to taunt them.

"Who is this wee mite you have with you?" He let out a menacing chuckle. "I know who she is! Yeah, I do. And you know who else wants to meet her, don't you? He has powers beyond your wildest imaginings, he does. You know who I mean. I'm not talking about Faulkner. The time has come, Lawrence. Someone has come whose power goes beyond anything you can comprehend. Your fancy moves will count for nothing when he finds you! He'll crush you like an insect, no matter what you try to do. And he'll do far worse to this wee girl here!" McCain let out an evil, gravelly laugh.

The laughter was short-lived. Anna's uncle made a move almost faster than the human eye. He was upon McCain in an instant, his cane landing a mighty blow on his right hand. The cruel blade went clattering to the cobblestones. At the same time, he aimed a powerful blow at McCain's aura, but his enemy's attention was more focused on that dimension. He shaped his own aura into a spike just a split second before the blow landed.

The impact on McCain was considerable. It wiped the taunting sneer from his face and sent him staggering backwards, panting for breath. However, the damage to her uncle looked more severe. He let out an audible gasp and dropped to his knees. He kept his eyes firmly trained on his adversary.

Anna was shocked as she watched the impact. To her enormous relief the spike had not penetrated too deeply into her uncle's aura, as it had been tightly clenched. But he was badly stunned.

McCain was certainly tough, and he recovered much more quickly than any of the other attackers. He made a lunge for his machete with his undamaged hand. The look on his face expressed precisely the lethal use to which he intended to put it. Anna needed to act, fast. His fingers had barely closed on the handle when his aura was struck by her blow. This time he was knocked clean off his feet and landed more than a yard away, stunned but still holding the machete. Anna hoped he might have had enough now, and that he would make a run for it. But he did not.

Wheezing heavily, he dragged himself to his feet once more. He began to walk slowly towards her again, leaning slightly, his head tilted to one side. His murderous eyes were trained on her, unblinking. His aura took the form of a spike again, and his machete was raised. Preparing herself for the attack and already planning her own counter, Anna took a step back. Her shoeless foot slid on the damp cobblestones. She lost her balance and tumbled backwards. McCain seized his chance, sprang forwards and swung his weapon downwards, directly towards her.

It never reached its target. Before it was even halfway down, his body convulsed. He was bent double and flung high in the air, backwards towards the railings behind him. Anna didn't see the blow that struck his aura with such a mighty force. All she saw was the cloaked figure of her uncle, standing tall once more between her and McCain. He was still in pain, but finally victorious. The scar-faced man was lying flat on his back in the road. His arms were outstretched and one leg was bent beneath him. His other leg twitched slightly, but he was otherwise motionless.

Anna glanced around quickly to make sure their other attackers had not recovered. And what a sorry sight they made. The first two to be felled by Anna's uncle were now making some attempt to move, but neither had progressed beyond their knees. Both were still bent double. The others lay completely motionless. None of these pathetic figures posed any further threat.

She looked back at her uncle. He was walking towards McCain. She checked his aura. It still shone vividly, showing no signs of lasting damage from the battle. But she did notice a subtle change. It remained basically blue, but the hue had changed slightly. It had taken on a hint of mauve. Uncle James picked up the bladed weapon and hurled it out of sight, beyond the railings that lined the far side of the square. Then he reached its owner.

McCain appeared to be unconscious, but as Anna's uncle bent down and grabbed him, the man groaned. Anna thought McCain's jacket lapels might come clean off, such was the force with which her uncle tugged his body up. He dragged him roughly towards the railings and shoved him hard against them. All the time he retained a tight grip on his foe's aura, rendering him powerless.

"Talk, McCain. Who did you refer to earlier? Who is more powerful than Faulkner?"

The beaten man was in no position to fight back, but he retained a remarkably defiant tone in his husky voice.

"I think you know who I'm talking about, Lawrence! He's got power beyond anything this world has known. And his *essence*..."

Anna drew close behind her uncle, listening with her breath held to catch every word. She saw a look of awe-struck fear cross the man's scarred face. His eyes lost their focus on his opponent, and he appeared to be looking into the far distance. He flinched as Uncle James increased the pressure on his aura, forcing him to continue.

"You, with all your fancy education and your high-powered friends, you may know more about what he is than I do. But I tell you this. He's going to have power beyond anything you've ever seen, power far beyond any of the masters we've had. I tell you, Lawrence, this world has *never* seen the like of him. It doesn't matter what you do to me. His day is coming, and there's nothing you, nor any of your beloved Order," McCain spat the word out, "can do to stop the rise of the Omega World now. The final victory is near. When he's ready to strike, that will be the end of you all!"

Despite his defiance and triumphant words, there was a curious absence of joy in his face. In the pale lamplight, Anna could only make out what looked to be a lost, haunted expression in his eyes, as they continued to gaze into the far distance.

"Where is he now?" Uncle James shoved the man roughly against the railings again. He applied more pressure to his aura. McCain tried to resist speaking further, but he was clearly in great discomfort. He gasped for air. Under further pressure, more words were forced out of him.

"I don't know where he is now. All I can tell you is he's not near. Not yet. But make no mistake, he will come. And when he does, he will slaughter you all without mercy. And he has special plans for her!"

McCain's attention suddenly returned to the here and now. His murderous eyes stared like daggers past her uncle, directly at Anna. She shrank back, trembling, knowing full well who it was they were talking about. The image of the red eyes from her dream returned. Then something inside her uncle seemed to snap. His aura glowed brightly again, now more purple than mauve. It was a colour Anna had never seen before in an aura. The idea of what it could mean frightened her.

McCain's body convulsed again. He let out a yell of pain. Uncle James appeared to be applying extreme pressure to his aura now, as if to crush the life out of it. At the same time, he had both his hands round McCain's throat, forcing his head hard against the railings. For a dreadful moment, Anna thought he was going to kill him right there on the spot.

"No, uncle, stop!" she cried, as McCain's body started to go limp. Just in time her uncle regained sufficient control of the fury that had gripped him. After a few more seconds that seemed to last an eternity, he slowly began to release the pressure in both dimensions. McCain's body immediately fell limply to the floor like a bundle of old rags. The almost imperceptible movement of his chest was the only indication that he was still alive.

Not looking at Anna, Uncle James stepped away and strode towards the nearest of the other attackers. All were conscious now, but none had moved yet. Anna was still in shock and unsure what to do. She stood motionless, watching, as one-by-one her uncle confronted the men. They all cowered and made no attempt to fight him. He made contact with each of their auras in turn, but with nothing like the pressure he had applied to McCain's. It was a subtle movement, to render them unconscious but nothing worse. He left them all where they lay in what looked like a deep sleep.

Finally, he returned to Anna. "Right, I've removed any risk of their following us. They will all survive, but they will be unconscious long enough for us to escape. Let's get away from here before any accomplices arrive." He paused. "I would like to take McCain with us, to question him further, and then to lock him up for good. That would also prevent him from telling his masters about tonight's events. But there's no way we can take all of them with us, so someone is sure to talk anyway."

"Might there be others out there now, hunting for us too?" Anna asked. She felt badly shaken. "It would really slow us down if we tried to drag him around with us, and we might get caught again. I just want to get away from here as fast as we can, uncle."

"You're right. And no taxi driver would pick us up if we had this unconscious lump with us." Uncle James gave McCain's body a disdainful poke with his toe. "We can't carry him all the way to Mr Warwick's, and they may be watching my rooms now. If we don't get away from this area fast, we could easily be attacked again. I cannot put your safety at any more risk. I'm afraid we have little choice but to leave them all here where they lie."

With that they set off, running down the side street ahead of them. "They will be gone long before I can get word to the Order to pick them up," Uncle James added, "but there will be plenty of opportunities to clear that rubbish up another day. My priority right now is to get you to safety, unseen."

Anna's feet were grazed and in serious danger of freezing on the cold, damp cobblestones, but she said nothing and hurried alongside him. All she wanted was to be away from that place. She looked again at her uncle's aura. She was relieved to see it had returned to its former blue colour.

They reached the far end of the street and emerged onto a wider avenue. The first thing Anna noticed was a gentle breeze on her face. There was still fog in the air, but it was thinning ahead of them. She breathed deeply for what felt like the first time since the stifling mist had descended. Within moments her uncle hailed a hackney carriage, and soon they were being whisked northwards towards still clearer air and more familiar streets.

Uncle James maintained a constant vigil on both sides of the carriage, but saw nothing. Anna's immediate fear lessened a little. With her legs and feet wrapped up in her uncle's cloak, her mind slowly turned to what that night's events might mean.

They had been directly targeted for attack. Or at least, her uncle clearly had. But had they known who she was when they planned this? Faulkner or Mortlock could well have orchestrated the assault, even if they were not in

London themselves. They could have ordered McCain to lead it. But there was no reason to think that any of them had known James Lawrence's niece was the girl sought by the Gorgal. Even Mortlock, who had encountered Anna once before outside Faulkner's mansion, had no way of knowing her identity, or where she had come from. McCain's surprise when he realised who she was seemed to confirm they had not expected the Gorgal's prized target to be there. If they had, from everything Mr Warwick had told her, Faulkner and Mortlock would also surely have been there to catch her. They must not have known.

But now they would know. Tonight's attackers would report what happened to their masters. Before the night was out, all their enemies would know that the Gorgal's target was connected to James Lawrence. Then they would surely find out who she was and where she lived. They would hunt her down at all costs. Her worries spread from herself to the others she cared about. They might be dragged into danger by association. Nothing would remain the same now.

By the time Anna made out the familiar trees lining the canal which ran past Mr Warwick's bookshop, the night air was clear. She was amazed how fast the weather had turned and the fog had dispersed. As quickly as it had arrived, in fact. She wondered if it had been entirely natural.

As always upon arrival at the shop, Uncle James dismounted the carriage first to confirm the coast was clear, before allowing Anna to alight. In all the weeks of her instruction, he had never seen anyone or anything untoward. Tonight, however, everything had changed.

These precautions now suddenly seemed vital, even inadequate. Anna's stomach began to churn.

With the clearing of the fog, the night was growing colder and crisper. A full moon rode high in the sky. When her uncle had satisfied himself that no-one was lying in ambush here, he ushered Anna rapidly across the street to the shop. Her senses were razor sharp. She peered all around as they crossed. She saw nothing. Her heart began to beat a little more steadily as they reached the door. She took one more backward glance – and the slightest of movements caught her eye.

Although difficult to tell in the moonlight, Anna thought she had momentarily glimpsed a man's face, near the base of a tree on the far side of the road.

4
A New Plan

Whatever Anna had seen, it was gone in an instant. She couldn't be sure it was not just her eyes playing tricks. Still, she immediately whispered a warning to her uncle. He span around and stared in the direction indicated. He made as though to investigate, then apparently thought better of it and decided to stay close.

Before long, Mr Warwick was at the door. With a look of grave concern, he let them in. He shut and bolted the door again immediately.

"Did you get my message?" he asked urgently.

Before responding, Uncle James turned to Anna and asked her to repeat what she thought she had seen.

"I may just have imagined it, but it looked like a man's face, staring at us from the other side of the street. It was at the bottom of the tree I pointed to, where the bank goes down to the canal. But it was gone straight away."

"Are you sure?"

"Well, no, not really. It was only an impression… but it did look like someone might be watching us."

Turning to Mr Warwick, her uncle said, "Master, I didn't receive your message, but we were attacked tonight. Six of Faulkner's hoodlums. One of them was McCain."

Anna saw the concerned look on the face of the old shopkeeper turn distinctly graver in the light of his lantern.

"And now Anna thinks she might have seen someone spying on us from outside. It may be nothing, but we can't risk it. Might I suggest you take Anna to the safety of the back room, while I return to check outside? I won't be long."

"Yes, of course," Mr Warwick replied immediately.

"The first thing to do is to get her warm again. She lost her shoes in the fight and has been shivering ever since."

Her uncle was right. Despite his cloak, Anna felt very cold. She could barely feel her feet. Uncle James took the keys from Mr Warwick and reopened the front door. Then he slipped back out into the night. Anna watched him disappear. She hoped fervently she had not just sent him out into yet more danger. The shock of that night was catching up with her, now that there had been a little time to reflect. She wanted to stay and watch from the window to make sure he was all right, but Mr Warwick would hear none of it. He ushered her briskly inside.

Once they had reached the back room safely, Mr Warwick told her to wait in her customary chair in front of the fire. Thankfully it was burning brightly, delivering some much-needed warmth. The tension in Anna's body lessened a fraction. She became fully aware of the pain in her frozen feet. It grew almost unbearable and was made no better by her proximity to the fire. Mr Warwick noticed the cuts and bruises on them, then looked even more disturbed as he examined her face.

"Oh, my dear child, what has happened to you?"

Anna raised her hand to her cheek. It was still stinging. Drawing it away, she saw blood on her fingers. She remembered being knocked to the ground.

"Don't worry, it's only a scratch," she said quickly. "To be honest, my feet are a little sore though!"

"My dear Anna," said the kindly old shopkeeper earnestly, "here, take this." He handed her a clean handkerchief to dab her face. "Now wait here while I get you something to warm your feet."

He hurried out of the room, retuning shortly with a bowl of warm water, a towel and some wool-lined slippers. The slippers were many sizes too large for her, but looked warm and inviting nonetheless. Anna slowly lowered her feet into the water. She bit her lip at the initial pain, then immersed them completely. She sat back in the chair, tiredness beginning to catch up with her, and waited as the pain gradually dulled. Feeling slowly returned. Meanwhile, the old man had disappeared again into another room.

Anna had always felt safe in this room, but recent events made relaxation anywhere impossible. She kept her eyes fixed on the different possible entry points, just in case. It was not long before the kindly old man came back with a cup of warm cocoa. Anna had barely taken a sip when there was a distant knock at the front door.

"That will be your uncle. Stay just where you are, don't move and I'll be back in a moment."

Anna did as she was told. She hardly moved a muscle, not even to take another sip of cocoa. Soon she heard hushed voices approaching. To her enormous relief, the door opened to reveal the shopkeeper, closely followed by her uncle. He appeared unharmed.

"I searched the canal side of the road some distance in both directions, but I couldn't see a soul out there. I think you must have imagined what you saw, Anna. Not that I blame you, after what we went through this evening."

"I'm relieved to hear that. Sorry to have made you go out there again," Anna replied.

Usually her uncle would have taken the opportunity to gently tease her, but not this evening. "No need to apologise. Evil times are upon us, and you are absolutely right to be vigilant and cautious."

The two men took their usual places in the heavily upholstered leather chairs, her uncle to the right of the fire, and Mr Warwick to the left, his chair angled towards the other two. The feeling had fully returned to Anna's feet. She dried them and put on the warm slippers. She was pleased to find the bleeding on her cheek had stopped.

"So, James," said Mr Warwick, his earnest expression brought into sharper relief by the firelight, "tell me what happened. You didn't receive my message? I hope you got the news from Miller about McCain and Grimes being back in London. As soon as I heard, I sent word to you at the concert hall to suggest that you come straight here. It looks like I was too late."

"Yes, I did get Miller's message. On reaching the Royal College, I decided we shouldn't stay, given the change of circumstances. That must have been before your message arrived."

"Good, James, you made the right decision."

"We left before the concert started, but still too late to avoid their attack. I'm kicking myself that I didn't bring Anna here directly from her house."

"Ah, don't be hard on yourself," the old man responded kindly. "It was new information. There was no way to know what McCain and Grimes's plans were, or that they would act so soon. You made your mind up quickly, and your judgement was correct. But tell me, what happened next?"

Anna's uncle wasted no time in recounting all the key details. He made Anna blush as he described the part that she played in defeating their assailants. Mr Warwick spoke little. For the most part he sat forward in his chair, his elbows resting on its arms and his chin on the backs of his interlocked fingers in front of him. His head was a little bowed, and his brows cast dark shadows over the hollows of his eye sockets. They gave him a slightly haunted look.

He responded to her uncle's concern at leaving their attackers behind, saying, "No James, you had no better options available to you. Had you been a Master Healer, you might have attempted to turn them away from the Omega direction. But you are not, and had no way of doing so. Nor did you have the time. And of course, had you rendered any of them, including McCain, um… 'beyond life'," Anna thought she saw the old man's eyes glance briefly at her from within their dark hollows, "as we know all too well, that would certainly have led to damage to your own essence. Probably irreparable damage, handing the enemy as a whole a great victory in the moment of their defeat. No, the absolute priority was to ensure Anna's safety. You chose the wisest course of action."

"Thank you. I hope so."

"We could send word to the Order now to see if we can still apprehend those men, but I feel sure they will have recovered and moved on before anyone can get there. Besides, we have an even more pressing matter that requires our full attention now. Namely, to get Anna to a new place of safety."

The old man broke off. Silence claimed the room as he ordered his thoughts. After a minute or so, he spoke again.

"Well, it would seem that the latest Satal war has now begun. It has happened sooner than we expected, or planned for. I thought we had a few more valuable weeks. I did not believe the enemy would launch an attack without either Faulkner or Mortlock in London to lead them. That is why I judged tonight would be safe. Anna, I am so sorry that I allowed you to come into harm's way. I am just deeply relieved that you are both such excellent fighters, and that their surprise attack failed. You did very well to escape. I commend you for it. Both of you!"

"Thank you," said Anna, blushing slightly. "I suppose Faulkner will know who I am now, though?"

"Alas, yes, you are right. No-one else your age could ever have done what you did this evening. They will certainly know who it was. And now they have the link to your uncle. For the foreseeable future, at least until the immediate conflict with Faulkner and his gang is resolved, I'm afraid it is imperative that you remain completely hidden from the outside world."

"Yes, I understand." Now was not the time to share how she felt about that.

"And James, if you were not already, I am sure you are now the most marked man in London. Having obtained a vital clue that could lead Faulkner and his henchmen to their ultimate prize, they will not stop until they have tracked you down."

Anna's uncle rocked his head back. "Ha! They can try!"

Mr Warwick raised up his gaze to look directly at him.

"I know you are better equipped than almost anyone to look after yourself, James, and it is evidently going to take more than six of the enemy to overcome you!" He allowed himself a brief smile, before the gravity of his words dragged his features back down to a frown. "I also know how much you cherish your freedom. But I must urge caution now. The war has begun, and our enemy's number in London is increasing by the day."

Uncle James nodded.

"I cannot afford for you to remain entirely concealed. We have important work to do to prepare for the battles ahead. But you must take the most extreme caution on those occasions when you must venture out. We must both disguise ourselves whenever needed. At all other times you must remain concealed until we are ready to strike. That time is approaching fast. You will not have to wait long."

Anna looked at her uncle. She knew how much losing his much-loved freedom would affect him. His expression remained impassive, but his eyes blazed in the firelight.

"Yes, master, I understand," he said.

"And so, to the most pressing matter at hand. That of where young Anna should reside." Anna listened intently. "You cannot return to your house, I'm afraid. That's quite clear. We should also make arrangements for your mother to spend time away from there, I think. Just to be on the safe side. We shall make it widely known that you are both out of town until after the Christmas season, to avoid endangering any of your household staff."

"Yes, I understand," she replied. "Could I ask where you have in mind?"

"Yes, of course. I hope you won't be upset that we had already made plans for your concealment when the time came, which we had agreed with your mother."

"No, not at all. Thank you for thinking of my safety."

"Obviously we had not expected to make use of these plans yet, though. The place we had in mind is deep in the countryside, far from here, with trusted friends. However, I must confess this idea is starting to give me forebodings now. Our enemies might find it difficult to track you down there, but they do have their ways and means. If you are found then I fear no-one in whose keeping we could place you would be able to withstand their attack."

"I agree. I would not want Anna any great distance from us at this time," said Uncle James.

"No," agreed the old man. He turned back to Anna. "Your uncle and I have important work ahead of us now, here in London. So do the other most senior and strongest knights, whom we trust in the Order. We are laying the groundwork for battle, and we can ill afford for any of us to be away. The broader ranks of the Order are still slow to move and have not yet fully awoken to the imminent dangers we face, even now. More importantly, I'm afraid I have serious reason to fear that their ranks may have been infiltrated by agents of our enemy. I would prefer to share your new location with no-one but our most trusted inner circle."

Anna nodded.

"Secondly, there is the matter of your instruction. We have reached the Practice phase of your training in double-quick time, and we must progress with it with the highest urgency now. We have less time than I expected, and I am not prepared to leave this most vital part of your training to anyone other than your uncle and myself. This is another reason for you not to leave London."

"Thank you. Yes, I would prefer not to leave the city at the moment if possible, and I am most keen to continue my training with you," said Anna. She wasn't sure that her views carried much weight at that moment, but she wanted them known anyway!

"Very good. So, all things considered, I believe we must conceal you not outside the city, but rather, buried somewhere unseen, right within its chaotic heart. Somewhere not devoid of people but, on the contrary, where they are so densely packed that one may almost become invisible amongst their vast number. If a pebble is cast alone upon a stone floor, one may easily find it if one knows roughly where to look. But if the pebble is, instead, cast amongst a thousand other pebbles, the task becomes altogether more difficult. And if our enemies must search for you amongst the millions of people who now occupy our great city, then we may have more confidence still. Of course, we shall do our best to make our enemies believe you are elsewhere, though."

"I agree," said Anna's uncle. "That way we can all remain close. But where do you have in mind?"

"Well, the Order has various safehouses in the capital where we might seek to hide Anna away. I'm afraid to say, though, that the times and recent findings are such that the number which are truly safe may be significantly fewer. Unfortunately, we cannot be sure which can be trusted now."

"I have an idea," said Uncle James.

"Yes?"

"What about Jeremiah Cartwright? He has rooms in a building just outside the eastern edge of the financial square mile, backing onto the East End. It is the most peculiar place really, situated on the top floor of the building. He inhabits it but a few hours per day, due to his long working hours. It seems to suit him."

"Yes, I think I remember him. Although, goodness, it must be years since I have heard his name." Mr Warwick looked thoughtful.

"The direction his life, and his work in the financial markets, have taken mean that he has little if any contact with the Order these days. Of all the Order members that I know, he is the least likely to have become involved with any recent plots or subversion by the enemy. He would be the last person they would target if they were seeking to turn someone against us to penetrate our ranks, as they would consider him of little use. But despite that, and in spite of his obsession with his career, I believe he still possesses a pure, if slightly weak, essence."

"I think Anna would need stronger guards with her though, in addition to Jeremiah," said the old man.

"Yes master, I agree. At least one of us would need to be there at all times as well. But I would rather have Jeremiah at my side in a tight spot than many I have known. He's a determined fellow, and he has always been very loyal to me. I feel certain he would deploy what powers he does possess to their maximum effect in our cause, should the situation require it."

"Hmm, that is an interesting idea. Anna would need a chaperone of course."

"Yes, she would. But one of us would be present at all times to act in that capacity. I realise it's unconventional for it not to be a woman in that role, but I am a close family member, and you are a former school master as well as an old family friend. I think that would be appropriate enough in these exceptional circumstances."

"Yes, I suppose you're right. We would need to confirm all those arrangements with Anna's mother. And with Anna herself, of course!"

"Thank you, Mr Warwick. Yes, I think that all sounds for the best," she replied. She would far prefer to have her two guardians as chaperones than someone she did not know.

"That's good. Jeremiah… likeable fellow, as I recall. Not strong in the Powers, but highly intelligent, and basically a decent man. I never felt that he had an important role to play in the Struggle, but I did think he might make a positive contribution to mainstream society one day, if only he would apply his mind and abilities in that direction. But alas, he always seemed too preoccupied with his career."

"What you say is true. He has devoted himself to something that he is very good at, but he makes little time for anything else. However, he remains someone I trust. In this particular situation his location, and his detachment from the Order, make him ideal."

"James, I believe you may be right. I agree that his complete detachment from Struggle in recent years does make this option an attractive one."

"What's more, he lives alone, as he is married only to his work, and he is about the only person who keeps such unsociable hours that he won't mind our intruding on his hospitality without warning, even at this hour!"

"Are you sure? It's quite an imposition."

"Yes, I feel sure he would agree. His rooms could hardly be located in a more heavily populated area, either. The sheer volume of people of all kinds is quite overwhelming. Someone could go unnoticed there more easily than almost anywhere else on earth. The more I think about it, the more I feel sure this is the safest place we could choose."

Mr Warwick paused just a moment longer. "James, if you trust Jeremiah, then I say we should take up your idea and propose it to him. But before that, I should like to hear what Anna has to say about it."

"Yes, it does sound like a good choice," she replied.

"Very well. We must also explain the change of plan to your mother, Anna, and gain her consent. She knows enough of these matters to understand that we must put your safety above all other concerns. I feel sure she will be in agreement."

"Yes, hopefully so!" said Anna.

"I will send word to her tonight that you are with us, and that we shall consult her fully on the plan tomorrow."

"Thank you, Mr Warwick."

"I suggest that you two travel to Jeremiah's straight away. I shall meet you there tomorrow, once I have packed up some essential items that I do not want to leave here."

Mr Warwick convinced the hesitant Anna that it would be all right to wear not only his slippers outside, but also a large and equally warm overcoat, which trailed on the ground as she walked. Her uncle was just about to head back outside to search for a taxi carriage when Anna recalled the person she thought she had seen outside the shop when they arrived. She wondered whether to say anything.

"Anna, is there a problem?" asked Mr Warwick.

She hesitated again. She did not want to appear foolish.

"Uncle, I know you checked outside and found no-one. But the more I think about it, the more certain I am that I did see someone spying on us when we arrived. We've already been attacked once tonight, so just in case, do you think maybe–"

"You are absolutely right," Mr Warwick interrupted, "and I praise your caution. James, might I ask you to circle around from the back door this time, and check again that all is clear before we leave the building?"

"Yes, of course, master."

"Thank you. Anna, I believe you said the person you might have seen was by the large tree on the other side of the road, on the bank leading down to the towpath. Is that correct?"

"Yes, that's right."

"James, I suggest you take not the first but the second or third street that leads back to the canal, to the point at which it meets the main road that passes the front of this shop. Then head this way towards the canal bridge. It's quite a long way and will take some time, but that should avoid your being spotted by anyone watching the front of the shop. It will also give you a good vantage point to see down the towpath. You can investigate further from there. Go slowly and carefully. Let's take no more chances."

"I shall go now." Anna's uncle turned to leave with an extravagant sweep of his cape.

"Uncle," said Anna, as he was about to step through the door, "please do be careful."

"Thank you. But don't worry, I am really very good at looking after myself!"

He winked, then disappeared once again into the velvety blackness. He seemed as confident as ever, but after the experiences of that evening, Anna had a lurking fear that she had sent him out into danger again. She felt a desperate urge to follow him, to know that he was all right.

"Mr Warwick," she said, turning to the old man, who was switching his attention to the log fire which was now burning low. "Do you think we could look outside, from inside the shop of course, just to make sure uncle is all right? I mean, just in case we need to go out there and help him somehow…"

Mr Warwick gave Anna one of his knowing looks and smiled. "He won't be there for a while yet. I've sent him quite a long way round! But I can sense just how much you are becoming involved in events now. And how much you apparently don't like waiting. Or following instructions!"

Anna looked to the floor, but Mr Warwick chuckled gently.

"I'm sorry, I don't mean to chide you. But I can see where some of the challenges will lie in your future instruction. There will certainly be no trouble motivating you. Neither do I have a terribly impetuous, foolhardy young spirit on my hands, as I did with a certain other person we both know well! You are calm, focused and extremely sharp, and yet you also show the right degree of caution when faced with danger. In fact, you display an unusual level of maturity for your age."

Anna averted her gaze again, embarrassed yet also undeniably flattered, even though she could tell there was a 'but' coming.

"But," continued Mr Warwick, "there are going to be times when you need to be prepared *not* to act, and to avoid dangerous situations altogether. And unfortunately, right now, those times need to be all the time. I say 'unfortunately', for I can see how much this goes against your nature."

Anna sighed and nodded.

"I understand that it may seem disloyal to you, or even cowardly, to let others face danger while you hold yourself back. Those feelings do you credit. But you must understand how important it is to complete your training before you face the enemy again. It is vital that you are ready and fully prepared. For, in all likelihood, the time will one day come when you have to face the greatest danger of them all."

There it was again. That reference to her eventual encounter with the man from her dream, who Mr Warwick seemed so determined she was going to meet. He might be right about her nature in general, but that particular danger was one she would be only too happy to avoid. Forever. She had vowed to play her part in stopping Faulkner, but the man from her dream was a different matter. The fear she held for him went so deep, right back to her early childhood, and her usual bravery evaporated completely at the thought of him.

She fell silent again. The silence crept slowly across the room, followed by its evil brother, tension. Anna began to worry about her uncle again, and her thoughts brought her to another topic that had been troubling her.

"Mr Warwick, can I ask a question about the attack earlier?"

"Yes, Anna, what is it?" He appeared relieved himself to have something to distract him from the invasive tension.

Anna hesitated. "It's about Uncle James. He was ever so brave tonight. And he was so strong in the battle. But…"

"Yes? Do go on."

"Well, when he was saving me from that horrible man, McCain, his essence was shining brightly. For a moment it turned a colour that I've never seen before in an essence. It was purple. It didn't last, but I wondered what it might mean…"

Mr Warwick looked at her unblinkingly for a moment, before lowering his eyes again and sighing gently.

"I suspect you may already have some inkling of what that means," he replied. "I'm afraid I have seen this before. For better or for worse, I shall explain. You deserve to know, and it may be important for the future. The explanation is, in fact, a very simple one." He paused. Then he asked, "As a child, were you ever taught to paint? With water colours and such like?"

"Yes. My mother used to paint occasionally, and sometimes she would let me try."

"Then, of course, I'm sure you know which two colours are mixed together to form purple?"

"Yes," replied Anna quietly, the question confirming her worst fears. "Purple is made by mixing blue with… red."

"Precisely. I'm afraid it was the same for your uncle's essence at that moment. The change is usually too subtle for most people to notice. I have a strong ability to see essences, which is why I have seen this before. You can see them much more clearly than anyone else though, so I am not surprised."

"But, red means evil…"

Not for the first time in a conversation with Mr Warwick, Anna found herself gripping the arms of her chair.

"First of all, Anna, please be in no doubt. Your uncle is a very good man. He is one of the finest men it has ever been my pleasure and privilege to know. I don't like to nourish his already over-fed self-confidence by saying this to his face though, of course!"

Anna smiled, in spite of the topic.

"But, like so many people, he is also wrestling with certain… demons. In his case, demons born out of his experiences in the Struggle. And, ironically, out of his hatred for anything associated with the Omega World."

"But surely, to want to stop the Omega World is a good thing?"

"To want to stop it, yes. But it is how we do it, and our real motivations when we do so, that are crucial. Alas, in the world as it is, our human nature is such that, no matter how good our initial intentions, we all have our frailties. Our points of weakness, which leave us vulnerable to doing things that fall short of the values and standards that we aspire to. To put it another way, we are vulnerable to the subtle, yet fatally divisive, methods of the Omega World."

"So, are these weaknesses caused by the, um, contamination of our world by the Opposing Energy, which you have described before?"

"Yes, exactly. The Opposing Energy is behind it all. It was the Opposing Energy that originally conceived the Omega World design, and it is that Energy which has been the driving force behind every evil effort to bring about the Omega World ever since. That includes Satals, the Gorgal, and all else standing in the way of our world reaching the pure Alpha State. And as we have discussed before, the Opposing Energy is still active in this world today, influencing people and events, nudging and luring them to follow the Omega direction. We shall return to the subject of the Opposing Energy and its contamination of our world very soon in your instruction, so let's hold further questions about those topics just for now."

Anna nodded.

"But yes, these weaknesses are amongst the greatest weapons of the Opposing Energy. Everyone engaged in the Struggle as deeply as your uncle has their character and their human weaknesses tested severely."

"And he was tested again this evening."

"Yes. And it is easy to understand why. You see, there were some particularly traumatic events in the last Satal war, for your uncle and for many of us."

"What happened? Did something bad happen to uncle?"

"Yes, it did. Something very tragic."

"Can you tell me what it was?"

Mr Warwick hesitated. "That is more than I can go into just now. But suffice to say it is entirely understandable that he bears mental scars from it. What you saw in your uncle's essence tonight, just momentarily until he conquered it, was hatred. Hatred which threatened to bring about a lasting change to his essence. Though thankfully, once again it failed to do so, I believe?"

"Yes, that's right. It went back to its normal colour after he'd finished with McCain."

"That is because he conquered his negative emotions. He did not act on them."

Anna nodded again.

"However, the truth is that a battle rages within your uncle, constantly. He has come to despise the Omega World and all that it stands for. If he ever allows himself to follow through on the hatred he feels, he risks doing serious damage to his own essence. And as you already know, the more damaged an essence becomes, the more open it is to further influence from the Opposing Energy. It's the ultimate, tragic irony that, in defeating Omega World forces, people can allow themselves to be dragged in the Omega direction themselves, by the way that they defeat them. If they do it in the wrong way."

"But how can we be sure we are fighting them in the right way? In that ambush tonight, for a while we were just fighting to survive. We had to do whatever was necessary to escape."

"Yes. It all depends on the necessity of your situation and the nature of your intentions when you act. Doing the minimum necessary to survive an attack on you does no damage to your own essence. Going further, for example to inflict unnecessary pain or injury on another person purely for revenge, would damage your essence."

"So, do you think my uncle might permanently damage himself one day?"

"This is a subject that he and I speak about regularly, at great length. So far, he has always mastered his more negative emotions admirably. But your uncle is a man of deep passions. He now walks a tightrope through life. It is not impossible that he will one day lose his footing."

"Oh, I hope not!"

"Indeed. It is my role, and the role of all the others who care about him, including you now that you are involved, to help prevent this from happening. And we must do all we can to catch him if he does fall."

Anna swallowed hard. "Yes, of course. I will do anything I can to help him."

Mr Warwick nodded his approval. "But please also let me reassure you on one point. Right now, certainly in relation to your safety and our immediate plans, we may rely on your uncle completely. As the daughter of his elder brother, whom he loved dearly, he would do anything to protect you."

"Yes, I know he would." She did not doubt that for a moment.

"Even if the fateful day should arrive when he can no longer control his rage, for example if someone else threatens you as McCain did tonight, then heaven help the particular foe he's facing at that moment. For unless they are a Satal, they will very likely perish in the face of his wrath. Whatever long-term damage he may do himself as a result, he will defend you to the end, be in no doubt about that. And it's a risk worth taking to ensure your safety."

"Oh, but I don't want to be the cause of that! I want to learn to defend myself fully, as soon as possible. Then no-one will need to defend me anymore. Please Mr Warwick, can we move on to mental combat in my instruction soon?" Anna felt the importance of learning all about combat using auras even more keenly than ever now.

The old man smiled. "Yes, Anna, don't worry. That time has come. That is the first topic we will cover in the Practice."

"Oh good. That's a relief."

The room went quiet again. Anna replayed the evening's events in her mind.

"Mr Warwick, do you have any idea what that strange violin music was that we heard? It was clearly connected to the attack."

"Ah yes, I'm afraid I do. I have heard that same music myself, on several occasions. Always bad ones."

"What was it?"

"It originated many centuries ago, in the kingdom of Bohemia. It was originally derived from gypsy music. However, it is not gypsy music, and please do not confuse the two, as many people do. The gypsies are people who have been much oppressed, unfairly, over the centuries. But the enemy derived and developed this music from some of the more obscure gypsy tunes, for their own purposes."

He explained that it was used to alert Omega forces to gather at the location of the player. This was usually in order to attack the Order, and also to instil fear in those they were about to attack. It was first used in the seventeenth century, when a small party of brave knights were hunted down by the enemy in Bohemia. They were hopelessly outnumbered, chased down and massacred in thick fog one night. The haunting, demonic violin music was the last sound they ever heard.

"It is fair to say that a more despicable, evil music has never been created," he concluded.

"Yes. It was horrible. It was very disturbing, even when I didn't know what it meant. It made me think of death."

"That's because it was created precisely to make their enemies think of their own impending death. What is most alarming is that it has now been heard again, in this very city. A further sign, if any were needed, that the new war has begun."

"You said there was fog that night the music was first played. There was fog tonight, too. It fell very quickly, then it seemed to clear again just as fast afterwards. And there was also heavy fog that night when the Beast captured Gillespie. I know we get a lot of fog in London, but there seemed to be something different about this. It felt almost like it was alive."

"Yes, another important point. Satals seem able to generate heavy fog when they are hunting their prey. We have no real understanding of how they do this. We think it is some sort of interaction between the climactic conditions at the time, their essences, and the Opposing Energy, which they can channel to a certain degree. They cannot always do it, but in a city like London the conditions are usually ideal."

"But why do they do it?"

"It is to slow down their enemies to make it harder to escape, and again to strike fear into them. It gives the Satal and its forces the upper hand, even before any confrontation starts. It also often provides the Satal with cover to transform into their true form, prior to a kill."

"But you said Faulkner is away from London at the moment."

"Nevertheless, given the speed with which the fog came and went, and that this happened just when you were attacked, I feel almost certain that Faulkner was responsible. Satals can create this effect at some distance. Tell me, did you see anything in the fog? Any strange, frightening images?"

"No, nothing like that. Just swirling mist. Why do you ask?"

"Satals sometimes use their powers to create images in the fog in their vicinity. The images are never completely distinct, they constantly move and change, but they can appear quite real and can be absolutely terrifying. Like evil hallucinations in the fog, if you will. But they can only create this effect for relatively short distances. The fact that you did not see any tonight rather confirms that Faulkner was some distance away, as we thought. But next time you find yourself out in fog, always ask yourself the question if it could have been created by a Satal. And always take the greatest of care."

"Yes, I see. I will!" So much about the world was not as it had seemed.

"On a related subject," the old man continued, "Satals can also sometimes induce hallucinations directly in our minds, not only using fog. It seems to require a lot of energy, so they only do this for short bursts of time, but it is another weapon they use against us."

The old man fell silent again. He prodded at the embers in the hearth, but his mind had clearly joined Anna's outside, wondering if Uncle James was all right.

"Oh, very well then!" he said suddenly. "Maybe you were right. Perhaps we should keep an eye out for your uncle, just in case he needs some help."

"Yes. It would be good to check," Anna agreed straight away.

"James is well able to look after himself, as you have already seen for yourself," Mr Warwick continued, "but… well, he has been gone for a while, and forewarned is forearmed after all."

Anna nodded. She needed no persuasion.

"There is an attic room upstairs, two flights up, with a dormer window that protrudes from the roof. It is quite broad, and I believe its curtains are still open. Provided we use no light and don't get too close to the window, we should be able to see much of the road and canal below without being spotted."

Anna followed the old shopkeeper to the staircase in the corner of the room, and up to the floor above. Reaching the foot of the next, narrower flight of stairs, Mr Warwick said, "Keep hold of the banisters and follow me." He extinguished his lantern.

At first Anna could see nothing in the complete darkness. Gulping, she gripped the banister tightly on either side. Slowly the stairs became visible in the dim light emanating from the floor below. They ascended into the darkness of the attic room above.

On reaching that floor, Anna could see nothing again initially. Then, slowly, she began to make out a faint light coming through a window some distance away at the front of the building. This attic floor seemed to be all one room. They edged towards the light.

The window protruded from a sloped roof at the front. Mr Warwick brought them to a halt a couple of feet from it. The full moon had been obscured by a cloud, but the gas lamps that lined the street and the distant stars afforded sufficient light to make out key features of the landscape below.

Anna surveyed the scene, trying not to get too close to the window. She could not make out a living soul. After a few moments Mr Warwick tapped Anna's upper arm gently and pointed to their right, towards the canal bridge. Peering intently, Anna just made out the half-concealed figure of her uncle.

Uncle James was pressing himself flat against a tree about halfway between the bridge and the shop, looking round the side of the trunk down the canal path. Anna was relieved to see him unharmed.

As she watched, he began to move stealthily forward to the next tree on the path in their direction, before concealing himself flat again behind that one. His stealthy movements reminded Anna of the cats she had seen stalking their prey in the gardens of her own neighbourhood. But who, or what, was he hunting? She could not see anything.

Almost as though in answer, Mr Warwick gestured towards the road edge, where the steep bank led down to the canal towpath. Anna's heart skipped a beat.

There were the prey. Two men with all but their heads concealed, lying flat against the bank and staring intently at the shop entrance directly below them.

5
Spies

Anna was shocked to find she had been right after all. But at least the spies seemed unaware that they themselves were now being tracked. The hunter was no more than ten feet from them. For an old man, Mr Warwick certainly had quick eyes. No doubt he already knew exactly what to look for, and where.

Anna held her breath as she watched her uncle peer again round the tree, appearing to weigh up his options. There were no more trees between him and his targets so his choices were limited. She looked back at the two semi-concealed figures and tried to focus on their auras. She did not expect to see much at that distance but was pleased to find she could discern something. Not that she liked what she saw. The impression was of quite damaged specimens, though neither was as large nor as vile as McCain's. One of the auras seemed to have an unusual, reddish hue to it.

Anna looked back in the direction of her uncle just as he made his move. He broke from his hiding place and sprang straight towards the duo, walking cane raised above his head. One of the men looked round as he bore down on them, but too late. They were stunned, unsure whether to run or stand and fight. Uncle James had time to strike one or both of them with his cane had he chosen to. Instead, he slowed down, towered over the prone figures and appeared to issue instructions. Anna could hear her uncle's voice was raised, although she could not make out the words.

Suddenly, the owner of the red-tinged aura, the taller and thinner of the two men, sprang up and lunged at him, swinging punches wildly. Uncle James deftly sidestepped the onrushing ruffian. With a downward shove, he sent him sprawling to the ground. The second man charged at him. He got within a couple of feet before doubling over in pain and hitting the ground himself. Anna hadn't been focused on it, but her uncle had clearly struck the man's aura hard to create such an effect.

Uncle James appeared to issue more orders. As there were two of them, Anna imagined they could have tried to make a run for it, or else try to fight him together. Instead, they moved in the direction he indicated.

Anna shifted her focus onto the auras of the trio, and sure enough, her uncle's was making contact with theirs. This was clearly affecting their ability and willingness to fight back. He was moving his aura rapidly from one to the other, applying pressure to each in turn. The taller man made one more half-hearted effort to resist, raising an arm and attempting to push Uncle James away again. With great ease, Anna's uncle grabbed the man's arm and twisted it behind his back. He jabbed the second spy in the back with his cane and manoeuvred the pair towards the road. Neither spy had attempted any form of defence or attack of their own with their auras, indicating that neither was familiar with the Powers.

"Well done, uncle!" Anna whispered.

"Yes, he took care of them very easily. He had a fine teacher, you see!" Mr Warwick chuckled quietly.

Anna followed the old man back downstairs. There was a loud knock at the front door. Telling Anna to wait just where she was, Mr Warwick made his way through to the front, carrying a newly-lit lantern.

Anna could not resist seeing what was going on. She pressed her eye against the crack in the door between her and the shop floor. Indistinctly, she saw Mr Warwick exchange a few brief words before opening the door. Uncle James shoved the two men hard into the room. There was plenty of cursing in return, but no more physical resistance.

"So, who do we have here, then?" Anna heard Mr Warwick ask, once he had re-locked and bolted the door.

The two young men said nothing, both avoiding eye contact. Anna strained to see through the crack. She could see their two auras much more clearly now. The shorter man's was mostly what she would have expected of a rough young man up to no good: somewhat disfigured with considerable discolouration and distinct brown smears. Happily, there was still some blue visible, too.

It was the taller man's aura that Anna was most keen to see. It, too, was significantly misshapen and discoloured. It contained far less blue than the first. But most interestingly, its surface was covered in small flecks of bright red. This explained the red hue Anna had made out at a distance. For the second time that night, this was something she had never seen in an aura before.

Faced with an initial wall of silence, Mr Warwick focused his questioning on the shorter man.

"What is your name?" His voice was much more powerful and commanding than the young man would probably have expected, from the old shopkeeper's appearance. More silence. Anna's focus remained on the auras. While Mr Warwick was speaking to the shorter man, his large, pure blue aura was already gradually moving over the surface of the red speckled one of the other man. In contrast to the sternness of Mr Warwick's voice, his aura seemed to be soothing its counterpart. The previously angry red flecks were starting to grow slightly fainter. Anna marvelled at the way Mr Warwick could divide his attention so effectively.

"I said, what is your name?" he continued. The ominously stern tone in his voice surprised even Anna.

The young man finally made eye contact with his inquisitor. Perhaps emboldened by the sight of the portly and much older man, he finally broke his silence.

"I ain't telling. What business is it of yours anyway, old man? You ain't got no business dragging us in 'ere."

"I have every business dragging you in here if I find you concealed, spying on me!"

"You want to be mighty careful, old man. You don't know what you're dealing with. If you don't let us go, your days will be numbered!" He was clenching his fists round his hat now, as though preparing for a fight.

"Is that right?" Mr Warwick fixed him with a fearsome stare. At the same moment, Uncle James flicked his aura like a whip at that of the shorter man. It was perfectly timed. The contact made the man physically recoil, but was not hard enough to cause any lasting damage. All the while, Mr Warwick's own aura had continued its soothing, healing motion on the other man's red speckled one.

"Well, I'm afraid I must beg to differ," Mr Warwick continued. "Whilst my days are indeed numbered, as are everyone's, I would venture to suggest that neither you nor your mob have any idea, still less influence over, what that number will be. Furthermore, I believe I do know exactly what I am dealing with. Two young men whose lives have gone astray. Men who have got involved with things they do not understand. They have found themselves in hot water, and they are getting well and truly out of their depth in it. They are probably in far greater danger than even they themselves realise."

The young man seemed to recover slightly. Mr Warwick had succeeded in drawing him into conversation.

"You certainly talk real brave, old man. But you don't know the half of it, you don't. If you knew who we work for, and how powerful they are, there's no way you'd talk so bold."

"But I think you'll find that I do know exactly who you work for. In fact, I know a great deal more about him than you do."

"Oh yeah, you do, do you? Then who is he?"

"You work for a man whom you call Mr Faulkner. And you live in fear of him because he is able to do things to people. Bad things, which you do not understand."

Mr Warwick's words seemed to hit their mark. The man's sneer was disappearing.

"However, Faulkner is not the only one with the power to do things you do not understand."

Mr Warwick looked him straight in the eyes. At the same moment he shifted his aura from the taller man and gripped the shorter man's hard. The effect was devastating.

"This is the kind of thing you mean, isn't it, young man? Faulkner can look into your eyes and threaten your very soul. You are powerless in his presence. You know he can hurt you badly, that he can inflict severe damage to your very core. You know he has the power to kill you as easily as look at you."

Anna had never seen Mr Warwick like this. She held her breath. He tightened his grip on the aura. The man was struggling for breath. He fell to his knees at Mr Warwick's feet. The old man lessened his grip, released the hold and returned his aura to its healing activities on the taller man's aura.

Anna breathed again. Surely he must have had good reasons for inflicting so much hurt on his opponent? Interestingly, his own aura remained pure blue throughout. There had been no hint of purple.

The shorter man may have been released, but his cockiness was completely gone. He remained crouched on the floor, head bowed, panting. Mr Warwick spoke again, his voice unchanged.

"You are right to fear Faulkner. He is a very dangerous man, and far more evil than you can ever guess. But you are quite wrong to believe that you must, therefore, serve him, and that you no longer have any choice. For you do have a choice. You always have a choice. And you still know the difference between right and wrong. I am going to ask you to choose the right path from now on."

Mr Warwick's aura returned to that of the crouching man, but this time the contact was very different. He appeared to be soothing his aura, as he had done with its red-flecked counterpart.

"You are utterly mistaken if you think that working for Faulkner somehow makes you strong. You really have no idea of the evil you are involved with. It makes you the opposite of strong. It makes you helpless. It makes you his puppet. Before long he will certainly crush you. Your life means nothing to him. The moment you have completed your usefulness he will snuff it out. If you continue to work for Faulkner, it will lead to your own complete destruction. And a miserable, desperate end it will be."

Mr Warwick paused. The man was still on his knees, but he was looking up now.

"It is not too late for you to make a change. I do not know how deeply you are in with Faulkner and his wicked business – not quite as deeply as your friend here, I perceive – but the hope I can offer you is this. As long as we still have breath in our bodies, it is never too late to change our direction. To turn our backs on the bad and hurtful things we may have done in the past, and to plot a new course. In your case, I say with great certainty that this is your only hope of survival.

"Yes, sir," the man replied.

"You have been drawn into wrongdoing and hurting others. That is the wrong way to live, and you must stop. You have been very fortunate. You were caught and brought here, to me. I am giving you the opportunity to mend your ways, to turn your back on Faulkner for good, and to start to build a new and honest life. I hope you have learned this lesson: the ways of evil can be seductive, but the further you pursue them, the greater is the evil that will ultimately come to you in return. So, listen well!"

"I promise, I will change, sir."

Mr Warwick had continued his work on the kneeling man's aura. Its owner had become quite transformed. All trace of the sneer was gone. He was like a child looking up at a revered teacher.

"Now, there are some questions I wish to ask you."

"Yes, sir."

"Were you two alone tonight?"

"Yes, sir. It was just the two of us."

"What did Faulkner tell you, and what exactly did he ask you to do?"

"Well, sir, it weren't Faulkner directly. He's out of town somewhere. We ain't seen him for days. It was one of his men, a new boss called Grimes, what gave us our instructions tonight. We was told just to keep an eye on this place, and on you, and to report back any comings and goings. Tonight's the first night. He never said nothing about why we was doing it."

"Are you sure?" Mr Warwick's tone grew sterner.

"Yes, sir. We was just supposed to report back what we saw, when you came and went, who else visited. That's all."

"Did he ask you to look out for anyone else other than me?"

Anna held her breath.

"No, he never spoke of no-one else to look for."

Mr Warwick stared into his eyes and began to grip his aura again, just gently.

"It's the truth! Please believe me, sir," the man whimpered.

Mr Warwick looked at him, then replied, "Thank you. I do believe you. And you are certain there wasn't anyone else sent to watch the shop, in addition to you two?"

"Yes, sir. It was just us two today. Then there'll be another two tomorrow."

"Were you the first to be sent here to spy on me?"

"Yes, as far as I know, sir." He paused, thinking. "Yeah, no-one else from the gang has been sent here before."

"All right. Now, what do you know of Faulkner's plans?"

The man hesitated. "I really don't know nothing, mister, honest I don't. They don't tell us nothing. Just tell us to do stuff, but no reasons. I seen a lot of old books being delivered to him, but I don't know why."

"And exactly when were you due to report to Grimes regarding your findings?"

"He told us to watch the place all night, then go to a house in Highgate at nine in the morning to report back."

"I see. Good."

The old man turned his attention back to the owner of the red-flecked aura. For the first time, he spoke directly to him. At the same time he engulfed the man's aura in his own.

"You have been listening to all of this, haven't you?"

The tall young man nodded.

"And you understand the truth of what I have been saying to your friend, don't you? For it applies even more gravely to you. I perceive that you have become more deeply embroiled in the affairs of Faulkner than your companion, to the point that you have probably felt no longer able to make decisions for yourself. Almost as though you have been under his spell. Am I right?"

The man nodded again, meekly.

"Well, you have been lucky, too. For I am going to break Faulkner's spell. I am going to restore your ability to make decisions for yourself. And I am going to give you the same choice I have given to your friend. You have the chance to cut your ties with Faulkner once and for all. You can make a clean break, mend your ways and lead a good and true life from now on."

"Yes, gov... sir," said the man. He had a deeper voice than the shorter man.

"As I told your friend, your only hope of survival is to change your ways and lead an entirely different life, far, far away from Faulkner and his gang. Do you understand what I am saying to you?" The massaging of his aura continued.

The second young man nodded again, vigorously this time. When he spoke again, his voice cracked with emotion.

"Yes, sir, I understand. And I will... I'll do as you say. And... thank you for the peace you've brought me."

Anna couldn't see, but it sounded as though the tall man was sobbing. All trace of red flecks was now gone from his aura.

"The time has come for you both to leave here, never to return. You have been given one chance to change your fates forever. But you must act fast. You will not return to the house in Highgate. You will leave London altogether, before Grimes and Faulkner realise you are no longer in their service. Leave, and travel as far away as possible."

"Yes, sir," said the taller man. His companion nodded.

"By the way, you never did tell me your names," added the old man.

81

"I'm Archer, sir," said the taller man, "Bob Archer. And this here is Ally Smith."

Smith nodded respectfully in Mr Warwick's direction.

"Thank you for giving us this chance, Mister," Archer continued. "I promise you won't regret it."

"For your sakes, I hope I will not. The day is coming when Faulkner and his gang will meet their downfall. After that, it may become safe for you to return, provided you have mended your ways. Until that day, unless you want to meet a terrible end at that man's hands, I suggest you stay very, very far from here. Now, be gone!"

Even from the next room, Anna was surprised by the masterful, booming tone of Mr Warwick's voice. The two young men required no second telling. They followed Anna's uncle to the front of the shop, then they fled into the cold night beyond.

Anna hurried back to her chair in front of the now extinct fire.

"My dear Anna," said Mr Warwick, as he entered the back room again with her uncle. His voice was now restored entirely to its usual, kind tone, as though nothing had just happened. "I am so sorry to have kept you waiting back here – and without even a fire to warm you!" He looked disapprovingly at the lack of activity in the hearth. "I presume you witnessed everything that just took place?"

"Well... yes," she admitted.

"I'm sure you have a number of questions. But before we discuss anything, we must prepare to leave here. If it wasn't already clear that we should no longer remain, it certainly is now. I am very confident that those spies will not return to Grimes in Highgate, and I also feel certain that Archer was telling the truth when he said they were the only ones spying on us. Nevertheless, it won't be too long tomorrow before their failure to report back raises suspicions."

"Yes, I agree," said Anna's uncle. "We should leave here straight away, and you should come with us, master."

"Yes. It is most inconvenient for me to leave the shop right now as there are some important items – books specifically – which I cannot risk losing or falling into the wrong hands. But I will just have to take the most valuable ones with us. We should all leave now, this very hour."

"We'll help you carry anything you need," Uncle James added.

"We still don't know what happened to your driver tonight. Might I ask you to find us a cab, while I make my preparations? The hour is late but I believe you will still find taxi carriages on the main thoroughfares, picking up gentlemen from their clubs and so forth. You are far more familiar with the streets at this hour of the day than I. I'm sure you will know where to look!"

"Yes, of course, Master. I shall leave at once."

As Uncle James left, Mr Warwick turned back to Anna.

"We have a little time while your uncle searches for a ride, so I will give you a brief explanation of what you saw. Then I will need to go to pack my essential belongings."

"Thank you. Yes, I understand," Anna replied.

"Did you see the red speckles on that man Archer's essence?"

"Yes, I did. What could cause something like that?"

"They were inflicted on him by Faulkner. Satals can manipulate a person's essence in such a way as to leave that person under their complete control, to follow whatever orders they give them. The victim essentially becomes their puppet. Or a Thrall, as we call them in the Order.

Anna nodded. She had heard him mention Thralls before.

"When they do this, it leaves a speckled effect on the essence like the one you saw. It always leaves the victim more sluggish and less powerful than they were before though, and it requires considerable effort on the Satal's part to do it. This is why they don't do it more often. It can also be reversed. I believe I was able to successfully remove Faulkner's control over young Mr Archer tonight by removing the hooks that Faulkner had placed in his essence. To complete the puppet analogy, I cut his master's strings."

Anna nodded again, her eyes wide.

"Now, I must make my preparations." With that, Mr Warwick hurried up the stairs with an energy that belied his years.

Anna sat back down. She wrapped Mr Warwick's warm dressing gown around herself, and within moments she had plunged into a deep sleep. She was woken by the reappearance of Mr Warwick. He was carrying a large box of old books, including one very old, very large one. He put it beside an equally large box he had already placed next to the door, together with what looked like a travel bag containing clothes and washing equipment.

"Your uncle will be here soon. I think I'm just about ready. Anna, I would like to take another look at the street, just to make sure no more of Faulkner's agents are around. I do believe Archer was telling the truth, as far as he knew it. But it is still possible that Faulkner arranged for others to watch me as well, without telling those two. I do not want to be caught out again. Would you care to join me?"

Anna nodded and got up immediately. She still had an inexplicable sense of foreboding, despite the capture of the two spies. The old man extinguished his lamp and they retraced their steps up the stairs and to the attic window. Anna peered down to the road again. As before she could make out no signs of life. Mr Warwick was also peering intently, his gaze sweeping the area below. Anna suspected he was making out all kinds of details that her untrained eyes were not. She tried to do the same, aiming to take in every minute detail. There was in fact a tremendous amount to see, from the shapes of what looked like discarded empty crates at one end of the street, to a small cat scaling a tree towards the other end. But there were no signs of human life.

Just then, the clouds parted. Anna surveyed the street and canal again, struck by how eerily beautiful everything looked in this new, ethereal light. Suddenly she felt sad, despite the strange beauty of the scene. This might be the last time she would ever be able to visit this place. Her eye inevitably strayed to the canal bridges, which held so many memories of happy times spent with her friends, and most of all, with Timmy.

Her first sighting of Faulkner was also right here in this shop, when Mr Warwick had suddenly hidden her away from him. Faulkner. He had appeared in their lives, and things had never been the same. He was like a terrible black cloud, casting a dark shadow over all that had been beautiful, ruining the lives of so many. His presence had become the backdrop to all their conversations and actions.

And now he loomed larger than ever. He was the reason she could not slip out to meet Timmy anymore. It was because of him that she could no longer return to her own home now, nor come back here to this place again, so filled with charm, mystery and fantastic stories. This shop, which had become a place of such freedom and learning in recent months, where extraordinary truths about the world had been revealed to her.

And now it had all suddenly come to an end. Her sadness deepened. Raising her head in an attempt to stem the tears that had unexpectedly filled her eyes, she looked at the silver-lit leaves in the upper branches of the dark trees which lined the canal. Then she saw something that made her heart freeze.

Beyond the trees, in the attic window of a tall house directly across the canal from them, there was a face. A contorted, white face, with a gaping mouth and ghastly, wide eyes. And those eyes were staring directly at her.

6
The Wraith

Quick as a flash, Anna ducked down below the windowsill. She tugged at Mr Warwick's sleeve for him to do the same. A more phantom-like vision she had never seen.

"I saw someone looking at us! In a window, in the house facing us across the canal."

"Are you sure?"

"Yes, I'm certain this time. It was a boy, about my age, I think. He was deathly white, like the face of a dead person. He had horrible, wide, staring eyes. There was something familiar about him, but I can't think why. Oh, Mr Warwick, it looked like – like a ghost!" She was trembling.

Crouching as low as possible, Mr Warwick led Anna hurriedly back through the room and down the stairs. Once there, he asked her to describe the face. He wore a look of real concern. Anna did her best to convey what she had seen. Mr Warwick did not reply. Instead he paced to the back door to look for her uncle.

"Where is he?" he said.

Anna had never seen him so agitated. At that moment there was a knock at the back door and Uncle James reappeared.

"Right, come on, quickly," said Mr Warwick immediately, "we must leave right now!" Anna held all further questions and hurried after him.

"What is it?" asked her uncle.

"Anna may just have seen a Wraith in a building across the canal. We must leave. Quick, please take one of these boxes. Anna, do you think you could manage my travel bag?"

"A Wraith? Here?" exclaimed Uncle James. "Right, let's go, now!" He grabbed one of the boxes and darted through the door.

Mr Warwick heaved up the other box and followed Uncle James. The sound of a window being smashed at the front of the shop reached them.

"It's breaking in!" cried Anna's uncle.

The old man locked the back door frantically. They dashed as fast as their legs and luggage would allow, to the waiting four-seater carriage.

"Driver, we have to leave, right now!" shouted Uncle James. Without hesitation, Mr Warwick and Anna clambered inside, whilst Uncle James gave further instructions to the cabbie. As soon as the luggage was stowed, Uncle James swung inside the carriage himself, slamming the door behind him. Anna took a quick peep outside the window before she was hauled back into the darkness by Mr Warwick. He warned her not to take any chances.

"Mr Warwick, what did you say it was?" she asked.

"First of all, are you certain that you saw someone up there? It couldn't just have been a trick of the moonlight?"

"No, this time I'm absolutely sure. It was a face. But not like any I've ever seen before. It was horribly misshapen, and a most deathly-looking white colour. Its eyes, they were so wide, like he was in shock, or mortal fear… if it was a person at all."

"Well, from your description I fear it was a Wraith. One of the Satal's most faithful and deadly servants."

As Mr Warwick spoke, the carriage began to slow. It came to a halt. Anna assumed they had reached a junction, but looking out of the window she could see that they were still well short of the next one.

"Driver, why have you stopped?" her uncle shouted out of his window.

"There's someone in the road sir, he waved us down to stop," came the reply. "Strange-looking fella… Wait a minute, where's he going?"

"What the…" started Uncle James, leaning further out of his window on the left-hand side to get a better look.

Suddenly, Anna's arm was grabbed through the open window on the right-hand side, by a bony, white hand. As she tried to pull her arm away, the gaping, salivating mouth and ghostly, wide-eyed face of the Wraith appeared at the window, inches from her own face. Despite the creature's dramatically altered appearance and her own panic, Anna recognised it now. Her panic morphed into utter shock. The features were unmistakable. They were horrifically changed, but they were undoubtedly those of Billy Gillespie! The face was a gruesome distortion of its former human form.

The creature held Anna's arm with a vice-like grip and tried to pull her from the carriage through the open window. Her scream alerted her companions. Mr Warwick was closest. He grabbed the white hand and began desperately to prise open the fingers. Anna's uncle bolted across from the other window and landed a mighty blow on the creature's jaw.

"Drive! Drive!" he shouted. The carriage began to move again. Despite the heavy blow, the Wraith continued to cling on to Anna. However, its grip had loosened a little, sufficiently for Mr Warwick to finally prise the fingers off. He immediately pulled Anna away and placed himself between her and the ghoulish creature. She refocused to search for its aura. But something was wrong. There was no aura.

The Wraith continued to hold onto the carriage, trying to haul itself in. Uncle James landed another crunching blow on the creature's head, properly stunning it this time. Mr Warwick gave it an almighty shove with the sole of his shoe. A third blow from Anna's uncle at the same moment finally caused it to lose its grip. It tumbled onto the road.

"Drive on driver, don't stop!" he yelled. "That man was trying to attack us. Don't stop for him again, whatever you do!"

The driver did as he was told, whipping the horses to go faster. Soon they reached the junction and careered round the corner. Anna peered through the back window and saw the ghoulish figure lying in the street, near a gas streetlamp. Just before buildings blocked their view, she saw it rise to its feet and start to run forward in their direction again. She sat back in her seat, breathing heavily.

"Are you all right, Anna?" Mr Warwick and her uncle both asked at the same moment. They were still standing, stooped under the ceiling and facing her in the swaying carriage.

"Yes, I think so. Thank you for getting it off me!" She was struggling to comprehend what had happened.

"That was a Wraith, all right," said Uncle James, returning slowly to his seat opposite her.

"Judging by its face, I think the victim was no more than about sixteen," added Mr Warwick. "A mere youth as you said, Anna. The poor, wretched soul."

Anna paused. "I – I know why it looked familiar, now. Its face… it was Billy Gillespie's!"

"What?" Mr Warwick and Uncle James spoke in unison again.

Anna nodded. "Yes. He was terribly changed, but it was definitely him."

"Good God. I see…" Mr Warwick said in a softer voice. "James, I don't want any risk of being followed. Please ask the driver to take us via a very circuitous route. Perhaps travel south first, maybe even over the river, before heading back east and north to our destination. And let's keep careful watch to make sure no-one's tailing us."

"Yes, master." Uncle James leaned out of the carriage to speak to the driver again.

Anna was deeply shaken. She was putting the pieces together in her mind.

"You said it was a victim. Do you mean that Faulkner turned Gillespie into that creature?" she asked.

"Yes, I'm afraid that's right," replied the old man.

"But how did he do that?" Anna was aghast.

"It's complicated, but we have some time now before we reach Jeremiah's. I'll try to explain."

Anna sat back deep in her seat, still stunned.

"Wraiths have featured in myths and legends of the general population for centuries as a type of ghost, or spirit of the dead. However, they are not ghosts. Not quite."

"So, are they still alive?" Anna asked.

"Yes, they are living people, but transformed into a kind of twilight existence by a Satal. People think they are ghosts because they still resemble their former selves, but always have contorted faces that lack any colour."

"How does a Satal turn someone into a creature like that?"

"It is sometimes able, briefly, to channel the winds of the Opposing Energy into a concentrated burst of energy, which it can direct through the essence of its victim. This has the effect of almost 'erasing' the essence. It leaves the victim as a Wraith. It's one of the cruellest acts a Satal can commit."

"That's why I couldn't see an essence! It was one of the things that shocked me most. So, it didn't have an essence because it's been blasted away by the Satal?"

"Well, no. Not quite. I said it almost erases the essence. The Wraith still has one – if it did not, it could not continue to live. But all the colour has been drained from it, leaving it transparent and effectively invisible. This makes Wraiths one of our most difficult enemies to defeat."

Anna's eyes widened. "Are there many Wraiths?"

"Fortunately not. It requires enormous effort and energy from the Satal to produce this effect. Far more than it takes to create a Thrall, for example. So they are thankfully very rare. Which is just as well. They are a far, far more fearsome enemy, and many times more dangerous, than a Thrall. It is many years since we have faced a Wraith. The Satal usually only does this when it has a specific target that it wants to hunt down."

Anna swallowed hard. She had no doubt who this Wraith's target was.

"From that moment on, a Wraith's life is no longer its own. It is not dead, but neither is it properly alive. It leads a desperate, half-life existence, and is a complete slave to the Satal's will."

Anna's arm was marked from where the Wraith had gripped it so hard, but thankfully there was no blood. Mr Warwick examined it to make sure there was no lasting damage.

"We are lucky that you did not sustain a worse injury. Contrary to its appearance, something in its transformation leaves the Wraith's physical body formidably strong – much stronger than it was before."

"Might it be possible to heal Gillespie's essence? To stop him from being under the Satal's control? Like you did with the Thrall, earlier?" Anna asked with faint hope.

"Alas, I'm afraid not. The damage is far too extensive for anyone to heal. And once given a mission by the Satal, the Wraith will not rest until that mission is executed. They are relentless. They are ruthless. They know no fear. They are a truly formidable enemy."

Anna gulped again. Without question it was after her. If it had been Mr Warwick, surely it would have broken into the shop much sooner. And it had unmistakably been her it had targeted in the carriage.

"Wraiths still bear resemblance to the living victim from whom they were transformed," Mr. Warwick continued. "But we cannot afford to think of them in that way, nor show them any pity. For they have been transformed into something utterly different, with all their former feelings and humanity burned out of them. They will not stop until they have fulfilled their mission, or until they themselves are killed."

"But that's awful!" said Anna. It had turned out even worse than she had feared when the Beast snatched Gillespie away.

"Anna, in the end we have to think of the killing of a Wraith as a blessing for it. It brings to an end the desperate, tortured misery of its existence."

Anna forced out one more question. She feared the answer, but she needed to know. "What happens to make the Wraith's face look like that?"

The old man's voice grew softer. "I'm afraid the experience of such an assault is deeply traumatic. The expression on the victim's face becomes grossly distorted during the attack. Tragically, it never leaves them."

"Oh…" Anna whispered.

The noise of clattering hooves and wheels on cobblestones was now the only sound as they sped through the night. Her uncle retook his seat.

"No sign of anyone coming after us," he said. "The streets are deserted. We didn't get out of there a moment too soon, though. My God, what a night!" He paused, looking out of the window again. "It seems the war is well and truly upon us, and our enemy's on the attack."

"Yes, indeed," responded Mr Warwick grimly. "We must accelerate our plans. And above all, we must track Faulkner's every move. His return to London will be the crucial moment."

The carriage continued to sway as it wound its way through the London night. Anna could not tear her thoughts away from what Gillespie had become.

"Why do you think those two men we caught didn't mention the Wraith?" she asked. "I mean, they seemed to be telling the truth."

"Yes, I feel sure they were, as far as they knew it. Wraiths are usually kept apart from everyone else. Only the Satal's most senior servants, such as Mortlock, and probably McCain and Grimes – people strong in the Powers – would be allowed to interact with it. Our enemies are as keen to keep their powers secret as we are. For regular people like Archer and Smith, seeing a Wraith would raise far too many questions. I doubt they even knew of its existence, let alone that it was watching the shop."

"Master, I assume Faulkner found out something about Anna from Gillespie?" said Uncle James.

"Yes. My theory now is that Faulkner interrogated Gillespie to find out how he had evaded him in that garden. He must have forced the information out of Gillespie that he had met Anna, and he will have realised that she somehow shielded Gillespie's essence from his reach. Of course, no-one Anna's age has ever possessed such powers, so Faulkner would have known straight away who it was who helped him."

Anna felt numb. She was obviously the reason Gillespie had been put through such a horrific experience.

"For the first time, Faulkner had found someone who knew something of Anna and knew what she looked like. He turned him into a Wraith in order to track her down."

The old man turned back to Anna. "Fortunately for us, however, it seems Gillespie did not know where you live."

"No," said Anna in a small voice. "I don't think Gillespie would ever have known that. My friends and I never talk with any of the Marylebone Street Gang, apart from when we're shouting insults at each other. I very much doubt Gillespie even knew my surname."

"Nevertheless, unlike any of Faulkner's gang, Gillespie knew what you looked like. That made him a valuable weapon Faulkner could use to catch you. One worth expending the tremendous effort required to turn him into a Wraith."

Anna's emotionally charged mind scrambled to take it all in. "Gillespie did know one person who knows where I live, though. Lizzy, one of the maids in our house. I don't think I mentioned it before, but I found out it was Lizzy who told Gillespie where to find me that night."

"What?" said her uncle, his voice suddenly raised. He knew all the household staff by name. "You mean to say Lizzy set that up? Why, that little… Why didn't you tell us this before?"

"I'm sorry, uncle. Now I see that I should have. I didn't want to get her into trouble – at least, not until I understood what was going on. Because Gillespie wasn't trying to cause me any harm that night. He came to me for help. I thought Lizzy might be acting out of good intentions. It's always hard to tell with her. But I knew the kind of trouble she would get into if everyone found out, and I didn't want to cause that if she didn't deserve it. I'm so sorry."

Uncle James was about to respond, but Mr Warwick interjected.

"Let's leave that for now, James. Unfortunately, we clearly cannot risk Lizzy continuing to work in that house now. I'm afraid there's no question about that. We can take care of that in the morning. But it would seem that Faulkner does not know about Lizzy. If he did, I feel sure he would have extracted Anna's whereabouts and we would have experienced a Satal attack on your house before now. Lizzy clearly did not come up in Faulkner's interrogation of Gillespie before he transformed him. For that, at least, we should be grateful."

Anna nodded, though she was struggling to feel gratitude for anything, amidst all the awful developments.

"The Wraith will have been scouring the streets looking for you," said her uncle, "including your former haunts by the canal. I hope you can now see how important it is to stay hidden away, out of sight!"

"Yes," she replied quietly.

"But how did the Wraith come to be in that attic?" he asked, turning to Mr Warwick.

"That I do not know. I'm starting to wonder if our enemies have adopted similar tactics to ours in Eagle Street. Having somehow come to suspect my true identity, they may have taken over those premises across the canal to watch me. But all the evidence still suggests none of our enemies knew of your identity or location until this evening, Anna."

"So how do you think Gillespie, I mean, the Wraith, came to be there?" she asked.

"I think it must have been taken there sometime after you both arrived at the shop. Otherwise, it would surely have attacked earlier, as soon as it saw you arrive. I am guessing it was taken there on McCain's instructions, as soon as he had recovered from the fight. For the first time, he knew the girl they sought was with James Lawrence. As they also suspected my identity by then, they might well have guessed that he would bring you to me. The Wraith's handler, maybe someone like Grimes, could have brought it straight there as soon as he got McCain's message."

"Well, be that as it may," Uncle James joined in again, addressing Anna. "What we now know is that there's a Wraith out there who knows you, and whose mission it is to find you. It will not rest until it succeeds, or it is dead. So, yet another reason to keep you hidden from the world, and to remain ever vigilant."

Anna finally sat back, deep in her carriage seat. Even after all the other dangers she had learned about, this new one was particularly shocking. She recalled the vice-like grip of the Wraith's bony white hands on her arm. The knowledge that this horrible, relentless creature sent to hunt her down was the undead remnant of what used to be Gillespie, made her feel physically sick.

And it was out there now somewhere, still restlessly roaming the night, searching for her. That was the only aim of its wretched existence now. It would never stop until it successfully completed its mission, or it was somehow eliminated...

It was too sad. She had failed Gillespie in his hour of need and allowed him to fall into Faulkner's clutches. His horrific experience at that man's hands, and his appalling state and tortured existence now, were her fault. She did not want any more injury to that poor, wretched soul. Her eyes started to swim, and so did her head. Overcome, she burst into tears.

It was Uncle James who noticed first. He moved instantly to put a comforting arm around her.

"Oh Anna. You've had a terrible experience tonight. Several, in fact. But please don't worry now. You are with the two people who can protect you most in the world. We will never let any harm come to you. You're going somewhere very safe now, where our enemies will never find you."

The tears ran in floods down Anna's face. She felt embarrassed, but once started, she could do nothing but let the emotion drain out of her.

"My dear," added Mr Warwick, "I am so sorry. With all that has occurred, I didn't stop to think what these experiences must have been like for you. I'm afraid I had forgotten just how young you are, and how new you are to the Struggle. You always seem so mature. But we must keep your emotional wellbeing at the forefronts of our minds, as well as your physical safety."

"Quite right," Uncle James added, giving Anna a final hug. "We're not used to managing that side of things, you know. I mean, we're only men after all, and therefore very limited! But we will do our best, I promise."

This finally helped to break Anna's mood. She was able to chuckle a little through her tears. She began to apologise, but the two men waved this away immediately. This time she knew they thought no less of her.

The carriage continued to weave its evasive path through the night streets. Anna watched a succession of unfamiliar building facades flit by, some of them very grand-looking indeed. The rocking motion of the carriage, combined with the hypnotic sound of horses' hooves and rattling wheels on the cobbled road, made it impossible for her to stay awake any longer. Her head dropped onto her uncle's shoulder, and she escaped the day's dramatic events at last.

*   *   *

A number of miles outside London, late the following day, Jake Grimes watched McCain cowering before Faulkner. To be fair to McCain, he had taken some brutal mental punishment for the previous night's failed ambush of Lawrence. Grimes knew it would be his turn next.

'Can't believe I came all the way outta London for this!' he thought to himself. But working for Faulkner was like a pact with the devil. Once you were in, you were in. If you crossed him, you were dead.

Despite this, he thought he disliked the leering figure standing next to Faulkner even more. Mortlock. If you did a job right for Faulkner, he would pay you well – better than anyone else. If you failed him, look out. But Mortlock, he was fork-tongued and slippery as an eel. Whether he was on your side or not depended solely on what was best for his relationship with his Satal master. Faulkner meted out pain for a purpose. Grimes himself would not hesitate to inflict injury when he needed to. But Mortlock – he would hurt people purely for the enjoyment and pleasure it brought him. A more loathsome but dangerous man, Grimes had never met.

In spite of the severe retribution dished out to McCain, Faulkner did not, in fact, seem too displeased. The mission to capture James Lawrence may have failed, but he had learned something new. Something of great value.

"Mortlock, we must use every means to track down this acquaintance of Lawrence. Every means! No stone must be left unturned until we have her identity and location."

"Yes, master. I shall start at once." Mortlock bowed deeply. A look of cunning had already appeared on his face.

Grimes braced himself, as Faulkner turned his dark eyes towards him...

7
Mental Combat

Anna awoke to find herself in a strange bed, in a room she did not recognise. She sat bolt upright and struggled to remember where she was. The events of the night before came slowly back to her. She had a vague recollection of arriving at this building, and of being carried in by her uncle, past someone she did not know. How embarrassing. She must have been very tired!

She peered around the room. It had a ceiling which sloped down almost to the floor to her right. Like Mr Warwick's attic room, it had a dormer window which protruded out onto the sloping roof of the building. It was the only source of light. The doorway was on the opposite wall, to her left.

This room clearly belonged to a man. From the dark suits hanging, to the tiny shaving mirror, to the lack of any kind of charm whatsoever – this room had not seen a woman's touch for quite some time, if ever. Then she remembered the conversation about her uncle's friend, whose house she presumed she must now be in, and whose bed she was afraid she must have turfed him out of. What was his name… Jeremiah? That was now two embarrassing things she had to apologise for, and she hadn't even met him yet.

It was then that Anna heard the sound of Mr Warwick's voice, coming from nearby. How reassuring it was. Under the bed covers, she was still dressed in yesterday's clothes. The beautiful sapphire dress now looked a lot less beautiful, and more like screwed up wrapping paper. Mr Warwick's dressing gown was folded over his slippers at the end of the bed. She got up, put both on and went to the window to see where she was.

They were a number of storeys up. The buildings opposite were slightly lower than the one she was in. Beyond their roofs she could see several church steeples, one or two smoking factory chimneys, and in the distance, the mighty dome of St Paul's Cathedral, topped with a huge cross. She gazed at it. She had seen St Paul's before, but not from this direction. This was a part of London to which she had never been.

She took a quick look in the shaving mirror. She was pleased to note that the graze on her cheek was already healing. None of the rest of what she saw pleased her, of course, but there was not much she could do about that. It was time to go and face the world.

Pushing through the barrier of shyness, she opened the bedroom door and ventured in the direction of Mr Warwick's voice. She found herself in a long, narrow corridor. There were a number of other doors, including one on the right which led to a bathroom. This place was completely unlike any home Anna had seen before, but she supposed it suited their purposes just fine. A door on the left was open, and it was from there that Mr Warwick's voice came. He sounded in good spirits. That was a promising start. Apprehensively, she knocked on the door.

"Anna, good morning!" he boomed brightly on seeing her. "How good to see you are up. I trust you slept all right?" The smiling figure of her uncle sat opposite him at the table.

"Yes, thank you," she replied, "I mean, I think I must have – I don't remember a thing! What time is it?"

"Around ten o'clock. Considering how late it was when we arrived, you haven't really slept all that long."

That prompted her to turn to her uncle. "Uncle, I have a feeling you had to carry me in from the carriage last night. I'm so sorry. I feel like a little child again!"

"Don't be silly, Anna. You'd had quite a day," he said good-naturedly. "I'm not surprised you were exhausted, and you were probably in shock too. You really were very tired, though – it was like carrying a dead weight! And there were so many stairs…"

"I'm sorry, uncle!" she said again, but she was able to laugh along with him.

She took a seat and happily accepted a bread roll, some cheese and a glass of water. She learned that Jeremiah had still been up when they arrived. He had no objection to their staying. He had left for work again early that morning. She was also informed that word had been sent to her mother that she was safe. Her uncle would be paying her house a visit that day to explain everything, and to gain approval for Anna to remain here. Assuming Anna's mother agreed with the plans, Uncle James would bring Anna's essential belongings back with him. He would also recommend that her mother move to another place of safety herself.

Anna was impressed to hear that her uncle and several other Order members had already been to the scene of the previous evening's ambush to see if there were any signs of McCain or any of the other gang members. They had all made a clean getaway, as expected. She wondered whether he had actually had any sleep at all. She asked what was going to happen next.

"The most important thing for you," said Mr Warwick, "is that we begin the next stage of your instruction straight away. The Practice. Although one might say you have already had considerable practice recently!"

Her uncle left the building before noon, and returned in the early evening completely transformed. He wore different clothes much shabbier than his usual ones, a flat cap pulled low over his eyes and a false beard. He reassured Mr Warwick that he had taken a very circuitous route back to Jeremiah's building. He was sure he had not been followed.

He had brought with him a large trunk of clothing and other essentials for Anna. Her mother had apparently agreed that she should stay here until it was safe to return. She had also written Anna a letter.

The thought of her mother, and the worries she must now have, made Anna's chest tighten. She beat a hasty retreat to the room she was staying in under the pretence of unpacking. She wanted to read the letter, and she couldn't cry in front of her teachers again! Tentatively opening it, she saw her mother's distinctive handwriting, and she thought she could see signs that the paper had been damp in patches. She sat on the bed and started to read.

"My dearest Anna,

Your uncle has informed me of the events of yesterday evening. This is a cause of great worry, but I am relieved beyond words that you came to no harm. I have given Edmund and James my permission to act as both guardians and chaperones during this dangerous time, on the condition that they keep you safely hidden.

I am conscious that relations between us have become very strained in recent years. I am also aware that my attempts to protect you and to keep you safe have caused you frustration. Circumstances are now such that I am uncertain when we shall next be able to meet. I am therefore committing to paper certain things that I know I should have spoken to you about before, but for which I could never find the moment.

Above all else, I want you to know how much I love you. I am deeply sorry that I have found myself unable to say this to you in person in recent times. It has become painful for me to do so, for everyone else whom I have ever allowed myself to love has been lost to me. However, please know it to be true, and felt from the very bottom of my heart.

I would also like to explain my wish to protect you so securely. The reason for this, as for so much of my behaviour, has been the Alpha-Omega Struggle. The Struggle has inflicted grievous injuries upon our family. I sought to spare you the details until you were old enough, but I see that the time has now come. When we are able to meet again, I promise that I shall do so. Until then, suffice to say that the Alpha-Omega Wars have caused me suffering almost greater than I can bear. I have done all I could to shut the Struggle out of our lives. In particular, I have attempted to shield you from it. The idea that harm could come to you, as it has to so many others, is one that I simply could not face. This is the reason for the strictness of my rules, including those forbidding you from leaving the house. I hope that you will one day come to understand, and to forgive me if you think I went too far.

However, it has become apparent to me that, regardless of my efforts, I cannot prevent you from becoming involved. Even if you do not seek the Struggle, it will find you. I must recognise that it is your destiny. Edmund and your uncle have spoken with awe of your potential in the Powers, and the unique gifts that you possess. If it were in any field other than the Struggle, I should feel most proud. It is time to put the good of the world ahead of my own worries, and to place the fulfilment of your destiny above my desire for your safety.

If I cannot avoid your becoming involved, then I wish for you to be as prepared and ready as you can be. You are with the two people whom I trust most in the world to guard you, and to instruct you in the skills that you will need. Please learn all they have to teach you, and follow every word of advice they give. I want you to know that, although becoming a knight is the last thing that I had wished for you, I am nevertheless extremely proud of the young lady that you are becoming. You have a spirit within you that reminds me very much of your father. This spirit was one of the many things about him that I loved most dearly, and it is something that I must not seek to dim in you.

Please take the greatest of care in the dangerous times ahead my darling. I hope most fervently that we may safely meet again very soon."

The ink of the signature looked as though the paper might have become particularly damp in that area. Anna put the letter to one side to avoid her own tears adding to the effect. She was experiencing a complex cocktail of emotions, but overriding all others was her love for her mother. She wished more than anything that she could see her, to tell her in person. Instead, she borrowed writing equipment from Mr Warwick, who always had some to hand, and wrote a reply that same day. Her uncle promised he would deliver it at the first opportunity.

"Uncle," she said, "in her letter, my mother mentioned injuries inflicted on our family in the Alpha-Omega Wars. What did she mean? Was... was she talking about my father?" Anna had always been told that he died in an accident when she was very young. Now she felt sure there was more to it. Sensing he did not want to answer, she added, "Uncle, please, I need to know."

Uncle James's face darkened for a moment. Then his expression became unreadable. Eventually he responded, "Your mother has experienced more than one injury in these wars. She has suffered greatly in her life as a result of them. But this is a subject that you must discuss with her directly. Both Mr Warwick and I have given her our most solemn word about this." Anna was about to protest when he continued, "I'm afraid that is final. It is a promise that I simply cannot break."

He withdrew before she could press him any further.

Jeremiah returned home very late that evening, at an hour that was apparently nonetheless very early for him. Anna learned that she had indeed taken over his room.

She was taken by the kindness in this blond man's face, but also struck by the look of absolute tiredness on his features, especially around his blue eyes. He was thin, and he carried the look of a man who, although still only in his thirties apparently, was tired to his bones. He had slicked-back hair which Anna could imagine had once contained a golden lustre, but any former shine was now gone and the hair itself was visibly beginning to thin. Jeremiah's aura was predominantly blue, especially at its core. It became fainter and more watery towards the surface, adding to the overall impression of exhaustion.

Jeremiah was extremely gracious in welcoming Anna. He was also filled with apologies for everything, from its neighbourhood to its highly unusual location on the top floor, to its size and condition, all of which he seemed convinced were beneath them.

"Mr Cartwright, please don't apologise," said Anna as politely as she could. "My bedroom in my house is also on the uppermost floor, which I am told is unusual, but it suits me just fine. You have been so kind, allowing us to stay here at such short notice. We are most grateful to you. And I do feel so awful about taking your room!"

"Please, Anna, call me Jeremiah, and not at all. It is the least I can do."

This little dance of politeness continued for a while, and cemented in Anna the feeling that she liked Jeremiah. Having had all further protestations about using his room rejected, Anna finally accepted it and retired for the night.

Mr Warwick and Uncle James began Anna's instruction again the following morning. This time Anna started the conversation.

"Mr Warwick, would you mind if I asked you a question?"

"Why no, not at all. I regret now that I deferred confirming to you that Faulkner is indeed a Satal, when you asked me about that. I must not repeat the mistake! Please, go ahead."

"Thank you. It's about the Gorgal. You've said that you believe it's a long way from here at the moment. I was just wondering if we can be sure about that, and whether we have any idea where it is?"

"Ah, yes," the old man replied. "I'm not surprised you've been wondering where it has been in the years since it first appeared. In answer to your first question, yes, for now we are certain it is a great distance away."

"And McCain told us as much after the ambush, if you remember," added Uncle James.

Anna nodded, recalling the vicious scar-faced man's words.

"We do not know the answer to your second question, about where it is," continued Mr Warwick, "but it will be somewhere distant, hidden away."

This took Anna by surprise. "But... why should a creature so powerful need to hide?"

The old man smiled. "I thought you would ask! From the pieces I've been able to put together from some of the more ancient Histories, it seems that when a Gorgal appears in this world its essence is highly unstable at first."

"Why is that?" asked Anna. This sounded hopeful.

"It is partly because it was not properly born of our world, and its essence contains none of the Alpha design. It is a mutation of the Omega design. Of course, that is also true of Satals, but Gorgals' essences are more unstable than Satals' are – at least, when the Gorgal first arrives. This seems to be due to the significantly greater size of its essence, and certain other characteristics related to the fact that Gorgals represent the Omega World in a far purer and more powerful form than Satals do. Alas, the process whereby the Gorgal's essence becomes stable is not documented. What the ancient texts do convey is that it takes a great deal of time and energy to complete the process."

"Do we know how long it will take?"

"Well, I cannot be exactly sure, but from my extrapolations I believe it could take anything up to twenty years from its first appearance. That could mean that even now it may only be halfway through the process. This really is only a rough approximation though. It cannot be relied upon."

This was the first time Anna had ever felt better for learning something about the Gorgal. If Mr Warwick turned out to be right, at least it would be some time yet before it came looking for her. She sprang to the next question.

"If the Gorgal is in a weaker state now than it's going to be in the future, or at least, if its essence is in a more fragile, um, unstable state, why don't we hunt it down now? I mean, why wait for it to become more powerful?"

"Anna, bravo, that is precisely the right question! If only some of your more senior colleagues in the Order would share your insight. Yes, it would be infinitely preferable if we could fight the Gorgal now. Our chances of victory would be greatly enhanced. However, without the backing of the Councils of the Order, the resources we have been able to deploy to search for the Gorgal have been too few. So far, we have failed to locate it."

"Do we have any guesses about where it might be?" asked Anna, her spirits slowly falling again.

"Well, I believe it will be sheltered in a remote corner of the world somewhere, far from any of the centres of the Order, while its essence slowly stabilises. It is probably being guarded by at least two of the Satals who accompanied it into this world. Unfortunately, we have no real idea exactly where that might be. But fear not. Our search will resume again in earnest, just as soon as we are safely through the forthcoming battle with Faulkner."

"I see. Thank you." The answers had raised yet more questions, but it was enough for now.

"So, the time has come to commence your Practice."

This was what she had been waiting for. She redoubled her focus. The sessions were to take place in the dining room, as it offered the most space. Mr Warwick and her uncle had moved the furniture away to the sides for the purpose.

"Under any ordinary circumstances we would have spent much longer on the theory of the Powers and its underpinning philosophies before reaching this point. We have skipped much, and what we have shared has been selected specifically to bring you to this point. I should add that you have been a fine student thus far, especially being so young. If only all my students had been so diligent and dedicated!" Mr Warwick winked.

"Well, if only you'd moved with similar speed through my own training and kept up with my lightning-quick mind, perhaps I wouldn't have grown so bored!" Uncle James retorted, making Anna smile.

"Anyhow," Mr Warwick feigned exasperation, "we shall now start to equip you with some basic techniques for defending yourself from mental attack, and to attack yourself when necessary."

Anna nodded. She was feeling both excited and nervous.

"I won't try to hide anything from you. The Practice can have its dangers. It can also be a frightening experience for new students. Some pupils find it deeply unpleasant and do not wish to continue. However, the art of mental combat is the most essential part of any knight's training. If you do not receive the full experience now, you will not be ready when the time comes to face the enemy for real. Is this all right with you, Anna?"

"Yes, Mr Warwick." Anna noticed her palms were perspiring.

"Very good. In this morning's session you will spar with your uncle, whilst I instruct you how to combat his actions. As you have already seen, James is highly adept in mental combat. Please do not be alarmed if, at first, you feel overwhelmed. Every student feels this way at first. Over time you will find that the techniques of defence come to you more and more naturally."

Anna nodded, her apprehension growing.

"We have discussed the importance of controlling and channelling our emotions in daily life, and the implications of not doing so for the state of our essence. This becomes absolutely vital in mental combat. There is no emotion that, if controlled, converted and channelled in a positive way, cannot be turned into something that can strengthen us. Just as in life there is almost no obstacle that cannot be converted to a new opportunity and way forward, so it is with channelling emotions positively in a battle. This will be the most important ability you will ever develop for combat. I hope this theory is clear?"

"Yes, I think so." She did understand. Whether or not she could trust herself always to put it into practice was a different question.

"Very good. So, let us commence. In the first exercise, your uncle will launch a practice attack on you. He is going to replicate something of what it feels like to face an attack from a Satal. Of course, it will not be the same as a real one, but there will be distinct similarities in how it feels."

Anna nodded again, swallowing.

"It is important we start with this for two reasons. One is to provide the initial context for teaching you the defensive techniques we shall go on to cover. The other is so that, when such time comes as you must battle with a real Satal, that will not be the first time you have experienced the terrifying feelings that contact with its essence can induce. The more familiar those feelings are, the better you will be able to manage them, and the less likely you will be to fall into a blind panic. We always do this first, before students have learned the methods of defence, to make sure that they receive the full experience at least once.

"Anna, you are much younger than anyone we have ever taught in the art of mental combat, but I am convinced you have the strength of mind to withstand it. However, please answer me honestly. Do you feel ready to go ahead?"

This was the moment that she had been waiting for. The experience she was going to need. But now the time had come, truth be told she was wracked by nerves. She recalled the appearance of Gillespie's lacerated aura after Faulkner's attack. She also remembered how the remote contact with the man from her dream had felt. Her insides seemed to freeze.

Then she recalled feeling sick with fear when Faulkner had her and Gillespie cornered in the garden. Even worse had been the utter helplessness when the Beast snatched Gillespie away. She had vowed to be ready next time. This was how she would become ready. Become someone no longer helpless and needing constant protection. Someone who could play her proper role in the Struggle. She steeled herself.

"Yes, I'm ready. I'll do my best."

"Very good," said the old man.

He gestured to her uncle to start the session. Uncle James nodded simply, gracefully removed his jacket, then immediately approached her. He was slightly crouched, his muscular frame ready to pounce. His hands and bent arms were raised in front of him, as though preparing for a physical fist fight. His concentration was complete. Anna's pulse quickened.

She switched her focus straight to his blue aura. It was already moving directly towards her, its shape changing. Then she felt it: a sudden inner jolt as it came into contact with her own. Uncle James applied pressure in that mental dimension. She started to feel as though her physical body was being crushed. A force was pinning her down, stopping her from moving or responding. She was powerless. Thoughts flashed through her head: this must be how Gillespie felt when she first used her aura to subdue him, and how the spies outside Mr Warwick's shop had felt. This was why they could offer so little resistance.

Then the sensation changed. The opposing aura started to push her, remorselessly. It felt as though she was being driven backwards. Back to the edge of the world, somehow. To the edge of her own existence. It was a feeling rather than something she could actually see, but she knew without doubt that beyond that 'edge' lay something terrible. Oblivion. Fear gripped her. And she had experienced this fear before. In the here and now, she was starting to relive the horror of her dream so many years before, when the demonic eyes of the largest of the five had bored into her. In that nightmare, she had felt purest evil, looking into her soul. Now she was being pushed closer and closer to the edge of this world, beyond which, somehow, the same kind of evil resided.

Terror welled up. They didn't realise what they were doing. They couldn't know the effect that revisiting that traumatic dream would have on her. They didn't understand. She was in real and absolute danger. Something had gone wrong. Badly wrong. Her very existence was now teetering on the verge of obliteration. She had to act right now or be lost forever.

Mustering all the might she could in that state, Anna pushed back with her own aura against the force pinning her down. Her dreaded progress towards annihilation slowed immediately. Then it stopped. Using the entire force of her will, she manoeuvred her aura rapidly and loosened the grip that was holding her a little. Then she pushed again, with redoubled effort and focus. The opposing force gave way some, then some more. Slowly she started to push the other aura steadily backwards, forcing herself away from the abyss.

The terror of what lay beyond remained. She focused and channelled that fear into a new rush of power and resolve not to be driven back towards it. Suddenly she felt strong, in control. She saw things with startling clarity. She could see not only the shape and blue colour of the opposing aura, but she could now make out every individual contour, every minor undulation on its surface, every tiny ripple of movement. With a single-minded determination not to fall victim to the horrors she had been exposed to moments earlier, she struck back.

She moved her aura at great speed to finally break away from the other, evading its grip completely. Then she clenched her aura tightly and jabbed it back at her opponent with lightning speed, striking a powerful blow. With tremendous acceleration, she moved her aura over her uncle's, instantly finding a strong grip amongst its contours. In a continuation of the same movement, she created a powerful twisting motion, entirely changing the other aura's shape and axis of rotation.

Power surged through her. At that moment she knew she could inflict the most terrible damage upon her opponent's aura now if she chose. But her purpose was only to bring the encounter to an end and to eliminate the danger, not to cause harm. She retained control, making sure her grip was not so powerful as to cause lasting damage. She flipped the opposing aura entirely and launched it as far away from her as she could, to where it could threaten her no more. At the same time, she pushed her adversary's physical body.

Breathing heavily, Anna returned her focus fully to her normal vision. It was then she noticed that the physical form of her opponent was no longer in front of her. In fact, it was nowhere near. She gasped as she realised that her usually imperturbable uncle was now lying on the ground several yards away, motionless, his head pointing in her direction and his legs crumpled up against the far wall.

"Oh, my goodness!" Anna cried out, rushing to him. To her enormous relief, he started to move, first reaching to rub his head, then shifting gingerly into a sitting position.

"Oh uncle, I'm so sorry! I really didn't mean for you to end up down there! I am so sorry."

She looked round at Mr Warwick, fearful he would be furious. In fact, he seemed to be trying hard to suppress a grin. Her uncle rubbed his head and back, then started to rise to his feet, shakily. He pressed one hand against the wall for support.

Mr Warwick spoke. "James, I don't suppose you decided to just let her do that to you by any chance, did you? Out of some kind of uncle-like fondness, or some such thing?" He continued to try to keep a straight face. He failed.

Uncle James's expression, a complex mixture of shock and hurt pride, conveyed the answer before his words could.

"No, master. As it happens, I did not. I did not decide to just let her do anything." He shook his head. It was taking him longer than usual to share the joke with the old man.

"I see." Mr Warwick finally managed a more serious expression. "Are you all right?"

"Yes, I think so." He was still rubbing his head. "No lasting physical damage, I don't think. Hopefully you'll be able to confirm that no significant damage has been done to my essence. I imagine there may be the odd telltale sign of damaged pride and humiliation in there somewhere though!" At last he managed a small, rueful smile.

"Please believe me," said Anna, "I really am so sorry. I didn't realise quite what was going to happen, and, well, I was terrified! I lost sight that it was you I was fighting with. I think must have panicked. I am so sorry. Please forgive me!"

"Anna, you have nothing to apologise to me for. Nothing whatsoever. I am not angry with you for what just happened. Certainly, I am experiencing a flurry of other emotions, but anger is not one of them." He took a breath. "But if it helps you, then I will say it. Anna, I forgive you for throwing me across the room and landing me on my head!" This time he managed a proper smile.

No-one spoke for a moment, as Uncle James set about dusting himself off and confirming that all his limbs were still working. Mr Warwick looked on with a curious expression that Anna could not quite read. Anna stayed exactly where she was, now feeling too timid to say anything more until she was spoken to again.

Eventually, Mr Warwick put his arm round Anna's uncle's shoulder and led him towards the corner of the room. He appeared to be asking him questions in a low voice. It was too quiet for Anna to hear. However, her uncle's response was more animated, and his voice was loud enough for her to make out his words.

"Master, I assure you that was no joke or act of kindness. Yes, she may have taken me by surprise, and I'm sure I could have withstood her a little better had I been fully on my guard. But the force she hit me with – it was immense! I have very seldom felt anything like it. Not only that. The speed at which she moved was astonishing. I could barely follow her. Now I understand how she stunned Mortlock outside Faulkner's mansion. We're dealing here with something quite extraordinary. Something beyond any of our experiences."

The two men re-joined Anna. Mr Warwick spoke first.

"Well, well. We ought to know better by now, but it seems you never lose your ability to surprise us. Your uncle was far from being my best student in, well, frankly any other subject…"

"Are you trying to make me feel even worse?" Uncle James smiled.

"…but mental combat was something at which he excelled from the start. He has been in more scrapes and tight corners than most people ever live to see – possibly because he seems to positively seek them out, mind you – but he always gains the upper hand and survives to tell the tale."

Uncle James chipped in, "I'm not just trying to make myself feel better when I say that what you just did was unprecedented. It could have been the work of a master fighter. Everyone else I have ever seen in their first Practice session has been totally overcome, overwhelmed and defeated."

"What was most impressive," Mr Warwick resumed, "and encouraging, was not your power and speed, but the control you displayed. I feared your uncle's essence might suffer real damage. I was preparing to intervene. But it seems to me you have already learned and applied the key lesson: controlling and channelling your emotions. That takes most students months, often years, to master. And we have barely begun!"

Anna felt herself blush. She was unsure where to look.

"There was only one area for improvement. Your initial perception of the situation. Remaining calm, perceiving and understanding the challenge correctly for what it is from the start, and not under or overreacting. These are key to entering into the battle in the most effective way technically, and also in the most appropriate frame of mind. This is true in every situation, but never more than when facing a Satal, who can play all manner of tricks with your mind and your emotions."

Anna understood. And he was right. She had not perceived the situation correctly at first. It was a lesson that she would remember.

"But you would not have been human," the old man added, "had you not struggled with that in your first session. Wouldn't you say, James?"

"Absolutely, I would. I won't deny it, you've given my pride a real dent today. But as I slowly recover," he smiled again, "what excites me, indeed, what fills me with awe, is how formidable you might one day become – once you've actually had some training! And once you have learned all that we can teach you, and you reach your full maturity."

"Thank you," said Anna. This time she managed to look them both in the eye.

"And heaven knows, in the war ahead we are going to need all of that strength," said Mr Warwick. "Anna, you are a remarkable young lady. Please never doubt yourself. I cannot tell you how much I am looking forward to seeing the knight that you will one day become."

8
The Lost Book

So began Anna's training in mental combat. Mr Warwick explained with a smile that, despite her unexpected success in the first session, they would stick to the plan and steadily build up to the techniques for defeating Satals. Their objective would be to add theory and structure to her obvious, instinctive talents. To begin with, she was to learn about the basic principles of mental defence against other humans.

First, she learned the impact of gaining a strong hold on the opponent's aura. As Anna had seen and experienced for herself, if an aura is gripped by another, with sufficient pressure applied to enough of its surface area, its owner could be prevented from retaliating in the physical world. Next, Mr Warwick and her uncle demonstrated basic aura attacks and the theory of how best to defend against them. Anna watched with fascination as they launched practice attacks on each other. She absorbed their full range of moves.

In one early session, Uncle James appeared to harden his aura before striking out at Mr Warwick's. The old man made his own aura malleable enough to absorb the blow without experiencing any ill effects. Then he flexed it to repel the attacker. In another, Mr Warwick was the aggressor. He lunged forward to get a mental grip on his opponent's aura, as though aiming to crush the life out of it. Anna's uncle manoeuvred his aura deftly to one side at the key moment, and, flexing it, dealt a blow to the side of its counterpart. This stunned the older man and Uncle James was able to push his physical body gently away.

There were many variations of attack and defence, and the demonstrations grew increasingly complex. As Anna took in every detail, she grew to understand the relative strengths of the two men. Mr Warwick's aura was the larger and more powerful of the two. When the two came into direct mental contact with each other, Mr Warwick would always be able to force his adversary back. Anna's uncle seemed able to manoeuvre his aura slightly more quickly and execute delicate moves a little more deftly than his stronger opponent.

Anna also came to understand that she was probably seeing the detail of the combat better than either of them could. Naturally, neither could see their own aura, but their moves seemed to her a bit slow and clumsy, as they grappled for a hold. Sometimes they would miss altogether what she considered clear chances to gain a grip, or an opening to strike.

The time came for Anna to join in the sessions. Her anxiety returned immediately. Watching was one thing, but she had not forgotten how the first practice attack had felt. The first bout was against her uncle again, with Mr Warwick looking on. 'Uncle looks even more apprehensive than I feel!' she thought.

When it started, he took her by surprise, striking suddenly. She was momentarily stunned. This was the fastest move she had yet seen from him. She knew she needed to respond fast or else be overpowered completely. Applying the blocks and evasion techniques she had been taught, she was able to ward off the next attacks strongly and successfully. Most importantly for her own confidence and peace of mind, this time she retained an accurate view of the situation right from the start. She managed to avoid inflicting any unintended physical damage on her opponent – to the great relief of them both!

In the next bout, Anna faced Mr Warwick himself for the first time. It was her turn to attack. She was able to get the upper hand immediately, through her greater speed and ability to see holds. Ultimately, however, she was beaten by a subtle combination of attacks and feints from Mr Warwick. His moves were slower than her visualisation of her own aura, but they were more cunning, with feints and dummies, and followed up with his considerable power. Anna was able to fend him off for quite some time, but eventually the old man overcame her and pinned her physical body gently against the wall.

For the first time, Anna had been defeated in mental combat. It was a feeling she did not enjoy one bit. Immediately, she went through her mistakes in her mind to learn from them. It was only some time later that Mr Warwick confided it had taken every ounce of his effort to overcome her. He admitted he had barely been able to see some of Anna's early moves, so fast were they. He had deployed some of his most advanced techniques, learned over many years, to finally get the upper hand. That made her feel a little better.

The trio held long training sessions every day, and Anna learned increasingly advanced fighting techniques. These included the most effective ways to deal with the types of spike and blade aura attacks she had already seen from their enemies. She had never been more focused. Soon, Mr Warwick told her she had already mastered all the basic combat techniques that it would take an ordinary new student months to learn. It was also notable that, after her first bout with Mr Warwick, she was never again overwhelmed by either of her teachers – often despite their best efforts.

Mr Warwick observed that, unlike every other student he had taught before, in Anna's case he was not so much teaching her as honing and refining an innate ability that she already possessed. For her part, Anna could feel her own strength and speed increasing by the day.

The combat sessions were interspersed with further related theory and history. She learned of the close relationship between the philosophy of the Powers and elements of ancient Greek and Roman philosophy, such as Stoicism. She also had her first practical lessons in the elementary skills of a Healer, and the basic principles of 'Foreseeing', the skill of a Seer. Anna was told it was very rare for any knight to possess both these powers alongside a decent level of combat competence. Mr Warwick was one of those rare cases who did. According to her teachers, in these subjects too she displayed an instinctive ability, the likes of which they had never seen.

One evening in early December, Mr Warwick judged they were ready to return to the subject of Satal combat. Anna's uncle was away that evening, meeting Order members who had been watching the house in Eagle Street.

"We know of only one way to defeat a Satal. Essentially, it requires reversing the process by which it comes into our world. And to explain that, we must go right back to the beginning.

"As we have discussed before, at the moment the universe was created, two fundamental energies existed."

"The Elemental Energy and the Opposing Energy," said Anna.

"That's right. And each moved to create a universe according to its own design at exactly the same instant."

Anna nodded, remembering her first lesson with Mr Warwick.

"The Elemental Energy sought a harmonious universe," the old man continued.

"The Alpha World."

"Yes. And of course, the Opposing Energy moved to create something altogether different. The Omega World, where nothing in our world today could survive. Now as we know, the Opposing Energy failed. The universe that was actually created fundamentally followed the Alpha design."

Anna nodded again. She was familiar with these concepts by now, no matter how hard she still found them to visualise.

"However, now we return to a topic that we have discussed several times before. The Opposing Energy's action and influence at the moment of the universe's creation led to what I call 'contamination' being present in the universe. As a result, our universe fell short of the pure Alpha World. This Omega contamination has made our universe less harmonious, with more suffering and injustice than the Alpha World would have."

"And until we reach the Alpha state," Anna added, "it is still possible for the Opposing Energy to turn our world into the Omega World. Which it is still seeking to do, through its direct influence, and through the Gorgal, the Satals and the other Omega forces."

"Yes, that's right," said the old man, looking pleased with her understanding.

"Mr Warwick," she continued, "you've told me before that Satals have nothing to do with the design of the Alpha World. So, if the Opposing Energy failed to create its universe, the Omega Universe that is, then how do Satals still appear? Is it something to do with that contamination again?"

"Ah, no, actually. Not in the case of Satals," he replied. "The Opposing Energy's initial attempt to create the Omega World failed, but a shadow of that world did, in fact, appear."

Anna grappled with what this might mean.

"This shadow universe," he continued, "exists in a real space, separate from ours. But it is not a fully-fledged universe. It is only partially formed. It's like a twilight universe, a mere echo of what the Omega Universe would be. We call this the 'Beta Universe', or more often, the 'Beta World'."

Anna thought back to what she had learned before. "You've told me before that pure creatures of the Omega World could not exist in our world. Is that different for this Beta World, then?"

"Yes, it is. Beings from the Beta World can, and sometimes do, come to exist in ours."

"So Satals come from the Beta World?"

"Yes, precisely. Being only partially formed, the Beta Universe itself cannot support proper life as we know it. It can only support what we might consider to be embryos of life. As long as they remain in the Beta World, they can never develop beyond that state. These embryos have adapted themselves from the Omega design. There are various types of embryo, but it is from the largest of them that Satals, and very occasionally Gorgals, appear."

"So, the Beta World is separate from our world. How do the Satals get here from there?" Anna was pushing much harder for information than she used to. She hoped it was not impolite, but she sensed strongly how important this knowledge was for her.

"Cast your mind back to your dream all those years ago. You described seeing strange, horizontal lightning, followed by the appearance of the five figures."

"Yes, that's right."

"Immediately before the lightning, there was in fact a great coming together of the winds of the Opposing Energy, into a single point. This confluence of winds caused the fabric of the universe to rupture."

"Sorry, Mr Warwick... what does that mean?"

"Well, it means a hole was created. We don't understand the science of this, but what we do know is that when this happens, on the other side of the hole is the Beta Universe. In your dream, you saw that very moment, when the two universes were connected."

If Mr Warwick did not understand the science then she certainly did not. But struggling though she was with the concepts, she now felt the full enormity of what she had seen in her dream.

"The hole only exists for a moment. Then the winds drop and the gap reseals. But for as long as the two universes are connected, embryos from the Beta Universe can come into ours. At the moment they pass through, they are born into fully-fledged life for the first time. And this is in a form that can survive in our world."

"And in the case that I saw, a Gorgal and four Satals passed through."

"Precisely. Now, they first appear here in their natural form. We call this their 'true form'. This form varies from creature to creature. The only common theme is that each appears utterly terrifying and abhorrent to our eyes."

"Like the Beast of Highgate," said Anna, recalling the horrific, horned beast.

"Yes, exactly. But to fulfil their evil works, Satals need to infiltrate and assimilate into the world of humans. To do this, they use a human 'host'."

Anna scrambled to catch up again. "So, do you mean that the man we know as Faulkner already existed, before the Satal arrived?"

"Yes, I'm afraid so. Soon after its arrival, the Satal captures a poor victim, destroys that person's essence and takes possession of their physical body. Sadly, this is what happened to an innocent man, named Marcus Faulkner, about eight years ago. Of course, it retains its own, very alien essence, as you have seen in Faulkner's case."

Anna started to feel slightly nauseous at this thought. But she needed to stay focused. She simply had to understand it.

"A Satal typically returns to its true form to kill its prey. It can then see much more clearly than in its adopted human form, and it is far more powerful in both the mental and physical dimensions."

"So, how do we defeat these monsters?"

"Ah yes, the key point. We only know of one way to kill them."

"You said that was by reversing the process they use to come here. Do you mean we somehow have to send them back to the Beta World?"

"Yes. Or to be precise, send their essences back. As I mentioned, the Beta Universe cannot support fully-fledged life. Once the Satal has come to life fully in our world, even its essence cannot survive back in the Beta World, when it returns."

It was time for a question Anna had often pondered. "Why can't we just kill the Satal with a gun, or another weapon?"

"Ah, if only it were that simple! Unfortunately, that will not work with a Satal."

"But I don't understand. Why not?"

"Well, you see, it is possible to kill the body of a Satal, when it's in its human form, and also when it's in its true form. But unlike the essence of a human, a Satal's essence can continue to survive separately from its body. The Satal simply moves on to a new host – and potentially to the person who killed the last host's body. So we must be extremely careful about that. Once it has a new human host, it can generate its true form again. So, killing the body does not kill the Satal."

"I see. What about killing its essence?"

"You've seen Faulkner's essence. It's huge, very powerful, and very well protected by those spikes. We cannot kill it by striking it with our own essences. That generally does us more harm than the Satal."

"How about trying to crush the life out of it, as you can with a human?"

"Now you're getting closer. But no individual has an essence remotely large enough to surround a Satal's essence and crush it. Nor can they match the immense power that the Satal can generate from within its essence."

"Oh, I see."

"However, crushing the Satal's essence is, in fact, a vital step towards defeating it. Just not in the way you're probably imagining. It is a step towards returning their essence to the Beta World."

Anna was confused again. "Mr Warwick, I'm sorry. I think you've lost me."

"Yes, this part is complicated. Let me try to explain it as simply as I can."

"Thank you!" said Anna. This was the crucial point she most needed to understand.

"A Satal's essence is developed and adapted from the Omega design. It contains none of the Alpha design. As a result, the essence is not fully adapted to our world. It is unstable. Not as much as the Gorgal's essence when it first appears here, but unlike the Gorgal's case, a Satal's essence does not grow more stable over time. So, despite being inhumanly powerful, the Satal's essence contains certain structural weaknesses. Flaws within its structure. This makes it vulnerable. If enough pressure is applied to it from all sides it can be made to collapse inwards."

"But you said they can't be killed by crushing their essences?"

"I did. Crushing the essence is not the end. It is just an important step. If the pressure can be applied until the Satal's essence contracts beyond a certain critical point, a chain reaction starts. The Satal's essence begins to collapse in on itself, until it becomes a small, extremely dense mass."

"Is that when the Satal dies?"

Mr Warwick laughed. "No, Anna. I can see how much you want the Satal gone, and I applaud you for it! But this is still not enough to kill it. When the essence becomes very dense, it attracts the winds of the Opposing Energy towards it. The denser it becomes, the stronger these winds are. When they converge on the single point where the essence is located, they can cause a rupture in the fabric of the universe again."

"Another hole, like the one the Satal first appears through?"

"Exactly, yes. Another hole connecting us with the Beta World. We must push the Satal's compressed essence through the hole to return it to the Beta World. Then it will die."

Anna struggled to visualise it. "But if a hole appears again, doesn't that mean more Beta World creatures can pass into our world?"

"Excellent question! The answer is no. Because of the way the rupture occurs this time, the pressure and the direction of the winds is *towards* the Beta World. So, at this time, passage is only possible from our universe into the Beta Universe, not vice-versa."

"All right," said Anna. She didn't understand the detail of course, but she followed enough to accept what Mr Warwick was saying. For now. "So, crushing the Satal's essence into a dense ball and then sending it back to the Beta Universe is the only way to kill a Satal?"

"Precisely. At least, it's the only way we know of."

"But," Anna jumped to the next problem, "you said that no-one has an essence big and powerful enough to crush a Satal's. So how can we kill them in the way you described?"

"A-ha! Yes, now we come to the crux of the matter. One knight alone is never enough to defeat a Satal. This is why I say it always requires a number of strong knights to do it. If the number is sufficient, together they can surround the Satal's essence and apply the pressure needed."

"Yes, I see," said Anna.

"Of course, this is much, much easier said than done. Not least because the Satal's physical body in its true form is usually very dangerous. It can cause considerable damage before its physical movements can be prevented by pressure on its essence."

"Yes, right." Anna was beginning to appreciate just how difficult this would be.

"Alas, there are usually severe casualties before the job is done. A considerable number of knights are needed, and tragically, some usually do not make it. Everyone involved must be prepared for this."

Mr Warwick's face fell briefly. Sensing the conversation was starting to bring back painful memories, Anna moved the subject on as gently as she could.

"Um, Mr Warwick, what happens to the Satal's body, once its essence has died in the Beta World?"

"All that remains in our world is the dead body of the person whom the Satal possessed. No evidence remains of the presence which had possessed it. The true form of the Satal disappears, along with its essence."

Anna let the conversation pause for a moment. Mr Warwick soon began again.

"There is one more thing I really should mention. It is not pleasant, but it would be wrong for me to withhold it from you. Satals have a very specific way of killing enemies who have the Powers."

"Oh. How do they do it?"

"There's no nice way to explain this. They don't just want to kill us. They seek to send our essences into the Beta Universe."

"But... why? Isn't the result the same, however it chooses to kill a person?"

"Well, no it isn't, in fact. It's different in one important respect. In the essences of those with the Powers, it seems there is invaluable energy which can provide enormous nourishment to the embryos in the Beta World. Nourishment they can get from no other source."

"Only from essences of people with the Powers?"

"Yes, so it seems. We don't fully understand the reason. But only in our case do Satals make the considerable effort required. Never with regular members of the population."

Anna hesitated. She dreaded the answer to her next question. But she needed to understand.

"So, what happens to us if the Satal sends our essence into the Beta Universe?"

"Well, it appears that the essence is devoured by the embryonic half-life Beta creatures that inhabit that dimension. Those creatures are not properly alive, but they are able to feed, to take on sustenance. They convert this into stored energy somehow. The more energy they receive, the more formidable the Omega forces will be that burst through the gap next time, into our universe. More formidable, both in terms of their individual powers, and of their numbers."

"So, in sending our essence to the Beta world, they not only kill us, but they make their own forces stronger for their next attack as well?"

"Yes, exactly. And the greater the power of the knight, hence the greater the size of their essence, the greater the nourishment."

This was the most horrific thing Anna had heard in all her instruction. The idea of an aura being feasted on by those embryonic twilight beings made her feel physically sick. Perhaps seeing her shocked expression, Mr Warwick continued rapidly.

"I know this sounds truly abhorrent. I can give you a little comfort. We believe the owner of the essence does not remain alive for more than the briefest time once it has entered the Beta World. So the conscious experience is mercifully short."

That felt like scant consolation. Anna had been picturing the conversation vividly. She felt a bit overwhelmed. But there was no more important subject for her to learn about than Satal combat. She had to push on.

"So that's the reason that Faulkner and his men don't just try to shoot us."

"Precisely. The fuel that we represent to their cause is too valuable. Now you can see why mental combat remains such a vital aspect of the Struggle, for both sides."

"Yes, I see." Then she remembered something else. "In my first practice session, with my uncle…"

"Ah yes," said Mr Warwick, smiling for the first time in a while as he recalled that memorable bout.

"Well, it felt like I was being pushed to the edge of existence somehow. Towards oblivion... At the time you said that my uncle was replicating the feeling of a Satal attack. That edge that I was sensing, was it actually the edge of our world, and the start of the Beta World?"

"Yes, Anna. Yes, that's right. Of course, we can never truly replicate it, but yes, that is exactly the feeling he was creating."

'About the worst feeling imaginable,' Anna thought to herself. She shuddered at the memory.

"As we have discussed before in relation to Wraiths, Satals can channel the winds of the Opposing Energy through their own essences. By doing this, they themselves are able to create a brief hole in the fabric of the universe. The direction of the wind is towards the Beta World again, so no Omega creatures can enter our world when they do it. They cannot sustain it, but they can do it long enough to force our essence through."

Anna said nothing now. If the experience was worse than that of the practice session, she could not possibly imagine a more terrible end. There was a sound from outside. Then the front door opened and Anna's uncle entered.

"Is everything all right, James?" asked Mr Warwick.

"Yes, master. The plans for the attack are progressing very well," he responded.

"Excellent. You must update me fully after this session. Actually, you have arrived at the perfect time." Just when Anna thought the evening's discussion couldn't get any more disturbing, he added, "You are just in time for the final topic of the day: the Gorgal!"

Then things got worse still. Turning back to Anna, Mr Warwick said, "Now, this is where we have a slight challenge. And that is that neither your uncle nor I have any idea how the Gorgal can be defeated!"

Anna looked back at the old man, stunned.

"Obviously, no-one alive has ever faced such a creature, but usually we would expect to have written texts from former times to provide guidance. In this case, we have none. All I have been able to glean is that the method I have just described to defeat a Satal will not work in the case of a Gorgal. This is due to the stabilisation of the Gorgal's essence that we discussed previously. That stabilisation process, once complete, removes the flaws in the structure of its essence that we exploit in the case of Satals."

Anna was shocked. For all her uncertainty and fears, she had always felt that her uncle, and particularly Mr Warwick, would be able to teach her what she needed to know, and explain how to deal with the dangers ahead. Could this really be true? That on this most important, and personal, point of all, concerning that man from her dream, was there a crucial gap in their knowledge? More like a yawning chasm. If the day really was coming when she would have to meet that 'man', it would be quite helpful to know what she was supposed to do!

"However, that does not mean that this knowledge from times long past does not exist somewhere. It was documented in a famous book, by our ancient predecessors in Rome, in ancient Greece and further back, right back to ancient Egypt.

"This book came to be held in secret by the Order in Rome from the height of the Roman Empire onwards, before the last European Gorgal struck. One copy of the book was made, and held by another branch of the Order in Constantinople, the capital of what had become the Eastern Roman Empire. That book was destroyed in the destruction of that city by the fourth Crusade in the thirteenth century – an event in which, incidentally, a Satal of that time played a major part. The original book remained in Rome until the time of the Renaissance, when it was transferred to the hidden library of the Order in Florence. It has remained there ever since. Or rather, it had. The challenge we have now is that this book has gone missing!"

Now Anna's uncle joined in. "After Mr Warwick interpreted your dream, I paid a visit to the Order in Florence myself. At the instruction of Signor Delvecchio, an old colleague of Mr Warwick's, the Order there allowed me complete freedom to search their extensive secret library. The Book of the Gorgals is nowhere to be found. None of the Order members could shed any light on what had happened to it. Indeed, they seemed as perplexed as I was, and visibly shocked."

"This was indeed a great and unexpected surprise," Mr Warwick added. "To me it's scarcely believable that a library as important as that of the Order in Florence could have allowed such a book simply to disappear. In fact," he lowered his voice, "I do suspect some kind of conspiracy…"

His voice trailed off briefly, as though the sound had been momentarily crushed by the weight of his thoughts.

"It is my intention," he resumed, presently, "as soon as circumstances permit, to pay a visit to Florence, to follow this up myself. I shall meet with my old friend, Signor

Delvecchio. He is one of the best knights I have ever known, and one of the finest men. His family has a long and proud history in the Order of Florence. I must see if he can help make some sense of it."

Anna wondered if this lost book was what Faulkner was searching for, and the reason his gang were gathering books for him. Perhaps they were trying to find it, to destroy it forever? But the mood of the discussion had changed distinctly. Now no longer seemed the time to ask. Silence filled the room again. It was Uncle James who spoke next.

"There are many in the Order who do not believe that Gorgals have ever existed. I must confess, before Mr Warwick's interpretation of your dream, I was one of them. They think they are mere legends, grown out of stories of very powerful Satals from times long past. For that reason, most in the Order do not consider it a priority to find this book."

"After we learned about the dream," Mr Warwick continued, "your uncle and I travelled to meet various leaders of the Order – not only in Florence but throughout Europe, including this country. We were shocked that so many amongst them remained cynics, even when they were presented with compelling evidence to the contrary." Worry was etched on the old man's face.

Uncle James added, "I'm afraid many of them consider your dream to have been merely a child's nightmare, and nothing more."

"What is most frustrating," said Mr Warwick, "is that they fail to see a connection between what you saw, and what has been predicted. Several of our most prominent and powerful Seers have predicted that the coming twentieth and twenty-first centuries are set to be the most momentous the human world has yet seen."

Anna sat forward in her chair.

"They have the potential to be truly unprecedented for mankind. In the most wondrous ways, or in the most catastrophic. In the next two centuries, they say, mankind may achieve utterly astounding feats, moving towards the pure Alpha state. But there is an alternative future foreseen, in which men, women and children may be massacred on a scale never before seen. Destruction on an unimaginable scale, by forces of evil unleashed by the Opposing Energy in a descent towards the Omega state."

Uncle James spoke again. "They tell us that both these possible outcomes have been foreseen for the coming centuries. Either direction is still possible."

"If the Gorgal is given the opportunity to execute its plans," Mr Warwick resumed, "it will nurture the conditions and set in motion a chain of events which will lead directly to that immense future destruction I mentioned. It has been foreseen that certain men, who are going to be born in the coming years, may go on to inflict the most appalling carnage on vast numbers of people in the twentieth century, throughout Europe and beyond. These individuals will seize upon and drive that chain of events initiated by the Gorgal.

"All of this potential future that has been foreseen will be set in motion by this Gorgal, if it is not stopped. As long as the Gorgal lives, it will drive the destruction directly, itself. But even if we can manage to defeat it eventually, if that defeat takes too long, the Gorgal will have sown the seeds for those others I mentioned to lead the mass-destruction themselves from then onwards, driven on by the influence of the Opposing Energy. And the Gorgal could start this whole process very soon, Anna – as soon as its essence has stabilised sufficiently."

Anna nodded, wide eyed.

"As we have discussed," the old man continued again, "the current state of the universe is highly unstable. One day, either the pure Alpha or the pure Omega state will finally be realised. From that point, whichever it is, there will be no return. The future is now balanced on a knife-edge. The world could start to follow the Alpha or the Omega path at a speed never before imagined, to its final state. What more important role can the Order of the Knights of the True Path have than to ensure the balance is tipped in favour of the Alpha World?"

"None whatsoever is the answer!" said Anna's uncle, his own frustration clearly visible. "Seeing as that has been the sole purpose of its existence for thousands of years!"

"Yes, exactly," Mr Warwick agreed. "The appearance of this Gorgal, at this precise moment in history, cannot be a coincidence. It could foreshadow the most fundamental shift of our world that mankind has ever known, towards the Omega state. It might be far, far worse than the Dark Ages after the fall of the Western Roman Empire. It could bring the most horrific events the human world has ever seen. I do not exaggerate when I say I fear that within your lifetime, Anna, and certainly within that of your children and grandchildren, it could mean the final descent to the Omega state. And as you know, that would ultimately mean the destruction of every living creature in the world, to be replaced by something very different…"

There was silence for a moment. Eventually Uncle James resumed, "Whether or not this happens depends entirely on whether we can defeat this Gorgal, and on how long that takes. The stakes are staggering. Yet, so many in the Order simply do not see it!"

"It may just be that the Order's complacency turns out to be the greatest weapon our enemies have against us," Mr Warwick concluded. "Or there might be other, more sinister reasons for the rejection of our findings... but, that is for another time."

The old man examined his pocket watch. "The time has moved on. We have covered a lot of territory, so I suggest we draw this session to a close. James, you and I must discuss the immediate battle plans. Then, I think I will write again to my old friend in Florence. We simply must find that book..."

He fell silent again, chasing down the remainder of his thoughts in the privacy of his own head. Then he rose from his chair and made his way to the door, followed by Uncle James.

Mr Warwick appeared stooped as he walked, as though he were carrying a great weight on his shoulders. Anna thought she had never seen him looking so old.

9
Battle Plans

Anna's instruction continued, but the timing of the sessions became increasingly erratic. They were often cut short too, as one or other of the men had to leave the house for battle preparations. Anna was amused to see the elaborate and convincing disguises the men would wear each time. At least one of her mentors always remained in the house for Anna's protection but the training sessions often stopped until they were both present again. They shared no details of the plans with her, but it was clear the attack on Faulkner and his gang was now imminent.

Whenever her instruction was paused, Anna was left with plenty of books to study. However, it was never long before her mind began to wander. At first, she would wonder how the preparations were going and what the next few weeks held in store, but she had no new information to build on. Since receiving her mother's letter, she had burned to know more about her father's fate, but her mentors were unable to answer those questions either, due to the promises they had made to her mother. Starved of anything else to occupy it, her mind would always head straight back to the subject of Timmy.

Where was he now? What was he doing? He had not shown up the last time they were due to meet, and she had never received an explanation. It was very soon afterwards that she was moved to this house. All possible connections with the outside world were severed. Anna could only conclude that Timmy had moved on from her. The possibility of whatever future they might have had together seemed lost. The raw pain of this had dulled with the passing weeks, but it did not go away. Now that she found herself more and more on her own, she began to dwell on the subject again.

Timmy was the only boy she had ever felt strongly for. Their brief moments together had been the most joyous of her life. She just could not let go of her dream that they might one day be together again, despite all reason to the contrary. And beyond that, she just wished she could see all her friends again. In her short life she had grown well used to being stuck on her own, but she did miss having someone around her own age to chat and laugh with.

Early one afternoon less than two weeks before Christmas, Anna's uncle came to see her. There was more than a hint of urgency in his voice.

"I have just spoken at length with Mr Warwick. He agreed I may share certain aspects of our battle plans with you, provided you promise not to breathe a word to anyone. It may literally cost all of us our lives if you do. Do I have your word?"

"Yes, uncle, of course. I promise."

"Good. If we had explained more about the dangers lying in wait in the past, I think you would have taken more care."

Anna nodded. She looked down.

"Especially in times of war, the influence of the Opposing Energy is always active. As Mr Warwick likes to describe it, it's like a mighty wind, blowing on our essences, trying to move us in its direction."

"Yes, I understand." This was something Mr Warwick spoke about a lot.

"Look, I know this is sometimes hard to visualise, or maybe even to believe. But please trust me. It is real. I have felt it, and fought it, enough times to know."

Anna nodded again, not speaking this time. The memory of his aura turning purple was fresh in her mind.

"So, unless Mr. Warwick or I explicitly say so," he continued, "or unless your life is in significant danger, you must not leave this house. Do I have your most solemn promise?"

"Yes uncle, you have it. I promise."

She did not say the words lightly. The recognition that the Opposing Energy might be trying to interfere with her thoughts now, on the very eve of battle, hit her hard. She could not deny that ideas of trying to see Timmy and her other friends had started to enter her mind again. Is this what happened before, when she ended up almost caught by Faulkner? This time she must be stronger.

"Thank you," he continued. "So, the day is almost upon us. Faulkner has been out of London for some time, but he is going to return the day after tomorrow. That is when we attack."

Anna let out a long breath. So, the time had finally come.

"Mr Warwick and I have given up trying to work through the Councils of the Order. We cannot afford to wait any longer for them to reach a consensus. Our enemy grows stronger by the day. We must attack while we may still achieve some element of surprise. I share Mr

Warwick's view that the Order may have been infiltrated at a senior level by the enemy, so it's no longer advisable to depend on their support anyway. Without the knowledge of the wider Order, we have quietly been mustering carefully selected members of the Order ourselves, but only people we are very close to and know we can trust implicitly."

"Right, I see. So what's going to happen?" Anna asked. She was filled with a mixture of excitement and apprehension. Things were finally starting to move.

"Faulkner is due to meet his gathered troops late in the evening the day after tomorrow, in the house in Eagle Street. So, we plan to ensnare him there. It will be in that battered old house that the first Satal shall fall!"

Anna's pulse was racing now. "But is it a good idea to attack Faulkner on his own territory, when he has all his men with him? Especially if you don't have all the support you wanted?"

"I understand your caution, Anna. But believe me, we have thought long and hard about this. We are sure Faulkner will know from his sources that the Council of the Order is dragging its feet. Indeed, his agents may themselves have been the cause of the opposition and the delays. Mr Warwick and I have been extremely careful to give every impression that we will not act without the Council's support. So he should not expect an attack yet. We ought to have the critical element of surprise. Also, Faulkner hasn't yet assembled his full forces. By striking now, we can take him down before further gang members arrive to join the murderous characters who have already gathered."

"So what are you going to do?"

Uncle James walked silently across the room to the only door. He tugged it open, checked outside then closed it again.

He continued, in a quiet voice, "The gang members are due to arrive at the house at different times through the day. They will have individual briefings with Mortlock. We plan to enter the house before they start arriving. We will eliminate Mortlock first. Then we'll take out the rest, one-by-one as they arrive, all before Faulkner gets there. With the element of surprise, the trusted forces we have assembled should be more than sufficient."

"How many people do we have?"

"There's Sir Stephen Walsingham and Tobias Blackthorn, two battle-hardened veterans who are held in great esteem within the Order. They are powerful, senior knights who fought with Mr. Warwick and I in the last Satal war. They understand the need to act fast, and they can be trusted completely."

Anna nodded.

"In addition, we have a band of other, more junior but very strong and highly-skilled knights. Then we also have a number of advanced students, some of whom you have already met. Together, we should be more than a match for the likes of Grimes and McCain – and Mortlock. We will have knights stationed at both ends of Eagle Street, in case any of them manage to escape."

Anna's voice was also hushed now. "What about Faulkner?"

"We know for a fact that he has important business in the City in the late afternoon and early evening. He will be watched. We have contingency plans to detain him should he try to make an earlier appearance. There will be more than enough of us to take him down by the time he arrives. A battle with a Satal is like no other battle though, of course. They are so powerful and resourceful that nothing can be predicted with absolute confidence. But we have the necessary experience and numbers on our side. With Mr Warwick at our head I am very confident we will finish the day triumphant."

Uncle James's words were positive, but the expression on his face remained deadly serious. Anna understood the danger this brave band was committing itself to. She was desperate to fight alongside them. It felt wrong to stay behind, hiding in this house while the rest of them went out and risked their lives taking on Faulkner. She was also starting to sense something bad about this impending battle. She began to worry for her uncle's safety.

He could not have been clearer in his message, but she was no longer prepared just to stand by and be 'protected'. She could not just submit to instructions when they felt wrong.

In a calm voice she said, "Uncle, I want to join the attack with you."

He looked at her for a moment. Then he raised his voice. "Have you not been listening to anything I've said? This is not the time for you. Your day will come, but it is not yet."

"Before you get angry, please hear what I have to say." She looked him directly in the eyes. "I have been listening. But I can't just stay here while you all go and fight this battle. You and Mr Warwick have trained me. I feel ready. And I want to… I must play my part, in bringing down Faulkner."

Her voice was measured, but a passion had flared within her. And her fear for her uncle's safety in the battle was growing. Uncle James stared back at her.

"Listen to me, Anna. This is no longer about whether you are ready, or whether you have the ability to play a part. Your instruction is still at its early stages, but the fact is you are already very capable in combat. But the point is this: we don't need to use your powers yet, not in this battle. We already have sufficient strength. We have the numbers. There's no need to risk the Satal identifying you during the confrontation. For if it does, that is likely to change the course of the battle, even if not the final outcome. If it realises you are there, there may be nothing you, nor any of us, can do to prevent it from…" He paused. "What I mean is, the Satal could wreak all kinds of damage before we finally overcome it."

He broke eye contact and moved away before continuing.

"Mr Warwick has foreseen that you have a pivotal role to play in the war ahead. He is a great Seer. We must trust him. There is no need to take this risk at such an early stage when we do not need to. You must save yourself for–"

"No, Uncle," Anna's own voice was raised now. "No. I will not save myself while others go out to fight the enemy. Not any more. You and Mr Warwick have said it's my fate to play my part in this war. And I sense it's my fate to play my part in ridding the world of Faulkner. I want to fight by your side now, when I can help prevent anyone else getting unnecessarily hurt, or killed…"

Her uncle did not respond. He paced the floor in front of her, repeatedly clenching and unclenching his hands.

He looked as though he was searching for the right argument but it was evading him. Then he snapped.

"Damn it, Anna," he shouted, turning back to her. "Now is not the time! I do not mean to belittle your powers in any way, or to suggest that you could not be a great asset to us in battle. Of course you could. You are already a strong fighter. But you must see the whole picture. Faulkner is not the most dangerous enemy we will face. Far from it. This battle is just the first skirmish in a much larger, much more dangerous war. The reason we are shielding you now is not because you are not ready for this battle. We are doing it because we need you in the far bigger battles ahead. I need you to be mature enough to see that!"

He resumed his pacing, a look of fierce determination on his face. He continued, "Just moments ago, you made me the most solemn promise that you would not leave this house without permission. If you want to be respected, as a knight, then your word must be your bond. You must prove yourself trustworthy. Were they just empty words?"

"No uncle, not at all. I did not say I would leave without your permission." Anna's tone was quieter again. "I wanted to leave with your permission."

"Well," her uncle's voice remained raised, "I do not give it!"

They both fell silent. Anna was still in no mood to take orders on this topic, and her powerful forebodings about the battle remained. But some of her uncle's words did register. It was surely true that greater challenges lay ahead. Was she being selfish and immature, demanding to be part of this first fight? Might she put them all in greater danger by being there and becoming the target of the Satal, as no doubt she would?

Her uncle seemed to have regained control of his own temper. "Anna," he said, "I apologise for raising my voice. I have deep passions when it comes to the Struggle, but I should not have shouted at you." He paused again.

"Your bravery does you enormous credit. You have seen the Beast with your own eyes, so you know exactly how dangerous this could be. You are only partially trained, yet you still want to volunteer. I recognise a brave and indomitable spirit when I see one. And I see one in you. I could not feel prouder. Please keep that bravery stored up, for the day is coming when you will need every ounce of it, in battles far greater than the one we face now.

"It will take more strength of character for you not to join us than it would to do so. I shall admit, it would be the same for me if I were in your shoes. I am asking for you to show that strength of character now. Will you accept what I am saying?"

Anna bit her lip. The flame still flickered brightly inside her. But she would not argue with him anymore. She had spoken her mind. He was now asking for her agreement, no longer demanding it. Reluctantly, she would go along with his and Mr Warwick's judgement this time. She had vowed that Faulkner would be stopped. She had to trust that they would fulfil that mission.

"All right. If you will not take me with you, I shall do as you say."

He took a deep breath, then he looked her in the eyes again.

"Thank you. Your maturity is yet another thing that does you credit." He broke into a smile. "Also, please don't worry so much. We do not intend to fail! Have faith in Mr Warwick and me. This will not be the first time we've faced a Satal together and emerged triumphant. We know what needs to be done. We are a formidable force when we stand shoulder-to-shoulder in the face of the enemy. With the help of our comrades, we will win the day. So, fear not!"

Anna returned his smile, in spite of herself. She had seen her uncle in combat enough to know what a powerful opponent he was. She did not doubt for one moment that the combination of her two mentors would indeed make for a formidable force against anyone. But she could not shake the sense of foreboding. The sense that somehow, things were not going to turn out as well as her uncle thought.

She looked at him. She had grown to know him well over these last few months. In his eyes she saw clearly the deep care that he had for her. He was one of Anna's very few blood relatives, and the only one she felt she shared anything in common with now. Despite his sometimes unpredictable ways, he was the closest she had to a father. What if she never saw him again?

Her chest began to tighten. She turned away to hide her eyes.

Anna woke unusually late the next morning. Flustered, she dressed and got ready as fast as she could. When she entered the corridor, she could hear voices coming from the dining room. She was about to turn back in a vain attempt to improve her appearance when Mr Warwick appeared and asked her to join them. She forced herself forward, and into the room.

Mr Warwick resumed his seat at the head of the dining room table. Sat next to him, beaming at her, was Jim, her house's junior butler with the startlingly pure blue aura. Anna had been very pleasantly surprised to discover that he had the Powers during their visit to the cricket match at Lord's in the summer. His presence on the eve of battle made her feel better. It also put her more at ease right now.

To her surprise, next to Jim was Emily Barmby. Anna had met her at the cricket match with Jim. She was a very pretty and pleasant young lady with large brown eyes, light brown curly hair and a charming smile. Her aura, too, was bright blue and pure, similar in shade to Jim's. It was not quite so blemish-free as his, no-one's was, but it was actually considerably larger. Anna was one of the very few who knew that Emily was Jim's girlfriend. If she was here too, did that mean that she also had the Powers? Anna's jaw dropped slightly at the thought. She could not be happier if that turned out to be so.

Next to Emily was a young man with blond hair, blue-grey eyes and a slightly pointed face. He looked somehow familiar to Anna, but she could not quite place him. His aura was also blue, though looking in more detail, she could make out certain blemishes on its surface, and a slight wateriness to its colour.

Finally, sat next to him was a very serious-looking young lady who Anna had never seen before. She had high cheek bones, light blue sparkling eyes and long, dark hair which shone glossily, tied up on top to hold it away from her face. She looked a little younger than Emily but was every bit as pretty. In fact, it would have been no exaggeration to call her beautiful, but there was something in her demeanour that suggested she was completely unaware of that fact herself. Shifting her focus again, Anna found the aura to be pure, sky blue in colour, and of a considerable size, too. If anything, it was even larger than Emily's. Anna was intrigued to learn who this was.

No doubt the fact that they were gathered here meant they all had some part to play in the battle ahead. Uncle James was nowhere to be seen.

"My dear Anna, I hope you had a good night's sleep?" said Mr Warwick. "After all your intense studies and recent worries, it is about time you had a proper one!" Anna appreciated the excuse.

"Now, I believe your uncle has explained that events are gathering pace. The current episode will come to a head tomorrow. The time has come to bring together some of the forces who will have parts to play in the plan in one way or another. They have to be people in whom we have absolute trust, in these troubled times. Our guests here are amongst that number. Of course, you already know Jim."

"Good morning, Anna!" Jim stood and gave her a polite bow followed by another broad grin, which Anna returned.

"And I believe you have already made Miss Emily Barmby's acquaintance, at Lord's in the summer?" continued Mr Warwick.

"Yes. Very pleased to meet you again," said Anna. She gave what she felt was a slightly clumsy curtsey. It was met by an infinitely more graceful one in return.

"Delighted to see you again too, Anna," Emily responded, smiling brightly, her eyes twinkling.

"Emily was trained by your uncle," Mr Warwick went on, "and she is quite a rare phenomenon." Then he turned to Emily and quickly added, "I do hope you don't mind me referring to you as a phenomenon, Emily!"

"No, no, not at all, master," Emily replied, laughing.

"The reason I refer to Emily in such a way is that the number of fully-fledged knights who are women is still relatively small, even in this country. Though there have been some notable pioneers as exceptions. In many other countries, the number is almost non-existent.

"I am pleased to say that we in the Order are somewhat ahead of society as a whole with regard to the participation of women, but the number is still much lower than it should be. Especially given the significant role that women have played in the Struggle throughout the centuries. However, there are some, and you are looking at the newest and youngest of them. And a very bright prospect she is."

Emily began to protest modestly, but Mr Warwick would have none of it. Then he moved on.

"I would also like to introduce you to one of your uncle's promising current students. Mr Percival Gladstone. Percival tells me you two have met briefly once before too, is that right?"

Anna froze, smiling a little awkwardly as she desperately wracked her brains.

"Yes, that's right," said the young man, just in time, "it was my great pleasure, and honour, to meet Anna at Alexandra's wonderful piano recital at the Royal College. A great delight it is to see you once again, Miss Lawrence – a true honour indeed!"

Then she remembered. The effusive greeting brought back to Anna their brief introduction before the concert. She also remembered his leaving the auditorium before the concert started. Right before she and her uncle were ambushed. She wondered why Mr Gladstone should feel quite so 'honoured' to meet her both times. Somehow it just didn't ring true. His presence worried her.

"And last, but by no means least," Mr Warwick concluded, "may I introduce you to another of your uncle's brightest young students, Miss Alexandra Greenwood. It was most unfortunate that you had to leave the piano recital before Miss Greenwood played. I am told it was the most magnificent performance. But I'm sure there will be other opportunities in the future."

"Very pleased to meet you, Anna."

The young lady stood and gave a much better-executed curtsey than Anna had yet managed. She smiled for the first time, and her stunning light blue eyes shone radiantly. Then she quickly returned her glance to the table ahead of her, looking very serious and quite self-conscious again. That was something Anna could identify with. It had been a while since Anna had spoken to anyone new, and it took her a while to take it all in. Her concerns about having Percival there lingered.

"Where's Uncle James today?" she asked.

"He has gone to meet up with another of his students who will be joining our forces for this mission. Young Greg Matthews."

Gregory Matthews. The swashbuckling, not to mention rather handsome, hero with the 'heart of a lion' who had faced down the bully Higgins in the cricket match at Lord's in the summer. Anna glanced at Emily, who had been as impressed as Anna by the young cricketer. She shot Anna a knowing grin with a twinkle in her eye, just sufficient to make Jim tut and shake his head in mock disapproval, before also smiling. In the months since Lord's, Anna had reflected many times on Matthews's bravery, determination, and above all, his focused calmness in the face of outrageous provocation. She suddenly felt a lot better about the battle ahead. Faulkner and his gang did not know what they were taking on!

"Greg's still in Oxford where he's studying at the university, but your uncle has gone to meet him partway, to accompany him back and to brief him."

"Ah right, I see," said Anna.

"I shall need to leave this afternoon to catch up with the other members about the plan. It was too risky to ask them to come here."

"Yes, I understand," said Anna.

"The reason Jim, Emily, Percival and Alexandra are here is to make sure you have companionship this afternoon."

Of course, by 'companionship', Anna knew he meant protection.

"It will also be a chance for you to make their acquaintances properly. You will be spending more time in their company in the future as your study progresses, and when you one day become a knight yourself."

The group began to chat amongst themselves. Mr Warwick took Anna to one side.

"I am aware this will be the first time that neither your uncle nor I will be here with you. We are on the eve of battle, so we have no choice now. That is why we have arranged for four companions, in whom we have complete faith, to join you in the house. Additionally, Jeremiah is going to come home early from work today. And for the first time in living memory, he will be taking the day off work tomorrow! The five of them together are a much more formidable force than either your uncle or me."

"But I feel so bad about taking people away from you, just when you need them most..." Anna started.

"Oh, thank you Anna, but please don't concern yourself. We will have enough numbers to win the day. Now, this evening I will need to ask Emily and Alexandra to join me for some specific battle preparations that I need their help with. They will return in the morning and remain with you throughout the battle itself. I shall ask Jim and Percival to remain here with you too, together with Jeremiah. That should afford ample security. In addition to your own, considerable powers, of course!"

Anna was grateful to him for that last comment, at least. But she still was not comfortable.

"I said to my uncle yesterday that I want to fight with you–"

"Yes, your uncle did mention your discussion!" Mr Warwick cut in. Anna felt herself blush, but the old man smiled warmly. "I commend you for your bravery and willingness to fight alongside us. That day is coming Anna, have no doubt. But thank you for your understanding that this is not the time."

Before she could say any more, he moved straight on.

"These arrangements will only be for today and tomorrow. Our enemies will be very much occupied, and we have been extremely careful to keep your location a complete secret. I am confident all will be well. Your uncle has spoken with your mother, and she is agreeable for you to be in the company of this group just for a short time."

"I see. Thank you," said Anna.

"Jim will need to leave this afternoon for a while to tie up loose ends and hand over responsibilities to the other staff at your house. He will return this evening. He will then remain here for as long as needed until the battle is over. You already know him well. There's no braver, more trustworthy ally to have at a time like this."

Anna nodded. "Yes. It will be great to have him here."

"Percival will remain here throughout the time we are away. He is surprisingly tenacious in combat. Deceptively so, in fact."

This time Anna did not nod. She tried to speak, but Mr Warwick moved straight on again.

"Finally, as I mentioned, Jeremiah is going to come home early from work today. Since getting to know him these last few weeks, I must say I have been very pleasantly impressed, not to mentioned surprised, with that young man's strength of character. He is showing great commitment to our cause now. He wants to help in any way he can."

Anna nodded again. "Yes, he seems a very good man, and I am most grateful to him." She wanted to return to the subject of Percival, but Mr Warwick was hurrying.

"We can't safely risk detracting from our attack force any further, but you will have highly capable support here throughout. In the exceptionally unlikely event you should need it, of course!"

"Yes, of course. Thank you."

The topic of Percival was not an easy one to raise. Mr Warwick was already moving away to speak to the others. But she forced herself to speak again.

"Mr Warwick?" She managed to catch his attention again without being noticed by the rest of the group. She gestured for him to follow her out of the room. He seemed in two minds. There were evidently pressing conversations he needed to have with the rest of the group, but he followed.

As soon as they were out of earshot, Anna said, "Thank you for making plans for my protection. You have been so thorough. I do appreciate it. There's just one last thing."

"Yes, Anna. What is it?"

"Well, it's Percival…"

He looked surprised. "What's the problem? I know Percival can be a bit much sometimes, but please believe me when I tell you I have found his powers to be stronger than you would think."

"I'm sure you're right. It's not that. It's just, well, each time I've met him he has seemed just a bit too… well, what I mean is, he doesn't quite seem genuine. It's as though he's hiding something."

"But Anna, I hardly—" Mr Warwick started.

"And on the evening of the concert, I saw him speaking to someone very suspicious looking. Then he looked around as though trying to avoid being seen, before slipping out. That was just before the concert was due to start, which was a strange time to leave. Then straight afterwards, Uncle James and I were attacked. It may only be coincidence, but isn't it possible that it was Percival who alerted our enemies and directed them to ambush us that night?"

Mr Warwick stood in concerned thought. "Anna, it's wise to be cautious. Especially in times like these. But on this occasion, I do believe you are mistaken. Since that night, I have found out that McCain and his hoodlums planned the attack on your uncle well in advance – well before our agents first saw him in Eagle Street. They aimed to take James out of the Struggle once and for all before the war began, when he was alone. There are really no grounds to believe Percival had anything to do with it. I do think that was purely a coincidence. I feel sure he may be trusted implicitly."

Anna nodded and said no more. Maybe she was reading too much into what she had seen. Also, the explanation sounded final. Mr Warwick's expression softened.

"Take heart, Anna. By tomorrow night, this episode will be all over, and the world will be rid of Faulkner for good!"

"Oh, I hope so! And I hope you will all be careful." She paused. "Mr Warwick… you will look after my uncle, won't you? I know how strong he is in mental combat, but I just have this feeling, and it won't leave me…"

For the briefest moment a look of concern flickered across his face. Unlike her uncle, Mr Warwick had the power of a Seer. He had praised her on her own natural abilities in that field. She wondered if he sensed that she was foreseeing something that might become true. The look was gone in an instant though, replaced by a more jovial one.

"My dear, yes of course! Don't forget, your uncle and I have been through such battles before and emerged more or less unscathed. We know how to defeat the Satal, and we have the forces to do it."

Anna nodded, trying to reassure herself.

"And your uncle is one of the best fighters I have ever seen. I mean it. There is no-one who knows better how to look after themselves. He has fought a Satal before, and I can tell you from first-hand experience that he played a major role in winning that battle last time." Then he paused. "But yes, I promise I shall be extra vigilant." He smiled. "Just a little more patience now, Anna. We will soon be through this!"

Despite her fears, Anna was comforted by the old man's words, and his confidence. He was wiser and more experienced than anyone she had ever met. She trusted his judgement.

Breathing a little more easily, she dared to look forward two days, to a world that was free from Faulkner, forever.

*   *   *

Many hundreds of miles away, in the flickering torchlight of the underground cave, the body of the giant figure began to move. The chanting of the three figures that knelt before it intensified. The evil sound twisted its way into the dark spaces of the deep cavern around them.

The mind of this being, whose purpose was to destroy everything that was and everything that would ever be in this world, had been slowly awakening for some time. It was now approaching full wakefulness. It was beginning to focus its full attention on its objective. And on one aspect in particular.

The mind began to probe deeply, into a realm far away from that in which its body lay, seeking out its prey… The disciples chanted on.

10
The Attack

Mr Warwick and Jim soon left, both in disguise. Anna spent the afternoon in the very pleasant company of Emily and Alexandra. They had completely different personalities, Emily lighter hearted and Alexandra more serious, yet somehow the three of them seemed to strike up a friendship rapidly. Anna was surprised how unusually relaxed she felt in their company. Dearly though she loved her uncle and Mr Warwick, it was nice to have some female company somewhere near her own age. Percival appeared out of his depth in this group, but he did his best to join in when he could. Especially when he could think of something to say to Alexandra. Anna could not help but notice his enthusiasm was not returned.

Evening came in no time. Once everyone had eaten, the two young women had to leave to assist Mr Warwick. Jeremiah returned home just before they departed. Anna watched on with great amusement as they donned their disguises. Both were dressed as much older ladies. Alexandra's wig was of such a silvery-white colour that it made her look ancient. She walked with a low stoop towards the door, helped by a slightly younger-looking Emily. Anna was amazed by the transformation. There was no way anyone who didn't know could tell who they really were.

Once the pair had gone, Anna took her leave of Percival and Jeremiah and retired to her room. Jim was due back soon, but she decided not to wait. She had talked a lot more than she was used to that afternoon and felt tired. She prepared for bed and got under the blankets. Her thoughts inevitably turned to the following day, and what it would bring for her two guardians and the rest of their force.

The room was very warm from the large fire which blazed next door. She slipped into a fitful sleep. Before long, her dreams became strange and troubled. One restless scene after another tumbled through her mind. But there was one that she kept returning to in different forms and guises. It was Timmy, refusing to see her, then slipping away from her forever.

Anna woke from a bout of restless turning, her hair damp with sweat. The room was even stuffier than before. Thirsty for air, she went to the dormer window and opened it a little. The cold wintery air of the night caressed her skin. She took in several chilly, fresh breaths, then left the window ajar to cool the room.

Returning to her bed, she dozed off again. Still her sleep was uneasy. Her strange dreams returned. This time they were haunted by images of Faulkner, lying in wait to trap her companions. She began to toss and turn again, before lying on her back and forcing her eyes slightly open.

The room, although still very dark, had started to take on a dim, red hue. It struck her that the fire in the next room might somehow have got out of hand, and that the building might be ablaze. She strained to open her eyes and look about her. There were no flames and no smoke, nor any other obvious source of the light. Struggling out of bed again, she checked the corridor. There were no signs of fire, nor anything else untoward. Perspiration dripped from her hair as she returned to her bed. The room looked normal again.

She fell back into her restless slumber with a deepening feeling of lethargy. Perhaps it was the heat she was still feeling. Maybe she was coming down with a fever. Her dreams grew ever more disturbing. A sense of dread started to slowly crawl across her sleeping mind.

In her dream, she found herself walking down a road. It led past a giant building that she recognised. It was St Paul's Cathederal. Above its dome was a fierce, stormy sky. Trees on either side of the road thrashed violently in the wind. The clouds above seemed to be alive, driven by the force of the gale. The clouds began to gather and accumulate, growing darker in two places. The dark patches swirled. The centre of each started to open, revealing blue sky behind. The openings looked like eyes. Threatening, angry eyes, looking down on her.

Then, behind her, she saw Faulkner. He did not appear to have seen her yet, but he was shouting furiously and slashing at the air with his cane. Desperately, she looked for somewhere to hide. Then the colour of the sky behind the clouds began to change. The wind howled, tearing at the trees, bending their mighty trunks and snapping branches. The blue sky turned, slowly, to red. Everything around Anna grew darker, bathed in the same, deep crimson colour. And the menacing red eyes stared directly into her…

Anna lurched back to wakefulness with a jolt. She realised it had been a dream. She struggled desperately to open her eyes again. Her body felt like lead. She was unable to move her limbs, or her head. It required a tremendous effort even to force her eyelids apart. When she did manage to, the red hue had returned to the room. Indeed, if anything, it was growing brighter. Not only that. The far wall of the room seemed no longer to be still. It was barely perceptible at first, but it appeared to be starting to slowly undulate. The whole structure of the far side of the room was moving.

Anna tried to get up. She found that she could not. It felt as though her body had sunk into the bed and was now trapped. Her eyelids, too, were heavier than she had ever known them. She could not keep them open. More waves of alarming images flashed through her unconscious mind. She returned to consciousness again with a start and fought to open her eyes. She hoped to find that the disconcerting movement of the wall had just been another part of her strange dreams. But it had grown even worse. The wall was starting to bulge outwards, towards her.

Alarm filled her mind. But the more the fear welled up, the stronger was the grip that seemed to hold her in place. It felt like something physical on her limbs. As though something – or someone – was holding her down. Her alarm turned to panic. She felt cold, bony fingers tightening their grip on her arms and legs, making any further movement completely impossible. She fought with all her remaining strength to raise her head, which was by now drenched with sweat. Skeletal fingers crept slowly from somewhere unseen behind her, onto her face. They held her cheeks and forehead in a vice-like grip, forcing her to look towards the bulging wall. She tried to let out a desperate scream, but no sound escaped her mouth.

Then a breathy, inhuman voice echoed around her head. "Look, look!" it breathed. Her eyes had closed, but she forced them open again. She looked in the only direction that the unseen hands would allow – towards the glowing, dark red wall. The bulge was now very pronounced. A crack started to appear across its length. Anna's eyes closed themselves again, even as she wrestled futilely with the hands that held her. "Look! Look!" the sickly voice in her head continued to urge her. Involuntarily this time, her eyelids opened again. What she saw sent a rush of utter terror through her. She finally understood what it was she was looking at.

This was not a wall at all. It was an eye. An enormous eye, which was beginning to open. Anna screamed again in uncontrolled terror until her lungs were empty, but still no sound came. She strained every sinew in her body to escape who or whatever it was that held her down. To no avail. The ghastly, cold fingernails dug deep into her skin until she felt her arms bleed. It was like she was shackled with barbed wire. More unseen fingers caressed her face and scalp, sending shivers of fear and revulsion through her. "Look! Look!" the hissing voice continued. Anna watched the opening eye, utterly powerless, consumed by the deepest dread she had ever known. She knew what she was looking at, because she had seen it before, in a dream when she was six years old…

The enormous eyelids continued to part, causing the dim red light that filled the room to grow brighter. What lay within came into sight. Where there should have been white, there was blood red. The iris slowly came into view, and it was blackness itself, darker than the night, an infinite void without light, colour or end. The fingers tightened further on her arms, her legs and her face, as the pupil began to appear. Blind panic drove the last rational thoughts from her brain. From within the inky blackness emanated a deep, dark, menacing red glow. It came from a living being, though not one created of this world. It was something that was never meant to be here. Something utterly abhorrent. Something with power beyond measure, whose sole abominable purpose was to annihilate everything that had ever existed in this world. And this infinitely powerful being was looking directly at her. It was looking directly into her. She felt its emotion. A sheer, utter hatred and loathing, for her and for everything else that existed. It was an emotion with strength beyond anything she had ever felt or could possibly have imagined.

Anna screamed blindly and insanely – and this time there was sound, although no way to know if it was audible beyond her own mind. For a tortured time of unknown duration, the purest living evil that had ever walked the earth looked into her and scrutinised her soul. Her aura was laid bare. There was nothing in her nature, in her character, in her very being, that it could not see. She was utterly powerless. One final, gut-wrenching scream escaped from her mouth.

Suddenly, the hands which had gripped her arms so tightly began to move, to shake her. A new voice filled her head. A voice she knew.

"Anna, Anna, wake up! Wake up!" Her arms and legs finally came free. She sat bolt upright, able at last to thrash out for all she was worth at those who had held her down. Her swinging fist made contact with something physical.

"Anna, stop! Please! It's me, Percival! You've been having a nightmare, and you've been screaming in your sleep. It was just a dream Anna!"

Anna lashed out once more, but this time Percival caught her wrist and held it. 'Was this the same hand that had been holding her down moments earlier?' the thought flashed in her mind. The contact felt different though, much warmer than those cold, evil fingers, and not as strong. She pulled her hand away and looked at her arms. There was no blood, nor even marks where the nails had gouged her.

"It was just a dream Anna, just a terrible nightmare. Everything will be all right, now. Everything is fine." Percival appeared to be doing his best to console her, but she did not trust him. She stared wildly through the semi-darkness, through eyes that were wide open now. She saw Jeremiah appear in the doorway, dimly illuminated by a lantern.

"Is everything all right?" he asked. "I thought I could hear screaming."

As Percival explained that Anna had been having a nightmare, she leapt from her sweat-drenched bed and reached out for the opposite wall. The one at which she had been forced to look. She placed her hands flat against it and ran them over its surface, searching for any kind of crack or opening, desperate to know if what she had seen was real. There was no more red, no sign of a bulge and not a trace of any eye. And yet, it had looked so real.

Despite the evidence from her own hands that the cold structure was as solid and unmoving as it had ever been,

Anna could not believe it had only been a nightmare. It had been like her experience as a young child, which Mr Warwick later confirmed had been more than a dream. This was the same. It had been even more vivid and intense. What might it mean? She still felt deep unease to her very core. But the relief was immense that the ordeal was over and there was no longer an immediate physical threat to her.

Percival looked awkward, but Jeremiah moved to her side and tried to put a comforting arm around her, telling her that everything was all right. Anna was not ready to be consoled, though. "Is Jim back yet?" she asked, urgently.

"No, not yet. He should be here any time now," replied Percival.

Anna thanked them both and told them she would be fine now. She accepted a glass of water from Jeremiah, then after several more assurances they left her alone again.

"I shall remain in the room next door, just in case you require any further assistance," Percival said. His voice grated inside her head. 'I wish you wouldn't bother,' she thought, but merely nodded. His presence left her feeling less comforted. Once the men had withdrawn, it was with more than a little trepidation that she pulled the covers up and slowly closed her eyes again. She was terrified by what she might see. But this time she fell into an exhausted slumber, troubled by no further disturbing visions.

She did not know how long she had been asleep when a sound partially roused her again. Lying motionless in a state of semi-consciousness, she listened. She could hear nothing more than the sound of a distant church bell through her slightly-open window, signalling some hour of the dead of night that she did not count. But then she heard the sound again. Carried on the breeze through that same window, came the faint noise that had woken her. It was the sound of a violin.

Meaning took shape in her mind. She sat bolt upright. She knew exactly where she had heard that sound before. A fragment of the eerily discordant melody reached her ears again, just as it had done right before she and her uncle were ambushed by McCain and his men in the fog. And it was growing closer.

She was overtaken by a new fear. This time she was certainly not dreaming. She was wide awake. The sinister tune of the enemy seemed now to be coming from right outside the building. Anna was momentarily rooted to the spot, her mind racing. Had their hideaway been found? Was it anything to do with the eye she had just seen in her dream? And if the enemy were already outside the building, how could she escape? If she tried to hide here, they would surely find her, and then she would be done for. The pace of the music grew faster and faster as it approached a manic crescendo. Then suddenly, it stopped.

As if in response, from somewhere above her, there was a soft, scratching, shuffling sound. Something was moving across the downward-sloping roof, directly above where she was sitting. It was moving in the direction of the open attic window. She screamed and bolted out of bed, reaching it just before the intruder on the roof did. She slammed it shut and locked the latch.

At that same moment, Percival came to the door again, carrying a lantern. "Anna, have you had another bad dream? I heard you scream again, and–"

"Percival, there's no time, we've got to get out of the building – right now!" Anna yelled, grabbing her cardigan and outdoor overcoat which lay folded on a chair, and finding her shoes.

"What? But it's the middle of the night! Anna, you've been dreaming again. You can't go outside now." He was holding his arm out across the doorway to stop her leaving.

"This is not a dream. The enemy is outside, and one of them is on the roof. Quick, run!" Anna was now rushing towards him, preparing her aura to fight him. "Don't try to stop me Percival. Are you one of them?" she yelled.

Percival held out his hand to stop Anna. He looked over her shoulder towards the window – and then his expression changed. Wheeling round frantically, Anna saw the outline of a figure, darkly silhouetted against the night. It was crouched on the rooftop outside the dormer window, looking directly at them. In his hand he held something that looked like a knife. 'McCain?' thought Anna, although this weapon looked considerably shorter than that of the man with the scar. She knew she should run, but in spite of herself she shifted her vision to see the man's aura. There was none.

Suddenly the figure thrust its head forward and pressed its face against the windowpane. Illuminated by Percival's lamp, Anna saw it clearly. The familiar face was ghastly white, its eyes wide and its mouth gaping open. The Wraith had found her.

She had already waited too long. She could not risk letting Percival prevent her escape. She smashed his aura with her own, causing him to crumple to the floor. She darted over his prone figure and through the doorway, taking his lantern.

She heard a crack from behind, as though something had hit the window. It was followed by another, then the sound of shattering glass. Anna half ran, half stumbled down the corridor as she forced her shoes on, knowing the relentless creature would be on her in seconds. "Jim, Jim!" she shouted in desperation.

She approached the other end of the corridor just as Jeremiah appeared through a doorway at the end. His eyes were blinking in the light of a candle he had lit, and his sleeping cap was at a crooked angle on his head.

"W-what on earth is going on?" he stammered.

"We're being attacked! There's a Wraith breaking into my room. They're outside too. I think Percival's in on it. Quick, run!" she yelled as she flew past him, opening the door that led from Jeremiah's home to the main stairs of the building.

Jeremiah seemed to grasp the situation immediately. "Don't leave by the front door of the building, then," he hissed. "There's a small window in the porter's lodge on the ground floor that leads to a back alleyway. Go that way and escape by the back streets. I'll hold them off as long as possible. I'll catch up with you if I can!"

Anna had slowed to hear the end of these instructions, then she plunged through the door and headed for the stairs. Immediately there was the sound of a scuffle breaking out behind her. As she bounded down the stairs, she heard the cry of a voice which sounded like

Jeremiah's. She stopped. She could not leave him up there to face the Wraith. She had to do something. But with no aura visible, what could she do against that creature? Her physical strength alone would be useless. As the noise behind the door grew louder and more frantic, an idea came to her.

"Gillespie! I'm down here! It's me you want, not him. Come and get me!" She alone was the Wraith's target. Her best hope of saving Jeremiah was to lure it away from him. "Gillespie, it's Anna Lawrence. I'm going to escape!"

The door above burst open. In the pale light of the lantern Anna was carrying, the ghoulish face of the creature that was once Gillespie appeared. Its wide eyes stared horrifically at her, and its mouth dripped blood. At the same moment an arm appeared over its shoulder from behind, grabbing it round its neck and starting to drag it back inside again. It was Jeremiah. He had what looked like a severe bite mark to his neck, but he was holding firm.

The Wraith slashed wildly at him with its blood-stained knife. Jeremiah grabbed the wrist of the hand holding the weapon as the Wraith struck him with his other fist. Jeremiah fell, but he pulled the Wraith down with him to the ground. He kept a firm hold of its wrist.

"Quick Anna, run for it!" he yelled as he wrestled desperately with the creature. "I'll hold it back. You have to escape now or all will be lost. All this will have been for nothing!"

Anna hesitated a moment longer, then she did as she was told. She would be of no use to him if she could not use her aura. And Jeremiah was right. If she delayed long enough for the other gang members to break in from below, they would all be done for. It was her they were after, not Jeremiah, so the best thing she could do for him was to get as far away from him as she could. These thoughts flashed through her mind as she flew down the remaining flights of stairs.

"Gillespie, I'm escaping! Come now or you'll never get me!" she yelled behind her as she ran.

She charged through the porter's lodge, which was empty at this time of night, slamming the door behind her. At the other end of the main room was a single, filthy window, which did not look to have been opened for many years. At first the latch would not budge at all.

There was a crash from not far away, followed by another, then another. It sounded like someone was trying to smash down the front door of the building. Anna tugged at the window again with all her strength. Finally, it moved a little. Desperately she gave it another mighty heave. It gave, then it opened fully. She was hit by a rush of cold night air.

Despite her desperation, she poked her head out first, looking one way then the other to check no-one was lying in wait.

At first, she noticed little apart from a very unpleasant stench. Peering harder, she made out a dim, fogbound light at the end of the alleyway to her left, and the ground some feet below her. To her right was nothing but blackness. No signs of life, but no way to be sure. She did not dare to hold out the lantern for fear of being seen. She extinguished it and set it aside. She pulled her cardigan and heavy overcoat on over her nightdress and readied herself for the plunge.

The sound of splintering wood came from the front of the building. Holding her breath, she manoeuvred herself through the window onto the ledge on the other side. She pulled the window back into a closed position, then took the plunge into the cold darkness.

The alley was lower than the porter's room, and she had to drop a couple of extra feet to the damp ground, causing her to stumble. She put her hands out to stop herself falling. They sank a little into some kind of cold, thick sludge on the alley floor. The smell was worse now, but the only sound was that of her landing, echoing down the narrow, man-made canyon – then nothing. Anna pressed herself back against the wall. She looked down the alleyway towards the dim light to check if anybody had been attracted by the sound. There was no-one.

Anna decided it would be better to head for the distant light, however risky, than the utter darkness in the other direction. She slipped and slithered over the sludge, grazing the back of her hand on the wall as she hurried. She looked towards the light ahead. It was coming from a streetlamp on a road that crossed the end of the alley. It was surrounded by billowing fog again.

Drawing to a halt just before the road, Anna looked behind her. She could hear nothing. Cautiously, she peered round the corner. The street ran uphill from right to left, towards the place where it presumably met the main road that passed the entrance to Jeremiah's building. She peered through the mist up the hill. At the top she could see several figures gathered near another streetlamp. It was late for a group to be stood around on a cold, foggy night like this…

She began to sense danger all around. Every second could be of the essence, before they realised she had escaped the house. Nonetheless, something made her hesitate. She had started to see things in the fog. They were only very faint, but shapes which looked like the outlines of people appeared, grew more distinct for a while, then disappeared again. The harder she looked, the more solid they became. Some appeared to be normal people. Others took on more sinister forms. All were soon obscured again by the grey mist.

She was beginning to feel strange. It was almost as though she had lost the sense of what was real and what was merely in her head since she had been disturbed so badly by that dream. The feelings of terror were coming back.

She fought to remain calm. Mr Warwick had told her that a Satal could manipulate the Opposing Energy to generate fog. When it was nearby, it could use it to create hallucinations in their victims, to disorientate them as it hunted them down. Was this what she was seeing? But that would mean a Satal was very close. Faulkner was supposed to be out of town until tomorrow. Had he returned sooner than expected? Was he hunting her down, right now? She started to panic.

She broke cover and bolted towards the opening of another alleyway on the far side of the wide road. From all around her, the cold fog suddenly swirled, as though caught by a gust of wind. Within that swirling, white mist, Anna saw the shapes of individual faces. Indistinct at first, then sharp and horribly real – terrible, twisted faces, some of them contorted in fear or pain, others snarling, revealing vicious fangs as they swept past her face. 'I'm imagining it!' she told herself, over and over. But they seemed so real.

As she approached the far side of the road, the fog ahead of her suddenly drew together from all sides and then upwards, to take on a single, very solid-looking form. It was an all too familiar one, with talon-tipped wings and long horns... the Beast of Highgate.

It burst forward, its jaws opened wide to devour her. She dived underneath it onto the freezing cobbles of the road, covering her face with her arm. She was gripped by deep, irrational panic now. She covered her head with both arms as she lay, but still she could see, and almost feel, the Beast standing over her, about to strike. Demons swooped all around it.

Anna contracted into a ball on the ground, her arms wrapped round her head as the images grew still more intense. In her mind's eye, the hideous, wrinkled, snarling face of Mortlock appeared, slowly opening his mouth to reveal uneven, jagged teeth. He hissed at her through the swirling mist. His expression contorted into a sneer, and he began to laugh. Hideous laughter, directed at her and her pitiful state, a malicious, hateful sound conveying a malevolent insanity.

Mortlock's face began slowly to shift and transform until it became recognisable as something else. The piercing black eyes in the darkly handsome, but menacingly evil, face of Faulkner. As the image moved and swirled in her mind, Faulkner slowly but threateningly reached out a cloaked arm through the fog, his hand raised, ready to grab her by the throat... Anna closed her arms even more tightly around her head. She just managed to hold in a scream.

Just then, a distant sound reached her ears again. A violin, playing a discordant, deadly melody. The sound brought her back to reality for a moment. She forced her eyes open. The fog still swirled angrily above her, but there was no Faulkner, or Beast.

She peered back up the street in the direction of the junction. Alarming visions remained, but the fog was thinner this close to the ground. She could just make out the figures under the gas lamp again. This time she saw something which finally brought her back to her full senses.

From round the corner of the building, the figures already there were joined by two more men, one of them very tall. Unlike the others, both new arrivals wore top hats and long cloaks which reached almost to the road. The tall man suddenly raised his cane and brought it down violently on one of the group, sending him to the ground. There was no mistaking who this was. Faulkner had returned to London ahead of schedule. He was there right now. The Satal had struck first.

Then Faulkner appeared to freeze, as though deep in concentration. The visions returned with renewed force. Anna could not stop them, but she told herself repeatedly, 'They are not real. They are not real. It's Faulkner trying to get to you. You cannot let him. You must overcome it!'

Immersed in fog again, she rose to her knees in spite of the deadly visions, then stooped to run. She forced her way towards the dark entrance of the next alleyway.

The images grew even more hideous, of violence and death, but Anna just about retained control over her emotions this time. She recognised them for what they were. She focused on the here and now and forced the fear of all she was seeing away from her. She plunged into the darkness of the alley, feeling her way on the damp left-hand wall with her hand. Had they seen her? No way of knowing, but they were sure to scour the streets for her once they knew she had escaped.

The darkness in this new alleyway was absolute. A new fear crept into her head. What if this one led to a dead end? Might she be trapped in here, with no possibility of escape? But she would not risk turning back. All she could do was to press on, and if necessary, hope to conceal herself somewhere deep in this blackness.

She forged ahead, the cold brickwork of the wall her only guide. The darkness added to the terrifying effect of the visions. But having come through a real moment of crisis back on the road, she felt stronger, and more in control. She resolutely kept hold of the one fact that she now knew to be true: she was being viciously attacked in her mind by a Satal, but no matter how real the visions appeared, they were mere tricks of the mind. 'They can't harm me if I don't let them,' she convinced herself. If she could maintain that grip on reality, she would be all right.

She soldiered on and on through the inky blackness. The visions continued, but they grew slightly less vivid. Was it because she was putting more distance between herself and Faulkner? That hope spurred her on. The terrifying things she had been seeing were definitely receding. 'Just keep going,' she told herself.

Eventually, when her eyes had grown fully accustomed to the darkness, she paused for breath. Peering in front of her, she thought she could see the faintest of glows up ahead. Was there another end to this alleyway after all, through which she might escape?

Then from behind her she heard the faint echoing sound of men's voices. She looked back. There was a distant, moving pinprick of light. The gang was coming after her.

She dashed onwards. The dim light ahead was slowly growing brighter. Eventually she emerged into a narrow street. It was very narrow, but it contained doorways, and the odd light – signs of life.

The fog was a little thinner here, and after passing several buildings she began to see people. All of them were shabbily dressed, some of them laughing and staggering about, swigging out of bottles, whilst others sat huddled on the ground, mumbling to themselves. Everyone appeared to be very intoxicated and none of them paid much attention to her.

She did not dare pause, and pressed on. The street grew busier and better-lit the further she went. She had absolutely no idea where she was now, but gradually this place started to present its own dangers. As she passed one particular group of rough-looking men, a fight broke out amongst them and a bottle whistled past her head. It smashed on the ground nearby. A melee ensued, consumed by the mist behind her as she rushed on.

Soon she could tell from brighter street lighting ahead and the first sight of a carriage that she must be approaching a junction with a larger road. Suddenly the vision of a foggy demon swept in front of her, causing her to duck involuntarily. It had been the first for some time. She stopped in her tracks again.

Ahead of her, where she assumed the larger road to be, she caught the indistinct outline of a group of figures coming towards her. Two of them appeared more smartly

183

dressed than anyone she had so far seen on this street – tall top hats, walking canes and long cloaks, silhouetted against the dimly-lit fog.

Anna stumbled back in the direction she had come from, desperately considering her next move. Glancing behind her at the approaching men, she searched for their auras. Even with the poor visibility, she caught the unmistakable impression of bright scarlet. The only other way out of this street was the long alleyway, down which more gang members were approaching. There was no means of escape. She was surrounded.

11
The Den

She retraced her steps desperately, keeping her aura as small and nondescript as possible. She had to think fast. There was a large building with a lit-up doorway. It had a small group of men and women staggering around and laughing outside it. She could see no better option than to go inside and search, either for a means of escape or a hiding place, before her pursuers closed in.

As she passed the laughing group, a vivid vision of the Beast of Highgate opened its jaws and lunged at her. Taken off guard she ducked at the last second, lost her balance and tumbled into the nearest woman. That had been too real. She looked all around her, wide eyed, to check there was really nothing there.

The woman she had collided with had large gaps between her teeth, which caused a sucking sound when she spoke. "Poor dear. The opium's got hold of this one real young. The poor mite."

Anna had no idea what that meant. She was just grateful it was kindness, not hostility. Apologising, she darted forward again and dived inside the building. Whatever this place was, it could not be any more dangerous than the street outside had now become.

The first thing that hit her was the smell. It was pungent and almost overpowering. Terrified she might have been seen entering, she dashed straight through the small entrance hall and past another room where men were drinking, laughing and singing loudly. No-one seemed to notice her. She reached another doorway towards the rear of the building and passed straight through it.

The fumes were even stronger in this new room. Indeed, this place seemed to be their source. The air was thick with smoke which made Anna cough straight away. Peering around desperately, she saw what appeared to be beds of a sort, each with its own oil lamp on a small table next to it. All the beds bar one in the far corner contained a person, either sitting or lying.

She caught sight of the man nearest her, who was reclining, propped up on one elbow. He was smartly dressed, but his face was covered in a layer of sweat, which also dripped from his hair. His hands were shaking visibly. His eyes looked crazed as they stared into the far distance. He was holding a long pipe, in which was burning whatever it was that filled the room with this dense smoke. She could not begin to imagine what was going on in the man's head, but whatever he was smoking was clearly not doing him any good. Nonetheless, he raised the pipe to his mouth again and inhaled some more.

Anna began to feel light-headed herself from the fumes. Her eyes probed the gloom, looking for any possible means of escape. She could see none. Suddenly, a hand grabbed her shoulder from behind. Wheeling round and bracing herself, she was relieved to find not Faulkner but an old man, with wide eyes and wild white hair sticking out in all directions.

"And what have we got here then? This ain't no place for young ladies!"

His words were slurred, and he swayed slightly as he spoke, but his tone was inquiring rather than dangerous.

Anna thought fast. She looked at his aura. It was a very odd specimen indeed, quite misshapen, with enormous undulations on its surface. Although it contained strains of greenish-yellow and a little brown, the overall impression was one of watery blue. There was no red or black. Slightly encouraged, no better options came to mind than to ask for help.

"Please, I'm being chased. I need a way to escape. Or at least somewhere to hide."

"Do you, now? And why should I help you? You had no business coming to a place like this…"

His words were growing slower and slower, but still his voice contained no malice. The look in his eyes was growing more distant, as though he was already forgetting who he was speaking to.

"I know sir, I'm sorry, but please help me." She paused. Her words were barely getting through to the man. "Please, I'm in great danger. I think the men chasing me are going to kill me if they find me!"

At this, the man reeled his mind back in from the distant place to which it had travelled. He looked at her again.

"Do you know my daughter?" he asked, some focus returning to his eyes.

"Your daughter? No, I don't think I know her," Anna replied. She was already starting to think of her next move. She could not afford to spend any longer on this lost conversation.

"No, you wouldn't know her. Nobody knows her now. I have no daughter no more. I did have a daughter once, but she's long gone. I weren't there to help her. Nobody helped her." His voice and his gaze both drifted off sadly into the distance again.

There was a noise in the room next door, followed by the sound of raised voices. One voice in particular was very loud and spoke in a commanding tone. This clamour seemed to penetrate the smoke that filled the old man's mind, and it brought him back a second time.

"Sounds like they're coming for you," he whispered, more urgently now. "I won't let them take you again, my dear. Not again!"

Anna wondered what he meant, and whether he was now confusing her with his own daughter in his muddled state. However, she was not about to turn down any possibility of help. The man led her to the back of the smoke-filled room, to the one bed which lay vacant in the far corner. The other patrons of the establishment appeared completely oblivious to her presence, and probably even to the room itself, so lost were they in their own worlds.

"Quick my dear, hide under here. They'll never find you there. I'll never let them take you again. It's so good to have you back, dear!"

Anna had no other choices left. She wasted no time and slid under the bed. It was terribly dusty, causing her to quietly sneeze once before she brought it under control. There were various rags and pieces of rubbish under there, but at least it was dry and relatively warm, both an improvement on outside. The next moment, the wooden slats of the bed above her head creaked as the man climbed onto it. A blanket came down the side, blocking all but the bottom inch of her view of the room. There was movement above her on the bed. The table next to it was moved closer and she could hear the sound of a match being lit. The wild-haired old man was lighting his pipe again, possibly shocked by the sudden re-appearance of his daughter. Anna felt faint. She lay her head down briefly on the dusty wooden floor. At least the visions had stopped.

The sound of shouting and glass being smashed came from the next-door room. It was followed by gruff voices growing nearer. Then, one stern, familiar voice rose loudly above all the others again. It was Faulkner.

"I am warning you, my man. I am certain a girl came into this building. If she is not in the bar, and if there are no other exits apart from the front door, then she must be in here!"

"I swear mister…" came a new voice, "I mean, good sir… I ain't seen no girls in 'ere. Look for yourself. It's only these 'ere, uh, customers in this room. An' they're all regulars, honest they are!"

Anna strained to see through the gap between the blanket and the floor. Her view in the dim light was obscured by the bed in front of her, but she could hear what followed all too clearly.

"Please sir, please, I beg you. Take a look for yourself. I swear I ain't hiding no-one. No. No! Argh–!"

His sentence descended into an anguished cry, as some form of excruciating pain was inflicted on him. Almost certainly an attack on his aura. There was the sound of a body slumping to the floor. Then Faulkner spoke again, his voice now the only sound.

"Listen to me, all of you. I want to know if a girl entered this room in the last ten minutes. If you saw her, you must tell me now. If I find that any one of you is concealing her, I will kill you dead, right where you lie. Am I making myself clear?"

There was the sound of murmuring.

"Master," came a hissing voice. Anna was certain it was Mortlock. "I do not mean to question you, but these men are ruined on opium. I do not think they would have noticed the girl even if she had come in here. Look at them, the wretched, worthless specimens."

There was a hard slap, followed by pained groaning and mumbled, unintelligible words. It sounded as though Mortlock had slapped one of the defenceless men hard about the face. Anna felt anger rise inside her, despite her fear. Why strike one of these men? There was clearly no way they could defend themselves in their state. Mortlock had just said himself he did not think they were hiding anything. Anna was revolted afresh by the old man.

"I still don't believe she came into this building, master. I fear that she may be escaping at this moment, as we tarry here. If we are going to search the place, please, let us do so quickly."

"Very well," replied the deeper, stronger voice of Faulkner. "Men, search the room. And make sure you check under the beds!"

Anna's heart stopped. This was it. She was cornered, with no hope of slipping away. If she were to reveal herself now, they would be on her in seconds. She would certainly be done for, with a Satal there as well as Mortlock and the others. She could only watch and wait, helpless. As she heard the sound of men's boots starting to move about the room, Faulkner spoke again.

"I am going to give these worthless creatures some new, very real visions to occupy their minds. If any of them knows anything, they will speak soon enough."

Suddenly Anna saw a ghostly white face pressed against hers, its mouth opening to reveal sharp, jagged teeth. It took every ounce of self-control to hold in the scream that longed to burst out of her, as the face snapped its jaws as if to bite her face. But there was no pain, and then the face was gone. She had controlled her mind. The awful shouts, screams and wails from above told her that the men on the beds were experiencing similar visions, but without any notion that they were hallucinations. She was horrified.

"Tell me where the girl is!" shouted Faulkner to the room at the top of his voice.

Anna felt something heavy sliding over her feet. Then her legs. It reached her waist, then began to slither towards her head, hissing as it moved. The giant snake opened its jaws wide to reveal large, venomous fangs. Panic threatened to overwhelm her, but again she controlled it. 'It's not real,' she told herself over and over. The men above her were now screaming and thrashing about in blind panic, as they fought the demons induced by Faulkner in their own minds.

Then Anna became aware of a scraping noise on the floor ahead of her. Blocking the visions, she peered desperately through the gap under the blanket. She saw the scuffed, dirty boots and the hand of a man searching under the bed next to her. In the hand was a long, bladed weapon, which moved under the bed in long, savage swipes. Slasher McCain. The blade found only the wooden bed legs. The searcher moved on to the next one, across the room from Anna. There was only one bed left after that. She would be discovered in moments. The visions in her head once again intensified.

"Stop! Stop! Please stop!" came the desperate voices of several of the remaining men, presumably too weak or too far gone to try to make a run for it. They were evidently suffering appallingly now. Then the searcher's boots reached Anna's bed.

With no more time to think, Anna made one last, desperate attempt to evade capture. She slipped her feet silently between the slats and the mattress above her legs at the end of the bed. She grabbed hold of the slat immediately above her with both hands and hauled herself up until her body was flat against the underside of the bed. There was a clear space between her and the floor below. Moments later, the searcher's blade came scraping below her, seeking out its victim. Anna held her breath. Her arms and legs started to ache as the blade continued its slow, stabbing and slashing progress immediately beneath her.

Anna blocked more mental attacks. She was only concerned about the physical pain in her limbs now. The blade, inches below her, seemed to take an eternity to complete its journey. Just when she thought she could hold on no more, finally the searcher stood up straight again and spoke up.

"Nothing under these beds. I've checked them all," came the rasping voice of Slasher McCain.

He moved away. Anna finally dared to take a breath. She lowered herself to the floor as gently as her failing arms would let her, biting her lip at the pain in her fingers. The sound as she reached the floor was inaudible amid the hubbub of the room.

"I tell you, she is not here, master," came Mortlock's voice again. "Time is of the essence. Quick, let us resume our search outside."

Mortlock's opinion finally appeared to have won. The visions in Anna's head suddenly stopped. The horrible screaming and cries from the room turned to quieter, exhausted groans. Anna began to breathe a little more easily.

Then the bed above her creaked, and the wild-haired man spoke up in a croaking voice.

"You'll never find her. Never! I'll never let you take her away from me again!" he shouted defiantly.

Anna's blood froze in her veins. The sound of the men leaving the room stopped abruptly. Then Faulkner's voice sounded, loud and clear. "What did you say?"

The old man did not repeat his assertion, but quickly leaned forward and lit his pipe again, perhaps already regretting his brief outburst. Slow, heavy footsteps approached them. Anna saw a pair of large, mud-spattered but highly-polished shoes come into view.

"I said," Faulkner spoke again, in a voice that dripped menace, "what did you say?"

"I said you'll never find her," replied the voice above Anna. It was weaker now. The old man sucked desperately again on his pipe.

"I will never find whom?"

The man was already drifting back into oblivion as he replied, faintly, "My daughter. You'll never find her. I'll never lose her again…"

Suddenly he was hauled back from wherever his mind had gone with a jolt. He let out a horrific cry. It was the sound of someone undergoing a mental assault. The Satal was now standing right over the bed under which Anna was concealed. She lay frozen to the spot, inches from his feet.

"It wasn't your daughter that you meant, was it?" Faulkner shouted at his defenceless victim. "It was the girl whom we seek. Anna Lawrence. It was her to whom you referred, was it not?"

Faulkner apparently lessened his attack, allowing the old man to respond. Anna continued to hold her breath. She was terrified at what the crazed old man might say next.

"I'm done for," he started rambling, "the opium's done for me this time. Seeing awful things in my head, I am. And feeling even worse and all. Reckon I'm on my way to hell, where I belong. But I'll never let them take away my daughter again. Never!" He remained defiant, even as his voice finally gave out.

"I suggest we forget about him, master." Mortlock spoke up again. "He's just a rambling old fool, out of his mind. He doesn't know where he is or what he's talking about. He isn't hiding anything from us."

Faulkner leaned forward. Anna felt the bed above her start to move as he lifted the poor man halfway off the bed and began to shake him. "Don't you dare pass out, old man. Where is the girl? Your… daughter? Tell me where she is now, or you shall die a more painful death than you have ever imagined. And so shall she!"

"His daughter died years ago," another faint voice spoke up from the direction of the bed next to theirs. "Always rambling about her, he is, when he's had a pipe. Disappeared on the streets apparently. Never been seen since. Never got over it, he ain't."

A brief silence followed, then Faulkner finally let out a yell of anger and threw the old man back down on the bed. It gave a loud creak above Anna's head, but held together.

"Come then, let us see if the men outside have had more success than we have in this pathetic hole." His voice was edged with deep anger.

He swept from the room, his accomplices close behind him. There was no sound of any resistance from the adjoining bar this time.

Anna lay her head back down on the floorboards. All the energy seeped from her tired limbs, but her mind still raced. She could hear comings and goings in the room as, one-by-one, the men either dragged themselves out of the place to elude its horrors, or relit their pipes to seek escape by those means instead.

She waited for things to die down again, hoping against hope that the poor old man above her, who had saved her life, was still alive himself. He might not really have known what he was doing, and he was clearly mistaken about who it was he was saving, but he had shown tremendous bravery in the face of the Satal. She dared not move a muscle though. Not until enough time had passed for Faulkner and his evil henchmen to have left the area entirely, and for everyone else who remained in the room to have returned to their own little worlds. Time passed. Anna finally began to doze herself, exhausted.

She had no idea how long she had been asleep when she was woken by a gentle tapping on her shoulder. She jumped, banging her head on the wooden slats of the bed above her. Then she remembered where she was. She shoved the hand away and pushed herself tight against the wall to avoid its reach. She saw the outline of a head leaning over the side of the bed. Wild hair stuck out in all directions.

"Are you all right, my dear? Didn't scare you did they, them nasty men?"

"Are you sure they've gone?"

"Yeah, they're long gone, now. Owner's just been in here, effing and blinding about them. Woke me up, he did. He's a right coward that one. There's no way he'd be talking like that about them if they was still here!" The old man gave a little chuckle, his head still upside down, looking at her.

"Are you all right?" asked Anna, wondering how much he would remember.

"Yeah, I'm all right. Tough as old boots, your old dad is."

Anna hesitated. "Is it safe for me to come out now? What about the others?"

"Don't worry about them. They're all back on the dream stick. Don't know who's coming or going, they don't."

Anna decided to trust him. He was convinced she was his daughter, and he had just faced death without giving her away. She shuffled and slid her way sideways out from under the bed, then dusted herself down vainly as she peered around. The room had returned almost entirely to its former state – sleepy and smoke-filled, with no-one paying her the slightest bit of notice. Half the beds were now empty.

"Thank you for saving me. I am most grateful to you," Anna said. She felt very light-headed from all the smoke in the room.

"You're welcome, my darling." The old man beamed, making him look even more crazed. "Oh, how I've missed you. There's no way I was going to let them take you again."

Anna faced a new problem. She could not stay here. But how could she break the news to the old man that she had to leave? It was trivial in comparison to the dangers she had faced that evening, but from the bottom of her heart she did not want to make things any worse for this poor old man who had been through so much. She sat next to him on the bed as he gazed at her, his eyes slipping in and out of focus. She considered her words very carefully.

"I must leave you now. I only came to see you for a short time, and I cannot return again. But you have really helped me. I am so very grateful to you. You are a kind, brave man, and there is nothing more you could have done for me."

"Oh, my dear, d'you really have to leave so soon?" he replied sadly. "But I understand. I'm grateful for you coming to see me this once, and for your words. I've been so lonely these years, so filled with regrets, since…" His sad look gave way to tears.

He reached over and gave Anna a hug with his wiry arms. She was surprised to find tears running down her own cheeks at the words from this strange old man. She just wanted to bring him some peace. Who knew if the streets were safe to return to yet, anyway? Delaying a little longer might be no bad thing.

Anna looked at his aura again. Its shape was the same as before, but its colour had more of a hint of yellow now, and on its surface were fresh scars that were not there before. They were nothing like the deep gashes she had seen on Gillespie's aura, but they would still surely cause mental strife and discomfort to the old man.

She visualised her own aura reaching out. She began gently to move it over his in a soothing, healing motion, as she had done previously with Gillespie, but now applying some of the basic principles of healing she had learned from Mr Warwick. Immediately, the old man seemed to relax. His sobbing started to subside as peace came to him. She continued for a time until finally all traces of the slashes were gone. The yellowing had lessened. The old man's tired face looked peaceful at last.

"I must go now," said Anna. This time there was no protest, just a tired nod and another wiry hug. She added, "I really think you should stop smoking this, whatever it is. However it makes you feel, I think it's doing you no end of harm."

"You know, I do believe you're right. I seen and heard some wild things tonight, none of them good. In fact, they was terrifying. I'm sure mostly they was just in my head. This stuff," he tapped the pipe on the table next to them, "ain't never brought me the peace you've done tonight, my dear. In fact, it's ruined my life. I'm gonna try and do what you say. I'll try and kick it for good this time."

"That's good." Anna nodded.

She stood up. The old man did not attempt to stop her from leaving.

"Well, goodbye," he said. "And thank you. I feel peace at last. Please do take care. I'll never forget you." He lay back on his bed, closed his eyes and looked at her no more.

Wiping the last of the tears from her face, Anna left him. She reached the doorway and peeped round the corner. The next room had returned to its old self again, albeit with fewer people, now even more inebriated than before. She took one last look back at the figure with the wild hair in the corner. Anna silently wished the man well and vowed not to forget him, nor this place she had stumbled across.

She moved quickly through the next room, glancing only to check that no-one followed her, and hurried to the front door. She peered carefully outside in both directions. It was still the dead of night and very dark. Heavy fog hung in the air, but there was now no trace of the wind that had made it swirl so, earlier. There was no-one standing outside, and no sign she could make out that anyone might be lying in wait. She adjusted her focus to check for auras in the dark mist. There was nothing to see, red or otherwise. A long time had clearly passed since Faulkner had left, and she decided to risk a move. She pulled her coat about her and plunged back out into the night.

She had no idea where to head for. She just wanted to get as far away from this place as possible. She definitely could not risk returning anywhere near Jeremiah's building, so instead she headed as fast as she could in the opposite direction to the long, dark alleyway. Soon she reached the wider road that Faulkner and his men had approached from. She slowed, checked in all directions for people and auras, then darted across it, into another street.

There were very few people around. Just the odd figure slumped in a doorway, and one or two men still walking the streets, wrapped up against the night. There were no gangs, and no-one payed her any attention. Despite her ordeal, Anna did feel a little refreshed by the sleep under that bed. She pushed on and on, crossing more thoroughfares and making several turns. She did not pause until she had put a significant distance between herself and that place where she had almost been caught.

Eventually, the air around her began to change. There was a smell – a combination of salt and something altogether fouler. She approached one more drinking establishment that was still open, which had a picture of a ship hanging outside. A number of people, this time all men, were still drinking, both inside and out. She gave it a wide birth, ducking down a parallel side street. She pressed on a short way, the smell in her nostrils growing stronger until, passing between two large buildings that might have been warehouses, she finally found its source.

It was the mighty River Thames, the artery which fed the heart of London from its hinterlands to the west, and which, eastwards, connected the great city with all the other lands of the world. And what a foul, dirty specimen it was. In the heat of the summer it stank to high heaven, and even now it was bad enough. But at last, she had some means of getting her bearings and making a plan.

She knew that the river ran basically from west to east, albeit with twists and turns. She was on the north side of it, somewhere far to the east of where she lived. If she followed the river to her right, it should take her via a meandering course to the west. If she went in that direction, eventually she should be able to strike out north again and return to familiar territory around her mother's house and Mr Warwick's shop. That would take a long time, and her enemies might well be lying in wait at both those locations when she got there. On the other hand, clearly it was not safe to return to Jeremiah's, even if she could find her way back there. She had no idea where Mr Warwick and her uncle were staying that night and no means of finding them, nor anyone else from the Order.

The memory of Jeremiah battling with the Wraith came back with a jolt. She hoped against hope he had somehow defeated it and escaped. But what if the Wraith had overcome him?

If Jeremiah had failed to stop it, that single-minded creature would no doubt be scouring the night streets now, looking for any sign of her. Who knew how close it might be at that very moment? And would Faulkner, Mortlock and the rest really have given up their search, knowing how close they had come? Unlikely. A healthy sense of fear returned to her. Fear that might just keep her alive.

She looked to the east and saw that the fog was thinning slightly. The first dim hints of dawn were just beginning to appear. It was dangerous to stay where she was, and even more dangerous to head back to anywhere she knew. Tiredness was setting in. Finally, she made up her mind. She would find somewhere to conceal herself around here, somewhere completely out of sight, for as long as it took for her trail to grow cold.

Anna set off to her left for now, following the direction of the river. She looked for a means to get down to the water. Soon she found one – an opening in the wall next to a large dock building, through which there were stone steps that led down to the riverbank itself. She made her way down them, almost losing her footing once on the slippery surface.

The tide was out, leaving a wide, slimy expanse for her to make her way along. Holding onto the wall for both direction and balance, she pushed herself forwards, searching for somewhere she might hide and rest. The thinning mist was definitely growing lighter to the east. Anna made out the dark silhouette of a low building ahead, up against the wall just before the next dock. She could not tell what the building was for. Perhaps for storing boats.

She reached it. After some fumbling along its wooden walls, she located a door. It was locked. It did not have any windows as far as she could tell. She continued round it to the far side and found a small gap between it and the stone wall. The gap was narrow, but just wide enough for her to fit into. This would have to do. If her enemies could find her here, they could find her anywhere.

She sat down in the gap, wedged between the stone wall and the wall of the building, with her knees hunched up to her chest for warmth. She listened out for anyone approaching. There was no sound, save the gentle lapping of the river against the bank some distance away. There she sat in the semi-darkness, too tired to move another muscle. She rested her head against the wooden wall, began to doze, then fell into a deeper sleep.

* * *

Jake Grimes, cowering with the rest of Faulkner's gang in the early light of dawn, braced himself. Faulkner was extremely angry. He could lash out fatally at any one of them, at any moment.

"The girl is loose, somewhere in the city," he snarled. "She is separated from all her guardians. We must capture her now, fast. McCain, arrange to have that building she escaped from kept under constant surveillance, day and night. We shall also continue to watch her mother's house, the area around the old man's shop and around her uncle's home, as we have been doing.

"Grimes," he continued, "let the Wraith loose in the neighbourhood around her house. Keep it fed and watered, but do not allow it to rest until it has hunted the girl down."

Then he turned to Mortlock. "In the meantime, it's time to execute our new plan to ensnare the girl…"

"Yes, master. I shall arrange it right away." Mortlock bowed and withdrew.

12
Kidnapped

It was the cold that woke her. It had not been too bad when she was running through the streets, but despite her cardigan and thick overcoat, now she felt frozen to the bone. She shivered, reluctant to move from the tight spot she had wedged herself into, but also sensing that to stay might mean literally freezing to death. She was also conscious that the river could cut her off if the tide came in. She looked up. Beyond the edge of the building it was now properly light. Dawn had come and gone.

With great difficulty, Anna forced her stiff limbs to move from their cramped position. She raised herself and peered round the edge of the building. The fog had fully lifted, and there were signs of life around her, from boats moving up the river in the distance to shouts and other activity in the docks close by. There were no apparent signs of danger, and she was tired, cold and hungry. Like it or not, the time had come to move.

Anna slowly pulled herself up to her feet, leaning heavily against the wall. She had pins and needles in both feet, and she felt very stiff from her sleeping position, but mentally she felt rested. She began to warm herself up.

What to do now? Her thoughts retraced their tracks from the previous night, but with less fear and greater clarity. Then she remembered: today was the day planned for the attack on Faulkner and his men in Eagle Street.

Faulkner was not supposed to return to London until today, but he had come back and struck first. Had Jeremiah managed to escape and raise the alarm? What about Jim? Maybe he would have returned to help, or at least let the others know. Yes, there was hope there, just so long as he too had not been captured by Faulkner's men.

She was desperate to find Mr Warwick and her uncle, to tell them what had happened and to let them know she was safe. But how? She must assume their enemies would be lying in wait in Jeremiah's neighbourhood in case she returned, and also around her house and Mr Warwick's shop. The truth was that she had no idea where in this huge city her two guardians might be now. The only place she knew they had planned to be later that day was in Eagle Street for their attack on the enemy. They had rented some rooms in a building on that street for spying on them. But she had no idea which one. Besides, Eagle Street was their enemies' heartland. There was simply no way she could go looking for Mr Warwick and her uncle there, especially today of all days. That was the one specific place they had ordered her not to go. It was too much of a risk, regardless of the changed circumstances.

Anna's next thought was to try to get a message to her mother. But she too had been moved out of their house to somewhere safe after the ambush by McCain, and Anna herself did not know where that was. She hadn't needed to know, as she was never meant to leave Jeremiah's. There was no way to contact her.

Anna wracked her brains and tried to fight off a sense of despair. She had nowhere she could go where there was anyone who could help her. She ran through the possible options of friends and acquaintances of her mother, which she discounted one-by-one. Then she hit upon an idea which stood out clearly from all the rest. Rebecca and Timmy.

Her friends knew nothing of the Struggle, and they were unknown to her enemies. Of all her friends, Rebecca was always the most resourceful. She was the oldest in the group, and their leader. Also, the idea of finally being able to see Timmy again, of being able to talk to him and the possibility of feeling his support again, filled her heart with hope like no other idea could. She was in a terrible state and would need to come up with some explanation, but the idea was so powerful that she set off without further hesitation.

She knew the way to the Thompsons' house from her own home, but not from here. However, it was definitely westwards, and the river would lead her to landmarks she knew in that direction, from which she could navigate. She would have liked to walk along the riverbank all the way if she could, despite the slime and the stench, to remain unseen. But there were docks blocking her route, and even if she could somehow negotiate those, the tide was now coming in. At some point soon the way would surely become impassable.

Instead she returned up the stone steps and took the first road that followed the direction of the river westwards. Her hair was unkempt, hanging down loosely over her shoulders and covering part of her face, not tied neatly as she usually kept it. Her overcoat was covered in slime, dirt and dust from her night's exploits. In short, she looked quite a sight to be walking the streets, and nothing like Anna Lawrence. Perfect. Fortunately, her coat reached almost to the ground, concealing her nightdress.

She made fast progress, despite sometimes having to double-back on herself when the road turned out to be a dead end, or to turn in a different direction than she was expecting. In due course she passed a large building which she recognised as the Tower of London. Not too long after, St Paul's came into view in the distance ahead of her. Her nightmare of the previous night came rushing back. Instinctively, she looked all around her for Faulkner. There was no sign. In the morning sunshine, the cathederal's majestic dome looked very different from the way it had in her dream, and the sky was clear. She calmed her mind again. This landmark was good news, not bad. It meant she was heading in the right direction.

It was still some time before she finally saw a sight that she knew to be in the West End. It was Admiral Lord Nelson, perched atop his lofty column in the distance to her right, peering over London's rooftops. Then in the distance ahead she spied the mighty clocktower of Big Ben. From there it would be a simple matter to navigate her way to where Rebecca and Timmy lived, which was quite some distance south of her own home.

The bustle of city life was all around her and it took all forms, but from the more smartly-dressed ladies and gentlemen she received only disdainful looks. It was the state she was in, and probably the smell of the river, some of whose muck she still carried on her coat. It might be good camouflage, but it really wasn't great to be turning up at Timmy and Rebecca's in this state. With some trepidation, she headed in the direction of their home.

Eventually Anna reached the freshly painted front door of their terraced house. She hesitated. The full reality of what she was about to do hit her. She was dishevelled, dirty and smelly, and she was turning up completely unannounced. How would she explain it? She could not tell them about the Struggle. On the other hand, she was desperate and needed help, she was hopefully about to see her best friend, and also her best friend's brother...

Her heartrate quickened and her mind began to fog over, to the point that she could not think what to say. But what else was she going to do? Allowing pure instinct to take over, she reached up and gave the knocker a loud rap. Her tummy filled with butterflies. She heard the sound of footsteps behind the door, it opened, and her eyes met the surprised expression on the round face of Rebecca and Timmy's mother.

"Hello Mrs Thompson. I was wondering if you could help me. I've had some... trouble. Is Rebecca or Timmy around?" It was the best she could manage.

"Anna, can that be you? What on earth's happened? Look at the state of you! Come on child, come inside where we can get you warm and dry." Anna was relieved Mrs Thompson's motherly instincts had overridden any need for explanations – for now anyway.

"Thank you, Mrs Thompson," she replied. She followed the round lady inside, into the warm house.

Mrs Thompson ushered Anna in front of the warm fire in the main room, bustled into the kitchen, then soon returned with a large cup of warm milk. Next, she busily moved into another room to retrieve some fresh clothes belonging to Rebecca. They were too big for Anna, but they were dry and warm, and nothing else mattered.

Once all the immediate priorities had been seen to, Mrs Thompson asked, "So Anna, what brings you to these parts on your own, and how on earth did you get to be in this state?"

Anna hesitated. No coherent answer coming to mind, she replied simply, "Oh Mrs Thompson, I've got into some bother. Are Rebecca and Timmy around?"

"They're both out at the moment. Timmy went out early this morning. I'm not sure when he'll be back. Rebecca is out doing an errand for me but should be home any minute now."

Almost as if summoned by her words, the front door opened and in walked Rebecca.

"Hello love, look, you've got a visitor!" said Mrs Thompson brightly.

"Hello Becca!" said Anna, gleeful at seeing her old friend again after so long.

Rebecca said nothing at first, clearly startled to see her friend sitting there so unexpectedly, in her own living room and wearing her clothes. But rather than breaking into a broad grin and running over to her as Anna might have hoped, the pretty, dark-haired girl's expression turned from surprise to one of sternness. Her attractive brown eyes were filled with suspicion.

"So, what brings you here, then?" she asked.

Sensing that something was amiss, Mrs Thompson said, "Well, it looks like you two have some matters to discuss, so I'll leave you to it. I shall be in the kitchen if anyone needs me."

With that, the kind lady disappeared and closed the door behind her.

"I, uh, I've had some trouble..." Anna started, before drying up. She was stunned and worried by the older girl's response to seeing her. It was something she had never seen before. "What's the matter, Becca? What's wrong? I'm sorry to turn up here so suddenly, but I really wanted to see you... and Timmy."

At this, Rebecca gave a brief snort. "Oh, you did, did you? You wanted to see Timmy? Why? So that you could cause him more pain? Look him in the eye and twist the knife yourself this time? No doubt you've come to explain your actions. Well it's too late for that, now. The damage has been done. Timmy's gone and disappeared, and I've no idea where he's gone!"

Anna was shocked, and completely lost for words.

"Well, what've you got to say? Why did you come here?" Rebecca continued.

Anna finally found her voice, but it trembled as she spoke.

"Becca, what do you mean, Timmy's disappeared? And why is he in pain? What have I done?" Thoughts of her guardians and the Struggle left her for now.

Rebecca looked as though she was about to burst into another tirade, but she stopped. Instead, she looked Anna straight in the eyes as if trying to weigh something up.

"All right, Anna. You don't seem no different from when I last saw you. Except your hair's a right mess and you're wearing my clothes. Why are you wearing my clothes, by the way? Anyhow, I won't pass no more judgement until I've heard what you have to say." Then she cut straight to the heart of the matter.

"I thought you and Timmy had been getting on real well and growing right close. Well, as close as any two people can, when one of them's locked away all day. Timmy never said nothing to me in particular, but he didn't need to. I know that boy better than he knows himself, I reckon. You didn't have to be a genius to see that my little brother had fallen completely head over heels for you."

Anna sat, rooted to her stool. Her head started to swim. Timmy having those feelings for her was all she had wanted to hear for the longest time. But now she was hearing it, she was filled with trepidation.

"Becca, I feel the same way too." She had never spoken openly to her about this, but she had no choice now. "I think about Timmy all the time, even though I haven't been able to see him for so long. I go to bed at night hoping desperately that he feels the same way that I do. Nothing in this world would make me happier than to know he did. I would never do anything to hurt him!"

Rebecca's eyes did not leave her for a second. "Well, he's been a completely different person since the last time he saw you. At times he's been in a right desperate state. And do you know why?" Anna had no idea why. "Because his heart's been broken into thousands of tiny pieces, that's why! Plain as day. Always used to be so calm and steady, he did. I've never seen him in such a state."

"But… but why? I don't understand…"

"I kept asking him what was wrong, and he refused to tell. Said it was none of my business. But you know me, I can be very persuasive when I need to be, and my intuition isn't bad either. There was only one thing I could imagine that might make him so upset but unable to tell me about it. So I asked him directly if it was about you."

"What... what did he say?"

"I tell you, he started shouting at me in a way he's never done before – nor would he ever have dared to! And he tried to avoid answering me. But I wasn't having none of it. Something was tearing him up, and I meant to get it out of him. I didn't let up until he told me what it was all about."

Anna was motionless, trying to comprehend what was going on. Rebecca continued watching her. She seemed to be talking a little more calmly.

"What did he say?" Anna managed to squeeze the words out. She was deeply worried about what was coming.

"Finally, he told me. About you and Gillespie. How he'd heard you'd arranged to meet him, and how he'd seen the two of you together."

"But–" Anna started.

"Gillespie, of all people! I told him I didn't believe it, but then he said he'd seen the pair of you with his own eyes. Reckoned it'd been a foggy night, but there'd been no mistaking it was you. When I said there must've been some kind of innocent explanation, he told me he'd seen you holding Gillespie's hands and talking right close with him!"

Anna was utterly mortified. The youth in the baggy clothes she had seen running away in the distance after she parted from Gillespie that night... it must have been Timmy. Somehow, he had been there. And he had got completely the wrong end of the stick.

"But Becca, that wasn't what you think–"

"He said you were calling him 'Billy', not Gillespie like we all do." Rebecca seemed determined to finish what she had started. "And that the lout was saying what a special night it'd been, and how he didn't want to leave you, or some such. That's right, he said that Gillespie thanked you for that night, and that he would never forget it. Well, I didn't know what to make of that when I heard it, I'm sure I didn't! Timmy said you and Gillespie were right intimate, and you gave him a big hug before you parted. I just couldn't believe what I was hearing!"

"Rebecca, none of that was what he thought it was. Let me explain–"

"He said he still hadn't given up all hope at first. Convinced himself that even if you had somehow got together with Gillespie, maybe he could win you back. So, he asked that Lizzy girl to give you a message to meet him, in the usual place. But Lizzy came back later and said you didn't want to see him no more, because you were with Gillespie now. And that was that! We haven't seen you nor Gillespie since."

Anna's insides were churning. "Let me explain–"

Rebecca still had not finished. "Now I never had you down as a liar, Anna. But I know for sure my brother isn't one. Straight as die that boy. Pure as anything. Which is one of the reasons it hurts me so much to see him in this state. He just doesn't deserve it. And you didn't even have the decency to tell him yourself. You just used Lizzy to give him the message." Rebecca's words remained sharp as razorblades, but her tone had softened a lot, as though doubts were slowly creeping in.

For Anna's part, she felt pierced by an almost physical pain. After all she had been through in the last twenty-four hours, she felt almost broken. She had only been trying to help Gillespie in his wretched state, but now she imagined the scene through Timmy's eyes. She felt her own heart begin to crack at the thought of the hurt he had felt.

Timmy must not have seen Faulkner that night. He must have been there just long enough to observe her 'intimate' moments with Gillespie. And here also was final proof of Lizzy's treachery... The thoughts crashed through her mind. By the time she was able to put them into words, she was already pacing the floor.

"There's been a terrible misunderstanding! I didn't know it until now."

She relayed what had happened, starting with Gillespie approaching her for help. She spoke very rapidly, and desperately. She made no mention of auras, about which Rebecca knew nothing. She did, though, explain that Gillespie was trying to escape from Faulkner, who Rebecca did know about. She relayed their subsequent near escape from him in the garden, and then their parting. She left out his final capture by the Beast. That was just too much to explain right now.

"I thought I was going to meet Timmy that afternoon, not Gillespie. I had asked Lizzy to arrange it for me. But Timmy didn't turn up. And then Gillespie found me and asked me for help. He took me completely by surprise. Becca, he was really desperate.

"You know better than anyone how much I disliked Gillespie, and all the Marylebone Street Gang," she continued. "The last time I'd seen him, I ended up shoving him in the canal if you remember! But he had obviously been through a terrible time at Faulkner's hands. He was in an awful state. If you'd been there, I know you would have been sceptical, just as I was, but I think by the end you would have wanted to help him, too."

Rebecca still looked doubtful.

"It was like when we helped Watson and Green at that mansion in Hampstead. The Marylebone Street Gang might be our enemies, but when it comes to the world of Faulkner, everyone needs help. And as for Lizzy, well, I still don't know if she ever passed on my message to Timmy about meeting up, but she certainly never gave me any more messages from him."

At the mention of Lizzy's name, Rebecca's scowl returned.

"Oh Becca," Anna continued, "if I'd known Timmy wanted to meet me, I would have been over the moon! I would have been out like a shot to see him, no matter who tried to stop me. And as for what you say Lizzy's told him about me now being with Gillespie, well that's nothing but a downright lie. Becca, you must believe that!"

Rebecca still didn't speak, but her expression had softened a lot now.

"I've never told anyone this," said Anna, "but I need to tell you now. I love Timmy more than I could ever put into words. I can't sleep at night for thinking about him, and my stomach sometimes physically aches because I long to see him so much. I've dreamt a thousand times that one day he might tell me he felt the same way about me, and that one day we might finally be together.

"I was absolutely devasted when Lizzy told me he wasn't interested, and when he didn't show up to meet me. Becca, I would rather die than do anything to hurt him. You have to believe me!"

"So what was all that about you hugging Gillespie, then? You didn't catch me hugging Watson or Green when we helped them!"

"Yes, I did give him a hug. I really wish I hadn't now, but I was just trying to comfort him after all he – all we – had just been through, escaping from Faulkner. He was in a shattered state. I was trying to give him a bit of hope. There was nothing more to it. Nothing has ever happened between Gillespie and me. Surely you must believe that? Never in a million years would I have become involved with him in *that* way!"

Rebecca had started looking down at the floor. She looked up again. She did not look angry any more.

"Tell me you believe me! Please tell me that you do!" Anna was now standing in front of her, rooted to the spot with her hands clenched, tears running in torrents down her face. Rebecca looked at her for a moment longer, then finally she broke her position and hugged her friend.

"Oh, Anna, yes all right, I do believe you. I always thought you felt the same way about Timmy, though until now I suppose I didn't realise just how deeply. Nor did I really believe you could've had those kinds of feelings for Gillespie, of all people. But Timmy was just so convinced. I'm sorry I jumped to conclusions. And sorry I was so hard on you. I do believe you, Anna, of course I do."

Anna was relieved Rebecca was finally on her side. But she still felt desperate.

"I've got to see him. I simply have to explain everything to him, and just hope and pray that he believes me. Where is he?" She might not be in control of anything else in her life now, but this was one wrong she was going to put right, no matter what.

Rebecca's consoling expression changed again. "That's where we've got a real problem. I've got no idea where he is."

"But what do you mean? When did you last see him?"

"Last night. When I came home in the evening, I found him in his room, packing his bag. He was obviously planning on going somewhere, though God only knows where. I must've spoken to him for a couple of hours. By the end he was just real sad more than angry. When I went to bed, I thought I'd talked him out of running off. But this morning he was nowhere to be seen, and his things were gone!"

"But where can he have gone?"

"I don't know. I've been out searching but there's no sign of him anywhere. Nobody's seen him. I haven't told my parents yet because they're always first out of the house anyway with their work and they didn't know he was gone. I was still hoping to find him and bring him home before they found out. But I need to tell them now. I'm so worried! Who knows where he's gone, and what he's going to do…?"

"We'll find him! I'll search with you," said Anna.

It was Rebecca's turn to battle with her emotions. "I should've kept an eye on him. I should've slept downstairs or something so he couldn't leave. But I thought it was going to be all right. I let him slip away, and who knows where he might be or what might happen to him now!"

For the first time in her life, Anna saw tears run down her strong friend's face. It was Anna's turn to console. And it was time to act.

"Becca, listen to me. I'm sure he's going to be all right. We'll find him and I'll explain everything. And... well... I won't stop explaining until he believes me. Together we'll find him, and I'm sure we can make things right again. Where have you looked for him so far, and where shall we try next?"

"Well," Rebecca wiped her eyes, "I checked the usual places. You know, like the canal and so on. Then I caught up with Johnny and Charlie, but they haven't seen him for days. They said they'd go out searching, while I came back to tell my mother. I haven't done that yet of course, because you were here. Anyway, Johnny and Charlie are supposed to come here at lunchtime if they haven't found him by then."

Johnny Adams and Charlie Morgan were two of their loyal group of friends. They had both been part of the adventure to Faulkner's mansion in the summer, when they had all first encountered the Beast of Highgate. Johnny was the most impetuous of their group, whilst Charlie was slightly clumsy and always more cautious. Anna was about to suggest they go out straight away when Rebecca's mother appeared from the kitchen with two plates of food.

"Ah, glad to see you two have made up, then!" she said brightly. "It's still before lunchtime, but you looked like you could do with some food, Anna, so I've made you both some."

The aroma reminded Anna she that had not eaten a thing since the previous night. Rebecca had lost her appetite and did not eat much. Worried though she was, Anna devoured her own steaming plate of meat and various vegetables, then gratefully accepted Rebecca's as well.

Before long, she was gulping down the last of her water, steeling herself for the search for Timmy. Her tiredness seemed to show on her face, though. Rebecca said, "Tell you what, Anna, there's no point in us going out just yet, because Johnny and Charlie will be here soon. We mustn't miss them in case they've got news. Why don't you rest a while here, while I tell my mother about Timmy? Then we can all go out searching together when the boys get here, if they haven't found him by then. And then you can tell me what it is that's made you so hungry and tired, and... well, so messy! But first, get some sleep."

Anna was keen to start searching straight away, but after eating so much food and after the night she had had, she reluctantly agreed. Leaning back in the easy chair by the door, she fell into a deep sleep in no time.

She was not sure how long it had been, perhaps an hour, when she was woken by a knock at the door. Rebecca immediately appeared from the kitchen.

"I've told my mother about Timmy," she said as she hurried towards the door. "She's gone out to get my father to look for him. Says they won't come back until they've found him. Gave me a right telling off for not letting her know sooner, she did. Oh, I hope this is good news..."

Anna rubbed her eyes and struggled to her feet as her friend opened the door. Johnny and Charlie were there, but there was no Timmy.

Both boys looked gravely serious, and very out of breath. Johnny, who had brown eyes, brown curly hair and a wiry, athletic build, had a cut and bump over his left eye. Charlie, the plumpest member of the gang, with blue-grey eyes and mousy-coloured hair, was panting heavily but appeared unharmed.

"Timmy's been taken by some ruffians working for that man, Faulkner!" exclaimed Johnny, before Rebecca could say a word.

"We saw him struggling with three of them near that old bookshop by the canal. They've taken him away! We've got to do something!"

13
Return to the Mansion

Johnny's words hit Anna like bullets. Could this possibly be true?

"Wait, slow down," said Rebecca, taking control. "What do you mean Faulkner's men have taken him? Where to? Tell me exactly what happened."

The boys stepped inside the doorway and noticed Anna for the first time.

"Oh, hello! What are you doing here?" said Johnny, smiling.

"Never mind about that now," Rebecca cut him off. "Tell us what happened." It was just as well she did. Anna had lost all ability to speak.

Johnny talked at a fast pace as Rebecca closed the door behind him. She was hanging off his every word.

"We were out looking for Timmy around our meeting place at the canal bridge. There was no sign of him, so we followed the canal to see if he was further up. Just as we were approaching that bookshop, we heard a commotion ahead. Then we heard Timmy crying for help. There were three big blokes manhandling him and trying to drag him down the street to a carriage!"

"What? Was he hurt?"

"Not to start with. He was giving them one hell of a fight. Punching and kicking for all he was worth, he was. Well, we shouted and ran down the road to try and help.

We reached them just as they was bundling him into the carriage. Charlie and me both grabbed hold of him and tried to pull him out, but one of the men shoved Charlie to the ground, and another one hit me here with a stick!"

Johnny pointed to the bump above his eye, which seemed to be getting bigger. Blood was seeping from a cut that went across it.

"Real rough they was, and strong and all," joined in Charlie.

"Then what happened?" Rebecca pressed.

"We tried to fight them, but it was no good." Charlie continued. "After they pushed me over, I tried to get up. But when Johnny got knocked down, he landed at my feet, and I fell right over him. Timmy was still fighting back hard, but then one of the men knocked him over the head and he stopped moving."

"Oh no!" Rebecca gasped, as Anna put her hands to her mouth, unable to speak. "Was he badly hurt?" asked the older girl.

"Yeah, I think he was knocked out cold. I tried to reach him, but one of them shoved me and I slipped over again. I tried to stop them, but I couldn't. I'm just so useless. They should've taken me instead…"

The stout boy looked very downcast. Even in her stunned state, Anna became vaguely aware of the grazes on both Charlie's trembling hands from his falls.

"Don't be so hard on yourself, Charlie," said Johnny. "There was nothing you could've done. And I was out of it. I didn't know where I was for a bit."

"Yeah, don't blame yourself, Charlie," said Rebecca. "Sounds like you did all you could. Both of you did. Thank you for trying to rescue him. Did you get any clues where they were taking him? Wait a minute. How do you know it was Faulkner's men who took him?"

"Well, that's the thing," Johnny continued. "Just after they slammed the door shut, we both heard them mention Hampstead, and something about getting him locked up in the tower. And we both heard one of them mention Faulkner."

"We reckon they must've meant that creepy old mansion where we saw the Beast," added Charlie.

"Then they set off in the carriage," said Johnny. "We shouted, but there was no-one around to help."

"What did you do next? Did you try to follow them?" asked Rebecca.

"I ran after them until they went round the next corner," said Charlie, "but, you know, I'm not the quickest... by the time I got there they was gone." He looked down at the floor.

"I was still dazed," continued Johnny, "but Charlie came back and got me. We came straight here."

"But what would Faulkner want with my little brother?"

"Who knows," said Johnny, "but whatever it is, it can't be good. Especially with what we know about Faulkner, and after what we saw up at his old mansion last time…."

The room fell silent for a moment as that thought sank in. Rebecca was first to speak.

"Right, there's no time to lose. We've got to get Timmy back, real fast, before that Faulkner gets his hands on him. You're right, they must've been talking about the tower we saw at that mansion. Like it or not, we've got to get back up there."

"Yeah, let's go," said Johnny.

Charlie looked pale. "D-do you think that beast might be there again?" His eyes were wide.

"Maybe. Who knows?" said Rebecca with a hint of desperation. "But if it is, then all the more reason to get up there sharpish and save Timmy. We can't waste another minute. Here, Johnny, grab this cloth to stop the bleeding from that cut on your head. Do you think you'll be all right to come with us?"

"Yeah, I'm fine," he replied without hesitation. "It's just a graze."

'It's a lot more than that,' thought Anna, impressed by his bravery. She had yet to speak, but while the others had been talking her mind had been racing. All her worst possible fears were coming true. Timmy, kidnapped by Faulkner. She knew it must have something to do with her.

Everything had gone so badly wrong since yesterday. Their enemies seemed to be striking from every direction now, taking them by surprise at every turn. Faulkner was only supposed to arrive back in London today to go to a meeting in the City, then travel to the house in Eagle Street tonight. He was back in London unexpectedly yesterday. She had to hope that the rest of his plan was unchanged, and that he was not at his mansion now.

She recalled with horror the Wraith into which the Satal had transformed Gillespie. She had helplessly watched Gillespie be carried off to that fate. There was no way in the world she could stand by and risk that same thing happening to Timmy. She had put him through so much pain already. It was probably her fault his life was in danger now. It made no difference if this was some kind of trap or not. If it was, they would just have to get round it. She would not let him come to harm, not while there was a breath left in her body. All hope lay with getting Timmy out of that mansion before Faulkner returned. These thoughts all flashed through her mind as she found her voice.

"Right," she said. "Beast or no beast, we go back to the mansion, now. Timmy's life depends on us!"

Rebecca needed no second bidding. "Are you two in?" she asked the boys.

"You try and stop us!" said Johnny with characteristic enthusiasm. Charlie also nodded, a determined expression on his face.

"Right. Thank you. Both of you."

"Do you think we should try to get the coppers?" Charlie added. "Or at least some grown-ups? Our parents? Faulkner's gang are real rough. And you remember what happened the last time we went up there!"

"We don't seem to have much luck getting the police to listen to us," replied Rebecca. She was clearly recalling the disastrous results when she and Anna had tried the last time they had gone to Hampstead. "And yes, I'm sure we should get our parents involved, but I've no idea where mine are now. They're out looking for Timmy, and I've no clue where they've gone. Likely they won't be back until well after dark now, seeing as how they're not going to find him. We can't afford to wait for them. Any of your parents around?"

Johnny and Charlie both shook their heads.

"Anna, what about your mother?"

"No, she's away. I'm afraid it's down to us," said Anna, anxious to leave. She knew that no-one's parents, nor even the police themselves, would be equipped to deal with the situation if Faulkner was there, or if any of Timmy's captors possessed the Powers. It was only Knights of the Order who could help them if it came down to any kind of fight, and she had no way of safely reaching any of those. There was no better option than to use the cunning of children rather than the strength of normal adults. They needed to get in there and out again without a fight.

"Right, that's it then," said Rebecca. "We'll need to get taxi carriages up there. We've got most chance of getting two-seater Hansom cabs, so we'll need two of them. I'll go with Anna. You two have enough money?"

Johnny and Charlie both turned out their pockets. Anna had no idea what a taxi fare would cost to anywhere, but she very much doubted that the meagre pennies they had between them would be enough. Becca had the same view.

"All right, wait here while I get my wages from the laundrette," she said. She returned in moments with a purse. She gave Johnny a handful of extra coins.

"It isn't easy catching cabs, not being adults," she added, "so I suggest we split up and try different main streets. We're more likely to both get rides that way. You two try the big street at the end of this road. Me and Anna will take the next one."

"Will do," said Johnny.

"Meet us in Hampstead, on that corner where the main road down the hill from Highgate meets the road leading to the mansion. Whoever gets there first, wait in those bushes set back from the corner, where no-one can see us. There's only one road to the mansion. Whoever gets there first can check for anyone arriving or leaving. It's safer than waiting by the mansion itself."

"All right," said Johnny, already halfway through the door, Charlie right behind him. "Race you up there!" The door slammed behind them.

Rebecca scribbled a very quick note to her parents, then she and Anna also left. Running, Rebecca led the way to their agreed road, where they immediately saw a horse-drawn taxi approaching from the other direction.

"Good timing!" called out Rebecca as they ran across the street to hail it. The driver took one look at them and continued on his way. The same happened with the next one. Rebecca explained to Anna, who had no experience of these things, that this often happened. A lot of cabbies would be reluctant to pick them up without an adult with them, but eventually she was sure they would get one.

After a short while, a third taxi appeared. For a moment they thought this one too might just continue on its way. However, at the last moment the driver slowed down. When he had pulled up alongside them, Rebecca told the driver where to take them and agreed a price. Then he had second thoughts.

"You know, I'm not sure about this." He looked down on them from his lofty perch behind the carriage and horses. "I don't usually give rides to youngsters, you know. How do I know you can pay me, and you won't just scarper when we get there?"

"Because we give you our word!" was Rebecca's initial, forthright response, before realising she might need to do better than that. "And because I'll show you I've got the money." She showed the taxi driver the coins she had in her purse.

"All right," said the driver. "I can see you've got the money. But I still ain't got no guarantee you won't do a runner when we get there, have I? If you want to go up to Highgate then you'll have to give me the money now."

Rebecca's eyes narrowed. "But how do we know you won't just take our money and then not take us all the way? Tell you what, mister. I'll give you half now, and the rest when we get there, plus a little tip. How's that? Then we all get what we want."

Given the urgency, Anna would just have paid the man and got in, but Rebecca was right. They could not risk failing to get there.

"You drive a hard bargain, young lady. Go on then, give me half upfront and I'll take you."

Rebecca gave Anna a sly wink before reaching up to give a few coins to the driver. "Thank you, mister. We're in a hurry, so there's an extra tip in it for you if you get us there as fast you can!"

"Well done," whispered Anna once they were both inside the carriage. She watched the buildings start to slide past the window at increasing speed. "You said Highgate though. Faulkner's mansion is down the hill from there."

"Yeah, it is, but I don't know what that road's called. When he gets us to Highgate, I'll direct him the rest of the way." Rebecca gazed out of her window. "I just hope he earns his money and gets us there like the wind."

They both fell silent for a time, no doubt sharing similar worries about what they might find when they got there. Eventually Rebecca spoke, maintaining her gaze outside.

"Anna, why do you think Faulkner took Timmy?"

"I was wondering the same thing myself. I'm not sure…" Anna was certain it must be to do with her, but she could not share the reasons. It would lead inevitably to a conversation about the Struggle. She had made the most solemn promise she could give that she would never tell anyone about the Powers and the Struggle without the express permission of Mr Warwick or her uncle. These were the deepest secrets she could ever hold. And her uncle had gone to such great pains just recently to explain the importance of keeping her word. But she knew Rebecca would have a lot of questions. She braced herself.

"You said Faulkner had been chasing Gillespie, too. Did he say why? It seems like a very strange coincidence. Maybe there's some clue there about what he wants with Timmy."

"Gillespie said he thought Faulkner was trying to capture his brother, Kenny. He said Kenny had double-crossed him, and Faulkner was trying to track him down, using Billy."

"Well, Timmy and me haven't had anything to do with Faulkner. And why did Gillespie go to you for help, and not any of his Marylebone Gang friends? What made him think you could help him against Faulkner?"

A suspicious tone had crept into her friend's voice. She had now returned her gaze inside the cab to look at Anna. She was asking the questions Anna had hoped so much to avoid, but she should have known Rebecca was too sharp. Anna longed to be able to explain things to her, but she simply could not. Hopefully she would be allowed to one day, but that could not be today. Besides, it would make no difference to their plan anyway. They still needed to rescue Timmy, regardless. She thought hard about how far she could go, and chose her words very carefully.

"Well, I had no more idea than you did when Gillespie approached me. But Becca..." She stopped and took a deep breath. "You know how you sometimes mention that I seem to... to know more about certain things than other people? You've said that you trust me, even though you don't fully understand how I know those things. Well, it turns out that the trouble Gillespie had got himself into was related to those things."

Rebecca's eyes were suddenly alive. Like this was a topic she had been burning to ask about for a long time, but which had always been taboo.

"You have to tell me. What's all this about?"

"I really do want to explain to you, honestly I do. And hopefully one day soon I will be able to tell you everything. But my uncle, and other important people who I respect and trust completely, have sworn me to secrecy. Much as I'm dying to, I just can't betray that."

"But Anna," said Rebecca animatedly, "Timmy's life is at stake! You have to tell me what you know. You know you can trust me. I won't tell a soul. And when I say that, you know you can believe me."

"Yes, I do know that. I do trust you. It's not that. It's just that I can't break the promise I made. Imagine if I made the most solemn promise possible to you, not to share one of your secrets with anyone else. I would never, ever break that. This is the same."

Rebecca did not respond.

"So, it's me who needs to ask you to trust me," Anna continued. "I promise you, nothing I know about makes any difference to our plan to save Timmy. Look, there are some things going on that involve Faulkner, some very bad things, and my uncle and some others are trying to stop him. I would go to them to ask for help right now, but I don't know how to reach them. Believe me, I wish I did."

"Faulkner's connected with the Beast of Highgate, isn't he?" Rebecca pressed.

Anna hesitated. "Yes, he is."

"But I don't understand. What's any of this got to do with your uncle? And how have you got yourself messed up in it? Is it because of your uncle?"

"Yes. He's fighting against Faulkner and his gang, and he's trying to bring them down. But please don't ask me any more about this. This is getting into that promise that I can't break. You know me, Becca, I just can't do it."

Rebecca closed her eyes, thinking hard.

"You know Anna, I sometimes think I don't properly know you. Not really. But, I do trust your intentions. I know you're a good person. I've always known that."

Anna didn't have a response. She merely nodded.

"All right. Listen, I understand about your promise. But this involves my brother, who for all I know is probably in the greatest of danger. So, I'm going to keep on asking questions, and you answer them as much as you can. All right?"

"Yes, all right, I will try. Thank you for understanding."

"Right. Well, first off, do you have any more idea than me what we can do to rescue him now?"

"No, not really. From my last conversation with my uncle, I have reason to hope Faulkner may not be in his mansion at the moment, although I can't be sure. Our absolute best chance to rescue Timmy is to get there and to get him out before Faulkner arrives."

"Yeah, that much is clear. Do you know anything more about this mansion we're going to, anything that might help us rescue Timmy?"

"No. All I know is that it definitely belongs to Faulkner. Apart from that, I don't know any more than you do about that place, or how to get inside."

Rebecca paused, then changed tack slightly. "What about that horrible old man we saw in Highgate, and then again outside the mansion when we saw the Beast? He's definitely part of this, isn't he? Can you tell me anything about him? Is he going to be there, and will he do anything to hurt my brother, like he did to Watson and Green?"

"Yes, that man is involved, too. I've found out his name is Joseph Mortlock. He works for Faulkner, and he's another very bad man. Not that you probably needed telling that. He's another sworn enemy of my uncle's. I can't say any more about him than that. But, the same as Faulkner, Mortlock is not supposed to be in the mansion now either."

"How did your uncle get involved with these men, anyway? All right, all right, I know, you can't tell me!" Rebecca rolled her eyes, having obviously seen something in Anna's expression. "I reckon your uncle's one of them, what do they call them, detectives, or private investigators, or something. Is he working for the government? Like a secret agent? It's a real shame you can't reach him. I'm sure he wouldn't fob us off like the police would."

"You're right, he would certainly believe us, and his... his colleagues would, too. They would definitely help.

But the problem is, we don't have time to search for them."

"All this business has something to do with why you showed up at our house today looking a right state, hasn't it?"

Anna did not answer at first. Then she said, "Yes. It has. Oh, Becca, I'm so sorry I can't tell you any more. It's been awful..." Her emotions started to get the better of her again.

"It's all right." Rebecca's tone softened. "It's just I hate knowing there's things people aren't telling me."

"I know. I'm so sorry."

"It's all right. Of course, I've known for a long time there was things about you, things you knew, that I didn't know or understand. But you've never actually refused to tell me things before when I've asked you. That's not really... comfortable, I can't deny it. You know how I like to know everything that's going on!"

Anna smiled, despite the awkwardness.

"But I do trust you. And I do believe you'll do anything you can to help Timmy.

"Thank you, Becca. Yes, you can absolutely trust me. I will do whatever it takes to get him out of there."

"Right. So, let's go and get him."

Rebecca peered back out of the window, as the carriage rocked this way and that. The road was very busy. "It's taking ages, isn't it? This driver must not want his tip!" But they both knew he could go no faster in this traffic.

The pair fell silent for a time, watching the terrain between them and their destination slip steadily by. The passing of time weighed heavily on them both. Then Rebecca spoke again.

"About your trouble with Timmy. I'm certain Lizzy's behind it."

"Yes, I'm sure you're right. But what are you thinking?"

"Well, you know we see her around sometimes. Her parents are a bit friendly with my parents, so we bump into her from time to time. That's why I started asking her to get messages to you, to let you know when we were all meeting up. It seemed fine at first, and she didn't object. But after a while, I started to have my suspicions about her."

"Why? What happened?"

"Some of the things she said caught my attention. The odd snide remark about you, like those problems you had a few years back, and that she thought you were strange… you know, the kinds of things that ignorant folk, like the Maryleboners, say."

Anna looked down at her hands. She knew people talked about her that way, but it was never pleasant to be reminded of it.

"I stood up for you, obviously," her friend added straight away.

"Thank you, Becca."

"Of course! You know I always do that. But it seemed odd she would make a point of saying those things when they were nothing to do with the actual conversation we were having. And she always seemed to do it when Timmy was around."

"Did she?"

"Yeah. At first, I thought it might be because she was jealous somehow, you know, because we were friends with you, whose family she was proud of working for. But after a while I started to think there might be more to it."

"In what way?" A bad feeling was growing.

"You know I've known about how you and Timmy feel about each other for ages. Other people didn't seem to notice a thing of course, not being observant like me! Well, in the same way, I started to notice that Lizzy was taking a keen interest in Timmy, too."

The pieces were beginning to slide uncomfortably into place in Anna's head.

"She was always asking where he was, and she'd put on special airs and graces when he was around. It was like she was trying to impress him. And she was the only other one that seemed to pick up on the slight changes in Timmy when your name got mentioned. Like the way he'd suddenly look down at the floor, you know, like he does, and look back up all shy through that long fringe of his."

Rebecca did a quick impression of her brother. Anna laughed out loud, despite everything.

"And the way he would go red for no apparent reason when we talked about you. All tell-tale signs of his feelings, if you're looking for them. And I reckon Lizzy was looking, all right."

Anna swallowed. She had had no idea until now.

"So, I realised Lizzy held quite a candle for Timmy, and I swear she'd become right jealous of his feelings for you. And the surer she became that he liked you, the bitterer and nastier she would be about you in front of him."

"Really?"

"Yeah." Then Rebecca laughed. "You should've seen her face one time when, before I could get a word in, Timmy himself told her to shut up! Told her she didn't know what she was talking about, he did. She went so red I thought she was going to explode, and she stormed out the room!"

Anna grinned, a bit embarrassed. She felt a strange sensation in her stomach.

"In the end, it got so bad I decided I couldn't trust her no more. That's when I stopped asking her to give you messages from us. But it turns out you and Timmy were still using her as a messenger. And she started to twist the messages to turn you against each other."

"Yes," said Anna as the coach swayed, rounding another bend. She recalled her conversations with Lizzy. "When I asked her to set up a meeting with Timmy, at first she told me he didn't want to see me. Then later she said he did want to meet, but then he didn't show up. I can't tell you how crushing it was, waiting for him. I was so excited to see him. It's a bit embarrassing, but I even took a little cake, to celebrate our birthdays! But then he never came, even though I waited and waited. It was like the final confirmation. The final rejection. I was devastated."

"Except he never got that message! Oh, poor you. That must've been awful. It makes me so angry!" Rebecca looked quite fierce now.

"And that was the same day she told Gillespie where I'd be." Anna continued to recall the sequence of events. "When I asked him how he knew where to find me, he said Lizzy had told him."

"While she'd given Timmy a different message, to hide and look out for you and Gillespie. The devious cow!"

"I just can't believe she'd be so mean."

"Well, she was. Timmy said Lizzy had told him you were with Gillespie now, and that if he didn't believe her, he should go out and look with his own eyes. She told him where Gillespie would be waiting for you and the rough time. She told him to go and hide and wait, to see for himself. He said it was quite a while before you showed up."

It all made perfect sense, but Anna was shocked by the level of deceit. She wondered how she hadn't seen Timmy until right at the end, when he was running away.

"After Gillespie approached me," she said, "I was so worried about other Maryleboners out to ambush me, I made us walk a long way before I let him talk to me. I kept checking all around me to make sure we weren't being followed. I didn't see anyone at all."

"Timmy said Lizzy told him to hide himself away near a crossroads where you were going to meet Gillespie. He said he waited deep in some bushes, hidden. So, I suppose that's why you never saw him. Then he said you both walked off and disappeared. He said it was real foggy, and by the time he came out from where he was hiding, he couldn't find where you'd gone."

"Yes, it was very foggy. It was hard to see more than a few yards."

"Timmy must've been right desperate to talk, because he said he hurried off and waited around on a road somewhere near your house, on the way you would go home, so he could speak to you and confirm things for himself. Said he waited ages, he did. Then finally he saw you with Gillespie again. That's when you hugged him and all the rest of it."

Anna was about to protest but Rebecca cut in, "Yes, I know it didn't mean anything, I know that now, but I'm just saying those are the only times he saw you. So that's probably why you never spotted him."

"Yes." Anna felt desperate again.

"Lizzy's going to pay for this mind, I'll see to it that she does. But we've got much bigger problems to sort out first. Look Anna, we're almost there!"

Anna looked out again and saw that the surroundings were much greener now. They were close to Highgate. She hoped against hope that Faulkner had not yet returned. If he had… She swallowed hard.

Rebecca noticed. "You think we're going to see the Beast again today, don't you?" she said.

"Oh, I hope not. But yes, to be completely honest, I really think we might. We have to be so careful, Becca. We have to be ready for anything."

The carriage slowed. The driver opened a little door in the roof above them. "All right, we're in Highgate. Where do you want to get out?"

"Down that hill, please. We want to stop right down there, where that road turns off towards them big houses." Rebecca indicated as best she could through the little door.

"Wait a minute, that's not Highgate! That's further than we agreed!"

"Well, I did say I'd give you a tip!" replied Rebecca.

She sat back inside the cab, grumbling to herself as the driver closed the door again. "Taxi drivers! It's only another few hundred yards. What does it matter?"

Soon the cab was drawing to a halt again, just before the turning. "All right, we're 'ere," the taxi driver called down through the door again.

Rebecca reached through the opening and paid the balance owed, plus what looked like a generous tip.

"Why that's mighty kind of you, madam!" said the driver, his attitude transformed. He pulled a lever to open the carriage door at once. As the girls clambered out, he called down, "I shall be most happy to take you anywhere you'd like to go in the future. A good day to you!"

As he pulled away, Anna and Rebecca both laughed. "I told him I'd give him a tip! Perhaps he'll be a bit more willing next time."

Their smiles didn't last. There was no sign of the boys. "I do hope they won't be long," said Rebecca. They moved to conceal themselves behind the bushes and undergrowth, some yards from the road.

Time passed with nothing but the sound of birds singing to disturb the silence. As Anna looked around her, bittersweet memories filtered through her mind. Memories of the terrifying scenes outside the old mansion. But she also recalled the exhilaration of the time she had spent with Timmy that day, and the closeness that had grown between them. But even those happy memories were now tainted by a new fear. Was he all right? Would they get in there in time to save him?

Anna was not looking forward to going back to that house again, but waiting here was even worse. There were no signs of movement from any direction. No-one entered or left by the road leading to the mansion. Time passed, and Rebecca apparently shared her feeling.

"Oh, where are they? We may not have any time to lose, and they're dawdling around. If I find they didn't come here straight away, as fast as they could, there will be hell to pay!" The two girls looked at each other, immediately regretting that choice of words.

After what felt like forever, but in reality had probably been no more than fifteen minutes, they heard the sound of hooves on the road coming down the hill.

"Bet it's not them. Bet it's just another carriage," muttered Rebecca.

"Wait, it's slowing down," said Anna.

Sure enough, as the sound grew louder, the trot of the horses was definitely slowing. Finally, a black Hansom cab came into view and stopped right on the corner. It was them. Inside the taxi, Johnny seemed to be arguing with the driver through the door in the ceiling, before handing over some coins. The driver finally let them out, then pulled off, his cursing audible even from where Anna sat.

"Obviously not as good a tipper as me!" whispered Rebecca, relieved.

"I paid you what we agreed!" shouted Johnny after the taxi. He shook his fist as he watched the disgruntled driver disappear into the distance.

"Shh!" hissed Rebecca at him, emerging from the bushes. "Do you want Faulkner, the Beast and who knows what else to know we're here?"

The new arrivals immediately hushed up. Their relief at seeing their leader was short-lived after they had followed her back into the undergrowth, and she started berating them in a whispering voice.

"Where've you been? Didn't I tell you to get up here as soon as you could? We've been waiting here for... forever. What were you doing?"

"Becca, we were trying to get a cab," Johnny whispered back. "You know how difficult it is for us kids to get a taxi!"

"Well we managed it all right, didn't we, Anna?" She seemed to have conveniently forgotten the two cabs that had refused them before they got lucky. Anna didn't respond, looking at the ground instead. Rebecca finally calmed down and refocused on the mission ahead.

"Anyway, now that you're finally here, there's not another moment to lose." The pitch of her whispering dropped further, and her speaking grew more urgent. "I don't want to dally a moment longer than we need to when we get to the house. It's too dangerous there. So let's agree the basic plan now."

The others agreed.

"We don't know exactly what's lying ahead of us now. We need to be so careful – more careful than we've ever been. No-one's to take any chances they don't need to. I reckon we got real lucky last time we were here. We've got to use our heads. And most of all, we've got to look out for each other. If anyone gets in trouble, the rest helps them. No-one, but no-one, gets left behind. Is that clear?"

"Yes," replied the friends in unison.

"Right, so we need to get into that tower. Johnny, Charlie, did they say anything else about it?"

"No, nothing," said Johnny.

"All right. The tower was on the left-hand end of the building as we looked at it from the trees, wasn't it?"

"Yes, that's right," said Anna, "on the left-hand end, on the side of the building. We could only see the top of it from where we were last time."

"Right," continued Rebecca. "Now, we never even made it as far as the house last time before we came across a whole load of trouble. This time we've got to get inside there."

She paused, as though reflecting on her plan before continuing.

"We don't know where we can enter, or who's inside waiting for us when we do. But I still reckon our best bet is to get in through a ground floor window, somewhere round the tower side of the building, or else round the back. Anyone have any better ideas?"

No-one did.

"All right then. From what I remember, the undergrowth we were hiding in beneath the trees went right round the mansion. This time I reckon we go through that undergrowth all the way round to the left-hand side of the building, find the position that's hardest to see from the house, then approach from there."

Again, the others all murmured their consent.

"Now, whatever danger we may be walking into, it's no worse than what Timmy's in right now. We're just going to have to tread real careful and try to outsmart whoever we come across."

None of the others spoke. The tension was palpable once again. The memories of their last visit were still vivid. As they prepared to move, it was Charlie who finally raised the question that was at the forefront of everyone's mind.

"Becca, are you expecting... I mean, well... do you reckon we're going to see that beast again?"

His voice remained admirably steady, but his face lacked colour. For the first time since she started, Rebecca hesitated, thinking through carefully what she was going to say next.

"I'm not going to lie. I can't say for sure that we won't. And I remember that thing as clear as day. I'll admit that I've had more than one nightmare about it since. And that awful sound it made... it chilled me to the bone, it did. But we've got to remember that Timmy's probably in there right now, already facing up to whatever's there. If ever he needed our help, he needs it now."

Everyone nodded grimly.

"So, if we have to face the Beast again then we have to face it. And we all stand together, right?"

Rebecca looked each of them in the eye as she repeated the question.

Everyone agreed. Anna did not doubt the boys' resolve for a second. She was relieved it had been Rebecca answering the questions about the Beast, not her. There would be no more questions now.

Rebecca continued, in a softer tone, "I also want to say thank you, to both of you. I know you would come here to help your friend whether he was my little brother or not, but he is my brother, and it means the world to me that you're here. And I know it will to him, and all. Thank you."

Rebecca was visibly wrestling with her emotions, but she mastered them. Raising her whispered voice one last time, she said, "So, on we go!"

The group broke their cover. With Rebecca at their head setting a fast pace, the brave friends hurried stealthily along the edges of the tree-lined road, to whatever fate lay ahead of them.

14
The Break-In

The mood was nothing like the last time they had been on this road. That time there had still been some light-hearted banter and spirit of adventure, at least until they got nearer the ominous mansion gates. No such chatter this time, nor looking in awe at the size and grandeur of the houses they passed. No-one was looking forward to this mission. No-one was immune to the growing fear. But no-one would turn back.

Before long they reached the bend in the road, beyond which they knew they would see the gates. Rebecca gestured for them to stop. They crouched down and concealed themselves completely in the undergrowth at the side of the road. Rebecca moved forward to the edge of the bend to check the lie of the land. She quickly returned. No-one was there as far as she could see. There was a moment of quiet, and it was then that Anna noticed it again – the sheer and utter silence of this place. Even at the junction with the main road where they had waited, they could at least hear the sound of birdsong. Here there was absolutely no sound of any kind, save the heavy breathing of the friends.

It was cold now, not at all like that hot, humid summer's day when they were last here. In fact, it seemed colder here than when they were waiting at the junction. The cold began to penetrate the thick coat Anna had borrowed from Rebecca. It sent a shiver through her. Her breath was starting to freeze. The weak winter sun, which had provided a little warmth earlier, had now disappeared entirely behind dark, silver-grey clouds. Anna was well used to seeing grey skies over London, but somehow it looked different here. More threatening. And so did the dark, empty trees. They looked ominous. Almost evil.

'It's this place,' she thought, 'it plays tricks on your mind. Or maybe they're not tricks...' She fought hard to control her fear.

It was clear the others felt it too, just as they had the last time they were here. Time was of the essence, but all four of them, even Rebecca, were hesitating in the cold undergrowth. This was an evil place, no question about it.

Anna wondered again if those 'winds of the influence of the Energies', might be at play right now, in this very spot, driving them. But if so, which Energy was encouraging them in which direction? Was the Elemental Energy pushing against them, trying to turn them away from this place? Was the Opposing Energy playing on her aura right now, pulling her forwards into a trap laid by Faulkner? It could be. There was no way to know, and no point in trying to guess. For her, there was no choice anyway. Regardless, her course of action would still be the same. She was going in to rescue Timmy.

Anna rose to her feet, ready to galvanise the group again as she had done in the summer. This time, though, the others rose as one at the same moment, a renewed look of determination on all their faces. Each had probably just gone through their own fears and concerns. Each had come to the same conclusion. This was not about what they wanted to do, but about what they had to do. And they had better get on with it.

"Right, in we go then," said Rebecca. Her words were positive, but her face was as serious as Anna could remember. "Straight through the gates, into the bushes straight ahead and then turn left straight away. No talking unless it's to alert us that you've seen something suspicious or there's some kind of trouble. All right?"

Whether all right or not, they all nodded grimly and set off. They crouched and moved forward in single file along the edge of the road. Anna was at Rebecca's shoulder as they rounded the bend. There were the gates. They were every bit as large and imposing as she remembered. Tiny snowflakes had started to fall all around the carved statues of hideous winged beasts that topped each pillar. They had looked frightening the last time, but now they brought something altogether scarier to mind. Something very specific.

The feelings of trepidation seemed ten times worse now, pushing against them almost like a physical force, opposing their entry. Rebecca slowed down a little, but she pushed on through the gates. Adjusting her focus, Anna saw the bobbing auras of her friends. She felt a burst of warm comfort inside to see that each of them was blue and vivid.

They reached the point where the driveway swept to the right and out of sight behind the trees. Straight ahead, down a slope with tall trees, and then across a wider stretch of the driveway, stood their ultimate destination – the mansion. They followed Rebecca and plunged straight ahead, into the wild greenery beneath the trees. They did not stop, but immediately headed left and started their journey round to the side of the huge house.

The going was tough to start with. The undergrowth was thick, and above them the branches hung low, forcing them to duck continually. They forged on as fast as they could. Although little snow had yet penetrated the trees, looking to her right, Anna saw that the snowfall was thickening fast in the open air. Beyond the falling flakes, there was the sinister old house, lying in the silence of the hollow below.

Her eyes immediately followed the line of its many-chimneyed roof to the left-hand end, to the imposing four-sided tower. A single window was visible to them, looking out over the driveway towards the main gates. Anna wondered if Timmy was in there, hoping desperately that someone was on their way to save him.

'Hold on, we're coming!' she thought. But inside the tower was only darkness.

Her thoughts turned to the more practical matter of how to get in. She could not yet see the side of the building, so she had no idea as to the window situation, but the tower itself looked truly intimidating. The window she could see must have been at least 50 feet above the ground, probably more.

They ploughed on. Anna lost track of the number of scratches from brambles she received, but they kept up a good pace. She monitored their progress round the massive structure below. They rounded its corner, and finally they glimpsed its side for the first time. That side was lined with low bushes, separated from the house by a path that went all the way round the building. Beyond the path was a row of ground floor windows. Before long, they reached a point where they could look at the wall, square-on.

"All right, stop here," hissed Rebecca. Her voice was soon enveloped by the utter silence that surrounded them. They had seen no movement of any kind, human or otherwise, from the moment they arrived.

"I hate this place," whispered Johnny, pulling brambles out of his coat. "There's something wrong here. It's evil!"

No-one could argue. As one, they followed Rebecca's gaze through the trees and thick falling snowflakes, towards their target. Even though the ground floor was significantly lower than their vantage point, the tower still rose well above them. There was a window on this face of it too, but any faint hopes they might have had of somehow scaling the outside wall of the house were dashed immediately. There were no low roofs or anything else that they could try to climb up. As Rebecca had suggested, the best option appeared to be one of the ground floor windows.

"We could try and go further round, to see if there're any better entry points round the back, but I don't reckon we'd be able to tell from this distance anyway," said Rebecca.

"I think the stables must be round there," said Anna, pointing towards the rear of the building. "The carriage came back from this side of the building last time."

"Yeah, you're right," said Rebecca. "If we can't find a way in on this side, we'll try there next. But if there's stables down there then there's also more likely to be people. Let's try here first." Everyone agreed.

"Right, well let's get on with it then," said Johnny suddenly preparing to run for it.

"Stop!" hissed Rebecca urgently. "We're not all just going to run down there and try to smash our way in! I have a plan."

Johnny slumped back down again. "I'm sorry, Becca. I just want to get on with it now. I can't stand this place no more."

Rebecca's voice softened. "I know. But remember what we saw down there last time. One false move and we could all be done for. We've got to be careful."

"Yeah, all right, I'm sorry. So what's the plan, then?"

"One of us makes a run down to those bushes outside the building there, at the right-hand end. We check nobody's seen them, then they check the windows one-by-one for any left unlocked. If none on this wall are open, we try the back next. I just reckon if one person goes, there's less chance of them getting spotted."

"I'll do it", said an unexpected voice. It wasn't Johnny as Anna would have anticipated, but Charlie.

"Are you sure?" asked Rebecca, betraying a little surprise of her own.

"Yes. Well, no, not really. But, well, I made such a mess of things before. I feel real bad that I couldn't stop those men from snatching Timmy. I want to get down there and help get him back if I can. I won't mess it up this time, I promise I won't."

Rebecca smiled. "I know you won't, Charlie. That's very brave. Yes, all right, you go. I know you're up to it. It wasn't your fault at all that they took Timmy, and I know you'll be careful."

Charlie nodded.

"Right, so I suggest you start at that end," she pointed to the right-hand end of the wall facing them, "and at each window, you'll need to check there's no-one inside. I don't reckon there's any completely safe way to do that, you just can't see inside from any distance away, so you're going to have to get up close. Get right under the window, then bob your head above the sill and then straight down again." Rebecca demonstrated. "Just enough to get a picture of what's in the room, and that's all. With any luck, even if there's anyone in there, you'll be so quick they won't notice. If there's no-one in there, then you can reach back up and try and see if that window's unlocked."

Charlie asked the question on everyone's mind. "What if someone's looking straight at the window when I bob my head up?"

"Then you duck down as fast as you can, below the window where they can't see you anymore, then move fast to one side in case they open the window and try to reach out. Then look up here to me, and I'll signal what to do next. If I beckon you up here like this, then you run for all you're worth. If someone comes after you and you can't escape, we'll all go in. We'll all stand or fall together."

"All right," said Charlie. He looked nervous but determined. Anna, who had been planning to volunteer herself, was filled with new-found admiration for their friend.

"So, you keep doing that, going down the side of the building. If you do see someone in a room and it has more than one window, then obviously give the other windows in that room a miss. Let's see, what else…" Rebecca paused for a moment. "We'll be watching your progress from here and let you know if we see anything. We should agree on some signals."

Rebecca suggested a series of hand signals that they should both use in different situations. Charlie practiced to make sure he had got them.

"Right then. I think we're ready. No more time to waste. You need to go."

"Right." Charlie nodded, grimly.

He gulped, took a deep breath and braced himself. Anna gave him a small hug of encouragement, and Johnny patted him on the back. Then Rebecca added, "Charlie, thank you. It takes a lot of guts, what you're about to do. Timmy will really appreciate it. And so do I."

She smiled at him encouragingly, and with respect. Charlie puffed out his broad chest.

"Right, bye everyone. See you in a bit!"

He made his way as quietly as he could down the slope. The trees were denser and the undergrowth thicker on this side of the house, and it took him a little time to reach the bottom. All the while, Anna watched the house below, the driveway and the forest all around them. There was no sign of movement. At the edge of the trees, Charlie gave one quick look back up the hill to receive the all clear signal from Rebecca, then he burst forward across the driveway, which was now completely covered by a thin layer of snow.

Anna held her breath as their friend pounded for all he was worth through the falling flakes. From this distance at least, his tracks were not visible. Charlie wasn't the fastest runner, and her eyes moved anxiously back and forth from him to the house, hoping desperately that no-one would appear at the windows. There was no sign of anyone. He reached the snowy bushes at the far side of the driveway and dived for cover. There was an audible sigh of relief from the companions.

Charlie remained concealed in the low bushes for some time. Then he re-emerged at the far side of the shrubbery and crouched down low with his back to the wall of the house, near the corner. He brushed the snow from the bushes off his jacket and looked back up the hill in their direction. Rebecca was giving him a thumbs up sign to let him know the coast was clear, but with the falling snow it seemed he could no longer find her. Rebecca gesticulated more and more animatedly, risking standing up to do it. He made her out and gave the same signal back.

"Thank goodness!" breathed Rebecca, concealing herself again.

Charlie started the next phase. He crawled to the first window, stopped and looked in their general direction again. Once again, Rebecca had to stand up so that Charlie could see her. Slowly he turned to face the wall. He reached up to take hold of the edge of the windowsill. The group hardly dared breathe. Anna watched with unblinking eyes as Charlie prepared for his first check.

He bobbed up – and he was back down again almost before he was above the sill. Sitting back down and breathing heavily, he looked up in their direction and shrugged, as if to say it had been too quick for him to actually see anything. They trained their eyes on the window for any signs of movement. There were none. Receiving Rebecca's all clear, Charlie braced himself, bobbed again, this time getting high enough for long enough to get a proper glimpse of the room, then dropped straight back down. With his back to the wall again and still panting heavily, he gave the thumbs up sign. There was another huge sigh of relief.

"He's so brave!" whispered Anna.

"Yeah, he really is," Rebecca agreed.

Charlie reached up again and began fumbling around the edge of the window frame for somewhere to get a grip. Finding one, he tried to open it. He tried for a good twenty seconds, but no luck. He sat back down and gave the thumbs down gesture in their direction.

"Oh my, I don't think I can take a whole wall of this!" Rebecca whispered.

Anna realised it had been some time since she had breathed properly herself. Charlie repeated his routine on the second and third windows, each with the same outcomes – no people, but no way in. By the time he reached the fourth window he had sped up. He bobbed up – and then came straight down again with much greater urgency. He immediately made a crossed arm sign which they had agreed would mean someone was there.

"Oh no!" hissed Johnny.

He pressed himself tightly against the wall and shuffled several feet away to his right. They all stared at the vacant window, transfixed. Then a man's face appeared!

Rebecca immediately made the crossed-arm signal back to Charlie and gestured for him to stay where he was, then ducked back behind the undergrowth. He nodded stiffly and pressed himself even more tightly against the wall. They all held their breath. The watcher didn't appear to be acting with any urgency. He seemed neither to be looking around for Charlie, nor looking in their direction. His gaze was slow and measured, as though he was looking at the falling snow. He left the window again.

"I wonder if he's going to come out to look for Charlie?" whispered Johnny.

"I don't think so. I really don't think he saw him," Rebecca replied.

"I hope you're right!" said Johnny.

"I agree, Becca," Anna whispered. "He didn't look like he was searching for anyone."

Rebecca gestured for Charlie to wait. Charlie gave a thumbs up and remained as he was, frozen to the spot. They waited over a minute without any further sightings. Eventually Rebecca gestured to Charlie to move on, past not one but several windows, to put some distance between him and that room.

Charlie crawled as low as he could beneath the next two windows before stopping under the next one. He was approaching the left-hand end of the building. On receiving the all clear, he repeated his routine on that window and the next. There were no people and the windows were locked. Then it was the final window on that wall.

"Looks like we might be going round the back," said Rebecca, sounding slightly desperate.

Charlie checked. There was no-one in the room. He tried the window. He fumbled with the edge of it for a few moments, found a grip and tried to force it. Nothing happened. He gave it another heave... and it budged a little! He tried again, and managed to open it some more.

"Yes!" whispered Anna and Rebecca together, as Johnny punched the air.

Charlie returned the window to its closed position, crouched below the window and blew air from his cheeks. Then with a big smile, gave a double thumbs up signal.

The trio were elated. For a moment. Then they snapped sharply back to reality as they considered the next part of the plan. Rebecca signalled to Charlie to remain exactly where he was. Then she hissed instructions to Anna and Johnny.

"Right, we head down the bank together to the edge of the trees, as far as we can stay hidden. Then, one-by-one we run over to where Charlie is. When you get there, lie flat against the wall so you can't be seen from the windows."

They made their way down to the edge of the trees. Johnny was first to go. He sprinted like the wind towards Charlie and made it safely to the house. Anna saw no movement in the windows. Then it was her turn.

'Right, here I go!' she thought. She was very nervous as she set off. She was looking at the windows rather than where she was running, and almost lost her footing straight away as she slid on the snow on the lower part of the bank. However, she made it to the driveway, then pelted across it for all she was worth through the falling snow. It wasn't too deep yet, and she made it safely. Finally, Rebecca hared across the driveway herself and they were all together again.

"Well done, Charlie," she whispered, "that was great! Really well done."

She checked the end-room was still empty, then slowly opened the window. She wasted no time clambering inside, and beckoned to Charlie to follow. Anna was next. Without hesitating, she rose, got first one leg through the window, then her upper body, then the other leg. She was in.

She found herself in some kind of small drawing room. There were various pieces of ornate furniture dotted about the room, including a long, upholstered sofa just in front of them, with its back to the window. Anna ducked straight behind it, joining Rebecca and Charlie. Johnny closed the window behind him and completed the group.

"You three stay here out of sight, and I'll slip out and try to find the way," whispered Rebecca. She looked extremely nervous.

"I think we should stay together" said Anna. She didn't want Rebecca taking all the risk, and she didn't like the idea of getting split up.

"No, it's best if you three stay here. The more of us that go creeping around in there, the more likely we are to get spotted. Let me find the way, then I'll get you and we can all go together."

"What if you get caught? How will we know?" asked Anna. "There aren't many of us. I think we should stay together. That way we can help each other if we run into trouble. Remember, we stand or fall together."

"That's right!" said Charlie, as Johnny nodded.

Rebecca smiled. "All right. Thank you. Let's get going then."

She led the way, tiptoeing to the door. She checked no-one was on the other side, then slipped through. Anna followed, also on tiptoe. There were two corridors, one off to her right, leading towards the front of the mansion, the other straight ahead, across the back of the building. Both were lined with doors. Rebecca took the right-hand corridor.

The foursome moved as quietly as they could, Charlie shutting the door behind them. Rather than try the nearby doors, Rebecca headed straight towards the middle part of the corridor, directly under the tower. Looking ahead, Anna spotted that one door was open. They drew close to it, then Rebecca gestured to the rest of them to stay where they were while she checked that room.

Anna braced herself as she watched Rebecca reach the open door. The older girl did a sideways bobbing motion, then ducked back suddenly. Rather than retreat though, she hesitated. She repeated the motion, taking a bit longer to take in the view this time. Then she tiptoed back to the group, smiling.

"I think that's the way to the tower!" she whispered, quietly but excitedly. "There's a doorway in the corner. Through it I could see the bottom of a spiral staircase going upwards!"

Anna's heart skipped a beat. The companions grinned excitedly at each other.

"But there's a slight problem. There's two men asleep in there! They must be guards. I think one of them might be the man we saw at the window earlier. There's a bottle on the table. Looks like they've been drinking, so that's probably why they've nodded off."

"Are they deep asleep?" asked Johnny.

"Looks like it. I could hear one of them snoring! Come on, let's try and slip past them and see if we can find Timmy in that tower. Not a sound now!"

Nervously, they all agreed. They retraced Rebecca's steps to the room. Even before they reached it, Anna heard the sound of loud snoring. It would have made her laugh under different circumstances. But it was a good sign.

Rebecca checked the room again. She gave the group the thumbs up. Anna took a deep breath and moved forwards.

They crept into the room and headed immediately for the open door leading to the stone staircase. Anna, however, kept her eyes firmly fixed on the two men sleeping in the middle of the room. One was sat back in an easy chair with his boots on the table in front of him. The other was laid out on a sofa. Both were sound asleep and snoring in unison. There was a large flagon in the middle of the table and a tankard near each of the men.

The man on the sofa might have been the man who had looked out of the window earlier. She had never seen the one in the chair before. A long scar marked this man's face, but unlike McCain's scar, this one ran down the left-hand side of his cheek. As fast and quietly as they could, the friends reached the staircase and headed silently upwards.

Round and round and up and up they went. They soon passed a closed door which presumably led to the second storey of the building. On and on they continued for what seemed an eternity. Finally, they came to a closed wooden door with no windows. This blocked the end of the stairway. Anna's heart skipped a beat again. Was Timmy on the other side of that door?

Ever so slowly, Rebecca reached out and turned the handle. She gave the door a gentle shove. It did not move. She pushed it again, harder, but still no movement. She put her mouth to the door and whispered quietly, "Timmy? Timmy, are you in there?"

Anna put her ear to the door, next to Rebecca. There was no sound. Rebecca tried again, a little louder.

"Timmy, are you there? It's Rebecca."

There was the sound of shuffling coming towards the door, then they heard a whispered reply.

"Becca, is that you?" It was Timmy!

Anna and Rebecca hugged each other briefly whilst the others grinned. Anna was momentarily euphoric. They had actually found him.

"Yeah, it's me." Rebecca replied. "We've come to get you. Are you all right?"

"Well, I've got a big bump on my head, and I'm locked up in here, but apart from that, yeah, never better!"

Anna felt the familiar butterflies return to her stomach. It was so long since she had heard that voice.

"I'm so glad you're here. I thought I was in real trouble," he continued.

"Is there anybody in there with you?" Rebecca asked.

"No, just me."

"This door's locked. Do you have any idea where the key might be?"

"One of the men who locked me in here had it. I don't know where they've gone now."

"I think they're downstairs. They've been drinking and fallen asleep. We'll try and find the keys. Hang on. We'll be right back."

"Don't worry, I'm not going anywhere!" Timmy whispered back.

Rebecca gestured to Johnny and Charlie to stay where they were, then she and Anna hastened back down the steps.

As they descended, Rebecca whispered, "Now we've found Timmy and we know he's here, I feel like we should go and find the police."

"I know what you mean," replied Anna, "but I also have a bad feeling that Faulkner's going to come back. Then it might be too late. I really don't think we can risk it."

"No, you're right. Let's see if we can get him out ourselves first. We'll have to search for the key around where those men are."

They reached the ground floor, and once again the reassuring sound of snoring reached their ears. This time Anna led the way. She bobbed her head to check the room. The two men were exactly as they had left them.

"There are no keys on the table," Anna whispered. "You check the man on the sofa. I'll take the one on the chair."

Rebecca nodded. They both tiptoed as softly as they had ever done in their lives to the respective sleeping men. Anna approached the scar-faced man as close as she dared from the side, then peered at his trouser pocket. She could see nothing. She passed behind the chair and looked at the pocket on the other side. There it was! The end of a large key, thrust in loosely, attached to a large metal ring which hung down by the side. Anna gesticulated silently but frantically to Rebecca. She gave a thumbs up sign. Then it was down to Anna.

She braced herself. The sound of her pounding heart hammered in her ears. She moved right behind the chair in case the man woke. Placing one hand gently on the chair back for balance, she crouched down and leaned round the side of the chair, ever so slowly. She reached out for the large ring. Her hand was trembling badly. She touched the key ring and tried to get a grip. Her fingertips slipped off it.

She remained behind the chair, but leaned further round it. Stretching out her hand as far as she could, this time she managed to get a grip on it. Now for the most dangerous part. Very slowly, she began to pull the key from the trouser pocket. It moved partially out, then it seemed to get caught on the material inside. With some exceptionally delicate manoeuvring, it came free and continued to move.

Just then, the man stopped snoring and reached up to rub his nose. Anna pulled her hand away instantly. She froze, not daring to move. Her eyes remained fixed on the side of the man's face. His eyes remained closed. He settled down, and gradually his breathing grew deeper and steadier again. Anna looked up at Rebecca, who was also frozen to the spot. She silently gestured for her friend to move to the stair doorway, just in case the man woke up.

She tried again for the key. She got another grip on the ring. She pulled again. This time the key, which was already halfway out, came clear of the pocket. She remained stock still, just to make sure the man did not rouse. She looked across at the other man on the sofa. He was still fast asleep. She gave Rebecca, peeping round the doorpost, a look of triumph. Then she moved carefully away from the man and silently rejoined her friend.

"Well done, Anna, well done!" Rebecca whispered under her breath once they were safely ascending the staircase again. "I thought my heart was going to stop when he rubbed his nose!"

"You thought yours was? I'm not sure mine's started again yet!" Anna's hands were still trembling.

The girls scampered back up as quietly as they could, Anna in the lead. As she approached Johnny and Charlie, she silently held the key aloft. The two boys punched the air in soundless celebration. Then she looked at the door, and she hesitated. She wanted nothing more than to see Timmy again, but she was also deeply worried about how he might react, given everything he thought she had done. She handed the key to Rebecca.

"Right, let's get him, and then let's get out of here," whispered Rebecca, putting the key in the lock and turning it. "Timmy, we're coming!"

She opened the door with a shove. And there was Timmy. He had what looked like a painfully large lump in the middle of his forehead, visible even through his long fringe, but other than that he seemed unharmed. Rebecca dashed forward and gave him an almighty hug. He greeted Johnny and Charlie with a look of gleeful relief on his face. Then his eyes fell on Anna. He did a double-take, as if disbelieving what he was seeing.

"What's she doing here?" he asked, turning to Rebecca. She had clearly forgotten about this situation in her eagerness to get her brother out. She rapidly tried to make up for lost time.

"Timmy, I've spoken to Anna. There's been a terrible misunderstanding. What you saw was all set up by Lizzy. It wasn't how it looked at all."

"But I saw it with my own eyes, sis," replied Timmy, whispering. He was looking back at Anna with cold suspicion. She had never seen a look like that on his face before. She felt desperate again.

"Timmy, please believe me! There was never anything going on with Gillespie. Nothing at all!" She was dimly aware of Johnny and Charlie looking at them, completely nonplussed.

263

Rebecca interjected, her sense of urgency overriding all else. "Look, there is a whole lot you two need to talk about, but that'll have to wait. Timmy, please just trust me for the time being. Things were not how you thought they were. But right now, we've got to get out of here before we get caught."

Timmy did not argue. While they had been talking, Charlie had moved over to the window that faced the front of the house. Suddenly he hissed, "Oh no! Look, someone's coming!"

The others rushed to his side. The snow was falling heavily and the sky was darkening with nightfall. They followed the line of Charlie's pointing finger to the left, to where the driveway emerged from behind the trees on the bank. Then Anna saw it. A carriage, travelling at great speed. It careered round the bend, sending up a plume of snow behind it. Anna's heart started to hammer violently again.

Standing up and whipping the horses for all they were worth was a menacing, almost skeletal, black-cloaked figure, with long grey hair billowing behind him.

"Who is it?" whispered Rebecca desperately.

Anna thought she could even make out a hideous snarl on the driver's face as the carriage sped towards the house. It was a face that dripped pure murder.

Anna whispered, "It's Mortlock."

15
Revelations

Anna took off instantly after her friends, who were already heading through the door. Doing their best not to wake the guards below, the five companions hurried down the spiral of stairs. It seemed to never end. As they finally reached the room at the bottom, they heard the sound of running footsteps.

"Quick!" hissed Rebecca. It was too late. They were halfway across the room when the door was flung open. The old man stood in the doorway, flanked by two younger henchmen. Anna had seen Mortlock in the distance, but the sight of him up close, with his hideous face and gnarled, skeletal fingers gripping his raised, skull-tipped cane, still made her blood run cold. Her eye was drawn to his right hand. There was the loathsome black-jewelled ring, forged by a Gorgal of ancient times. The noise had finally roused the scar-faced man from his slumber. He quickly shook his comrade awake. They both looked dumbstruck at the scene into which they had awoken.

The young companions froze at the sight of the old man. Anna was at the back. As always, she contracted and disguised her aura. She made no move yet, but was thinking fast. They could rush their adversaries and try to get away. But the chances of them all escaping five grown men without anyone getting captured or hurt were extremely slim. All were rough-looking, and at least one was very strong and experienced in the Powers. They would need to find another way.

Mortlock looked at the group of intruders. His gaze picked out Anna, and a different look entered his eyes.

"So, what do we have here? Adcock, Bryant, if you'd slept any longer, our guests here might have left without saying goodbye!"

His mock-jovial expression cracked to reveal a furious one. "Well? Why are you just standing there? Get them!"

The pair sprang into life, followed by the two men who had been standing behind Mortlock. At the same moment Anna yelled to her friends, "Quick, back up the stairs!"

The group ran past Anna just in time for her to slam the staircase door into the first pursuer, buying them a few seconds. They sprinted upwards for all they were worth. Johnny, Timmy and Rebecca made rapid progress, but Charlie was slower. Anna, bringing up the rear, heard the first of the pursuers, the scar-faced man, closing on her with every step.

Suddenly, Charlie stopped and moved aside. Anna's momentum took her past him. Facing down the stairs, he shoved hard with the sole of his boot into the approaching attacker's chest. The man stopped and stumbled backwards. He recovered instantly, reached up and grabbed Charlie's ankle as he tried to escape. The large boy fell to his knees.

Quick as a flash, Anna darted back down and took a swing at the scar-faced man's brown-smeared aura. She made full contact. The man doubled up with pain, released his grip on Charlie's leg and fell backwards, towards the next pursuer. Charlie gave scar-face an extra shove with his foot, just as Anna struck the disfigured aura of the second pursuer with a downward blow. Both men tumbled helplessly backwards into those who followed.

"Quick Charlie!" Anna yelled. This time Charlie moved with renewed determination and purpose. The sound of the next chasing men grew louder, but they both made it to the top room in time. Johnny slammed the door behind them and slid the bolt across before the first of the pursuers crashed against it. He used the key he had taken from the outside of the lock to fully secure the door. Anna tried to catch her breath. Rebecca was already taking charge.

"The lock and the bolt should hold them out for a while, but let's take no chances," she said. "Timmy, bring that chair over."

Even as she was speaking, the men outside started wrestling with the handle and barging the door with their shoulders. Timmy shoved the top of the chair-back under the handle and wedged the chair firmly beneath it.

"Right," said Rebecca in a whisper that would not carry to their pursuers, "that should do it. Now let's look for another way out of here."

The main window opened onto a sheer drop at the end of the house, fifty feet or more to the ground. Anna was already checking the smaller window, from which they had spied Mortlock. It was less than ten feet down from this one to a short, sloping roof which might possibly lead to some means of escape. There were two bars in front of the window. On closer inspection she found them to be solid, thick and embedded deeply into the wall at top and bottom. As the hammering on the door echoed around the little room, she gave the bars a tug with all her strength. There was no way they were going to budge. The window itself was not large, and the gaps between the bars and the wall were too narrow for anyone to squeeze through. There were no other windows or doors. Whoever had made a jail cell out of this room had done their job well.

The pounding on the other side of the door suddenly ceased. They all stood stock still as the icy voice of Mortlock filtered through the door.

"You will no doubt have realised by now that there is no way out of that room, except through this door. You are trapped, so you might as well give yourselves up and accept the inevitable. I may just go easier on you if you do. But woe betide you if you do not!"

Anna gestured to the others not to say a word. The icy voice spoke again.

"So, you choose to defy me? That is something that you will come to regret. But so be it." His voice grew louder and more menacing. "Adcock, Bryant – burn them out!"

Anna and her friends exchanged alarmed glances. A muffled conversation from behind the door indicated that Mortlock and two of the men were to remain there to keep guard while the other two went to fetch fuel for the fire.

"I say we try to rush them now, while there's only three of them there," whispered Rebecca. "At least we can surprise them."

For some reason, all eyes now fell on Anna, including those of Rebecca herself. She hesitated. It was the presence of Mortlock that worried her most. She knew that the evil old man was very strong in the Powers, and it was surely only her that he wanted to capture, rather than the others. If she could just engineer a way for her friends to escape first, then she would take her own chances. But with their enemies about to burn the door down, there was no time. And three opponents were certainly better than five and a burning door.

"Yes, I agree. But listen, let me take on that old man. I will explain later, but I think I know how to deal with him."

In reality, whether or not she could even begin to deal with him in mental combat she had no idea, but it was their best chance.

"I'll try to detain him," she continued, "and you run past us. Whatever you do, don't wait for me. I will follow you."

"Anna, there's no way we're leaving you behind, so you can forget all about that," whispered Rebecca straight back. "But you can take on the old man, if you insist." She gave Anna a look conveying that she understood this was connected with their earlier conversation. "The rest of us should be more than strong enough to deal with the other two. We'll help you if you need us."

Turning to the other three, Rebecca continued, "I know it's a horrible thing to say, but knock them out if you can. Use the chair as a weapon. Do what you have to. Our lives depend on it!"

The friends silently removed the chair from the door. They managed to slide back the bolt so slowly that it didn't make a sound. On the silent count of three, Rebecca turned the key and tugged open the door in one movement. Immediately Johnny dashed through, thrusting the chair feet-first at the first man he came to.

The man was surprised and fell backwards down the staircase. Timmy, Charlie and Rebecca shoved the second man hard against the stone wall, stunning him. They all plunged down the stairs over the prone figure of the first man. Johnny had discarded his chair for speed.

They had made little more than a couple of turns of the staircase when they came to an abrupt halt again. Anna reached her stationary friends and saw Johnny being held roughly from behind by Mortlock. The old man was holding a knife tightly against his throat and had a disgusting sneer on his face. He also had a tight grip on Johnny's aura, rendering the boy helpless. They could not take any risks now.

"Well, well, well. We are a spirited bunch, aren't we? But the game is up. Back upstairs, now! And slowly. If any of you try to make so much as a move in any other direction, be in no doubt that it will mean the end of your little friend here. And you will be next!"

He shouted to the two men down below to rejoin him. This could not have turned out worse. They had lost their only advantage. Mortlock had them exactly where he wanted them. Anna felt desperate. She was just no use on her own, without Mr Warwick or her uncle to guide her. But she had to pull herself together. If she could just somehow get Mortlock away from her friends, she felt sure that would improve their chances of escape. The henchmen had hardly proved themselves the sharpest bunch so far. But how?

The five companions were forced back into the turret prison. None of them dared to try anything. Mortlock was joined by his four henchmen, two of them still rubbing the fresh injuries they had just received. Rather than looking angry with their captives though, they seemed to be cowering in the presence of the old man just as much as their prisoners were. Mortlock shoved Johnny hard into the room, landing a jab on his aura as he did so. Johnny fell to the floor and doubled up. His face had gone white and he looked terrible. Then Mortlock spoke again, his tone even colder than before.

"You will regret trying to defy me. You have not shown me the respect I deserve." His voice rose. "But mark my words, you will! I will kill you myself one-by-one if you do not cooperate. Indeed, I shall relish the task! However, it may still not be too late for some of you to save your lives. There is one of you that I am particularly interested to speak with. Would you like to tell me which one of you is Anna Lawrence?"

Anna's companions all looked straight ahead. It was clear they were all deeply frightened by this horrible old man, but none of them would give her away. This was Anna's chance to get Mortlock away from her friends. She took a slow step forward. "I am Anna Lawrence," she said.

A look of smug satisfaction appeared on the old man's features.

"I thought I recognised you from your last visit here! We have something very special planned for you. You will come with me. Baldwin, Capes, lock these other wretches up and guard them until I come back to finish them off myself. It is clear I cannot trust these other two imbeciles with the task."

He turned to the two men he had caught asleep. "You two are a pair of useless, worthless rodents. Now you will pay for your negligence."

Shifting her focus, Anna saw that he was already mentally attacking one of them. His very large, stained mutation of an aura was crawling over that of the scar-faced man. Suddenly he stabbed it with a thrust of a brown, barbed spike. To cover his tracks, he gripped the man's throat at the same moment. The man fell to his knees, yelling in agony. Then he slumped to the floor, a look of mingled pain and terror on his face. Mortlock did the same to the second failed guard. Then he returned his attention to the new men.

"Whatever happens, make sure none of them escape. I will be back."

He made eye contact with each of Anna's friends. As he did so, he sent a stinging whip crack to each of their auras in turn with his own, making them flinch terribly. Anna's fear of the old bully turned to anger, but she had to keep herself under control until the right moment. She could see her companions were terrified, not understanding what had made them feel such inner pain. But she also recognised a defiance in all of their eyes which gave her hope. She returned their gaze with an equally strong, determined and encouraging one of her own.

"Miss Lawrence," said Mortlock, turning back to her with a sickeningly sweet, false smile. "Would you be so kind as to step this way? We're going to take a little trip downstairs."

Anna briefly considered resisting the old man's aura. However, if they were about to move a safe distance from her companions then she would wait. She would look for an opportunity to escape his control later. She allowed his aura to grip hers tightly.

He shoved her hard towards the door. She heard movement behind her. Timmy had stepped forward to try to help, followed by the others. Mortlock forced them all back immediately at knifepoint. No-one doubted for a moment that he would use it.

"Don't worry," she said, looking at them in a way she hoped conveyed her confidence. Timmy returned the look. Even in this critical situation, it meant the world.

"Capes, Baldwin," barked Mortlock, "lock these children in. After that, neither of you leave your post, no matter what you may hear from downstairs. You stay here and make sure no-one enters or leaves. If anyone tries anything, kill them!"

As if to emphasise his words, he handed his knife to one of the men. To the other two men, he said, "You two, stay here as well. No more blunders or I promise you it will be the last mistake you ever make!"

Mortlock gave one of the crouching figures, the scar-faced man, a hard kick to the ribs as he passed him. He shoved Anna through the door, then down the stairs. The force he was applying to her aura was considerable, rendering her powerless for now. She could not tell if it was more powerful than Mr Warwick's or her uncle's aura, but without question it was very strong. She did not even try to resist yet. She was determined not to give him any impression she could be a threat. As long as he believed her weak, he might become complacent. At least she was achieving her first objective, that of putting distance between her friends and the most dangerous of their enemies.

She fought to remain calm. She did not believe Faulkner would actually want Mortlock to kill her. He would want to send her aura into the Beta Universe. Hardly a comforting thought, but at least that might give her more time.

No sooner had they reached the ground floor room than things got more difficult. Without loosening his grip on her aura, Mortlock took two strong pieces of rope from a cupboard. He used one to tie her hands tightly behind her back. The rope chafed badly, but that was clearly of no concern to Mortlock.

It was now almost completely dark outside, and a single lamp burned in the room. Mortlock took down a large candelabra and lit each candle meticulously. Then he pushed Anna through the door, in the direction he wanted her to move. They proceeded down the corridor, then turned deeper into the house. The flickering candlelight accentuated the deep lines and other ghastly, snarling features of the old man's face. Anna fought against the fear which crawled over her. The shadows, sent dancing by the candelabra into the dark corridors, added to the sense of silent eeriness in the place. All the while, Anna felt the loathsome touch of Mortlock's aura on her own.

They passed a flight of stairs leading into the dark upper reaches of the building. Finally, Mortlock shoved her through another doorway. She found herself in a hall so large that, lit only by the candelabra, she could not even make out the shadowy details of what lay at the far end.

He dragged her to one of the walls, then pushed her roughly to the ground, barking at her not to move. Still maintaining his tight grip on her aura to prevent her resistance, he produced the second length of rope and bound her ankles as tightly as her wrists. Anna battled the rising tide of fear again.

Once she could not run or even walk, the old man finally released his grip on her aura as he darted quickly into the hall to locate wall-mounted torches to light. She had not expected it, and he moved so fast that he was out of range before she could strike at his aura. But, finally she was free from his control. She would not allow her aura to fall under his power again.

Mortlock lit the wall torches one-by-one, as though preparing for some kind of ceremony. Once finished, the hall still contained some shadowy darkness, such was its size, but Anna could just about make out its key features. A long table stood close to the side of the hall she was on, lined with chairs. Much of the opposite wall was covered by a number of large bookcases. There appeared to be several suits of armour standing in the gloom against the back wall, and at the front, not far from her, was an enormous window, nearly two full storeys high. A high vaulted ceiling was dimly visible.

His task complete, Mortlock wheeled round and approached her again, like a giant spider now able to focus its full attention on its trapped prey. Anna fought her emotions again at the sight of this man who had turned to evil many decades ago, and who had been twisted beyond recognition in the service of at least three Satals. He drew closer, his shadowy leer conveying pure malevolence. But this time he did not come within range of her aura. He looked down at her kneeling form. Anna was ready to strike, but he was too far away.

"So, look at you, clever little Miss Lawrence. You don't look very clever now, do you? Not at all!" The sound of his mocking laughter echoed around the hall. "There has been an awful lot of fuss made about you. But now that I look at the pathetic specimen you are, I can't begin to think why. I captured you with such ease. I'm afraid my masters, in their infinite wisdom of course, have overestimated the threat you pose. And that is all to the good. For if you are the worst we have to fear from our enemy now, then victory must already be close at hand. How sweet that final victory over my old companions will be. And in particular, over that pathetic, misguided fool, Edmund Warwick!"

Anna contemplated diving forward to try to take a swipe at his aura. But bound and barely able to move as she was, she would be at a huge disadvantage. She did not want to reveal her true ability until the decisive moment. That was the one element of surprise she had left.

Instead, she simply watched, and listened. His words annoyed her. She wanted to challenge him, to contradict him, but instinct told her not to. Not yet. The less she spoke, the less he could dominate her.

"I now understand that you have been spending a lot of time with that weak old fool, Warwick," Mortlock continued. I imagine he may even have mentioned me to you. Although I very much doubt that he told you the truth."

Anna continued to take great care not to show any emotion.

"You see, Warwick has always lacked courage. He is always too weak and frightened at the vital moments. That is his downfall. Where is he now, for instance? While you are here, attempting, albeit pathetically, to rescue your little friend? He is conveniently off elsewhere, away from danger." His revolting sneer grew more and more pronounced. "I'm afraid your teacher is nothing but a weak coward!"

His words began to needle her. The urge to contradict him grew. But she remained silent.

"It was you, wasn't it?" he continued. "It was you who took me by surprise on the steps outside this very house. Now that I look at your face again, I can recall that same haughty expression you wore. Well, you only gained the upper hand because you took me by surprise. Do you understand me? And you are going to pay the price!"

Anna looked back at him, outwardly calm and impassive. Whether her silence was starting to irritate Mortlock or whether he was just warming to his subject she could not be certain, but the vile creature began to pace the floor before her, still beyond aura range. His demeanour was threatening, his eyes now wide and glittering in the candlelight. He looked almost crazed.

"Do you know what I am going to do now, before my master arrives to finish you off? I am going to show you what real mental power is. What real strength feels like. I am going to inflict mental pain on you the like of which you have never before imagined. And you had better believe me when I say that I am a master in that art. You don't doubt it, do you?"

Anna did not doubt it for one moment, but she said nothing. She maintained her air of calm.

"I know that you can see essences, girl. I am sure that you have looked upon mine. I expect you found it repulsive to your delicate, pretty sensibilities, based on your teachings from the old coward Warwick and that idiot uncle of yours. What you will not know about, for I am sure they would not tell you this, is the immense power that I am now able to wield through it. Far more power than either of your pathetic teachers. *Blue* essences contain fatal weaknesses, which I have entirely eliminated in mine. I'm sure your teachers never told you that, did they?"

He was trying to provoke a response from her. She would not bite. She looked back in her captor's eyes, impassive and unwavering.

"With this essence of such formidable power, I can inflict the most terrible damage imaginable on a person. And indeed, I have, many, many times!"

The odious old creature's boasting about inflicting pain and damage was starting to anger Anna, despite her best efforts. It was not the threats. It was the fact that this abomination of a man appeared so willing to ruin other people's lives for his own twisted ends, and even gratification. It was as though he thought he somehow had the right to do it. He did not. No-one did. The desire to take on this master of injustice was strong. But she sensed that such a reaction was precisely what he wanted. For some reason, despite his dominant position, he was trying to anger her. Rather than subdue her, was he trying to *turn* her?

She recalled Mr Warwick's words of caution. When anger becomes a person's master, rather than the other way around, that's when they become most vulnerable. Anger clouds judgement and leads to the wrong actions. It was a weapon the Omega World used to defeat its enemies from within themselves, to turn them in the Omega direction. She must not fall for it. She said nothing.

"I am going to use my immense power on your pathetic essence. And for your arrogance, I intend to show you no mercy. I will take you to within an inch of your pathetic little life before my master comes back to finish you. He will be pleased with me for warming you up for him, but that is not why I will do it."

He paused, looking for a response. Again, she gave him none.

"Do you want to know why I am going to do this to you? Because I don't have to, you know. I could spare you that. But I am going to do it because I can! I want you to know just how easily I can crush you. It will bring me great pleasure to reveal your mental weakness compared to mine, before you die!"

Anna fought hard to remain outwardly unmoved.

"Do I frighten you, little girl? Inside, I know that I do. I terrify the life out of you! You will beg for mercy, for me to take your life to spare your pain. But I shall show you no mercy!"

Even from this distance, Anna could see that the man's mouth was starting to drool. She watched him contort his filthily contaminated aura into a deadly, red-and-brown barbed spike. He began to move it back and forth with menace, still at a distance for now. Anna braced herself, ready for the onslaught that was surely very near. Fighting to control the anger and fear which she knew his words were designed to create, she remained a picture of confident calm. When they fought, it would be on her terms.

His snarl grew even more abhorrent than before, his eyes even wilder. She realised that she was now actually getting to her captor, rather than the other way round. He was starting to become enraged himself. The old man's ugly features had become so twisted they made him look completely insane.

For a brief moment, fear began to get the better of her again at the reality of what she was facing and what he might do next. She could not block the feeling entirely. But she knew what she had to do. She had to control it and then use it. To channel it. She chose this moment to finally break her silence – and not in the way that Mortlock had hoped.

"Actually, no. You do not scare me. Not in the least. I don't fear you at all." She kept her voice as confident and strong as she could manage. And as she spoke, the words became truer and truer. She started to master her fear again, driven by a stronger force from within. "In fact, the only feeling I have for you… is pity."

For a moment the crazed old man ceased his prowling and stared at her, as though trying to absorb what she had just said.

"But I do have a question for you," she continued steadily. "How do people turn out like you? What happened to you, to make you such a broken person? Such a failure of a man? Something has obviously gone badly wrong. Your brain doesn't seem to function as proper people's do. The fact that you seem to think this broken state of yours gives you some kind of power – well that just shows how malfunctioning you really are. It's laughable. I wonder what it was that broke you and caused you to become such a... a misfit? I find you a rather pathetic, pitiable old man. I feel genuinely sorry for you."

Anna's words were born out of her channelled anger and fear, but they were not delivered with either. She shaped them deliberately and spoke them with ice-cool calm. She knew the attack was coming, and she was determined to face it from a position of strength, in greater control of her emotions than her opponent.

Mortlock stood rooted to the spot. The look on his features betrayed his shock. Whatever response he had been hoping to provoke, this clearly had not been it.

"You... you dare to mock me?" He almost choked on the words. "You, who know nothing, dare to call me a failure? A *failure*? How dare you! I am infinitely superior to you. As I will show you!"

He wielded his spike-shaped aura even more aggressively. Anna braced herself again, ready. She was certain she was in greater control of herself than he was now. Still the assault did not come. He was hesitating. Why? Did he not dare to strike if she was still in full control?

Anna was very calm. She had the upper hand, at least in terms of composure. She was still cautious, but ready to launch her own counter to his attack at any time. She watched her enemy's every move. Then she saw a subtle change in his expression. A slight return of cunning in his eyes. He had just about mastered himself again. As he spoke, the fury in his voice was gone, but his every word still dripped with poison.

"You know, little girl, I must confess to some surprise. Not at your blind, unjustified arrogance – that has always been a Lawrence trait, and a fatal character flaw in your family. But I am surprised that you choose to use such arrogant words with me, of all people. When I have already proved myself so superior to your family, against those who meant the most to you. When I have already inflicted such profound damage on your own life. Anyone would think that the loss of your father meant nothing at all to you, to hear the way you talk."

This took Anna by surprise. Her mind scrambled to understand. Was he implying what she thought he was? Could it be true? Or was it just another meaningless boast to provoke anger? She wanted to pretend she did not care either way. But this was something that she did care about. She had to. She feared her outward expression had shown a hint of weakness for the first time, before she could control it again.

For all his insane appearance, Mortlock was watching Anna's features every bit as closely as she had been watching his. Sure enough, he had read the brief sign. The downward curl of his ugly snarl began to twist upwards. He sneered, evilly.

"Well, well, well," he began again in a slower, softer voice, like cotton wool, wrapped around barbed wire. "You didn't know, did you? Your teachers didn't tell you! I should not be surprised, I suppose. Yet more cowardice from the old fool. Couldn't bring himself to tell you the truth. But this does help to explain your lack of emotion.

I had expected to see stronger, more impressive feelings in you. I have been most disappointed in your lack of passion. But now the reason has become clear!"

Anna's mind raced. Mr Warwick had referred to her uncle's emotional scars from the traumatic events of the last Satal war. A war in which this man had fought on the opposite side. Her mother had written of the injuries inflicted on their family by the Alpha-Omega Wars. Was it Mortlock who had inflicted the most grievous one of all?

He had turned the tables on her. It was possible he was just bluffing, alluding to something that did not exist, to draw her out. But her deepest instincts told her otherwise. And her reading of this old villain told her he knew he had just found a new weapon to deploy against her – a truth that she had been unaware of until now. Completely calm on the outside, she felt a terrible apprehension at what was coming next.

"Poor little Anna Lawrence," continued the soft, taunting voice. "Do you remember your father?"

Anna did not respond. She could not stop her breathing from growing shallower and sharper though.

"Do you know how proud everyone was of him? Of what a fine and brave young man he had become? 'The future hope for the Alpha World' they called him. Quite outshone his younger brother, your poor, inferior uncle, he did. Although that is hardly an accomplishment of note. Well, Anna, it seems that your teachers have left out one important detail from your instruction: what became of your much-loved father."

Anna strained to retain her facade of composure. Fierce anger was rising now. Anger laced with confusion.

She wasn't sure she could control it this time. It was clear her captor was enjoying himself immensely with this new toy he had found. She hated that he should take such pleasure in this subject. She wished she did not want to hear any more. But she needed to hear the rest. His narrative now held her in its grip.

"Well, how ironic that it should fall to me to fill in this missing piece of your education! For, Anna Lawrence, it was I, the much maligned, 'broken', 'pitiable' Joseph Mortlock, who *killed* your father!"

He hissed out the final words, his face contorted into the most hideous snarl. Anna had by now known this was coming, but it still set her head spinning. It explained her uncle's aggressive reaction every time Mortlock's name was mentioned. Her composure was fatally fractured now by a whirlwind of confusion, anger, and hatred for this man.

"He was brave, I'll give him that," Mortlock continued. "Unlike his worthless younger brother and the old coward, Warwick. They turned tail and ran like frightened rats in the face of my might, abandoning your doomed father to his terrible fate at my hands. Your father did at least fight valiantly." The old man's mad eyes sparkled as he continued to twist the knife. "But he was simply no match for my immensely superior power! I crushed him, just as I shall crush you!"

Mortlock had taken the ground from under her feet. How much of it was true? Once again, deep down her instincts told her that there was indeed some truth in these words. This monster had killed her father, and now he was gloating to her about it.

Deep-seated feelings from the distant past had been unleashed inside her, and they were starting to run wild. She just about managed to retain the disguise of her aura, for now. But bound though she was, she struggled to her feet, extreme rage bursting its shackles. Whatever the truth, beyond any doubt the time had come to rid the world of this tormentor that stood before her. This murderer. This killer of her father.

Slowly and deliberately, the sneering Mortlock moved his aura into her range. She could see that her rage was what he had wanted. Yes, he had got to her. He was now calm, while she was finally consumed by anger. But she didn't care. She would destroy him anyway.

No longer worried that her state was exactly what this crafty enemy had intended all along, finally she removed her aura's disguise, revealing its true size and form, ready to strike him down. She might not be able to see her own aura, but she felt it. She knew it was conveying the full, massive power she was feeling at that moment.

Mortlock had been preparing his barbed spike, ready to side-step when Anna's aura attacked, then stab and slash it viciously from the side. But his eyes suddenly widened. There was a look of genuine shock on his face at what he was seeing. It was just enough to make her hold off from striking, for a moment. Her fierce look penetrated his. Mortlock had succeeding in goading her to the very brink of lashing out and attacking him. But now, at the key moment, he realised for the first time just what it was he was up against. And he had real doubt in his eyes. Doubt that he could overcome what now faced him. Doubt and, unmistakably, *fear*! Anna began to channel her emotions again. She remembered the lesson about not striking in hatred. She had almost fallen. But she had not.

They stood facing each other, neither moving. She remained strong, fearless and ready for anything, but she calmed her mind. She would fight with control. Her opponent, on the other hand, now appeared lost in indecision. Finally, he broke eye contact. He skipped suddenly away from her, sweeping his aura out of her range again.

"Little girl," he called out, trying vainly to regain the upper hand, though his face could not hide his humiliation. "You are nothing but an impudent child. I could finish you off right now, easily, just as I finished off your father. But you have a much more exciting end ahead of you. It was my job to detain you here, which I have done with the greatest of ease, until someone else comes who is going to complete the work. We shall wait for him. It won't be long now. Then the fun will really begin!"

Almost as if summoned by his words, there was the sound of distant, running footsteps. Mortlock started to laugh again. Facing the old man was one thing, but if the Satal appeared now… She dived at Mortlock as far as her bound legs would allow, and took a massive, desperate swipe at his aura. If she could overcome him, maybe she could force him to untie her, or at least eliminate him from the battle. But he was too far away, and he danced further from her reach. She could not get to him.

The door flew open. But it was not Faulkner. It was a much shorter man, wearing a coat and hat both covered with snow.

"It's Lawrence!" shouted the man. "James Lawrence is here! I got here just before him, but he's already here…"

No sooner had he spoken than more footsteps could be heard. A second, taller figure appeared in the doorway behind him. It was her uncle! Anna could have cried with joy. The first man attempted to sidestep him and escape before the fighting broke out, but Uncle James engaged first with his aura to render him powerless, then flung him easily to the ground, his head crashing against the wall. He did not get up.

Mortlock darted in the opposite direction, towards the wall lined with bookcases. Uncle James headed straight for him. Then both men stopped. They stood facing each other, still some way apart. If Anna had any shadows of doubt remaining about Uncle James being a coward and frightened of Mortlock, they were dispelled by his words as he squared up to the old man.

"Finally, the day I have been longing for all these years. The day I get to defeat you in a fair fight, you old monster. No more sneaking up and attacking us from behind. This time I shall eliminate you from the Struggle, once and for all!"

He advanced, a look of fearless determination in his eyes. In contrast, the crazed look had returned to Mortlock's face. Whatever internal debate was raging in his twisted mind, it did not last long. He snarled, then turned and fled.

He reached a section of the wood-panelled wall just beyond one of the large bookcases. With a single, swift movement, he pressed the wall panels in several places. The wall swivelled open to reveal a hidden door. He darted through and pulled it shut behind him with a loud click, just as Anna's sprinting uncle reached it. 'Interesting that someone so powerful, brave and superior should turn tail and run at the very sight of my uncle!' thought Anna. Her contempt for the old man could not be more complete.

Uncle James pushed the panels with all his might, then pounded it with the side of his fist. He attempted to mimic the movements Mortlock had made on the panelling, but to no avail. Cursing, he gave the wall one last whack with his cane, then he dashed over to Anna.

He spoke very quickly as he set about untying her.

"Faulkner's on his way. He knows you are here and he is coming for you. He'll be here any minute. I wanted to finish off Mortlock first. That wasn't my preferred way to get rid of him, but it will do for now. But this is not the time of our choosing to fight Faulkner. We need to get out of here, right now."

"But my friends are still here. They're locked in the tower, guarded by Mortlock's men. We can't leave here without them!"

"But Anna, we must get you out of here first, and then I'll come back for–"

"I will not leave here without them!"

Her uncle uttered another curse, but he grasped the situation.

"Very well, then we'll try to free them first. But we may have no choice but to face Faulkner if we can't get them before he arrives."

His eyes were more deadly serious than Anna had ever seen them. He wrestled with the tight bonds on her legs, which would not come undone.

"Sir Stephen and Greg are on their way and will be here soon. Faulkner is travelling here directly from the City. He did not appear to have his men with him. The snow has slowed him down, fortunately."

Anna nodded. Finally, the last knot came undone.

Not a moment too soon. In the distance, a large door slammed. If it was Greg or Sir Stephen, surely they would have taken greater care not to be heard?

"He's here!" breathed her uncle. "Whatever happens, we cannot risk him finding you. I shall have to face him in this room."

He looked frantically around. Grabbing Anna's arm, he led her, running, to the far end of the room, to where the open curtains of the large window stretched to the floor. He concealed them both behind the curtain nearest the left-hand wall, then spoke quietly and very hurriedly.

"This is not how any of us planned this battle. We wanted you to be nowhere near when it happened. But we have no choice now. I must ask you to do everything in your power to remain concealed, and to escape at the first safe opportunity, rather than to fight. This is not your time. You have a bigger mission to fulfil, another day."

"But uncle–"

"Listen to me, Anna. I will detain Faulkner long enough for you to escape, and you must do so, unnoticed. Do you understand? It's your escape that is paramount. Our entire future in the Struggle may depend on you surviving this day. If he captures you, my fight will have been in vain. You must promise me. Promise me!"

Anna had never heard her uncle so desperate, but there was no way she could leave him to his fate. She did not reply.

He peered round the curtain towards the door. There was no sound of footsteps yet from the corridor.

"Look, Anna, I am not asking you this for yourself, but for me, and for everyone else whose future is going to depend on you."

Anna still did not reply. She just could not agree to what he was asking.

"There's no more time to argue. If you will not escape, at least promise me this one thing: that you will not join me in the battle until I give you a signal. When I shout 'Now'. Whatever happens, and whatever you are seeing, under no circumstances must you enter the fight until you hear that word. That will be critical to our advantage. I will judge the right moment. There are various ways in which I can fight Faulkner, and your joining too early could disrupt the flow. I will create the right moment for you to have maximum impact. At least promise me that!"

There was such urgency in his eyes that Anna nodded this time.

"Yes, all right, uncle. I will wait for your signal."

"Thank you. And listen to me." He took hold of both her shoulders and stared fiercely into her eyes. "You have a power within you, the like of which I have never seen. If you will not or cannot escape, be confident, stay strong and fight like the lioness I already know you to be. Fight like you have never fought before. You cannot let them take you. You must not. The fate of the world depends on what you do right now."

Heavy footsteps became audible from the corridor. Footsteps of the one who had come to kill her. Uncle James said no more. He put his finger to his lips and was gone, leaving Anna fully concealed. Unlike the footsteps that had come before, these were slow, measured and very loud. A stifling tension filled the air. It was difficult even to breathe. Anna's stomach started to churn. Her uncle dashed back to the centre of the hall. He faced what was coming, brave and alone.

Peeping through the tiniest gap, Anna watched as a tall, cloaked figure appeared, filling the doorway and blocking any possible escape. The Satal was there.

16
The Battle

Faulkner stepped slowly forwards, into the room.
"Lawrence. I thought I would find you here. Where is the child?"

Uncle James said nothing at first. Then he replied in a strong voice, "She's somewhere far away from here. Somewhere you will never find her." He stood his ground, watching every movement like a hawk.

"Ah, but I know that's not true," replied the deeper, sterner voice. "Events have rather overtaken us both today, have they not? I had not expected my plans to be so successful so quickly. Neither the capture of the boy, nor the luring of the girl here. Had I expected it, I would have come sooner."

Uncle James said nothing. He continued to watch, alert, ready for any sudden attack.

"Nevertheless, I am here now. I have not yet found Mortlock, but I am sure he is entertaining himself at the girl's expense here somewhere. She must still be here, otherwise you would not be. So, I shall eliminate you first, then I shall take the girl."

"I'm afraid you won't find her. I am here to rescue her friends in the tower. She is nowhere near. But I will let you discover that for yourself."

"Do not lie to me, Lawrence!" Faulkner's voice suddenly grew louder. "You have been a constant irritation to me in recent times. I am pleased that it will be here, in my own house, that you shall die."

The deep voice filled the huge room. He started to advance slowly, brandishing his walking cane. Uncle James continued to stand his ground.

"I have some news to share, before I kill you. I have received word that your master, Warwick, who we now know was masquerading as that infernal bookseller, Mr Barton, has already been captured. Four of my best men, all with the Powers, are now holding him securely in the City. He cannot escape. I had set a trap for anyone who attempted to follow me. Apparently he was foolish enough to try. As soon as I have killed you and the girl, I shall return to execute him as well." He paused to let the news sink in. "Dear, dear, it doesn't seem to be a good day for you, does it? This particular episode of the war is about to be over, almost before it has begun!"

Anna gasped as he spoke. Not Mr Warwick. Everything was going so badly wrong. They simply had to rescue him somehow. But to do that, they would have to survive themselves first.

If Anna's uncle was disturbed by this latest development, he gave no indication. He continued to watch Faulkner's every move, as the two enemies had started to circle one another slowly. Anna's uncle cut the same tall, strong figure he always did, but now she saw them together for the first time, Faulkner was significantly taller and more powerful looking. Her uncle was face-to-face with evil personified. She had seen Uncle James in action and she knew exactly how strong, skilful and devastating he could be in combat. But she also knew that no knight in history had ever fought a Satal on his own and won. She watched the two men, waiting for his signal to join him.

Suddenly, Faulkner took a powerful swipe at her uncle with his thick cane. Uncle James managed to parry it successfully with his own stick, although the power of the blow made him stagger backwards. Faulkner laughed. He was starting to toy with him. Anna noted that not for one instant did he take his eyes off her uncle, though. Uncle James immediately regained his balance and continued to move slowly around his adversary. His face showed absolute concentration.

Anna focused on the men's auras. Even from a distance she could clearly make out the fearsome, scarlet-tipped spikes covering the massive black ball of the Satal's aura. The sight of it made her stomach turn. Then the real combat began.

Faulkner's aura first feinted one way, then swung round at great velocity to strike from the other side. Anna's uncle reacted with the tremendous speed of his own that she had seen in training. His aura perfectly sidestepped the main impact of the blow, receiving only a glancing contact. There was no significant damage. Immediately he lunged with his own aura, to try to get a grip on the enemy's. But it moved too fast and it evaded him. Then came an altogether more aggressive assault.

Faulkner's aura started to strike from one side then the other repeatedly, gradually gaining in speed. As it did so, Faulkner himself strode forward and began to drive his opponent back. Uncle James formed his aura into a tight ball to withstand the impact of the blows and he took what evasive action he could. Faulkner was building up a terrible momentum. Anna's uncle was forced further backwards. He looked like he would be overwhelmed completely. The attack was relentless. Anna grew desperately worried. She prepared herself to join him at any moment. But no signal came yet.

Her uncle's back was just feet from one of the large wooden bookcases that lined the far wall when he counter-attacked. Anna gasped at the speed with which he manoeuvred his bright blue aura. It was faster than anything she had seen from him before. He deftly avoided the latest blow from Faulkner's aura, then seized one side of it by its spikes. In a continuation of the same movement, he twisted it in a way that clearly took his opponent by surprise. Faulkner howled with rage. At the same time, Uncle James lunged the silver-tipped end of his walking cane directly at Faulkner. It stabbed the taller man squarely in the chest, sending him staggering backwards. He immediately struck again in the mental plane. He landed a fist-like blow with his powerful blue aura on his much larger foe. Anna feared the damage it might suffer from the red-tipped spikes, but being clenched, the markings it received were only slight.

Uncle James took up his own defence again straight away. Wisely, as it turned out. A savage counter side-swipe missed his aura by a fraction of an inch. Faulkner had been surprised by the speed and deftness of the man he was fighting, but he had not been seriously hurt.

"You know what I am," he roared, "and you know what is about to be unleashed on you. Prepare for annihilation!"

The booming threat was delivered with such venom that it shook Anna to her core. She stood ready to help, however inadequate that help suddenly seemed. Still no signal yet.

Then Faulkner launched a blistering attack. The speed of his spiked aura was much faster now, its thrusts savage. He was contorting its shape, pulsing its spikes this way and that. He landed blow after stabbing blow on the pure blue of his opponent. Anna was filled with admiration for her uncle's bravery and his skill. He defended this way and that, steeling his aura against what was becoming a blizzard of scarlet-tipped swipes and thrusts.

As he was forced back again, he seemed to be manoeuvring the battle further and further away from where she was hidden. Possibly in the hope that she would escape. But he was taking more and more hits. Despite the clenching and rapid evasive movements of his aura, Anna could see that the damage to its surface was growing rapidly. He faced up to the barrage, counter-jabbing when he could, first from the right, then from below. Each time he slowed the bombardment a little, but the onslaught did not stop. He tried in vain, several times, to gain another grip on the opposing aura. But his enemy's movements were just too fast now, and the slashing of the spikes too lethal.

Uncle James still battled on bravely. In the physical dimension he landed an effective strike with his walking cane on Faulkner's hand, causing him to drop his stick. He followed it up with the biggest swinging blow on the Satal's aura he could still muster, again pausing his enemy's advance just momentarily. But each time, Faulkner simply resumed again immediately. Uncle James's counter-strikes finally began to lessen. Faulkner forced him right back towards the bookcases again. The blue aura was sustaining significant damage now. Anna stood, poised. Still the signal did not come. Her premonition about her uncle and this battle returned to her like a hammer blow. And then she understood.

There would be no signal. Her uncle had never intended for her to be involved in this fight. He had planned to do his best to defeat the enemy, but he had known all along that this would eventually be doomed to fail. He fought it nonetheless, purely to draw attention away from her and to buy her time. He was about to lay down his life so that she might escape. He was moments from death, and she had just stood there and let it happen. All these thoughts flashed through Anna's mind as she broke cover and pelted towards the melee a long way ahead of her. Was she already too late? Were her worst fears about to be realised, right in front of her?

At that same moment, the main door to the hall, which was much closer to the fighting, was flung open. Another man dashed in.

"James! James!" the man yelled.

From his embattled position, Uncle James yelled back, "Sir Stephen! To me, to me!"

Sir Stephen Walsingham, veteran of the last Satal war, sprinted towards the battle, finally relieving some of the terrible pressure on Uncle James. Faulkner turned to fend off this new attacker. He had his back to Anna as he fought both opponents at once with mighty, crashing sweeps of his aura.

As she dashed towards them, the section of wall panelling by the bookcase opened again. Amongst the deadly, dancing shadows of the three combatants, the silhouette of a crooked, long-haired figure slipped out from its place of concealment, a cane raised above its head.

"Uncle, behind you!" yelled Anna, still too far away to stop it.

Her voice could not be heard by anyone over the din of the fighting. The silver skull at the end of the cane glinted for a moment in the flaming torchlight before it came crashing down with full force, directly onto the crown of Uncle James's head. It was a fateful blow. Her uncle's back had been turned to him, and he dropped to the floor like a stone.

"No!" cried Sir Stephen, seeing his comrade fall. But he could do nothing for him. Faulkner immediately launched a fearsome attack, driving him back.

As Anna drew close to her motionless uncle, she saw blood already appearing from a severe wound on his head. Rage exploded inside her. Her sole focus moved to his attacker, who was raising his cane for a second blow on the unconscious figure. Clenching her aura into a mighty fist, she swung with full force at the vile old creature who had struck in such a cowardly fashion. Mortlock spotted her at the last moment. He moved his aura partially out of the way, reducing the impact, but it was still sufficient to propel his physical body violently backwards. He hit the floor a number of feet away, coming to a halt just in front of the large bookcase near the secret door.

Faulkner was now at the end of the room, near the large window, bearing down on Sir Stephen. Anna decided to take Mortlock out of the battle first, to protect her uncle and prevent any further intervention. Then another figure burst through the door. Anna hesitated. Was it friend or foe? His features were obscured by the shadows at first, but then Anna made him out. It was Greg Matthews! He wore a grave expression as he tore forward towards them. She could not have been happier to see more help arrive, but she immediately returned her focus to eliminating Mortlock.

The old man was using the tall bookcase to haul himself to his feet. Anna darted towards him, preparing the final knockout blow on his aura. Suddenly he heaved the giant bookcase away from the wall, sending it toppling over in her direction. Focused as she was on his aura, Anna only realised when it was already falling towards her.

It was at that moment that Greg reached them. With a dive, he grabbed Anna. They both went sprawling to the floor as the bookcase crashed down on top of them. One section caught him squarely on the head, and he disappeared under the wreckage of the shelving and books. He did not move. His momentum had sent Anna just clear of the falling objects.

Still focused on Mortlock, she saw him stagger through the secret door again. In an instant she had reached the threshold herself. She thought of pursuing him through it. But it was pitch black on the other side. Dazed though he might be, Mortlock could easily trap her if she followed him in there. Faulkner would surely defeat Sir Stephen at any moment and return to finish off her uncle. They had to be her priority. Instead, she slammed the secret door shut again. She grabbed a wedge-shaped wooden chunk of smashed bookcase and jammed it roughly into the gap between the floor and the door to prevent any further opening.

Breathing heavily, she looked back at the scene in the torch-lit hall. At her feet lay the fallen bookcase, its shattered remains and contents scattered into the middle-distance. It covered most of Greg's prone figure. Some way beyond him, over in the middle of the room, lay the figure of her uncle. He had not moved an inch since he was felled. In front of the large window, Sir Stephen was lying on the ground, clutching his leg. He looked as though he had just taken a severe beating. But he was still alive at least. Anna could see no sign of Faulkner.

"Sir Stephen, are you all right?" she called as she started to move towards her uncle to tend to him.

Sir Stephen looked up, revealing a stream of blood running down the right-hand side of his face.

"Anna, is that you? Quick, you must run for it! Now, before it's too late! Please, I implore you! I will hold it off for as long as I can!"

"Where's Faulkner?" she asked.

The air was rent by an ear-splitting scream, which echoed deafeningly around the old hall. Anna flinched and crouched down. She tried to locate the source of the sound. It seemed to have come from all around. Then she saw it.

From the dark shadow of the far end of the hall, furthest from the large window, emerged a huge, demonic creature over ten feet tall, with long horns and enormous, talon-tipped wings. 'A Satal returns to its true form to kill its prey.' Having defeated its enemies, that moment had come.

"Run Anna, run! Escape before it's too late!" Sir Stephen yelled desperately once more. He struggled vainly to get to his feet, but slumped back down, unable to stand. "It's coming!"

The Beast let out a second almighty shriek that made Anna crouch even further down, her hands over her ears. The Beast was advancing towards the motionless body of her uncle in the middle of the room. It was moving its wicked aura to either side, as a medieval knight might have wielded a ball and chain. It was preparing to smash the life out of the aura of her unconscious uncle.

Anna sprang up and scrambled desperately to make up the distance before the Beast got to him. She was too far away. There was only one thing in this world that could stop the Satal now. The discovery of its most sought-after prize: Anna herself.

She yelled, in the mightiest voice she had ever mustered, "Satal, be gone!"

The sound was mighty indeed, almost as though it could not possibly have come from her. It echoed all around the chamber. The Beast slowed and turned its huge, horned head in her direction, snorting. Anna dashed headlong to cover the remaining distance to her uncle.

The Satal decided to finish off Uncle James first before turning its attention to this new, unexpected arrival. It swung its aura. As she dived towards them, Anna envisaged hers pushed forward from her, between that of her uncle and the slamming ball of spikes heading straight for it. She flexed it as hard as rock and braced herself for the blow.

When it came, it was a terrible one. She felt the spikes embedding deeply into her aura and watched them come to within a few inches of her uncle's motionless one. They slowed. They did not reach it. Anna felt as though nails had been driven deep into her chest, and she gasped in agony momentarily. But, having flexed her aura so hard against the blow, the pain eased as the spikes withdrew. She was able to refocus.

Rising to her feet, she seized the moment. She could not let the Beast kill him. That thought triggered a massive surge of power. Envisaging her aura once again like a clenched fist, she moved it at lightning speed and smashed it into the spiked ball with all the power she had. Never before had she hit anything so hard. She felt the pain again in her own chest as her aura struck the red-tipped spikes. She withstood it. She stood her ground and kept her focus solely on her enemy.

She had certainly gained the element of surprise. The giant beast was not only stopped in its tracks, but its enormous physical body actually staggered backwards several steps before coming to a halt. Then it reared up to its full height, regarding the child before it with something akin to shock. Quick as a flash, Anna positioned herself between her uncle and the Beast. She flexed her aura and braced herself.

The Satal did not advance. It began to crane its neck forward as if to take a closer look at this new, unexpected adversary. It moved its head, first to the left, then to the right, grunting and hissing all the while. Then its eyes narrowed. It let out a hissed sound in her direction. It seemed to be saying, "*You!*"

Behind her, she could again hear Sir Stephen's voice from his prone position. He yelled at her to make her escape. His words brought her to her senses a little. Fear crept back into her mind. The moment they had all sought to avoid so desperately was now upon her. The moment when the Satal, one of the five from her dreaded dream, found her. And here she stood, facing it alone. The Beast of Highgate, which had so terrorised London, towered over her.

As the enormity of this moment in her life sank in, a spirit ignited within her. It was stronger and more forceful than any fear she felt. Mr Warwick and her uncle had told her many times that she had a vital role to play in the Struggle. Deep down she had known it to be true. This confrontation was part of that destiny, whether they wanted it to be or not. She had been born to fight in this war, for as long, or as short, as her life lasted. She would face up to the enemy before her, and she would not stop fighting while she still had a breath left. Rising in stature, she channelled every emotion that was racing through her. She visualised her aura expanding to its full size. Then she spoke in words that would have been alien to her at any previous time in her life, and with a boldness that would have stunned anyone who knew her.

"Satal, you shall pass no further. You may know who I am, but you have not seen my like before. You will not take my uncle. I will not allow it. If you attempt to, I will fight you to the death. You will not be victorious this day." She felt massive power coursing through her aura. The usual doubts of the old Anna Lawrence were banished.

Whether it was her words or her aura, she seemed to be having quite some effect on the beast before her. Where the Satal had not hesitated to take the attack to her uncle and Sir Stephen, and had aggressively beaten them both down into submission with relative ease, it maintained its distance from her. It seemed to be contemplating its next move very carefully.

Anna pictured the unconscious body of her uncle lying behind her, and thought of what the Satal intended to do to him. She thought of Mr Warwick, captured and now awaiting execution at this monster's hands. She thought of Gillespie and the appalling, irreversible injuries inflicted on him by Faulkner in an attack she had failed to prevent. She thought of all the other people whose lives this beast had ended or ruined, and all those it would end in the future if someone did not stop it. It had to be stopped. Feelings of still greater power surged through her. She spoke again, her voice mighty.

"Satal! Be gone!"

The Beast observed her for one more long moment. Then it slowly expanded its wings to their full span. It bent its legs and rocked its head back slightly, tensing its wings as if to take off. Was it going to fly away? Was it actually going to leave them? A new flicker of hope appeared in her heart. Then the Beast opened its jaws wide, let out the loudest, most blood curdling, most unearthly scream that any in the room had ever heard, and it lunged forward in attack.

Anna reacted instantly. She darted to one side to avoid the slashing of the lunging beast's claws, drawing the creature away from her uncle. She focused her attention on its aura. Her best chance of survival lay in getting a hold on the Beast's aura and applying sufficient pressure, before its talons tore her to shreds. If she failed, she was certainly dead. She manoeuvred the duel further and further from her uncle's body with her nimble movements.

"Hold on Anna, I'm coming!" yelled Sir Stephen.

He was struggling bravely to get to his feet, but he was unable to. Anna was not distracted. She was seeing everything very clearly. She continued her manic, erratic movements to avoid the creature's physical lunges, all the time searching for her opportunity in the mental dimension. Suddenly the Satal swung its giant aura at her viciously. It came at her with tremendous velocity. With a speed of thought bordering on pure instinct, she visualised her own aura flattening and curving round one side of its attacker, slipping around its outer contours and avoiding its impact. Then she accelerated her aura back to catch up with the spiked aura as it passed. Like a hand catching a flying ball, she grabbed it. The Satal's attack had been fast as lightning, but her movement was even quicker. She got a hold.

She felt her aura engulfing a portion of the deadly spiked ball. The monster immediately attempted to tug its aura away, pulling this way and that. Anna held on mentally for grim death, certain that if she were to lose her hold now it would be the end. The Satal heaved and twisted with enormous strength, but she held on with every ounce of the power she felt. It did not escape her grip. And sure enough, the movement of the Beast's slashing claws slowed, then stopped.

The spikes stabbed and scraped at Anna's aura. She did not lessen her hold. Then the Beast stopped tugging and twisting. It started to exert pressure back onto Anna's aura. At first, she thought she could withstand it. But slowly and inexorably, it increased the pressure until she could find no way to prevent it from pushing her aura backwards, and downwards. Her physical body was forced to its knees by the extraordinary pressure in the other dimension. The Satal, rather than being held, was beginning to engulf the edges of Anna's aura with its own. It was starting to grip her.

The spikes sank in. The pain became almost excruciating. She resisted the oppressive force as best she could. She hoped beyond hope Sir Stephen would reach them in time to help. Despite a savage wound in his leg, from which blood was pouring, he half limped, half crawled towards her, wearing a look of utter determination. She could not focus on him, but from the corner of her eye she spotted a familiar, long-haired shadow appearing behind him, not from the direction of the secret door this time but from the main doorway. A cane was raised above its head.

So huge was the force being applied to her aura, she could not even breathe a word of warning. As her final hope began to fade, Sir Stephen caught sight of Mortlock. He turned just in time. Their auras locked and they became embroiled in their own deadly fight. Sir Stephen was unable to come to her rescue, but he held Mortlock back and stopped him from being able to join the Satal to finish her off.

Anna continued to resist with all her might. The Satal's monstrous physical form edged forward until it towered over her tiny frame. Gradually, she started to succumb to the ruthless, relentless pressure on her aura. Finally, the Satal broke Anna's grip and it tore its aura free. It sent the spiked ball crashing straight back into her aura, stunning her completely. Then it took another grip and began to press her again. Anna was already on her knees. Now her body was being bent slowly backwards towards the floor.

Her whole focus was trained on the auras. She started to feel the chill of an invisible wind. She understood what it was. The fabric of the world she knew was beginning to come apart.

The evil wind grew stronger. The Satal must have created the opening between the universes. It was pushing her aura towards the Beta World. She gripped its aura desperately. It was the only thing that could prevent a physical attack. But her grip was weakening. It was not enough to stop the Beast edging forwards with its talons and slowly taking hold of her shoulders. It pushed out its stinking snout until it was within a foot of her face. It opened its jaws, revealing long fangs, rows of razor-sharp teeth and a coiled tongue. The stench of its breath hit her full in the face as it let out another unearthly shriek. Rather than her physical body, it was her aura that it wanted to kill. To feed it to the Beta World. It pressed still harder. The sound, the smell and the endless pressure on her aura began to drive Anna's consciousness from her, even though she continued to push back.

Sir Stephen, still battling desperately with Mortlock, was horrified by the murderous spectacle unfolding before him. Their bitter enemy was gaining the final upper hand on the girl who had been their greatest hope. But she was still only a child. She looked tiny, frail and defenceless compared to the monster that was dominating her, about to end her young life. It was a travesty of all that was right in this world. She should not have to face a creature so terrible, all alone.

He managed to fend off a knockout blow from Mortlock, but he could not escape him. The inhuman spectacle in the centre of the room was about to reach its ghastly climax and there was nothing more he could do.

"Hold on, Anna, hold on!" he yelled, his voice starting to crack.

Anna heard the words distantly as she held on desperately to consciousness. Her aura inched closer and closer to the gap between worlds. She felt the real, true desolation of the Beta World for the first time. The evil winds blowing against her aura began to howl as it neared the tear in the universe's fabric. She thought she could even hear the embryonic creatures of the Beta night, buzzing and chattering like large, hideous insects, hungrily waiting to devour her aura.

The horrific feelings of terror from her childhood nightmare returned, fivefold. Panic threatened to consume her final attempts at resistance, just as those feelings in the dream had completely overwhelmed her all those years ago. But Anna was no longer that child. She had grown, both in power and in knowledge. Now she was armed with an understanding of what was happening. She had already experienced something of what this felt like. She had fought back before in the Practice and won. She would fight back now.

Anna focused her mind, her thoughts and her very being on preventing the horrific fate that lay inches away. As she teetered on the edge of existence, from somewhere deep inside her soul, inside the very heart of her aura, she found the life force to push back on her enemy again. She felt another massive surge of power. She pushed with every ounce of her might.

The jaws of the creature were inches from her face now. They opened again, this time letting out not a scream, but a sharp hiss. The sound registered somewhere in her head. It was the sound of surprise. Her back was already touching the floor. Her legs were bent double beneath her. But the aggressor's aura had stopped moving forward. Through all the pain and fear, Anna started to believe. She would not allow her uncle to die. Nor Mr Warwick. The evil Omega tide must finally be turned. Now was that time. She channelled every emotion into another surge of enormous power. She focused it all onto the opposing aura. And it shifted. Not so far before it came to a halt again, but enough. Sufficient to move her away from the edge, from that gap between worlds. The winds lessened. Finally, they stopped. The hole had resealed.

It had taken an almost superhuman effort to achieve that much. She did not have the power to force it back any further. But energy still coursed through her and she held her ground. Her resolve was granite. She would not be forced back towards that desolate place again. Defeat of the enemy might be beyond her, but she would give no further to this beast which had destroyed so many before her. It had finally met something it could not defeat. They remained there, locked in a titanic, deadly stalemate.

"That's it, Anna! Well done, my girl!" cried Sir Stephen as though he could not believe his eyes.

"Shut up, you fool," Mortlock hissed in his ear. "Her resistance is utterly futile. It will only be moments before her life is snuffed out forever. Her beautiful essence," he sneered, "will be fed to the Beta World, and there's nothing you can do about it. Nothing!"

Then events took another turn. There was a tremendous crash at the end of the hall. The middle section of the huge window shattered into a thousand pieces. A figure leapt through it, landing on the floor within Anna's line of sight.

It was Mr Warwick.

17
The Brave Knight

Apart from his face, the figure bore little resemblance to the kindly old bookseller Anna knew so well. He looked strong and powerful, his movements were fast and agile, and his were eyes ablaze.

In no time he was within feet of the battle. He opened his heavy, snow-covered cloak, exposing the jewelled hilt of an ancient sword. Like a knight of old, he drew it with a single, graceful movement. Anna noticed a sash of bright blue running diagonally from his left shoulder across the front of his white shirt.

She remained locked in her mental duel with the Satal, but the Beast hissed in the direction of Mr Warwick. The old man raised the sword in both hands then swung it in long, slow, downward diagonal arcs in front of him, alternately to his left and to his right. He could not kill the Satal using a sword, but he could defend himself from its physical attacks.

The monster's attention was divided. Its pressure on Anna's aura lessened just slightly. She should have reacted and struck straight away with all her remaining strength. But the flood of relief caused her to lessen her own grip on the Satal's aura momentarily. It was a fatal error.

The Satal suddenly tugged its aura away, breaking her grip. Then she was hurled violently backwards as a vicious, stabbing pain exploded deep in her chest. It had been an immense, lightning-fast strike from the Satal's aura. As she hit the ground, she rolled over onto her front a split second before the Beast's stamping talons smashed onto the stone floor where she had been. But the Satal's back was already turned. Its focus was now on Mr Warwick.

Anna was unable to move. She could barely breathe. There had been something different about this blow from any she had taken before. She had been knocked to the ground previously, been severely winded and felt huge bursts of pain. She had always been able to move again afterwards. This time, she could not. Unable even to raise her cheek from the cold stone tiles, she watched Mr Warwick.

His face was pure, determined calm. Unblinking and never shifting his gaze from the Satal's deadly aura, he took slow, steady paces forward. The Beast drew itself up to its full, awesome height, spreading its webbed wings to their full span. The vast, demonic shadow cast on the wall was the stuff of nightmares. It towered over the old man.

Still unable to lift her head, Anna shifted her focus. There was the massive, spiked ball of an aura, blood red at the tips. She winced again at the continuous pain from its last, paralysing assault. Within feet of it was Mr Warwick's aura. It was its full, natural size, and alive with a blazing, pure blue colour. It was the largest, most powerful human aura Anna had ever seen. But it was dwarfed by that of the Satal. Mr Warwick stepped stealthily from side to side. All the time he continued to swing the sword in front of him in case of any sudden physical strike. He seemed to be waiting for the monster to make the first move, and the first mistake.

The Satal followed his every move. It had clearly decided to kill this new intruder first before it returned to finish Anna off. It tilted its head back and gave another death scream. It beat its wings and clawed the air savagely in the direction of the old man. Then it crouched, preparing to strike. Mr Warwick's expression showed not the tiniest flicker of fear. Anna wanted to shout, but she couldn't make a sound. The piercing pain in her chest remained unabated.

Then it came. A sudden lunge, wings beating, talons lashing at the old man. With swift moves of his sword he repelled the blows. Simultaneously came the aura attack, which Anna knew would be the more deadly. The force of the blow was tremendous. With the distraction of the physical assault, Anna felt sure it would have done for almost anyone else. But Mr Warwick flexed his aura, moved it at the crucial moment and reduced the strike to a glancing blow. The spikes did not fully pierce the surface of his aura.

Anna still could not move. She wondered what the Satal had done to her. She had a growing fear the damage might be permanent. But she was desperate to help her beloved old mentor. The pain remained, but she forced herself to raise her head slightly from the tiles.

The next moves happened very fast, as Mr Warwick countered. The moment the spiked ball drew back for a second swing, the blue aura followed it and grabbed it like a flash. Holding on like a limpet on a rock, it immediately began to expand across its surface. The Satal attempted to pull away, but Mr Warwick held on, engulfing more and more of the larger aura.

Anna heard more shouting and scuffling from the side of the room, where Mortlock now had Sir Stephen pinned against the wall. The knight was attempting again to free himself, to help his old friend. Mortlock held him back.

Anna raised her head further. She recognised what Mr Warwick was attempting. She dragged herself into a kneeling position, clutching her hands to her chest. Having no other options, he was trying to surround and compress the Satal's aura unaided. It was a truly heroic attempt, but something no knight had ever achieved on their own. Whatever permanent toll it would take on her, she had to help him.

She forced herself into a crouch, then she rose. Slowly, still holding her chest, she moved forward towards the battle. She started to focus on what she must do. She was beginning to control the pain. She caught sight of her uncle's motionless body, and he appeared not to be breathing. She tried to block that from her mind. She simply could not fail her other mentor.

The pure blue aura was now covering a full third of the surface of the vicious black and red ball, but its progress had stopped. The Satal was resisting with increasing power. The old man's face had contorted with the enormity of his effort. The Satal flexed its deadly talons, but the pressure on its aura was enough to prevent a physical attack. It was in the mental dimension where its real threat lay. The Satal tugged its aura ferociously, twisting and turning it in an attempt to break the old man's hold. He clung on for dear life, but it was only going to be a matter of time. The blue aura was stretched thin. He could extend it no further. It would not be enough to defeat the Beast. Anna had to engage now, decisively, or all would be lost.

The Satal had its back to her. She saw it flex all its mighty muscles, and it let out a deep roar. To Anna's horror, two, then three red-tipped spikes pierced the pure blue outer surface of Mr Warwick's aura. A fourth, a fifth, then more passed clear through to the other side. For the first time since she had known him, she saw a look of panic cross the face of her old teacher.

"Prepare to die, old friend!" rang out the crowing, taunting voice of Mortlock from his own battle somewhere at the side of the room. He was blocked from Anna's view by the Satal.

With no further thought, she lunged forward. Using every last remaining ounce of effort, she flexed her aura into the hardest fist she could envisage and smashed it into the exposed area of the Satal's aura.

There was an immediate effect. The fighting auras lurched a considerable distance. The creature jerked its snout towards her and let out another deadly shriek. This time, Anna did not hesitate. She immediately followed up the blow by lunging at the enemy's aura, grabbing it, then moving to surround it from her own side. She visualised it smoothing itself over the huge spiked sphere. At the same time, she kept her aura firm and impenetrable.

The Beast's aura started to writhe and twist again immediately. Anna held firm. She continued to expand. The deadly spikes scraped and scratched at her. But her resolve was hard as flint. Despite the Satal's frantic movements, she covered more and more of the surface. Finally, she made contact with Mr Warwick's aura. At first it was just on the left side. Then, gradually, the two auras joined up right across the top of their enemy's.

Her eyes met her master's. His were filled with utter determination, now combined with re-born hope. Hope, and also intense pride – in her. Anna glimpsed the familiar old glint in his eye, and even the briefest hint of a smile in the kindly old face. It had only lasted a second, but it meant everything. She was battered, bruised and exhausted, but now filled with all the resolve her small frame could hold.

Anna's arrival had breathed new life into Mr Warwick. As she continued to spread her aura, his began to appear around the right-hand side. The Satal fought back. It stabbed its spikes hard at them with a deadly, pulsing motion. Twice it managed to open up gaps in the join between their auras at the top. Each time they re-sealed it through their sheer, combined will. Anna felt power surging through her aura again. She pushed on and on. She joined with Mr Warwick's aura over an ever-greater area. By now she felt she was engulfing well over half the spiked surface herself. Finally, streams of sweat pouring from her brow, she closed the final gap with Mr Warwick. They had their enemy fully surrounded.

"Yes! You can do it!" came a cry from Sir Stephen, still locked in combat with Mortlock.

Even as the Satal writhed and hissed, Mr Warwick made eye contact with Anna again. His eyes blazed with the fire of a man who would not be defeated.

"Now!" he shouted.

Anna redoubled her effort, exerting tremendous pressure. She pushed, compressed and crushed, all the while maintaining unwavering contact with the aura of her master.

It was then that she felt it. It was very faint at first. Then it became more noticeable. The enemy's aura felt as though it had somehow, slightly, given way. Anna drove forward again with all her force, blocking out the ear-splitting screams and roars.

And it happened again. This time a jolt forward, as though the structure she was pushing was slowly fracturing. Anna began to feel the sensation of wind around her aura again. An unpleasant breeze, filled with hate and malevolence. The winds of the Opposing Energy were just beginning to converge. She pushed again for all she was worth. There was a further collapse, immediately followed by another, then another. It was gaining speed. The winds grew stronger, drawn in by the increasing density of the Beast's aura.

Then the Satal let out another death roar. The spikes of its aura suddenly stabbed out with savage ferocity. Anna felt their full force. The deadly piercing sensation from earlier returned at her core. For a moment it took all her breath away, completely. She pictured the spikes piercing right through her aura. The evil winds howled around her. She faltered. It was too much. She could not sustain her aura's pressure on her enemy. The pain in her chest turned to agonising fire. Her contact with Mr Warwick's aura was lessening. The pressure from her aura dropped. Her head fell forward and her consciousness began to ebb away.

"Hold on Anna! Hold on now!" Mr Warwick's voice reached her. "This is the moment. This is where all will be won or lost forever. We have it. Its defeat is within our grasp. But you must hold on!"

His words acted as a mighty anchor, stopping her consciousness from being swept away completely.

"I need your strength now, Anna. The Order needs it. The world needs it. Anna, you have it within you. You are the mightiest of us all. Fight back!"

It is possible that the words of no other man in the world could have brought Anna back from the brink at that moment. Such were the unwavering strength of his voice, the depth of respect she held for him and the meaning of his words to her, she somehow found the will to continue. She tried to focus. Mr Warwick came into view. His face was very pale, but still determined. She could see the red tips of the enemy's spikes protruding throughout his aura. There must have been more than a dozen, maybe twenty. The realisation that he was somehow able to withstand the overwhelming pain spurred her on. She forced herself through her own pain. She blocked it out as much as she could. She started to focus and began to muster the energy to push again.

But the delay had been fatal. It had taken too long. The momentary lessening of pressure on the Satal's aura after its stabbing attack had given it the chance it needed in the physical world. It lashed out furiously at her with its deadly talons. Anna threw herself backwards to the floor, avoiding the slashing blades by an inch. Then it raised its clawed foot to stamp the life out of her. She had no chance of fending it off. She could not escape. Time slowed down. In vain, she started to apply pressure again through her aura, which was still wrapped around its enemy. The power was enough to slow down the stamping motion, but not yet sufficient to prevent it. It was too late.

There was a sense of fatal inevitability as the blow came. She raised her arm in a final gesture of defiance and closed her eyes. She was focused only on crushing as much as she could of the remaining, hateful aura of the creature, before it killed her. She felt the heavy weight upon her. The final, searing pain came – but only from her leg. She opened her eyes. She was stunned to see the body of Mr Warwick lying across her. The awful talons of the Satal's foot protruded from his body. Only one claw had missed it, stabbing her thigh. The old man had leapt to take the killer blow, for her.

A hundred thoughts and emotions threatened to overwhelm her. She pushed them all from her head bar one. Finish the Satal. Nothing else. Otherwise all this sacrifice was for nothing.

The Beast withdrew its claws, ready for another strike. She channelled all her remaining power back through her aura, fuelled afresh by her master's bravery. This time it was enough to stop another physical attack, at least temporarily. She looked at the Satal's aura. It was considerably smaller, but no longer reducing in size. Mr Warwick's aura was still wrapped around part of it, but it had now lost much of its colour. It was fading, turning almost grey. 'He's dying!' she thought. She blocked out that realisation. The grief would leave her useless.

Anna tried to ignore the violent pain in her leg and continued to press with her aura. But the pressure from the side of the Satal's aura held by Mr Warwick was starting to fail. Her own head started to swim, possibly due to the blood she was losing from her thigh. The creature began to move again. Mr Warwick's pressure was decreasing rapidly now. It would soon be able to launch another physical attack. They had come so close, but there was no more she could do. The Satal was going to strike a decisive, defining victory for the Omega World after all.

Suddenly a powerful new blow hit the three battling auras, making the writhing mass jump several feet. The impact was enough to stop the physical movement of the Beast again. And it had come from a large, blue aura!

Anna refocused her exhausted mind. Then her heart cried for joy. It was her uncle! One side of his face was completely covered with blood from the gash on top of his head, but he wore the grimmest, most determined expression imaginable.

Anna renewed the pressure from her side of the Satal's aura. This time the force from the other side was strong. Her uncle's bright, powerful aura had already spread itself over a considerable portion of the enemy's surface. Then, faintly, the pressure increased from the areas still covered by Mr Warwick's aura. Her old teacher was still fighting!

The pressure on the trapped aura steadily increased again. The Satal let out a howl. And rather than indomitable power, this time the noise sounded like fear. As though the Beast had thrown everything into its final, ruthless attack, only for it not to be enough.

They drove against it, Anna's own strength returning by the moment. She pushed her own aura over all the remaining surface of the Satal's until there were no gaps once more. Then the three comrades pushed as one.

The evil at their centre began to collapse again. Anna did not let up. Her full power was gradually returning.

There would be no reprieve this time. The collapses within the enemy's aura were coming one after another. The chain reaction had started.

The size of the ball reduced visibly as the destructive process within it gained momentum. Now it was irreversible. The brightness of the red spikes began to dim. The hideous, high-pitched howls of the Satal echoed deafeningly all through the mansion as the creature from the Beta World faced its final destruction.

Soon its aura seemed to reach a critical mass, beyond which it could be reduced no further. The only movement Anna felt was the maelstrom of the malevolent winds which raged all around the auras. She pushed on, undaunted.

The auras started to vibrate. The trembling grew violent, as though they were being buffeted by a wild storm. Marks began to appear on the surfaces of the blue auras. She felt physically sick. Intense blackness ringed the small, compressed remains of the Satal's aura. Its dense composition had created another hole, connecting them with the Beta World.

The winds howled towards the hole and through it. Anna felt the pure evil and hatred emanating towards her from whatever lay beyond the opening. This time she pushed all fear aside and followed the example of Mr Warwick and her uncle.

The body of their obdurate enemy writhed defiantly to the end, but to no effect now. No more attacks were possible. The trio were not to be denied. The dense ball of the Satal's aura was forced into the aperture. It held itself on the brink just briefly, then it was gone. The hole was sucked closed behind it. The terrible wind on Anna's aura, and the dreadful hatred from that other place, ceased.

With no more aura to push against, a shattered Anna dragged her focus back to the physical world. The body of the Satal had begun to deform and shrink right next to her. Its figure returned to that of Marcus Faulkner, the poor man whose body the Satal had taken possession of many years before.

As Anna looked at the dying body, its face began to move. It twisted into one final, ghastly snarl. The look was more shocking than at any time during the body's possession by the Satal.

It raised its head off the ground, and it looked directly at Anna. Then its twitching, swaying, snarling features spoke in one terrible, drawn out, deathly hiss. The words did not belong to the Satal, but to another.

"I know who you are! Now I have found you! I am coming for you…"

As the words reached their crescendo, Faulkner's eyes glittered, ignited by a different, distant but altogether more terrible presence. For an instant the pupils glowed with a deep, menacing red. Then the head fell back to the floor, dead.

There was nothing. No movement, no sound, no feeling. Anna lay motionless, numb and unaware. She did not notice the movement at the edge of the room, as Mortlock finally broke Sir Stephen's grip and fled the scene. She could not respond to her uncle's desperate words as he held her.

The superhuman mental effort it had taken to banish the Satal, and the immense physical toll it had taken on her body, had left her completely spent. A wave of painful exhaustion swept her into unconsciousness.

18
Farewell

It was her uncle's blood-smeared face that she saw first. He looked gravely concerned. He seemed to be speaking, but she could not make out the words. Slowly, the sound began to filter through.

"Anna? Anna, can you hear me? Are you all right? Anna, please speak to me."

"Yes, uncle, I'm fine," she replied automatically. The deep pain which shot through her leg suggested otherwise. The memory of what had happened slowly returned. Urgency gripped her.

"Is – is it gone? Faulkner – the Beast – is it gone? Did we defeat it?"

"Thank God!" A look of untold relief crossed her uncle's face. "Yes Anna, we did it. Faulkner's gone. Never to return."

Relief swept over Anna as well, despite the pain. "Are you all right uncle? Your head?"

"I'm fine. Don't worry about me."

"Oh, what a relief. I thought…" Then she remembered. "What about Mr Warwick?" The urgency redoubled. "Is he going to be all right? Oh, please, tell me he is!"

Her uncle's expression changed. "Ordinarily I wouldn't try to move you in your condition. But I'm afraid we have very little time left now. Do you think you might be able to sit up?"

The meaning of this reply slowly sank in. Pushing down with her right elbow, she tried to raise herself. An immense stab of pain ripped through her right leg, forcing her straight back down.

"Anna, are you all right?" His look of deep concern had returned. "I'm so sorry to ask you this, after all you've been through. But can I try to raise you up?"

Anna had never felt anything quite like that bolt of pain. She hesitated. "Yes, all right, go ahead. But please, slowly!"

With the greatest of care, her uncle moved alongside her. He put his left arm gently under her shoulder for support. Slowly and carefully, he raised her. She could not stop another gasp of pain as she reached an upright position. Her gaze was drawn automatically to the pain's source. The entire lower-right side of her dress all round her leg was crimson. It felt like something had been tied around her thigh above the injury.

"I took the liberty of tying a tourniquet around your leg. You were losing so much blood, I had to stop it somehow."

"Thank you, uncle," said Anna.

"I used a long strip of material from the shredded remains of Faulkner's clothes. It was the least he could do for us." Uncle James forced a weak smile. It was gone in a moment.

"Where's Mr Warwick?"

"He's over there."

Several feet away, behind her, lay her beloved teacher and mentor. The hilt of the sword was clutched flat to his chest with both hands. The blade lay over his legs and reached almost to his feet. His face was still, his eyes closed. The floor between them was a sea of red.

"No! He can't be dead! It's not possible. He saved me. It should have been me. He can't be gone!"

"Anna, Anna," her uncle tried to soothe her. "He's not dead. But I'm afraid he doesn't have much time left. I tended to his injuries as best I could, but they are far too severe for anyone to heal. I'm afraid he is beyond recovery."

"No! That can't be!" Her voice strengthened. She struggled to move herself to see her old master more clearly. She felt more spasms of pain, but they were no longer her main concern. "There must be something we can do? We must try!"

"Anna," he said softly, "I have done everything possible to stabilise him for a short time. Beyond that there is nothing that can be done. He has sustained terrible injuries. No doctor alive could save him now."

"But—"

"Please Anna, listen to me. We don't have much time. Mr Warwick wants to speak with you now. That's why I had to wake you."

"Yes, please let me speak to him!" She tried to drag herself in his direction.

"Let me help you." As gently as he could, he lifted his niece to the old shopkeeper's side. Then he moved to the other side. The old man's chest was moving almost imperceptibly.

"Master, Anna is here. She is going to be all right."

There was a brief flicker of the eyelids. Mr Warwick slowly opened his eyes and looked at him.

"Here she is, master." He gestured towards her.

Anna reached out to place her hands on her teacher's, which clutched the hilt of his sword. The old man slowly turned his head in her direction. Despite the unbearable pain he must have been feeling, his eyes softened and his familiar old features broke into a weak smile.

"Hello, Anna." His voice was the faintest of whispers. "It is good to see you. You are all right?"

"Yes, master. Oh, Mr Warwick, please stay with us. Please don't leave!" Her voice cracked. The old shopkeeper had overcome so much in his long life. Surely, he could pull through this, too.

"I'm afraid I'm not going to make it this time." His voice strengthened a little. "But there are some things that I need to say to you. If you could indulge me, I should be most grateful."

"Yes, of course," she said. Her voice was hoarse.

"Firstly, I want you to know how proud I am. To have known you, and to have called myself your teacher for a time. And most of all, to have been able to fight alongside you once, before my time was done."

Anna tightened her grip on his hands.

"Since the first time I set eyes on you as a child, you have never ceased to be a source of amazement and joy to me. But tonight, you surpassed anything I could have imagined. Your bravery was beyond my comprehension. You remembered every word of your instruction. You executed it without fault."

"I would have been done for if you hadn't arrived when you did," she replied. "And you kept me going through the battle. You saved the day. You saved us all." Tears ran down her face.

"No. It was your strength, your might, which won the day. Your power... it matched the Satal's! Your uncle and I just tipped the balance. Without your extraordinary powers, all would certainly, without question, have been lost. And with it, the course of the Struggle could have changed forever. I feel sure of it."

Anna looked down. No more words would come.

"You know how I enjoy the Histories. I love the stories of our heroes from times past. I do not know of any knight in the whole of history who was able to stand alone against a Satal, to withstand its worst, as you were doing when I arrived. Your aura was a sight to behold! It was truly wondrous. Not only are you the most outstanding pupil it has ever been my privilege to teach, but I am quite sure you are the most outstanding pupil there has ever been."

"Thank you, Mr Warwick." She was struggling badly. "But you saved my life. You are lying there because of me. Those claws... they were meant for me. I've cost you your life..." She broke down completely. Her uncle moved round to console her.

"But Anna, please listen to me. I would far, far sooner have it this way. Please understand this. Yes, I acted through love for you, but also because you are our greatest hope for the future of the Struggle. You may still not perceive it even now, but I am certain that you will become so much more important in the history of the Struggle than I have ever been. Or ever could be. Had the Satal killed you this night, it could have been the fatal blow against the Alpha World. But it did not. We were victorious. And for me, that is a source of the greatest joy you can imagine. I would change nothing."

Anna gripped the old man's hands again. Her body trembled. Mr Warwick closed his eyes and took a breath.

"Anna, I have something very important I still need to say."

"Yes, master."

"Tonight, we have fought a great battle, and we have won an important victory. But this was only one battle, the first of many that will need to be fought, and won, before the world is rid of the unprecedented threat it now faces. I fear there will be far, far harder struggles ahead before that final victory is ours.

"However, as I have always aimed to be absolutely truthful with you, so I am now when I say this. As long as you remain true to the Alpha cause, and fight on the side of what you know in your heart to be right, I believe our side will win. So, I want you to make me one last promise."

"Yes, anything. I will promise anything you ask." Anna was sobbing uncontrollably.

"I want you to promise me that whatever happens, whatever obstacles and temptations are put in your way, of which there will be many, and however desperate and hopeless things may seem, you will never waver from the Alpha side. And that you will never give up. That you will keep searching until you find the way through. For there will always be a way. This, Anna, may be the most important thing I have ever said to you as your teacher. I want you to remember it, always."

Anna nodded.

"If you are lost, or if you give up, all hope may be gone. But if you continue to believe and to fight on, no matter how hopeless the cause may seem, just as you did tonight, then I am certain we will emerge victorious. Please, Anna, promise me."

A familiar fire had returned dimly to Mr Warwick's eyes, one last time. He raised his head slightly, clasped Anna's hands and looked directly into her eyes. She controlled her voice as best she could. "Yes, master. I promise you that, with all of my heart. Please rest peacefully, knowing that I will."

A look of calm finally came to Mr Warwick's face. He rested his head back down.

"Thank you, Anna. Thank you. Please believe me, I will die a happier man than you can ever know for hearing that."

Anna nodded. She looked desperately at her uncle, not knowing what else to say. His face told her that nothing more was needed. But Mr Warwick spoke again, his voice weakening, but still in that same kindly tone Anna had known and loved all her life.

"In all my dealings with you, I tried my best to be honest. There was only one exception. There was one truth that I knowingly misled you about. It was when you asked me about the appearance of your own essence."

He paused. He was struggling badly for breath, but he wanted to continue.

"If you recall, I mentioned its dazzling blue colour and other qualities, but I said that it was not yet of any great size. I chose not to burden you with the full weight of the expectations that we all had. For you were going to have to bear that burden soon enough. But in truth, even at the age of fourteen when your instruction first began, your essence had already grown to become the largest that I, or anyone else, has ever seen in a human being. Only in a

Satal have I seen larger. That was true at the time we spoke, and it is still growing now, all the time. This is why I was so keen to teach you how to disguise it at the very beginning of your instruction."

Any other time, the subject of her own aura would have fascinated her. But now it did not mean anything. Not if Mr Warwick would no longer be there. But slowly, as he spoke, she calmed her mind. There was almost no time left. He had things he wanted to say before he passed, so she would listen. This was the last time she would hear him speak. She would soak it in and make the most of every word, one last time, as the emotion poured out of her.

"Naturally, I have never seen my own essence, but I have heard it said that it is not an inconsiderable size. But even at an age when very few others have ever even begun to develop the Powers, they tell me that your essence is already far larger than mine. What's more, they tell me that it quite *outshines* mine! Certainly, I have never seen anything like it. Anything quite so beautiful, so marvellous. Not even in a Grand Master of the Order at the height of their powers.

"That is just one of the many, many reasons that I say it has been the honour of my life to have known you, and to have played even the smallest part in the wondrous story that will be yours. I no longer have any doubt that it will be amongst the greatest ever told in our Order."

Her tears streamed freely. She did not try to hide them, or feel ashamed. They were the purest expression of what he meant to her.

The old man's eyes closed and his face contorted. It looked as though a deep pain had taken hold. He opened them and looked at her uncle.

"James, please do not grieve for me. You were a fine pupil, and you have become a very great knight. And you have been a great friend to me. You know what must be done now. You are strong. Do not waver. Act with courage and true intentions, guide Anna, and help her see it through to the end. Go forth. My spirit will be with you."

He turned his head to look at Anna once more. For the last time, she saw the kindly expression that had so often warmed her heart in the most frightening of times. The one she had grown to love most of all. His smiling eyes held her tearful ones in its caring gaze for a moment longer. Then they gently closed, as life left the old man's body forever.

At first Anna could not take it in. She was sure he would open his eyes again. But the look from her uncle told her otherwise. Tears were also visible on his face. Uncontrollable desolation took hold of her. She could not remember her own father, but the kindly old man lying before her had mentored her as well as any father could have. He had literally changed her life.

Her short time in the world had been filled with more than its fair share of unhappiness, but Mr Warwick had shown her a new life, one in which she might actually mean something. One where she might become something in the future. And now, this most gentle yet inspirational of mentors had laid down his life to save hers. He had been torn from her so abruptly. It was more than she could cope with.

Her last memory of that awful mansion was of Timmy, Rebecca and the others pouring in, their captors having finally been overcome. But the image swam in her head even as it met her eyes. She fell back into deep unconsciousness.

19
The Spy Revealed

It was a week before Anna's mother would let anyone visit her, apart from the doctors and her uncle. Her delight and relief at her daughter's safe return were matched only by her shock and concern at her condition. Even Anna's uncle was only permitted to see Anna when her mother felt she was up to it. He was under the strictest instructions not to discuss anything that had happened until Anna was well enough, beyond letting her know the essentials. It was a rule that he stuck to religiously.

Uncle James had apparently been almost ever-present in the house since their return. Anna understood there were also other members of the Order stationed in and around the building at all times. However, with the defeat of Faulkner, the immediate danger appeared to have passed.

Anna spent large parts of that first week asleep. She had no memory of the journey back to her home, and very little of the initial days that followed. She was told that she had lost an enormous amount of blood from the wound in her thigh, and it had been touch and go as to whether she would survive. The gash was long as well as deep. It caused her continual pain, for which the doctor gave her pain-killing medicine. She understood it would be many weeks before she could leave her bed. As for whether she would ever be able to walk normally again, no-one could say.

Her uncle told her that her aura had also sustained damage. She was certain it was from the brutal blow from the Satal which had left her unable to move for a time during the battle. It had felt like nothing she had experienced before. Uncle James told her that scars remained where the spikes had struck her. He reassured her that they should fade somewhat with time, and that they should not have a lasting impact on her. But from his experience, it was likely that some markings would always remain.

Lucky though she felt to be alive, the loss of Mr Warwick hung like a big black cloud over her bed at all times. She was consumed by grief and guilt at the passing of her teacher. Her premonition that tragedy would strike during the battle had proved correct, but she had mistaken the person. She just could not imagine the world without Mr Warwick there.

What Anna did learn from the brief conversations permitted with her uncle was that her friends had escaped without serious injury. The forces of the Order had made it from Eagle Street to the mansion soon after the battle, and at her uncle's direction they had easily overcome the guards in the tower.

She was also relieved to learn that, despite a severe head injury from the falling bookcase, Greg Matthews was expected to make a full recovery. Sir Stephen's condition was slowly improving from the injuries inflicted on him by both Faulkner and Mortlock. To her enormous relief, when she asked her uncle about

Jeremiah, he said that although their friend had indeed been badly injured, he was sure he would be all right.

When she tried to tell her uncle about Percival, he had stopped her mid-sentence. He told her that he knew what had happened, and that there would be an opportunity to talk about it another time. Percival had been one of his students. Anna realised just how difficult this betrayal must have been for him.

Mortlock, McCain and Grimes had all apparently managed to get away. They had fled London, but most of the other gang members had been captured in Eagle Street. There had been no more sightings of the Wraith since the night of the attack on Jeremiah's home.

For her part, Anna sketched out the attack on Jeremiah's for her uncle. She relayed how she had managed to escape, and how she had eventually come to be at Faulkner's mansion. In relation to Timmy, she merely said that her friend had been taken. She could see that her uncle burned with questions, but true to his word he held them all back for now.

One morning, a week after the battle, when Anna was able to sit up in bed for the first time, her uncle visited again. He still had a bandage round his head, which did nothing for his stylish image. His blood loss had been less than Anna's though, and apart from headaches, which were becoming less frequent by the day, he was physically more or less recovered. He did, however, look far more tired than Anna had ever seen him. Large black shadows under his eyes suggested he had not had a proper night's sleep since the events at the mansion. That morning, he took the doctor and her mother to one side for a brief discussion.

"Yes, all right, I think she's ready," the doctor said eventually.

"But whatever happens, James," her mother added quickly and a little sternly, "don't overdo it. At the first sign that she's getting tired or distressed, you must let her rest at once."

"Yes, I fully understand. I shall certainly do so." He did not seem the indomitable character he had once been. It was Anna's mother who was in charge now.

"Very well, then," she continued. "Anna, don't let your uncle tire you out with all his talking! And make sure you don't try to overdo things yourself."

She kissed Anna on the forehead, then she and the doctor left the room. Uncle James quickly checked outside in both directions before closing the door again.

"The doctor tells us you're making good progress. He says you might be strong enough now to talk about things in a bit more detail. I'm sure you have a lot of questions of your own, too. It's probably better that you let some of them out, before you explode!"

Anna smiled weakly. She did have questions, but she did not have the stomach to ask them yet. All thoughts led her back to the death of Mr Warwick. That was still too raw to dwell on for long. Her uncle was the only person she could bring herself to talk to about it at all. He was probably the only one who could begin to understand how she felt.

He continued, "We have been able to piece together most of what happened now. I visited Sir Stephen yesterday. He witnessed the whole battle with Faulkner after I was knocked out, and has filled me in on the details. I must say, I thought I knew what you were capable of, but even I was astounded to hear what you managed to do. No-one I have ever known could have endured that kind of phenomenal power on their own." Then he smiled. "I shall overlook that you ignored my instructions to escape! It turns out that you knew better than me. You were brave beyond words."

"Thank you," said Anna, looking down briefly at her hands. "How is Sir Stephen now?"

"He's recovering. Like you, he sustained a serious injury to his leg from the Beast. He will walk again, although probably always with a limp. But he is devastated that he was unable to come to your aid in that battle. This is not the first time he has fought a Satal. He lacks nothing in bravery, nor skill. He feels desperate that he was unable to help you when you most needed it."

"Oh, but why, uncle? He has no reason to feel that way. We would never have survived a battle against both Faulkner and Mortlock. He saved both our lives by keeping Mortlock out of the fight, despite being so badly injured." Anna began to recall the battle more clearly. "His encouragement gave me strength too, just when I needed it. His words brought me back from the brink. Please do tell him how grateful I am to him. He did everything he could."

"I can't tell you how much your words will mean to him. I shall let him know. Thank you." He paused. "Before I go on, I must also thank you for myself. From Sir Stephen's account, it is clear that without your intervention, I would certainly now be dead. Which, in all honesty, was what I fully expected. The fact I am here now is entirely down to you. I owe you my life. I thank you most sincerely."

Anna did not know where to look or what to say. She would equally not be there had it not been for her uncle and Mr Warwick. Before she could find any words, he moved on again.

"There is something else I'd like to talk about. Something important, which cannot wait any longer. There are still some gaps in the information I have on the events leading up to the battle." His voice remained soft and undemanding, but a certain, unmistakeable tension had crept into it.

"Do you feel up to going back through the events between my leaving you at Jeremiah's home and the enemy's attack there? The last time we met was the evening I left to meet Greg, who was travelling back from Oxford. The following night, the enemy attacked. Do you remember if anything unusual happened during the day, before the attack?"

Anna thought hard. So much had happened since then. "Well, I woke up late that morning. By the time I went into the main room, Mr Warwick was already there. He was talking to Jim, Emily, Percival and Alexandra Greenwood. Mr Warwick and Jim then left, and I had a lovely afternoon with Emily and Alexandra," she hesitated, "and Percival. I can't think of anything strange."

"So, Mr Warwick, Emily, Alexandra, Percival and Jim. Did anyone else visit that day?"

"No. Well, only Jeremiah. He returned home earlier than I had ever seen him. That was the only unusual thing I can think of. No-one else came."

Uncle James rose from his chair and checked outside the room again. Then he resumed his seat, looking agitated.

Anna continued, "Mr Warwick left Jeremiah's to brief other Order members who were going to be part of the Eagle Street mission. I don't know where that meeting was."

"No, that's fine. Don't worry about that. It's Jeremiah's home I'm most interested in. So, no-one else went there as far as you know, apart from Jeremiah?"

"No, that's everyone."

"All right. So, who stayed with you, up until the house was attacked?" His tone was growing more urgent, which he seemed to notice himself. "I'm sorry Anna, I don't mean to press you. Please take your time."

"Percival was there. He was in the house the whole time, at least until I went to bed. Jeremiah stayed too, once he had returned. Emily and Alexandra left in the early evening to meet Mr Warwick. Jim left earlier on, around the same time as Mr Warwick, to tie up loose ends here in this house. He was due to come back later in the afternoon to stay at Jeremiah's overnight as well, but as far as I know he didn't make it back before we were attacked."

A fearful thought returned to her. She realised she hadn't heard about Jim since she had returned home.

"He wasn't ambushed by the enemy, was he? Is he all right?"

"Yes, Anna, don't worry, he's fine. He was accosted by members of Faulkner's gang, but fortunately he managed to escape them, eventually."

Anna heaved an enormous sight of relief.

Her uncle continued, "Could you relive for me the exact sequence of events during the attack itself? Only if you feel up to it of course. But in as much detail as you can manage at this point. Please be as accurate as you possibly can. There may be a lot riding on what you tell me."

Anna wondered what he meant, but she knew better than to ask him yet. She went through everything she could remember, from the dream, to the fiddle player, to the Wraith attack.

"Uncle," she said suddenly, "we haven't spoken much about that night, with all that's happened since. You said Jeremiah is recovering. The last time I saw him he was bravely battling that Wraith, but he was already injured. If he hadn't held that thing back, I don't think I would have made it out of that building. He is going to be all right, isn't he?"

Her uncle's expression changed. He looked down. Then he leant forward and gently put his hands on hers as they lay on the bed. His tone was suddenly very soft.

"I'm sorry. I couldn't tell you the full extent of his injuries when you asked me before. It was still too soon. I was under the strictest orders from the doctor and your mother. However, things have moved on, and it would be wrong to withhold something so important from you any longer. I'm afraid Jeremiah's wounds were very severe. He hasn't made it. He passed away yesterday."

The words hit Anna like rifle shots. She pulled her hands away from his. "No! No uncle, please, tell me that's not true!"

Her uncle appeared to be choking back his own emotions. He looked at her tenderly. "Anna, I wish I could tell you that it's not true..." Then he looked down again and gently shook his head.

"But he saved me! I stopped to help him, but he told me to run. I didn't at first, but then I thought... I thought that if I ran, the Wraith would chase after me and leave him alone. I thought that would give him his best chance. I called out to it, to Gillespie, to chase after me instead. Oh, no. He saved me! He helped me escape, and I just left him there to be killed..."

"It was not your fault. You did exactly the right thing. It was I who put Jeremiah in danger by asking him to let us stay. In the end, it cost him his life. I shall carry the guilt of that to my grave..."

But a fresh wave of grief erupted inside Anna. Only one thought penetrated it. "Have you dealt with Percival? He was on Faulkner's side all along, I'm sure of it. He must have told them where we were. He tried to stop me escaping. He caused Jeremiah's death!"

The words exploded out of her. Then she broke down into floods of tears, becoming hysterical. Uncle James tried his best, but he could not console her. The news about Jeremiah unlocked fresh feelings of grief, and guilt, for Mr Warwick as well. Two people had died to save her. It was just too much. Anna's mother soon reappeared, and she ushered Uncle James out of the room. The doctor returned to give Anna more medication. Eventually she fell into a deep sleep.

It was two days later before they were allowed to resume the conversation, Anna's mother having reluctantly agreed.

"I would much prefer to avoid further discussions until you are fully recovered," she said. Anna noted she was dressed for going out. "But having spoken to your uncle at length, I understand that there are certain important matters that do have to be resolved. I understand the importance, so I shall reluctantly permit one more conversation. But that's all. And I have told James that he must not upset you again!"

Uncle James looked very pale. He simply nodded his confirmation.

"I have to go out now," she continued. "It is the first time I have left the house since your injury, but I have some pressing matters to attend to that I cannot postpone any longer. Your uncle will remain with you until I return. I hope to find everything resolved when I get back."

Uncle James nodded again. "Yes, that is also my hope."

Once she had left the room, Uncle James again checked outside the door. The dark shadows under his eyes had deepened. Before long, the sound of the front door closing reached them from far below.

This time, Anna started the conversation by returning to the Wraith attack. "You said the Wraith has not been seen. Does that mean he… it survived?"

"We can't say for sure. There was a trail of blood leading from Jeremiah's rooms, down the stairs to the front door. The tracks stopped after that. It has not been seen since, but I think we must assume it survived."

"I see," said Anna quietly.

At her uncle's request, she continued the story from the point she left the battle with the Wraith on the stairs, to her long journey to Rebecca's house and the news that

Timmy had been captured. This time she shared everything, including, for the first time, something of her feelings for Timmy. It was still embarrassing to discuss, but after all they had been through it was no longer insurmountable. It felt far more important that her uncle knew all the facts now.

She explained that she had known it could be a trap, but that there was no safe way of reaching anyone in the Order, and that she could not allow any of her friends to meet the fate that had befallen Gillespie. Her uncle did not disguise his surprise on learning about Timmy. He agreed that it must have been a trap laid by Faulkner, but this time he did not rebuke her. The conversation turned to how he could have known.

"Please think very carefully. Who knew that you and this… Timothy Thompson… felt something for each other?"

"Well, Lizzy knew. She was helping us to meet up. Or at least, I thought she was." Anna explained how she had subsequently learned that Lizzy had given her and Timmy different messages, to create trouble between them.

"I see. We removed Lizzy from the household staff after she arranged for Gillespie to meet with you. Since then, it's possible she may have spoken about your… feelings for Timothy to others, and that Faulkner found out. Was there anyone else who knew?"

"Only Jim." She briefly relayed the time she had asked Jim to help arrange a meeting with Timmy in the early Autumn. She explained that he had refused, reiterating that she was not allowed to leave the house, but that he had also promised not to tell anyone.

"Please don't be angry with him, uncle. The reason he didn't say anything was to save my embarrassment, and because I begged him not to. I think he felt bad about refusing to help me."

"I see. All right. So, you went with your friends to rescue Timothy. What happened then?"

Anna explained how they had gained entry to the mansion, how they had located Timmy, and their capture by Mortlock. She learned that Uncle James had come to hear of Anna's arrival at the mansion from Miller, the Order secret agent. He had been concealed at the entrance to the Hampstead mansion's driveway and had seen them arrive. Faulkner had received word of Timmy's capture, and had left the City much earlier than expected. Fortunately for everyone, the progress of his large carriage was considerably delayed going up the hills by the deepening snow, and her uncle had reached the mansion first. Uncle James had seen light through the great hall window and headed straight there.

She also found out that Mr Warwick had indeed been shadowing Faulkner that afternoon, as Faulkner had told them before the battle. When Faulkner received the message to return to his mansion, Mr Warwick attempted to overtake him, to get there before Faulkner did. It meant he had to move fast and break cover, and that's when he was captured by Faulkner's men. The men were all strong in the Powers, as Faulkner had said, but Mr Warwick had eventually managed to overcome all four of them. Then he had headed for the mansion.

"So he had already been in one big battle, even before he got to us!"

"Yes, and a very tough one, too. I extracted this information myself, from one of those men. They were all hardened criminals with considerable strength in the Powers. Once Mr Warwick had defeated them, he left them tied up with their own rope, to be picked up by our Order colleagues. The man I questioned had ridden on horseback to catch up with Faulkner and give him the message about Mr Warwick's capture. Faulkner sent the man back, to help make sure our master did not escape. His help clearly wasn't enough!"

"I see," said Anna, wide eyed.

"This was why Faulkner did not have any men with him when he arrived at the mansion. If he had, I think we would have been done for. That is another thing we have Mr Warwick to thank for."

They both fell silent for a moment. Anna considered with some wonder what Mr Warwick must already have been through even to get the mansion, before the battle with Faulkner. Somehow it made his eventual fate even harder to bear.

Uncle James finally resumed. "And you know the rest. So, that more or less brings us up to date. But it still leaves the most important question unanswered. How did Faulkner and his gang find out that you were at Jeremiah's home? Whether or not Lizzy played any part in their using your friend as bait to capture you, there is no way she could have known about Jeremiah's."

"But surely it was Percival who told them?"

Her uncle did not answer directly. He looked very tired. His face carried a haunted expression. "I think there's only one person now who we can rely on to identify the culprit for sure. I need to speak to him somewhere private. Right now, the only place I trust completely is this room. Would you mind if I had that conversation here?"

Anna was self-conscious about her appearance, but she agreed. Uncle James left the room briefly. She heard him call downstairs to someone, asking them to fetch Jim. He also issued instructions that no-one else was to come within earshot of the room until further notice.

"Jim?" said Anna when her uncle re-entered. It would be the first time she had been allowed to see anyone apart from her mother, her uncle and the doctor.

"Yes. I believe he's the only one who can help us confirm the true identity of the spy who gave away your location to the enemy. But we have to move fast."

Anna's pulse quickened. She was suddenly more alert than at any point since the start of her recovery. As they waited for the faithful knight, Anna's uncle began to pace the room.

"It's getting very stuffy in here. Do you mind if I open the window?" he asked.

"No, not at all, please go ahead. It would be nice to get some fresh air. But are you all right, uncle?" He did not look his normal self at all.

"Yes, Anna. Please don't worry about me."

He unlatched the large window at the far side of the room and opened it wide, allowing a gentle, cold winter breeze to come in. He placed an upholstered armchair near the window. But instead of sitting, he continued his agitated pacing. Then there was a knock.

"Enter," he called out, immediately moving towards the door. Jim's familiar face appeared.

"Sir, you asked for me?"

"Yes, thank you for coming so swiftly, Jim. Please, do come in."

Jim beamed at Anna as he entered. "Mistress Anna, how good to see you looking well. We've been so worried about you. Emily asked me to pass you all her very best when I saw you next."

"Thank you, Jim. Do please send her mine, too," said Anna, beaming back. "Yes, I'm starting to feel better now. It's good to see you again. How are you?"

As she spoke, she looked at his aura to check for any damage from the attack on him by Faulkner's men. She was mightily relieved to find it as strikingly blue and blemish-free as ever.

Before Jim could respond any further, Uncle James, keen to get on with the conversation, shepherded him over to the far side of the room, to the armchair by the window.

"Oh, thank you for asking, mistress," Jim replied, taking the seat. "I'm all right. At least, as much as anyone can be at a time like this, when such truly tragic events have occurred."

"Yes, indeed," said Anna's uncle. He had remained standing, unable to wait for further formalities. "Jim, we need your help to unravel exactly how those events occurred. There may be no-one else we can turn to now."

"Of course, sir. Please ask me anything. There's nothing I wouldn't do to help."

"Yes, Jim, thank you. We really do appreciate your words. Now, I need you to think very carefully. Tell us what happened on the day before the battle, from the moment you left Jeremiah's home onwards. I know we have discussed this before, but I need to recap some of the details now."

"Yes, sir," replied Jim, thinking. "Well, I came straight here, sir. I spoke with other members of staff to make sure all my duties would be covered whilst I was away, so I could stay at Jeremiah's for as long as needed. It wasn't difficult, as Mistress Anna and her mother were both away from the house anyway, so there were fewer tasks to be done."

"Did you tell anyone where you were going to be?" Seeing a surprised look on Jim's face, he added, "I mean, could it have slipped out by accident, when you were talking to the others?"

"No, sir. I certainly never said a word about that. I knew how important it was. I was extremely careful not to say anything to anyone."

"Were there any other conversations that seemed to you in any way out of the ordinary, while you were in this house that day?"

Jim thought hard for several moments. "No sir, there was nothing I can think of. Maisy asked me where I was going at such short notice, and I told her I was going to stay with a sick aunt south of the river. The same story I agreed with you and Mr Warwick beforehand, sir."

"Very well," continued Uncle James. He was standing still in the middle of the room, halfway between Jim and Anna, his hands clasped tightly behind his back. He clearly had an idea on his mind and all his attention was focused on pursuing it. Anna could feel his intensity. She looked down at the bed covers as he continued. "And you have previously explained how you were then attacked by Grimes and other members of Faulkner's gang on your way to Jeremiah's home. We have already discussed that in detail, so no need to go over that again now. Then, finally, you escaped them."

"Yes, sir. I made absolutely certain I wasn't followed. And when I got back to Jeremiah's, that's when I found…" His face looked pale as he recalled what he had seen.

"What time would it have been when you got there?" Uncle James cut in.

"It was after midnight, sir, approaching one o'clock."

"And there was no sign of any gang members there by the time you arrived?"

"No, sir. I suppose they'd all gone off, hunting for Anna."

"Yes, no doubt." Anna's uncle paused, apparently thinking hard before finally making up his mind. "Thank you, Jim, that has been most helpful. Now, I think there is just one more thing I need to ask you. Then we should be able to resolve once and for all how Faulkner tracked Anna down to Jeremiah's. Please think very carefully about what I am about to ask. It may be the most important thing that I have ever asked of you. Indeed, I do not exaggerate when I say that lives may literally depend on it, this very day."

Anna jerked her head up and looked at him. What did he mean? Were they in danger again, right now? Jim nodded earnestly. His expression conveyed more powerfully than words that he would do anything to help.

"Jim," said her uncle, his voice calm, but his focus absolute. "Please remove your disguise."

Jim paused, as though searching for a meaning that eluded his grasp. "Sir… excuse me?" he said finally, nonplussed.

"I said, please remove your disguise." Uncle James's voice remained calm, but a hard edge had entered his tone.

"I beg your pardon, sir, I, I... I don't think I understand." He looked utterly bewildered now.

"Oh, but I beg to disagree," Anna's uncle responded. His tone began to grow ominous. "I think you understand exactly."

Slowly, he advanced on the confused younger man in the chair. "I shall ask you one more time." Then furious anger suddenly burst from him. "Remove your disguise!"

The poor butler began to grimace, as though suddenly in great pain. Shocked, Anna shifted her focus. Jim's pure blue aura was in the vice-like grip of her uncle's larger, more powerful one. It appeared to be squeezing its smaller counterpart mercilessly. And it had started to glow with a vivid, purple colour again.

"No, uncle! No! Stop!" Anna yelled. Something had happened to him. She had to stop him before he did something terrible. She attempted to raise herself from the bed to intervene, only for a bolt of pain to shoot through her from her leg. She fell back again, immobile.

"You are a traitor!" hissed Uncle James through clenched teeth. His face was now just inches from that of the cowering Jim, who sat rooted to his chair. "You have betrayed every faith placed in you by those who trusted you the most. Your treachery has been beyond belief. It has led to the deaths of loyal and true friends. To the death of our own, dear master!" His voice rose to a roar. "Judas, remove your disguise!"

Jim looked utterly terrified. He was unable to move or speak in the face of this assault. Uncle James's aura appeared to be crushing the life out of him.

351

"No, uncle! You must stop!" screamed Anna again. "You are wrong! Jim hasn't done anything! It was Percival who told Faulkner. He was the traitor. Stop, uncle – you're going to kill him!"

It was as though something had possessed him. Unable to move from the bed, she tried desperately to reach out with her own aura to stop the attack. It was no good. The confrontation was at the other end of the room. It was too far away to reach them. She was powerless to intervene.

"It was *you* who led Faulkner and his gang to Jeremiah's!" he yelled like a crazed maniac. "You practically served Anna up to the Satal on a platter! Poor young Anna, who trusted you completely. Your treachery, your barbarity, they know no end!"

Uncle James had both Jim's coat lapels in a tight grip and he was slamming the younger man repeatedly against the chair back. All the while, the death-grip of his purple aura on that of the young butler continued to tighten.

"Stop uncle, stop! He's innocent! You're killing him!" Anna cried.

With three final, mighty slams of the younger man's body into the back of the chair, Uncle James hissed the three words again. "Remove – your – disguise!"

Through tear-filled eyes, Anna watched on helpless as Jim began to lose consciousness. She made a final, desperate attempt to leave her bed, but the excruciating pain in her leg prevented her from getting more than halfway out of it. She watched the final moments, utterly distraught.

Then something strange happened. As Jim lost consciousness, his aura began to change. Large streaks of black and brown appeared, where there had only ever been bright blue before. Black, brown – and then red. Spots at first, growing into large, ugly, scarlet patches. Before long, all remaining hints of blue were gone completely, replaced by a vision of red, black and brown. And the colour was not the only thing that had changed. The shape had transformed, from a perfect sphere to a deeply cratered, horribly misshapen object. Anna was appalled. Had her uncle somehow caused this change in poor Jim's aura? What could it mean? When the transformation was complete, Uncle James flung the younger man back down into his chair for a final time.

He stepped away, sweat dripping from his hair, which he swept back from his face. Turning to Anna like some kind of deranged performer at the end of a horrific stage show, he gestured in the direction of the unconscious butler.

"And behold, the true essence of our friend, Jim!"

"You're not my uncle!" Anna yelled at him. "You are something else!" He must have been possessed in some way, or somehow have fallen under the enemy's control.

It was then Uncle James noticed that Anna was halfway out of her bed. He hurried over to help her. Terrified, Anna clenched her aura and fired a hard jab at her uncle's. She did not use full force, not yet, not until she understood what was happening. But it was still enough to send him crashing to the floor, doubled up in pain.

"Tell me what just happened! What made you attack Jim? What did you do to his essence?"

Her uncle looked up. No trace remained of the maniac she had witnessed moments earlier. Looking at his aura, the purple had already faded.

Uncle James made no attempt to strike back at her. Rising slowly and painfully to his feet, he gestured towards the unconscious figure in the chair.

"Jim's essence, which you see before you, is not my creation. You know enough about these things to understand that such a transformation cannot be inflicted by one person on another. Not in the course of such a brief interaction."

Anna remained absolutely alert, staring at him. "Explain what just happened!"

"Let me help you back into bed first. Lying in that position won't do your leg any good. Anna braced herself, her aura ready to smite him if there was any sudden movement. The gentle look in his eyes as he helped her back into a sitting position suggested that he posed no threat to her, but she kept her guard up. What had possessed him?

"Uncle, tell me what just happened."

"An essence with an appearance like that can only be created by the evil misdeeds and intentions of its owner, over a period of time. And to possess an essence as damaged as that one," Anna's uncle jerked his head in the direction of the hideous-looking specimen across the room, "the owner would have to have perpetrated some truly heinous acts, wouldn't you say? Treacherous acts, in fact."

The meaning of his words was clear. But Anna would not be deceived.

"You attacked him so viciously. You made it happen!"

"Anna," her uncle responded, his voice soft and his expression tender, "you know that is not possible."

"But…" Anna knew this was true. There must be another explanation. "But… but he must have transformed his own essence, like we do when we disguise ours. He must have made it look like that himself, somehow. Probably to stop you from attacking him."

"I would challenge you, or indeed anyone, to disguise their essence to that extent." He cast another disgusted look in Jim's direction. "Especially when they are unconscious! Didn't you notice? It only took on this appearance when he passed out. No-one can disguise their essence when they have lost consciousness."

"But—"

"I'm afraid it's not this appearance that's the disguise. It was the pure, blue, spotless one that was not real. It fooled every one of us. Me, Mr Warwick… even you, with your powers. And it's a disguise he has used to the most callous, deadly effect. I'm afraid our friend, Jim, has been well and truly turned."

Anna fought against what she was being told. There must be some form of evil sorcery at work.

"Uncle, I think you're being controlled. I think the Gorgal is doing something. It said it was coming for me. It can reach out over great distances. You… you were completely changed…" She checked his aura again. It had returned to pure blue.

"Anna." He spoke very softly now. "I am so sorry. I gave you a terrible shock. I admit, I almost lost control. But I was not possessed. I was correct. Think about it. Have you ever seen an essence that looked like Jim's did today when he arrived?"

There was something in these words that struck home. Jim's aura had always been bright blue with almost no blemishes, right from when she had first known him. If anything, when she saw him at Jeremiah's home, and again today, it had become more perfect still. Practically faultless, with hardly any of the subtle, unique undulations that were always present in others. It had been almost unique in that respect. Had it been uniquely perfect because it had not been real? Had it been merely a creation of its owner, a mask to deceive everyone around him?

She simply could not believe it. And then she remembered another reason to believe it was not Jim who had given them away.

"But it was Percival! He tried to stop me when I escaped from Jeremiah's. And he left the piano concert so suspiciously, just before we were attacked. I'm certain it was him!"

"Mr Warwick told me of your fears about Percival when I returned to London with Greg. But we can be certain it wasn't him." He stopped. He did not seem to want to pursue that line of conversation any further.

"What do you mean? All the evidence points to him! Why think it was Jim, when it was clearly Percival?"

He took a deep breath, then he spoke very softly. "Because, tragically, Percival was killed during the attack on Jeremiah's home. The Wraith stabbed him in your room. It seems he died trying to stop it from chasing you. I'm so sorry..." Her uncle looked distraught himself.

"What? Percival? This can't be right. He tried to stop me..."

"I was able to speak to Jeremiah in the days after the attack, before he passed away. As you escaped his rooms, he went to face the intruder. He saw Percival on the floor, holding on to the Wraith's legs for dear life, trying to pull it to the ground. The Wraith stabbed him ferociously, to get him off. He bought you some vital time. But tragically, he died at the scene."

This news came like a thunderbolt. She remembered striking Percival's aura to get him out of the way as she escaped. She had left him doubled up on the floor of her room. She recalled the moment. He had put his arm across the doorway, telling her she had just been having a nightmare. That was before he had seen the Wraith at the window. After that, had he in fact given his life to save her? After she had left him fatally weakened? She had blamed him for the attack. Was this actually yet another death she had caused? It was too much to take in. She could not tell what was true and what was not anymore. She put her head in her hands and closed her eyes.

There was a sudden sound of movement. Looking up, she was just in time to see her uncle block a savage blow aimed in her direction from a deformed, jagged, black, brown and red spike. He parried it easily, as though he had been expecting it. He gripped, twisted and cast it away from him with ease, then shoved the physical body back hard in the direction it had come from. Jim crashed back into the chair. He lay there, breathing hard, his face covered with sweat and drained of all colour.

Anna was struck dumb once more. Finally, the truth was clear. Had the blow from the spike been aimed at her uncle, she might still have given Jim the benefit of the doubt that it could have been self-defence. But the spike had been coming directly at her. Her uncle had been right all along. That was why he had ushered Jim straight to the far side of the room when he had entered, and why he had remained standing between Jim and her the whole time.

He had attacked Jim to force him to reveal the truth. Now she understood why her uncle's aura had turned purple. It was the hatred. Hatred towards this man who had betrayed them all to the Satal.

"But why?" she gasped.

"That is the question to which I also seek an answer. You may be assured that it is nothing that you have done – nothing whatsoever. Rather, it is certainly because of who you are. But *why*?"

They both looked back towards the man in the chair, whose head was now bowed. It was Anna who spoke.

"Jim, how could you do this to me? How could you do this to all of us?"

He slowly looked up. He had an entirely defeated, dead look in his eyes. He did not reply. Anna's mind began to race.

"But this makes no sense! You could have told him where I lived at any time. Or if you wanted to turn me over to Faulkner, you had opportunities. That time when I confided in you about Timmy, when I was desperate to get a message to him. I asked you to help me set up a meeting. You could easily have arranged for Faulkner to be there instead. You could have delivered me right to him!"

Jim's eyes and his voice were devoid of emotion as he started to speak. "At that time, there was nothing further from my mind. That was before everything changed."

"And exactly when did everything change?" asked Anna's uncle.

"It started after that night you were both attacked by McCain." Jim's tone was completely flat. "Until then, Faulkner had no idea that Anna was the girl they wanted to capture. But after that he knew, and he started to search for any way he could find to get to her. That's when he got his hooks into me."

Jim turned his expressionless face back to Anna. "By that time, I didn't know where you were. I tried to find out, but the secret was very well kept. I was terrified my short-lived usefulness to Faulkner might come to an end. And with it, my life. But he found other uses for me. As a source for learning the Orders' battle plans, which I was sometimes able to leak to him."

There was a strange quality to his voice. He sounded as though he were relaying a series of facts relating to someone else. Anna had the growing impression of a man whose soul had been burned out of him.

"Finally, Warwick invited me to Jeremiah's to look after you. At last, my perfect chance had come. It wasn't after the attack that I returned to Jeremiah's. It was me who led Faulkner and his men there. I told the Wraith's handler where your room was. I helped the gang smash the front door down to capture you. I was at the front of the group who chased you down that long alleyway. I was ready to catch you and hand you over to Faulkner. I would have done it willingly. But you escaped again."

Anna listened in horror. This man, whose face she knew so well and whom she had trusted completely, was speaking so dispassionately about his readiness to betray her. The basis for her faith in all she saw in auras, and in the world, and for her trust in all those she knew, was being ripped from her. How could she ever trust anyone again? Or trust her own judgement and instincts? Anna's uncle paced the room between her and Jim like a caged lion.

"Once you were on the loose and separated from all your guardians," the monotone voice continued, "I had one more thing to offer Faulkner. I guessed you would go to your friends to seek refuge and help. You had nowhere else to turn. And probably one friend in particular. So I got to use the knowledge you had shared with me about your love for that boy, Timmy Thompson, to lure you into a trap. You'd spoon-fed me with that gem of information yourself. It was perfect."

Her most intimate secret, the importance to her of which he knew full well, used against her without a qualm. The betrayal was complete.

"The gang captured the boy. Then they let him escape briefly, before staging his capture again in front of your other friends, to lay the trap. We told them exactly what to say about where they were taking him, and to make sure your friends heard them. No-one could mistake where you needed to go to find him.

"But that part of the plan worked too well. You got there much quicker than anybody expected. It took some time to get word to Faulkner that we'd captured the boy, and that he should get back to his mansion. We passed word on to Mortlock too, to keep the boy secure and wait for your arrival, until Faulkner could get there. I understand Mortlock got to the mansion before Faulkner, but not before you. You getting there so fast, that took everybody by surprise."

"Tell me something," said Uncle James. "While you were working for Faulkner, did you learn anything about the Gorgal?"

For the first time, a slight, wry smirk appeared on the defeated man's face. "You say that as though you think

Faulkner would share information like that with someone like me. He shared nothing with me. He just issued orders and took my information."

"Did he say anything that might give a clue as to where the Gorgal is now?"

"No. Nothing," Jim replied. "I'm not lying to you. I know you could force whatever information you like out of me now, but you don't really believe Faulkner would share the location of the Gorgal with someone as lowly in the ranks as me, do you? He never even mentioned the Gorgal in front of me."

"What about Lizzy? Has she been involved with Faulkner or his gang in any way?"

"No, not so far as I know. I'm the only one the gang's ever had on the inside of this house."

"Jim, what was it that caused you to change?" It was Anna who spoke this time.

Jim said nothing at first. Despite still being young, his demeanour was now that of a shattered, crushed and hopeless man who had reached his end. Eventually he replied, again in a tone without emotion.

"They have their ways and means. They prey upon your every weakness. They take everything that was good and turn it bad. They turn every emotion against you. I wasn't strong enough to resist. Nowhere near strong enough."

"But what happened?"

"It was Mortlock who approached me first. I didn't want anything to do with him to start with, of course. But he had found out who you were and that you lived here, and somehow, he found out all about me and Emily. And he knew certain things about me, some things about my distant past which weren't so pleasant. Things that were finished and done with long ago, but which I didn't want Emily knowing about, in case they changed the way she felt about me.

"Mortlock threatened to share them with her. I thought he was bluffing, but he showed me the evidence he had. I had no doubt he'd use it. He's a real nasty piece of work. I should've been brave enough to explain things to Emily. Should've trusted her to see beyond them, to see me for the good man I was trying to be. But I didn't have that confidence. I couldn't face the possibility of losing her. I was too weak. I took the coward's way out."

"Oh, Jim…" said Anna.

"After I'd helped Mortlock a little with some information, I tried to break it off and stop it going any further. Then he turned real nasty. He threatened to do all kinds of things – not just ruin everything between me and Emily for ever, but to do far worse things to her as well. I should've been stronger. I should've gone to you, Mr Lawrence. But I could only think of Emily." He stopped for a moment.

"Go on," said Uncle James, unmoved.

"Then, Mortlock introduced me to Faulkner. That's when things began to get really serious. Faulkner started to do things to me. He used that terrible essence on me. I can only imagine what damage it did. It was awful, like he was scratching away my soul with those blood-tipped spikes. Before long, I was their willing accomplice. It felt like my only choice left. Once I'd passed a certain point, it was like something had changed inside me. Something had died. My decency was gone.

"They had me at a point where there was no going back. Deeds that were once appalling and unthinkable have become things I don't bat an eyelid at now. I've done the most terrible acts without hesitation. I've lost all feeling. To have gone against their wishes would've been far, far worse…"

"But Jim," Anna asked, still unable to believe what she was hearing, "your essence always looked so pure, from long before you say Mortlock first approached you. How could someone like you be turned so quickly?"

"Like I said, I'd done some bad things a long time ago. I tried to mend my ways, but I was always weak. Always easily tempted to stray again. Once I really understood about the Powers, I was sure all those weaknesses would be showing themselves in my essence. So, as soon as I learned how, I disguised it to make it appear bluer and purer. It took me a long time to master it and keep it up – it's not easy – but I managed it."

Anna was stunned again. So, Jim's aura had never been as pure as she had thought. She had been misled all these years. She felt like an utter fool.

"What about Emily?" asked her uncle. "Did she know about any of this? Was she in on it?"

Jim's eyes shot a look straight at Uncle James. For the first time, there was genuine emotion in them. He did not reply at first. Maybe he could not. When he did finally speak, his voice, which had been so monotone until now, cracked.

"No, she doesn't know. I loved her, with all my heart. Despite everything I've done, I still love her. It was my love for her that was the weapon they used against me. That was the cruellest part…"

A single tear ran down the right cheek of his otherwise still emotionless face.

The room fell silent. Everything was still, apart from the movement of the curtains in the gentle, chilly breeze from the open window. The young man was looking down at the floor, his descent to the bottom of his life complete. Suddenly, without warning, he leapt to his feet and made for the window. Before Anna or her uncle could move, he had one leg through it. He was held only by his tight grip on the window frame at either side.

"Stop him, uncle!" Anna cried.

Uncle James made as if to move. Then he stopped. Jim hesitated long enough for her uncle to reach him, but he did not. The purple hue had returned to his aura.

Jim spoke again. "Please tell Emily this one thing. Through it all, despite everything, I never stopped loving her."

He moved his head and other leg out of the window, took one look below, then pushed himself outwards. Moments later, there was a sound from somewhere far below, then nothing.

Anna sat in complete silence. Her uncle also remained motionless for a time. Both stared at the open window where Jim had been just moments before. Finally, Uncle James walked over to the window, leaned out of it to glimpse the scene below, then closed it.

"It's over," he said.

20
Reunited

The following morning, Anna was visited by a police constable, in the presence of her mother. He asked questions about the circumstances of the butler's death. Anna confirmed that Jim had jumped without any physical coercion or encouragement.

Anna's condition had deteriorated. Physically, her leg wound had been opened again by her attempts to get out of the bed. Far worse had been the emotional impact. Her appetite was gone, and she did not want to see anyone. Her thoughts were in turmoil again. She was deeply shocked by the revelations about Jim, as well as by his sudden death. Her faith and trust in the world around her, and in human nature, were shaken to their very core.

Now more than ever she missed the solid, steady rock, the person she had always felt she could rely on. Mr Warwick. He was the one she would have turned to now. He was possibly the only person who could have helped her make sense of it all. He had been the kindest, gentlest man she knew. There was so much guidance he still had to give, so much more he would have taught her. She could not grasp that she would never speak to him again.

Mr Warwick had given her life a direction. Now she had to carry on in a world she was seeing in a new, very different light, without his wise hand to guide her. Even if she tried to hide and have nothing more to do with the

Struggle, as a large part of her wished she could, it would find her. This would never be over for her until the Gorgal and its Satals were gone, or she herself was dead. Facing one Satal had been truly terrible. It had brought so much pain and misery. How could she possibly face far worse enemies? It seemed completely hopeless and utterly beyond her. When she had been with Mr Warwick and her uncle together, there had always been hope. Now their cornerstone was gone.

All that day, Anna refused to speak to anyone. She heard it was the day before Christmas Eve, but it did not feel like it. Such things held little meaning for her now. It was late in the evening when there was a knock at the door. It was her uncle. Anna was not sure she wanted to see him at first. It was hard to forget his state when he had confronted Jim, even though it had turned out he was right. But he looked terrible himself. He appeared hesitant to approach her. When she saw his tired face, and when he smiled at her, weakly but kindly, her feelings softened.

"Oh, uncle," she said. "I wish Mr Warwick was here. He would know what to do now. I miss him so much!"

Looking into his eyes, she knew he understood. In all the world, he was the only one who could possibly understand.

"I miss him too," he replied. "More than I can start to express. I have struggled very much to overcome his loss, and to deal with what must be done next. I'm afraid I have been doing a poor job of it so far. I am not the man he was. But we have no choice but to go on. You know that that is what he wanted above all else."

Anna nodded.

"I'm afraid I can never be Edmund Warwick," he continued. "We may never see his like again. But I promise I will be the best teacher and guide to you that I can be. And while there is still breath in this body, I will protect you."

"Thank you, uncle." There was nothing more that could be said. They had each other. They would have to find their way forward in the Struggle together as best they could.

She was hardly feeling any better the following day when, late in the afternoon, there was another knock at the door. It was opened by her smiling mother, to reveal some very unexpected guests. It was Rebecca and the rest of the gang – all nine of them, including Timmy! Her uncle must have told her mother, and she must have understood. She had somehow understood that this was what Anna needed. She left them all alone.

None of Anna's friends had ever been inside her house before, and at first Anna could not believe her eyes. It was like two completely unconnected worlds, coming together. They were all very concerned to see her condition, but to Anna it was like the first breath of fresh air since she had set foot in Faulkner's mansion.

After a while, they began to laugh and joke, about how posh her house was, about the disapproving looks they had received from some of the staff as they had trooped through it, and about how clumsy Charlie had been as they came up the stairs, nearly knocking over an expensive-looking vase. Then talk turned to events further afield, of adventures that they had had, and of all manner of gossip that Johnny had heard, some of which possibly contained a grain of truth, most of it surely not. She laughed deeply for the first time in she could not remember how long, at Charlie's description of being covered from head to foot in flour in an incident at his dad's bakery. He had later been given a cake to make up for it, so he reckoned it was all well worth it. For a while, Anna was transported beyond her own troubles to far happier places.

Finally, the time came for them to leave. Rebecca spoke up.

"Right everyone, we've got to go. Anna and Timmy here have some unfinished business they need to talk about, so we'd better leave them to it. No arguments, now. Come on, get a move on!"

One by one the friends bade Anna farewell, before Rebecca ushered them all out of the room.

As the older girl reached the doorway herself, she looked back and said, "You'll be right as rain in no time, Anna. You're the bravest person I know. Get well soon. I look forward to seeing you down by the canal again before you know it!" Then she added, "Oh, and by the way, don't worry about Timmy. I've explained everything to him. He understands now. Timmy, do the right thing, won't you? See you later, little brother!"

She disappeared and closed the door behind her.

"Oh, Timmy," said Anna once they were alone. "It's so good to see you. It's been a tough time. But you do know there was nothing in all that nonsense about Gillespie, don't you?"

Timmy looked up at Anna through his long fringe in that way of his, making her stomach do its first somersault for months.

"Yes, I know it now. Becca explained everything. I'm sorry about how I reacted."

Then he pulled out from his battered coat a small package and an envelope, which he handed to her. "Merry Christmas, Anna," he said.

Opening the envelope, she found a squashed, but beautiful, pressed yellow flower. It was just like the ones he had given her in the summer, a lifetime ago.

"Oh Timmy, thank you!" The tears that came to her eyes this time were so different from the others she had shed recently. Timmy leant forward and gave her a kiss on her forehead. He lingered for a moment, then Anna reached up and kissed him on the lips. It was a feeling she had dreamt of a thousand times since the summer, but one she had thought she would never experience again.

It wasn't long before there was another knock at the door, and Timmy, too, had to leave.

"Merry Christmas, Timmy," she said as he moved away. "And thank you. Hope to see you again soon!"

"Merry Christmas, Anna," he replied, and grinned. "You will!"

Anna laid back in her bed once more. The sound of carol singers' voices found its way in through the open window. She looked over to it, the scene of such tragic events two days earlier. Snowflakes were gently falling outside. She closed her eyes, listened to the singing and shut out all other thoughts bar those of Timmy. She knew the moment could not last, but for now it was enough. Maybe there could be positive things ahead after all. She understood life differently now, but perhaps it was still worth taking its journey.

The next day was Christmas Day. From that day onwards, Anna's physical recovery progressed well, and the process of emotional recovery began. Her innocence of the world and its true nature were gone forever, but she saw that there was good there as well as bad. Perhaps a lot more good than bad, in fact. And that was something worth fighting for. She had only recently become involved in the Struggle, but she had already seen more than enough to know how important it was that the right side emerged victorious.

When Uncle James felt Anna was strong enough, he shared with her some more about Jeremiah's final days. He had battled very hard to recover from his terrible injuries, and he had survived a number of days before he lost the fight. Her uncle had visited him every day during that time. Jeremiah had revealed to him that he had spoken much with Mr Warwick during their stay at his home, about his plans to change his direction in life.

Anna was stunned to learn that meeting her had apparently been a true inspiration to Jeremiah. He had said that if a girl so young was prepared to face the greatest evil of all for the sake of everyone else, he could no longer continue his normal career, focused only on himself and his work. He had vowed to re-join the Order and to fight for the Alpha cause. His last words to Uncle James, when he realised he was not going to make it, were that he had no regrets. Apparently, he had said he would die content, knowing that he had done something to help Anna in her critical mission.

Anna was dumbstruck, and consumed at first by another wave of grief and guilt. There was no way she deserved such words. She could not imagine how she could be an inspiration to anyone. But the message stayed with her. The fact was that Jeremiah had laid down his life for her. So had Percival and, of course, Mr Warwick. They had made the ultimate sacrifice for the cause. And because they believed in her. She might not understand that belief, but she could not betray it.

The time to feel sorry for herself had passed. They had not died just so that she could wallow in self-pity. Whatever it was she was capable of, she owed it to them to do it. From now on, they would be her inspiration. It had been Mr Warwick's most fervent wish that she become a great knight in the Struggle one day. She would remain true to the promise she had made to him. She would seek out the help she needed, and she would become as strong as she could be. She vowed one day to become someone her old master would have been truly proud of.

Anna gradually started to feel differently about herself. She was no longer going to accept being treated like a little girl. And she would no longer put up with being kept hidden away. There were things she had to do. She was going to live life on her terms. She would talk to her mother about it, but she already sensed that they understood each other better now. Their relationship had changed. At last, she felt up to talking to her about everything, including what had really happened to her father, and the other experiences of her family in the Struggle that her mother had alluded to, however tragic. She would do so very soon. The time for that conversation had come.

At last, the day came when the doctor said it was safe for Anna to try to walk again unaided. Leaning heavily on a stick, she stepped forward from her bed. Her muscles were weak through lack of use, and her injured leg almost gave way twice. But with fierce determination, she made it clear over to the other side of the room without help, to the delight of her applauding mother, the doctor and her uncle.

When Anna and her uncle were alone again, he gave her a knowing look.

"Do you know what I think, Anna? Don't tell your mother quite yet, but I think you might just be ready to start your instruction again."

"Do you know what I think, uncle?" she replied, smiling. "I think you might just be right!"

Epilogue

In a distant land, deep in a cave illuminated by five flaming torches, the enormous form on the stone slab began to stir. Its mind had become fully active, observing, probing and influencing events at a great distance, in ways of which it alone was capable, amongst all the living creatures on earth. The stabilisation of its essence was not yet complete, but that day, too, was near. The day on which it could safely re-emerge into the world, to execute its apocalyptic mission.

The giant figure started to move. The Gorgal rose slowly to its full, terrible height in front of its three bowed followers. Their chanting ceased. An awed silence filled the shadowy cavern.

The colossal figure began to share its plans, in a form of oral and mental communication impenetrable to any living creature born of the earth. Plans for the annihilation of the entire world, starting with the single enemy whom it had identified first upon its entry into this world. The one who had just struck the first significant blow in the new war. The day of that girl's downfall was approaching, fast. It would be upon her far sooner than she knew.

The creatures of the Omega World began their preparations for all-out war.

Appendix

Further Background Information

(This appendix contains no spoilers. It reflects the position at the start of War Begins. It provides non-essential but additional detail, relevant to the book. The content is supplemental to that contained in the preface.)

The Elemental Energy, the Opposing Energy and the Alpha & Omega Worlds

At the time our universe came into being, two fundamental 'energies' existed. Each moved to create a universe according to its own design, both at that same moment. The Elemental Energy sought a harmonious universe, the Alpha Universe, more commonly referred to as the Alpha World. The Opposing Energy sought to create a very different existence, the Omega Universe, more commonly known as the Omega World.

The Opposing Energy failed. The universe that was actually created – our universe – followed the Alpha design. However, the activity of the Opposing Energy at the moment of the universe's inception left it 'contaminated'. As a result, the universe that we live in fell short of the pure Alpha Universe – it became less harmonious, with more suffering and injustice than the Alpha World would have.

The Alpha-Omega Wars and the Struggle

The current universe is not in its final state. Its fate is finely balanced. One day it will finally attain either the pure Alpha state, or the pure Omega state. In the Omega state, life of a very different kind would exist, and nothing that lives today would be able to survive.

Since the dawn of civilisation, a select group of men and women have fought with beings from beyond our world to bring about the universe's final state, either the Alpha or the Omega World. These conflicts are known as the Alpha-Omega Wars. The ongoing efforts of both sides to finally win these wars are referred to as 'the Struggle'.

The Elemental and Opposing Energies remain active in the world. Like mighty, unseen winds, they push and influence the thoughts and actions both of people directly involved in the Struggle, and of those in the general population who are completely unaware of it.

Each Energy is seeking to bring about its own final version of the universe, once and for all. Only when one or other final state is reached will the 'winds' of their influence finally cease.

Auras and Essences

Every human being possesses an aura. The aura's appearance varies by person. It is usually roughly spherical, and it is always translucent.

The aura's colour, appearance, shape, size and surface texture all reflect aspects of the person's nature, character and personality.

Auras can contain a range of different colours. Amongst these, blue indicates a fundamentally good person. Brown suggests someone who has been corrupted in some way. Black indicates that the person is willing and ready to harm others for their own benefit. Red always signifies evil. The extent to which these colours are present indicates the degree to which the person has these qualities.

The size of the aura corresponds to the person's power. The natural shape and surface texture provide further insights: generally, the more spherical the aura and the smoother its surface texture, the better the person's nature.

To see a person's aura, it is necessary to focus the vision and the mind in a particular way. For those that possess it, this ability is instinctive. No-one can ever see their own aura.

A person's aura is always located close to them, usually at a height between the top of their head and the bottom of their chest. It does not surround their body; it appears to 'float' close to it.

Even when in focus, the aura does not entirely obscure the view of the person's physical form, or of the physical world around them.

The extent to which auras are visible is generally proportional to the visibility of physical objects in that location, at that time. For example, auras cannot be seen through physical objects, such as walls or trees. They also become all or partially obscured by phenomena such as fog, just as physical objects do. However, unlike physical objects, auras can be seen in the dark.

The shape of the aura, and its location relative to its owner, are not necessarily fixed. Those with the ability to see other people's auras are also able to manoeuvre and contort their own auras. They cannot see their own auras but they can do this by visualising their movements, and sometimes by observing their effects on the auras of others that they come into contact with. However, it is never possible to move the aura more than a few feet away from the body.

Auras cannot come into contact with or 'touch' objects in the physical world. However, they can touch, grip or strike other auras, similar to the way that a hand touches a physical object. Auras cannot pass through each other.

Auras can be disguised. They can be made to appear smaller than their true size, and to appear purer or less pure than they really are. It is not possible to make an aura appear larger than its real size.

For those that possess it, the ability to see auras ordinarily develops around the time of reaching adulthood.

'Aura' is the word that Anna Lawrence found as a child to best describe what she could see. The correct term for aura, used by the Order and by everyone involved with the Struggle, is 'essence'.

The Powers

The Powers is the term used for the ability to see, to move and to contort auras, plus the abilities to heal damaged auras and to foresee certain aspects of the future.

People with the ability to heal others people's damaged auras are called Healers. Those with the ability to see aspects of the future are known as Seers. All Healers and Seers are able to see and manipulate auras. However, not everyone with the ability to see and manipulate auras has the powers of a Healer or a Seer.

For those who possess them, the powers of healing and foreseeing the future also generally reveal themselves only around the time of reaching adulthood.

Mental Combat

Auras can be used by those with the Powers to attack other people's auras, to defend against attack, and to subdue and control opponents. A mental attack can kill the victim if sufficiently severe. Fighting with auras requires the combatants to be in close proximity.

In addition to being used for striking and defending, the aura can be used to subdue an opponent. This is done by manoeuvring the aura to surround a sufficient surface area of the opponent's aura, and exerting sufficient pressure on it. If successful, this prevents the opponent from attacking or resisting in both mental and physical dimensions.

Mental combat is an essential skill for everyone involved in the Struggle.

The Order of the Knights of the True Path

Since the dawn of civilisation, the Order has comprised those rare men and women who are able to see auras. Their mission has always been to bring about the Alpha World, and to prevent a descent into the Omega World.

Edmund Warwick is a Grand Master of the Order. Other senior knights include Sir Stephen Walsingham and Tobias Blackthorn. Although younger, James Lawrence – Anna's uncle – is also a prominent knight. All four men fought in the last Satal War. Jim Heath, the junior butler in Anna's household, is a younger knight.

It takes a number of years of instruction for a student to become a fully-fledged knight. Gregory Matthews is currently being trained as a knight by James Lawrence.

Anna has now begun her training, led by Edmund Warwick and her Uncle James. She is the youngest student to begin a knight's training in the history of the Order.

Edmund Warwick

Edmund Warwick is an elderly bookshop owner, and an old friend of Anna's family. Amongst the general population, he is known by the alias of Mr Barton.

Mr Warwick is a Grand Master of the Order, and one of its most senior knights. He fought successfully in two previous Satal wars.

Mr Warwick is a keen scholar of 'the Histories', the documented history of the Struggle since the dawn of civilisation. He is amongst the Order's foremost experts in the subject.

Mr Warwick is leading Anna's instruction in the Powers.

James Lawrence

James Lawrence is a well-known socialite, and the younger brother of Anna's father. He is also a prominent knight in the Order. He fought in the last Satal War.

Uncle James has been entrusted by Anna's mother with the role of Anna's guardian when her mother is not present. He himself was originally taught by Mr Warwick.

James now trains other knights, and is assisting Mr Warwick with Anna's instruction.

Satals

In addition to luring humans with the Powers to fight for the Omega cause, the Opposing Energy is occasionally able to unleash more formidable enemies into our world – creatures born not of our universe, but mutated directly from the Opposing Energy's design. Amongst the most formidable of these are Satals.

These hugely powerful beings act directly to move the world towards the Omega state. They do this by corrupting individuals to act in ways that are wrong, and that do harm to others. This furthers the Omega cause by damaging the individual's own aura, by causing divisions and disharmony in society as a whole, and by causing or provoking wars within and between nations.

Satals cause untold death and destruction in the world, and can only be defeated through mental combat. It generally requires a significant number of knights to achieve this.

Satals' true forms vary from creature to creature. What is common to all is that they always appear horrific to human eyes. In order to pass unnoticed in the world, they can also adopt human form. Unbeknown to the general population, Satals actually lie behind legends of beasts and monsters in most cultures.

Satals' actions have been the cause of many of the most devastating wars and other tragic events in human history. They have often shaped the course of events by influencing people in positions of power. Sometimes they have taken on positions of leadership themselves, and some have even become leaders of countries, whilst in their human forms.

Always, they act to create division and hatred between peoples, to weaken society and civilisation as a whole. They do this to lead the world in the direction of destruction, violence and suffering – all steps towards the ultimate descent to the Omega World.

Anna's Dream

Aged six, Anna experienced a vivid nightmare. She witnessed five figures appearing, around a giant rock on a hilltop. One figure was much larger than the others. She was drawn immediately to its eyes. The 'whites' were blood red, the irises were black as night, and a deep red glow emanated from the pupils. Anna sensed that what she saw was real. It felt like the greatest evil imaginable. The dream still haunts her to this day.

Mr Warwick has interpreted the nightmare. He confirmed his belief that what Anna saw in her dream was real. He revealed that the four smaller figures were all

Satals. That in itself represented a threat of unprecedented scale. According to the Histories, no more than two Satals have ever appeared at the same time before. However, even this was not the most fearful aspect of his interpretation. Mr Warwick believes that the largest figure of the five was a being thought only to exist in the legends of the Order. A creature of untold power, known as a Gorgal *(see separate note)*.

Never have five such mighty creatures appeared in this world at one time. Mr Warwick believes that such a force could bring about a catastrophe far worse for civilisation than the Dark Ages that followed the fall of the Western Roman Empire. That era was instigated by the last Gorgal to appear in Europe and lasted almost a thousand years, until the Renaissance. To Mr Warwick, a keen scholar of the Histories, this new invasion appears to be a more fundamental move from the Opposing Energy than it has ever made before. It could be a truly devastating offensive, with the potential to instigate an irreversible descent into the final Omega state.

The Gorgal

Like Satals, Gorgals are not born of our universe. They too are mutated directly from the Omega design. However, according to the Histories of the Order, a Gorgal represents the Omega World in a far purer form than Satals do, and has powers of a far greater order of magnitude. The Gorgal is by far the most powerful and destructive weapon that the Opposing Energy is able to unleash upon our world.

A Gorgal has not been seen in the West for over a thousand years. As a consequence, it was considered a mythical creature by most in the Order until Mr Warwick translated Anna's dream.

According to the Histories, the last Gorgal in Europe appeared more than one thousand five hundred years before. Its actions led directly to the fall of the Western Roman Empire, and the decent of civilisation into the Dark Ages for a thousand years, until the Renaissance.

According to the ancient writings, Gorgals have the power to change the course of history far more profoundly than Satals can. One of the ways they do this is sometimes by channelling and driving the winds of the Opposing Energy on a huge scale, to influence people's behaviour in numbers far greater than any Satal could.

The Histories state that the introduction of a Gorgal is the most direct intervention that the Opposing Energy can make in the Alpha-Omega Wars, to bring about the Omega World. Mr Warwick believes that the state of the world is already far less progressed towards the final, pure Alpha state than it would have been, had it not been for the interventions of the Gorgals of the past, which have set progress back by centuries.

The last visitation by a Gorgal anywhere in the world is understood to have been in East Asia, in the first half of the second millennium AD. The actions of that Gorgal led to a relative demise in strength and influence of the civilisations of East Asia for over five hundred years, right up to Mr Warwick's time. Prior to that, countries in that region had led the world in terms of civilisation and technological advancement for significant periods of human history. Mr Warwick expects them to do so again in the future, but their advancement has been set back by centuries as a result of the events instigated by that Gorgal. The information about this has been received by the Order in the West from the Orders of knights in East Asia, with whom there has been increasing contact in recent centuries. It is understood that knights in the East Asian region have been engaged in the Struggle for as long as those in the West.

The Histories also tell of Gorgals having struck in Africa and the Americas in times past, to similarly devastating effect for the regions and peoples involved. In the worst cases, whole civilisations were wiped out.

From the Histories, it is understood that it requires an enormous, almost superhuman effort on the part of armies of knights to defeat a Gorgal. According to Mr Warwick's interpretation of Anna's dream, upon its arrival here, this new Gorgal appears immediately to have singled Anna out specifically as a threat, amongst the entire population of the world.

The Beast of Highgate

A horrific, demonic monster, sighted at the scenes of a series of savage killings in London, especially around the Highgate and Hampstead areas to the north. Named the 'Beast of Highgate' by the newspapers, rumours have spread like wildfire that it is a demon from hell, possibly Satan himself, prowling the night streets.

Mr Warwick has confirmed to Anna that this Beast is, in fact, a Satal. It is one of the five beings from her dream, with the mission to move the world towards the Omega state.

In its true Satal form, the Beast is around ten feet tall, has a horned head, a long snout and a large mouth containing long fangs. It has bat-like wings and long, razor-sharp talons. Its powerful, muscular body is covered with small, black scales.

Anna and her friends witnessed the Beast for themselves in the summer, whilst trying to save two boys who had been taken to the mansion of a man named Faulkner. They witnessed the Beast capturing and killing one of the boys' older brothers.

Marcus Faulkner

Mysterious owner of a huge mansion on the edge of Hampstead, not far from Highgate. Rumours are rife that Faulkner is behind the appearance of the Beast, conjuring its presence through evil rituals. Mr Warwick has confirmed to Anna that Faulkner is involved with the Omega forces.

Faulkner has recruited a gang of local criminals to carry out his work. Rough though they themselves are, they are known to live in fear of him.

Unseen, Anna has spied Faulkner's aura. It is unlike anything she has seen before. It is far larger than any other aura she has seen, and has the appearance of a giant, spiked ball. It is black at its core, becoming scarlet towards the tips of its long spikes. To Anna, it conveys the impression of purest evil.

Anna has learned from a boy called Billy Gillespie *(see separate note)* that he witnessed Faulkner transforming into the Beast of Highgate himself, to kill a friend of Gillespie's brother. If true, that would mean

Faulkner is a Satal, one of the five figures from Anna's dream.

Joseph Mortlock

An old man known to be an associate of Faulkner's. His large aura has colourings of black, brown and, most predominantly, red.

Mortlock was once Mr Warwick's best friend, and a very promising knight of the Order. Mortlock and Mr Warwick trained in the Powers together as young men. However, he is a 'Turner', a person with the Powers who has been converted to fight for the Omega cause, either by a Satal, or directly by the influence of the Opposing Energy. In Mortlock's case, it was the Satal of his early adulthood who successfully turned him.

The Order only learned of Mortlock's treachery years after he was turned, when he finally lined up amongst the Omega forces ranged against them in the great battle of that Satal War. Ever since that time, he has remained one of the Order's bitterest enemies.

Anna's Friends

A group of teenagers with very different backgrounds from Anna's. There are nine of them in total, four girls and five boys, and their leader is a girl two years older than Anna, called Rebecca Thompson.

Rebecca is Anna's best friend. Rebecca's younger brother is called Timmy. He is also part of the group. The other members include boys called Johnny Adams and

Charlie Morgan. For a long time, Anna has secretly been in love with Timmy.

None of Anna's friends are aware of the Powers or the Struggle.

The Marylebone Street Gang

A gang of rough kids around Anna's age, and sworn enemies of Anna's friends.

Some of the gang's elder brothers have been drawn into Faulkner's gang. They have begun to threaten Anna's friends' family members, to try to force them to work for Faulkner, too.

Now the Marylebone Street Gang members themselves have started to become involved in Faulkner's activities, running errands for him.

Billy Gillespie

Billy Gillespie is one of the Marylebone Street Gang. It was during a confrontation with him that Anna first discovered her ability to subdue an enemy using her aura. But instead of hurting him, she used her aura to soothe his, and to bring him some peace.

Kenny Gillespie is Billy's older brother. He was deeply involved with Faulkner's gang. On one occasion, he and his best friend failed to follow Faulkner's instructions. In response, Faulkner killed his friend and started to hunt down Kenny.

Billy Gillespie had no knowledge of the Powers himself. However, when Faulkner launched a vicious mental assault on him in order to force his brother's location from him though, Gillespie recognised that the nature of this contact was in some way similar to the contact that Anna had made with him, even though the effect and feelings were entirely different. For this reason, he thought Anna might be able help protect him against Faulkner. He approached her for help.

Countdown to 'War Begins'

Unknown to Billy Gillespie, Faulkner was following him using a connection he had made with Gillespie's aura. He was on the brink of catching them both in an abandoned garden when Anna realised, just in time. She managed to successfully shield Gillespie's aura and conceal them both from him. Once they thought Faulkner had gone, she urged Gillespie to escape London.

As Anna headed home, she glanced back at the retreating figure of the boy. Suddenly, from the swirling mist above his head, a giant, swooping shape emerged. From its head rose two horns, and below its wide, bat-like wings stretched powerful legs tipped with long talons. The Beast of Highgate. The giant predator closed on Gillespie like a massive, demonic bird of prey, snatched him up and carried him away. Anna was too far away and could do nothing but watch helplessly. She sank silently to her knees, powerless, as the horrific Beast disappeared into the misty night sky. Then there was just a silent, empty road ahead of her.

Anna knelt motionless on the ground, shocked and devastated. Thoughts and emotions ran wild in her mind. Amongst them, deep inside, that intuition about the future which sometimes spoke to her, told her that the day when she would come face to face with Faulkner in battle was now very near. With a steely determination forged out of that night's tragic experience, she vowed that when that day came, she would end the evil brutality of this Satal, and rid the world of it forever.

She had failed Gillespie, and her failure had cost the boy his life. Somehow, whatever it took, she would make sure that no-one else would ever again suffer at the hands of Faulkner.

Also by C.J. Hansen in the Alpha-Omega Wars series:

OMEGA AWAKENS

Printed in Poland
by Amazon Fulfillment
Poland Sp. z o.o., Wrocław